THE MAGNIFICENT AMBERSONS

BOOTH TARKINGTON

THE
MAGNIFICENT
AMBERSONS

THE MODERN LIBRARY

NEW YORK

1998 Modern Library Paperback Edition

Biographical note copyright © 1998 by Random House, Inc.

All rights reserved under International and Pan-American Copyright Conventions.
Published in the United States by Random House, Inc., New York, and
simultaneously in Canada by Random House of Canada Limited, Toronto.

MODERN LIBRARY and colophon are registered trademarks of Random House, Inc.

LIBRARY OF CONGRESS CATALOGING-IN-PUBLICATION DATA
Tarkington, Booth, 1869–1946.
The magnificent Ambersons/Booth Tarkington.—
1998 Modern Library ed.
p.   cm.
ISBN 978-0-375-75250-6
1. Family—Indiana—Fiction. I. Title.
PS2972.M25   1998
813′.52—dc21   98-19552

Modern Library website address: www.modernlibrary.com

BOOTH TARKINGTON

Newton Booth Tarkington, an enormously prolific novelist, playwright, and short story writer who chronicled urban middle-class life in the American Midwest during the early twentieth century, was born in Indianapolis on July 29, 1869. He was the son of John Stevenson Tarkington, a lawyer, and Elizabeth Booth Tarkington. His uncle and namesake, Newton Booth, was a governor of California and later a United States senator. In the essay "As I Seem to Me," published in the *Saturday Evening Post* in 1941, Tarkington recalled dictating a story to his sister when he was only six. By the age of sixteen he had written a fourteen-act melodrama about Jesse James. Tarkington was educated at Phillips Exeter Academy, Purdue University, and Princeton, where his burlesque musical *The Honorable Julius Caesar* was staged by the Triangle Club. Upon leaving Princeton in 1893 he returned to Indiana determined to pursue a career as a writer.

After a five-year apprenticeship marked by publishers' rejection slips, Tarkington enjoyed a huge commercial success with *The Gentleman from Indiana* (1899), a novel credited with capturing the essence of the American heartland. He consolidated his fame with *Monsieur Beaucaire* (1900), a historical romance later adapted into a movie starring Rudolph Valentino. "*Monsieur Beaucaire* is ever green," remarked Damon Runyon. "It is a little literary cameo, and we read it over at least once a year." The political knowledge Tarkington acquired while serving one term in the Indiana house of representatives informed *In the Arena* (1905), a collection of short stories that drew praise from President

Theodore Roosevelt for its realism. In collaboration with dramatist Harry Leon Wilson, Tarkington wrote *The Man from Home* (1907), the first of many successful Broadway plays. His comedy *Clarence* (1919), which Alexander Woollcott praised for being "as American as *Huckleberry Finn* or pumpkin pie," helped launch Alfred Lunt on a distinguished career and provided Helen Hayes with an early successful role.

Following a decade in Europe, Tarkington returned to Indianapolis and won a new readership with the publication of *The Flirt* (1913). The first of his novels to be serialized in the *Saturday Evening Post*, the book contained authentic characters and themes that paved the way for *Penrod* (1914), a group of tales drawn from the author's boyhood memories of growing up in Indiana. The adventures of Penrod Schofield, which Tarkington also chronicled in the sequels *Penrod and Sam* (1916) and *Penrod Jashber* (1929), seized the imagination of young adult readers and invited comparison with *Tom Sawyer*. Equally successful was *Seventeen* (1916), a nostalgic comedy of adolescence that subsequently inspired a play, two Broadway musicals, and a pair of film adaptations as well as Tarkington's sequel novel *Gentle Julia* (1922).

Tarkington broke new artistic ground with *The Turmoil* (1915), the first novel in his so-called *Growth* trilogy documenting the changes in urban life during the era of America's industrial expansion. William Dean Howells, the father of American realism, praised Tarkington's vivid depiction of the human misery generated by one man's worship of bigness and materialism. *The Magnificent Ambersons* (1918), the second work in the series, earned Tarkington the Pulitzer Prize. "*The Magnificent Ambersons* is perhaps Tarkington's best novel," judged Van Wyck Brooks. "[It is] a typical story of an American family and town— the great family that locally ruled the roost and vanished virtually in a day as the town spread and darkened into a city." *The Midlander* (1924) concludes the trilogy with the story of a real estate developer who is both a creator and a victim of the country's new wealth.

Tarkington won his second Pulitzer Prize for *Alice Adams* (1921), a novel often seen as an extension of the *Growth* trilogy. The unforgettable portrayal of a small-town social climber whose outlandish attempts to snare a rich husband are both poignant and hilarious, *Alice Adams* was later made into a film starring Katharine Hepburn. Tarkington's other memorable books of the period include *Women* (1925), a cycle of amusing stories about the flourishing social life of suburban housewives, and *The Plutocrat* (1927), a satire of an American millionaire abroad. In addition he turned out *The World Does Move* (1928), a volume of autobiographical essays, and *Mirthful Haven* (1930), a serious novel of manners inspired by his many summers in Kennebunkport, Maine.

In the late 1920s, Tarkington commenced a prolonged battle with failing eyesight and near blindness. After undergoing more than a dozen eye operations he regained partial vision, but he was forced to dictate his work to a secretary. His joy at being able once more to see colors maintained a lifelong passion for collecting art. The entertaining stories Tarkington wrote for the *Saturday Evening Post* about the art business were published as *Rumbin Galleries* (1937). In addition he completed *Some Old Portraits* (1939), a book of essays about his collection, which included works by Titian, Velázquez, and Goya.

During the final years of his life Tarkington again focused on Indiana. In *The Heritage of Hatcher Ide* (1941) he updated the family sagas of the *Growth* trilogy, while in *Kate Fennigate* (1943) he offered another social comedy in the spirit of *Alice Adams.* In 1945 Tarkington was awarded the prestigious Howells Medal of the American Academy of Arts and Letters.

Booth Tarkington died at his home in Indianapolis following a short illness on May 19, 1946. *The Show Piece* (1947), his unfinished last novel, profiles a young egoist reminiscent of the George Minafer of *The Magnificent Ambersons.*

TO
SUSANAH

THE
MAGNIFICENT
AMBERSONS

CHAPTER I

Major Amberson had "made a fortune" in 1873, when other people were losing fortunes, and the magnificence of the Ambersons began then. Magnificence, like the size of a fortune, is always comparative, as even Magnificent Lorenzo may now perceive, if he has happened to haunt New York in 1916; and the Ambersons were magnificent in their day and place. Their splendour lasted throughout all the years that saw their Midland town spread and darken into a city, but reached its topmost during the period when every prosperous family with children kept a Newfoundland dog.

In that town, in those days, all the women who wore silk or velvet knew all the other women who wore silk or velvet, and when there was a new purchase of sealskin, sick people were got to windows to see it go by. Trotters were out, in the winter afternoons, racing light sleighs on National Avenue and Tennessee Street; everybody recognized both the trotters and the drivers; and again knew them as well on summer evenings, when slim buggies whizzed by in renewals of the snow-time rivalry. For that matter, everybody knew everybody else's family horse-and-carriage, could identify such a silhouette half a mile down the street, and thereby was sure who was going to market, or to a reception, or coming home from office or store to noon dinner or evening supper.

During the earlier years of this period, elegance of personal appearance was believed to rest more upon the texture of garments than upon their shaping. A silk dress needed no remodelling when it was a year or so old; it remained distinguished by merely remaining silk. Old men and governors wore broadcloth; "full dress" was broadcloth with "doe-skin" trousers; and there were seen men of all ages to whom a hat meant only that rigid, tall silk thing known to impudence as a "stove-pipe." In town and country these men would wear no other hat, and, without self-consciousness, they went rowing in such hats.

Shifting fashions of shape replaced aristocracy of texture: dress-makers, shoemakers, hatmakers, and tailors, increasing in cunning and in power, found means to make new clothes old. The long contagion of the "Derby" hat arrived: one season the crown of this hat would be a bucket; the next it would be a spoon. Every house still kept its bootjack, but high-topped boots gave way to shoes and "congress gaiters"; and these were played through fashions that shaped them now with toes like box-ends and now with toes like the prows of racing shells.

Trousers with a crease were considered plebeian; the crease proved that the garment had lain upon a shelf, and hence was "ready-made"; these betraying trousers were called "hand-me-downs," in allusion to the shelf. In the early 'eighties, while bangs and bustles were having their way with women, that variation of dandy known as the "dude" was invented: he wore trousers as tight as stockings, dagger-pointed shoes, a spoon "Derby," a single-breasted coat called a "Chesterfield," with short flaring skirts, a torturing cylindrical collar, laundered to a polish and three inches high, while his other neckgear might be a heavy, puffed cravat or a tiny bow fit for a doll's braids. With evening dress he wore a tan overcoat so short that his black coat-tails hung visible, five inches below the overcoat; but after a season or two he lengthened his overcoat till it touched his heels, and he passed out of his tight trousers into trousers like great bags. Then, presently, he was seen no more, though the word that had been coined for him remained in the vocabularies of the impertinent.

It was a hairier day than this. Beards were to the wearers' fancy, and things as strange as the Kaiserliche boar-tusk moustache were commonplace. "Side-burns" found nourishment upon childlike profiles; great Dundreary whiskers blew like tippets over young shoulders; moustaches were trained as lambrequins over forgotten mouths; and it was possible for a Senator of the United States to wear a mist of white whisker upon his throat only, not a newspaper in the land finding the ornament distinguished enough to warrant a lampoon. Surely no more is needed to prove that so short a time ago we were living in another age!

. . . At the beginning of the Ambersons' great period most of the houses of the Midland town were of a pleasant architecture. They lacked style, but also lacked pretentiousness, and whatever does not pretend at all has style enough. They stood in commodious yards, well shaded by left-over forest trees, elm and walnut and beech, with here and there a line of tall sycamores where the land had been made by filling bayous from the creek. The house of a "prominent resident," facing Military Square, or National Avenue, or Tennessee Street, was built of brick upon a stone foundation, or of wood upon a brick foundation. Usually it had a "front porch" and a "back porch"; often a "side porch," too. There was a "front hall"; there was a "side hall"; and sometimes a "back hall." From the "front hall" opened three rooms, the "parlour," the "sitting room," and the "library"; and the library could show warrant to its title—for some reason these people bought books. Commonly, the family sat more in the library than in the "sitting room," while callers, when they came formally, were kept to the "parlour," a place of formidable polish and discomfort. The upholstery of the library furniture was a little shabby; but the hostile chairs and sofa of the "parlour" always looked new. For all the wear and tear they got they should have lasted a thousand years.

Upstairs were the bedrooms; "mother-and-father's room" the largest; a smaller room for one or two sons, another for one or two daughters; each of these rooms containing a double bed, a "washstand," a "bureau," a wardrobe, a little table, a rocking-chair, and often a chair or two that had been slightly damaged downstairs, but not enough to justify either the expense of repair or decisive abandonment in the attic. And there was always a "spare-room," for visitors (where the sewing-machine usually was kept), and during the 'seventies there developed an appreciation of the necessity for a bathroom. Therefore the architects placed bathrooms in the new houses, and the older houses tore out a cupboard or two, set up a boiler beside the kitchen stove, and sought a new godliness, each with its own bathroom. The great American plumber joke, that many-branched evergreen, was planted at this time.

At the rear of the house, upstairs, was a bleak little chamber, called "the girl's room," and in the stable there was another bedroom, adjoining the hayloft, and called "the hired man's room." House and stable cost seven or eight thousand dollars to build, and people with that much money to invest in such comforts were classified as the Rich. They paid the inhabitant of "the girl's room" two dollars a week, and, in the latter part of this period, two dollars and a half, and finally three dollars a week. She was Irish, ordinarily, or German, or it might be Scandinavian, but never native to the land unless she happened to be a person of colour. The man or youth who lived in the stable had like wages, and sometimes he, too, was lately a steerage voyager, but much oftener he was coloured.

After sunrise, on pleasant mornings, the alleys behind the stables were gay; laughter and shouting went up and down their dusty lengths, with a lively accompaniment of curry-combs knocking against back fences and stable walls, for the darkies loved to curry their horses in the alley. Darkies always prefer to gossip in shouts instead of whispers; and they feel that profanity, unless it be vociferous, is almost worthless. Horrible phrases were caught by early rising children and carried to older people for definition, sometimes at inopportune moments; while less investigative children would often merely repeat the phrases in some subsequent flurry of agitation, and yet bring about consequences so emphatic as to be recalled with ease in middle life.

... They have passed, those darky hired-men of the Midland town; and the introspective horses they curried and brushed and whacked and amiably cursed—those good old horses switch their tails at flies no more. For all their seeming permanence they might as well have been buffaloes—or the buffalo laprobes that grew bald in patches and used to slide from the careless drivers' knees and hang unconcerned, half way to the ground. The stables have been transformed into other like-nesses, or swept away, like the woodsheds where were kept the stove-wood and kindling that the "girl" and the "hired-man" always quarrelled over: who should fetch it. Horse and stable and woodshed, and the whole tribe of the "hired-man," all are gone. They went quickly, yet so silently that we whom they served have not yet really noticed that they are vanished.

So with other vanishings. There were the little bunty street-cars on the long, single track that went its troubled way among the cobble-stones. At the rear door of the car there was no platform, but a step where passengers clung in wet clumps when the weather was bad and the car crowded. The patrons—if not too absent-minded—put their fares into a slot; and no conductor paced the heaving floor, but the driver would rap remindingly with his elbow upon the glass of the door to his little open platform if the nickels and the passengers did not appear to coincide in number. A lone mule drew the car, and some-times drew it off the track, when the passengers would get out and push it on again. They really owed it courtesies like this, for the car was genially accommodating: a lady could whistle to it from an upstairs window, and the car would halt at once and wait for her while she shut the window, put on her hat and cloak, went downstairs, found an umbrella, told the "girl" what to have for dinner, and came forth from the house.

The previous passengers made little objection to such gallantry on the part of the car: they were wont to expect as much for themselves on like occasion. In good weather the mule pulled the car a mile in a little less than twenty minutes, unless the stops were too long; but when the trolley-car came, doing its mile in five minutes and better, it would wait for nobody. Nor could its passengers have endured such a thing, because the faster they were carried the less time they had to spare! In the days before deathly contrivances hustled them through their lives, and when they had no telephones—another ancient vacancy profoundly responsible for leisure—they had time for everything: time to think, to talk, time to read, time to wait for a lady!

They even had time to dance "square dances," quadrilles, and "lancers"; they also danced the "racquette," and schottisches and polkas, and such whims as the "Portland Fancy." They pushed back the sliding doors between the "parlour" and the "sitting room," tacked down crash over the carpets, hired a few palms in green tubs, stationed three or four Italian musicians under the stairway in the "front hall"— and had great nights!

But these people were gayest on New Year's Day; they made it a true festival—something no longer known. The women gathered to "assist" the hostesses who kept "Open House"; and the carefree men, dandified and perfumed, went about in sleighs, or in carriages and ponderous "hacks," going from Open House to Open House, leaving fantastic cards in fancy baskets as they entered each doorway, and emerging a little later, more carefree than ever, if the punch had been to their liking. It always was, and, as the afternoon wore on, pedestrians saw great gesturing and waving of skin-tight lemon gloves, while ruinous fragments of song were dropped behind as the carriages rolled up and down the streets.

"Keeping Open House" was a merry custom; it has gone, like the all-day picnic in the woods, and like that prettiest of all vanished customs, the serenade. When a lively girl visited the town she did not long go unserenaded, though a visitor was not indeed needed to excuse a serenade. Of a summer night, young men would bring an orchestra under a pretty girl's window—or, it might be, her father's, or that of an ailing maiden aunt—and flute, harp, fiddle, 'cello, cornet, and bass viol would presently release to the dulcet stars such melodies as sing through "You'll Remember Me," "I Dreamt That I Dwelt in Marble Halls," "Silver Threads Among the Gold," "Kathleen Mavourneen," or "The Soldier's Farewell."

They had other music to offer, too, for these were the happy days of "Olivette" and "The Mascotte" and "The Chimes of Normandy" and "Giroflé-Girofla" and "Fra Diavola." Better than that, these were the days of "Pinafore" and "The Pirates of Penzance" and of "Patience." This last was needed in the Midland town, as elsewhere, for the "æsthetic movement" had reached thus far from London, and terrible things were being done to honest old furniture. Maidens sawed whatnots in two, and gilded the remains. They took the rockers from rocking-chairs and gilded the inadequate legs; they gilded the easels that supported the crayon portraits of their deceased uncles. In the new spirit of art they sold old clocks for new, and threw wax flowers and wax fruit, and the protecting glass domes, out upon the trash-heap. They filled vases with peacock feathers, or cat-tails, or sumach, or sunflowers, and set the vases upon mantelpieces and marble-topped tables. They embroidered daisies (which they called "marguerites") and sunflowers and sumach and cat-tails and owls and peacock feathers upon plush screens and upon heavy cushions, then strewed these cushions upon floors where fathers fell over them in the dark. In the teeth of sinful oratory, the daughters went on embroidering: they embroidered daisies and sunflowers and sumach and cat-tails and owls and peacock feathers upon "throws" which they had the courage to drape upon horsehair sofas; they painted owls and daisies and sunflowers and sumach and cat-tails and peacock feathers upon tambourines. They hung Chinese umbrellas of paper to the chandeliers; they nailed paper fans to the walls. They "studied" painting on china, these girls; they sang Tosti's new songs; they sometimes still practised the old, genteel habit of lady-fainting, and were most charming of all when they drove forth, three or four in a basket phaeton, on a spring morning.

Croquet and the mildest archery ever known were the sports of people still young and active enough for so much exertion; middle-age played euchre. There was a theatre, next door to the Amberson Hotel, and when Edwin Booth came for a night, everybody who could afford to buy a ticket was there, and all the "hacks" in town were hired. "The Black Crook" also filled the theatre, but the audience then was almost entirely of men who looked uneasy as they left for home when the final curtain fell upon the shocking girls dressed as fairies. But the theatre did not often do so well; the people of the town were still too thrifty.

They were thrifty because they were the sons or grandsons of the "early settlers," who had opened the wilderness and had reached it from the East and the South with wagons and axes and guns, but with no money at all. The pioneers were thrifty or they would have perished: they had to store away food for the winter, or goods to trade for food, and they often feared they had not stored enough—they left traces of that fear in their sons and grandsons. In the minds of most of these, indeed, their thrift was next to their religion: to save, even for the sake of saving, was their earliest lesson and discipline. No matter how prosperous they were, they could not spend money either upon "art," or upon mere luxury and entertainment, without a sense of sin.

Against so homespun a background the magnificence of the Ambersons was as conspicuous as a brass band at a funeral. Major Amberson bought two hundred acres of land at the end of National Avenue; and through this tract he built broad streets and cross-streets; paved them with cedar block, and curbed them with stone. He set up fountains, here and there, where the streets intersected, and at symmetrical intervals placed cast-iron statues, painted white, with their titles clear upon the pedestals: Minerva, Mercury, Hercules, Venus, Gladiator, Emperor Augustus, Fisher Boy, Stag-hound, Mastiff, Greyhound, Fawn, Antelope, Wounded Doe, and Wounded Lion. Most of the forest trees had been left to flourish still, and, at some distance, or by moonlight, the place was in truth beautiful; but the ardent citizen, loving to see his city grow, wanted neither distance nor moonlight. He had not seen Versailles, but, standing before the Fountain of Neptune in Amberson Addition, at bright noon, and quoting the favourite comparison of the local newspapers, he declared Versailles outdone. All this Art showed a profit from the start, for the lots sold well and there was something like a rush to build in the new Addition. Its main thoroughfare, an oblique continuation of National Avenue, was called Amberson Boulevard, and here, at the juncture of the new Boulevard and the Avenue, Major Amberson reserved four acres for himself, and built his new house—the Amberson Mansion, of course.

This house was the pride of the town. Faced with stone as far back as the dining-room windows, it was a house of arches and turrets and girdling stone porches: it had the first porte-cochère seen in that town. There was a central "front hall" with a great black walnut stairway, and open to a green glass skylight called the "dome," three stories above the ground floor. A ballroom occupied most of the third story; and at one end of it was a carved walnut gallery for the musicians. Citizens told strangers that the cost of all this black walnut and wood-carving was sixty thousand dollars. "Sixty thousand dollars for the wood-work *alone*! Yes, sir, and hardwood floors all over the house! Turkish rugs and no carpets at all, except a Brussels carpet in the front parlour—I hear they call it the 'reception-room.' Hot and cold water upstairs and down, and stationary washstands in every last bedroom in the place! Their sideboard's built right into the house and goes all the way across one end of the dining room. It isn't walnut, it's solid mahogany! Not veneering—solid mahogany! Well, sir, I presume the President of the United States would be tickled to swap the White House for the new Amberson Mansion, if the Major'd give him the chance—but by the Almighty Dollar, you bet your sweet life the Major wouldn't!"

The visitor to the town was certain to receive further enlightenment, for there was one form of entertainment never omitted: he was always patriotically taken for "a little drive around our city," even if his host had to hire a hack, and the climax of the display was the Amberson Mansion. "Look at that greenhouse they've put up there in the side yard," the escort would continue. "And look at that brick stable! Most folks would think that stable plenty big enough and good enough to live in; it's got running water and four rooms upstairs for two hired men and one of 'em's family to live in. They keep one hired man loafin' in the house, and they got a married hired man out in the stable, and his wife does the washing. They got box-stalls for four horses, and they keep a coupay, and some new kinds of fancy rigs you never saw the beat of! 'Carts' they call two of 'em—'way up in the air they are—too high for me! I guess they got every new kind of fancy rig in there that's been invented. And harness—well, everybody in town can tell when Ambersons are out driving after dark, by the jingle. This town never did see so much style as Ambersons are putting on, these days; and I guess it's going to be expensive, because a lot of other folks'll try to keep up with 'em. The Major's wife and the daughter's been to Europe, and my wife tells me since they got back they make tea there every afternoon about five o'clock, and drink it. Seems to me it would go against a person's stomach, just before supper like that, and anyway tea isn't fit for much—not unless you're sick or something. My wife says Ambersons don't make lettuce salad the way other people do; they don't chop it up with sugar and vinegar at all. They pour olive oil on it with their vinegar, and they have it separate—not along with the rest of the meal. And they *eat* these olives, too: green things they are, something like a hard plum, but a friend of mine told me they tasted a good deal like a bad hickory-nut. My wife says she's going to buy some; you got to eat nine and then you get to like 'em, she says. Well, I wouldn't eat nine bad hickory-nuts to get to like *them,* and I'm going to let these olives alone. Kind of a woman's dish, anyway, I suspect, but most everybody'll be makin' a stagger to worm through nine of 'em, now Ambersons brought 'em to town. Yes, sir, the rest'll eat 'em, whether they get sick or not! Looks to me like some people in this city'd be willing to go crazy if they thought that would help 'em to be as high-toned as Ambersons. Old Aleck Minafer—he's about the closest old codger we got—he come in my office the other day, and he pretty near had a stroke tellin' me about his daughter Fanny. Seems Miss Isabel Amberson's got some kind of a dog—they call it a Saint Bernard—and Fanny was bound to have one, too. Well, old Aleck told her he didn't like dogs except rat-terriers, because a rat-terrier cleans up the mice, but she kept on at him, and finally he said all right she could have one. Then, by George! she says Ambersons *bought* their dog, and you can't get one without paying for it: they cost from fifty to a hundred dollars up! Old Aleck wanted to know if I ever heard of anybody buyin' a dog before, because, of course, even a Newfoundland or a setter you can usually get somebody to give you one. He says he saw some sense in payin' a nigger a dime, or even a quarter, to *drown* a dog for you, but to pay out fifty dollars and maybe more—well, sir, he like to choked himself to death, right there in my office! Of course everybody realizes that Major Amberson is a fine business man, but what with throwin' money around for dogs, and every which and what, some think all this style's bound to break him up, if his family don't quit!"

One citizen, having thus discoursed to a visitor, came to a thoughtful pause, and then added, "Does seem pretty much like squandering, yet when you see that dog out walking with this Miss Isabel, he seems worth the money."

"What's she look like?"

"Well, sir," said the citizen, "she's not more than just about eighteen or maybe nineteen years old, and I don't know as I know just how to put it—but she's kind of a *delightful* lookin' young lady!"

CHAPTER II

Another citizen said an eloquent thing about Miss Isabel Amberson's looks. This was Mrs. Henry Franklin Foster, the foremost literary authority and intellectual leader of the community—for both the daily newspapers thus described Mrs. Foster when she founded the women's Tennyson Club; and her word upon art, letters, and the drama was accepted more as law than as opinion. Naturally, when "Hazel Kirke" finally reached the town, after its long triumph in larger places, many people waited to hear what Mrs. Henry Franklin Foster thought of it before they felt warranted in expressing any estimate of the play. In fact, some of them waited in the lobby of the theatre, as they came out, and formed an inquiring group about her.

"I didn't see the play," she informed them.

"What! Why, we saw you, right in the middle of the fourth row!"

"Yes," she said, smiling, "but I was sitting just behind Isabel Amberson. I couldn't look at anything except her wavy brown hair and the wonderful back of her neck."

The ineligible young men of the town (they were all ineligible) were unable to content themselves with the view that had so charmed Mrs. Henry Franklin Foster: they spent their time struggling to keep Miss Amberson's face turned toward them. She turned it most often, observers said, toward two: one excelling in the general struggle by his sparkle, and the other by that winning if not winsome old trait, persistence. The sparkling gentleman "led germans" with her, and sent sonnets to her with his bouquets—sonnets lacking neither music nor wit.

He was generous, poor, well-dressed, and his amazing persuasiveness was one reason why he was always in debt. No one doubted that he would be able to persuade Isabel, but he unfortunately joined too merry a party one night, and, during a moonlight serenade upon the lawn before the Amberson Mansion, was easily identified from the windows as the person who stepped through the bass viol and had to be assisted to a waiting carriage. One of Miss Amberson's brothers was among the serenaders, and, when the party had dispersed, remained propped against the front door in a state of helpless liveliness; the Major going down in a dressing-gown and slippers to bring him in, and scolding mildly, while imperfectly concealing strong impulses to laughter. Miss Amberson also laughed at this brother, the next day, but for the suitor it was a different matter: she refused to see him when he called to apologize. "You seem to care a great deal about bass viols!" he wrote her. "I promise never to break another." She made no response to the note, unless it was an answer, two weeks later, when her engagement was announced. She took the persistent one, Wilbur Minafer, no breaker of bass viols or of hearts, no serenader at all.

A few people, who always foresaw everything, claimed that they were not surprised, because though Wilbur Minafer "might not be an Apollo, as it were," he was "a steady young business man, and a good church-goer," and Isabel Amberson was "pretty sensible—for such a showy girl." But the engagement astounded the young people, and most of their fathers and mothers, too; and as a topic it supplanted literature at the next meeting of the "Women's Tennyson Club."

"Wilbur *Minafer*!" a member cried, her inflection seeming to imply that Wilbur's crime was explained by his surname. "Wilbur *Minafer*! It's the queerest thing I ever heard! To think of her taking Wilbur Minafer, just because a man *any* woman would like a thousand times better was a little wild one night at a serenade!"

"No," said Mrs. Henry Franklin Foster. "It isn't that. It isn't even because she's afraid he'd be a dissipated husband and she wants to be safe. It isn't because she's religious or hates wildness; it isn't even because she hates wildness in *him*."

"Well, but look how she's thrown him over for it."

"No, that wasn't her reason," said the wise Mrs. Henry Franklin Foster. "If men only knew it—and it's a good thing they don't—a woman doesn't really care much about whether a man's wild or not, if it doesn't affect herself, and Isabel Amberson doesn't care a thing!"

"Mrs. *Foster*!"

"No, she doesn't. What she minds is his making a clown of himself in her front yard! It made her think he didn't care much about *her*. She's probably mistaken, but that's what she thinks, and it's too late for her to think anything else now, because she's going to be married right away—the invitations will be out next week. It'll be a big Amberson-style thing, raw oysters floating in scooped-out blocks of ice and a band from out-of-town—champagne, showy presents; a colossal present from the Major. Then Wilbur will take Isabel on the carefulest little wedding trip he can manage, and she'll be a good wife to him, but they'll have the worst spoiled lot of children this town will ever see."

"How on earth do you make *that* out, Mrs. Foster?"

"She couldn't love Wilbur, could she?" Mrs. Foster demanded, with no challengers. "Well, it will all go to her children, and she'll ruin 'em!"

The prophetess proved to be mistaken in a single detail merely: except for that, her foresight was accurate. The wedding was of Ambersonian magnificence, even to the floating oysters; and the Major's colossal present was a set of architect's designs for a house almost as elaborate and impressive as the Mansion, the house to be built in Amberson Addition by the Major. The orchestra was certainly not that local one which had suffered the loss of a bass viol; the musicians came, according to the prophecy and next morning's paper, from afar; and at midnight the bride was still being toasted in champagne, though she had departed upon her wedding journey at ten. Four days later the pair had returned to town, which promptness seemed fairly to demonstrate that Wilbur had indeed taken Isabel upon the carefulest little trip he could manage. According to every report, she was from the start "a good wife to him," but here in a final detail the prophecy proved inaccurate. Wilbur and Isabel did not have children; they had only one.

"Only one," Mrs. Henry Franklin Foster admitted. "But I'd like to know if he isn't spoiled enough for a whole carload!"

Again she found none to challenge her.

At the age of nine, George Amberson Minafer, the Major's one grandchild, was a princely terror, dreaded not only in Amberson Addition but in many other quarters through which he galloped on his white pony. "By golly, I guess you think you own this town!" an embittered labourer complained, one day, as Georgie rode the pony straight through a pile of sand the man was sieving. "I will when I grow up," the undisturbed child replied. "I guess my grandpa owns it now, you bet!" And the baffled workman, having no means to controvert what seemed a mere exaggeration of the facts, could only mutter "Oh, pull down your vest!"

"Don't haf to! Doctor says it ain't healthy!" the boy returned promptly. "But I tell you what I'll do: I'll pull down my vest if you'll wipe off your chin!"

This was stock and stencil: the accustomed argot of street badinage of the period; and in such matters Georgie was an expert. He had no vest to pull down; the incongruous fact was that a fringed sash girdled the juncture of his velvet blouse and breeches, for the Fauntleroy period had set in, and Georgie's mother had so poor an eye for appropriate things, where Georgie was concerned, that she dressed him according to the doctrine of that school in boy decoration. Not only did he wear a silk sash, and silk stockings, and a broad lace collar, with his little black velvet suit: he had long brown curls, and often came home with burrs in them.

Except upon the surface (which was not his own work, but his mother's) Georgie bore no vivid resemblance to the fabulous little Cedric. The storied boy's famous "Lean on *me*, grandfather," would have been difficult to imagine upon the lips of Georgie. A month after his ninth birthday anniversary, when the Major gave him his pony, he had already become acquainted with the toughest boys in various distant parts of the town, and had convinced them that the toughness of a rich little boy with long curls might be considered in many respects superior to their own. He fought them, learning how to go baresark at a certain point in a fight, bursting into tears of anger, reaching for rocks, uttering wailed threats of murder and attempting to fulfil them. Fights often led to intimacies, and he acquired the art of saying things more exciting than "Don't haf to!" and "Doctor says it ain't healthy!" Thus, on a summer afternoon, a strange boy, sitting bored upon the gate-post of the Reverend Malloch Smith, beheld George Amberson Minafer rapidly approaching on his white pony, and was impelled by bitterness to shout: "Shoot the ole jackass! Look at the girly curls! Say, bub, where'd you steal your mother's ole sash!"

"Your sister stole it for me!" Georgie instantly replied, checking the pony. "She stole it off our clo'es-line an' gave it to me."

"You go get your hair cut!" said the stranger hotly. "Yah! I haven't got any sister!"

"I know you haven't at home," Georgie responded. "I mean the one that's in jail."

"I dare you to get down off that pony!"

Georgie jumped to the ground, and the other boy descended from the Reverend Mr. Smith's gatepost—but he descended inside the gate. "I dare you outside that gate," said Georgie.

"Yah! I dare you half way here. I dare you—"

But these were luckless challenges, for Georgie immediately vaulted the fence—and four minutes later Mrs. Malloch Smith, hearing strange noises, looked forth from a window; then screamed, and dashed for the pastor's study. Mr. Malloch Smith, that grim-bearded Methodist, came to the front yard and found his visiting nephew being rapidly prepared by Master Minafer to serve as a principal figure in a pageant of massacre. It was with great physical difficulty that Mr. Smith managed to give his nephew a chance to escape into the house, for Georgie was hard and quick, and, in such matters, remarkably intense; but the minister, after a grotesque tussle, got him separated from his opponent, and shook him.

"You stop that, you!" Georgie cried fiercely; and wrenched himself away. "I guess you don't know who I am!"

"Yes, I do know!" the angered Mr. Smith retorted. "I know who you are, and you're a disgrace to your mother! Your mother ought to be ashamed of herself to allow—"

"Shut up about my mother bein' ashamed of herself!"

Mr. Smith, exasperated, was unable to close the dialogue with dignity. "She ought to be ashamed," he repeated. "A woman that lets a bad boy like you—"

But Georgie had reached his pony and mounted. Before setting off at his accustomed gallop, he paused to interrupt the Reverend Malloch Smith again. "You pull down your vest, you ole Billygoat, you!" he shouted, distinctly. "Pull down your vest, wipe off your chin—an' go to hell!"

Such precocity is less unusual, even in children of the Rich, than most grown people imagine. However, it was a new experience for the Reverend Malloch Smith, and left him in a state of excitement. He at once wrote a note to Georgie's mother, describing the crime according to his nephew's testimony; and the note reached Mrs. Minafer before Georgie did. When he got home she read it to him sorrowfully.

Dear Madam:

Your son has caused a painful distress in my household. He made an unprovoked attack upon a little nephew of mine who is visiting in my household, insulted him by calling him vicious names and falsehoods, stating that ladies of his family were in jail. He then tried to make his pony kick him, and when the child, who is only eleven years old, while your son is much older and stronger, endeavoured to avoid his indignities and withdraw quietly, he pursued him into the enclosure of my property and brutally assaulted him. When I appeared upon this scene he deliberately called insulting words to me, concluding with profanity, such as "go to hell," which was heard not only by myself but by my wife and the lady who lives next door. I trust such a state of undisciplined behaviour may be remedied for the sake of the reputation for propriety, if nothing higher, of the family to which this unruly child belongs.

Georgie had muttered various interruptions, and as she concluded the reading he said:

"He's an ole liar!"

"Georgie, you mustn't say 'liar.' Isn't this letter the truth?"

"Well," said Georgie, "how old am I?"

"Ten."

"Well, look how he says I'm older than a boy eleven years old."

"That's true," said Isabel. "He does. But isn't some of it true, Georgie?"

Georgie felt himself to be in a difficulty here, and he was silent.

"Georgie, did you say what he says you did?"

"Which one?"

"Did you tell him to—to— Did you say, 'Go to hell'?"

Georgie looked worried for a moment longer; then he brightened. "Listen here, mamma; grandpa wouldn't wipe his shoe on that ole story-teller, would he?"

"Georgie, you mustn't—"

"I mean: none of the Ambersons wouldn't have anything to do with him, would they? He doesn't even know *you*, does he, mamma?"

"That hasn't anything to do with it."

"Yes, it has! I mean: none of the Amberson family go to see him, and they never have him come in their house; they wouldn't ask him to, and they prob'ly wouldn't even let him."

"That isn't what we're talking about."

"I bet," said Georgie emphatically, "I bet if he wanted to see any of 'em, he'd haf to go around to the side door!"

"No, dear, they—"

"Yes, they would, mamma! So what does it matter if I did say somep'm' to him he didn't like? That kind o' people, I don't see why you can't say anything you want to, to 'em!"

"No, Georgie. And you haven't answered me whether you said that dreadful thing he says you did."

"Well—" said Georgie. "Anyway, he said somep'm' to me that made me mad." And upon this point he offered no further details; he would not explain to his mother that what had made him "mad" was Mr. Smith's hasty condemnation of herself: "Your mother ought to be ashamed," and, "A woman that lets a bad boy like you—" Georgie did not even consider excusing himself by quoting these insolences.

Isabel stroked his head. "They were terrible words for you to use, dear. From his letter he doesn't seem a very tactful person, but—"

"He's just riffraff," said Georgie.

"You mustn't say so," his mother gently agreed. "Where did you learn those bad words he speaks of? Where did you hear any one use them?"

"Well, I've heard 'em serreval places. I guess Uncle George Amberson was the *first* I ever heard say 'em. Uncle George Amberson said 'em to papa once. Papa didn't like it, but Uncle George was just laughin' at papa, an' then he said 'em while he was laughin'."

"That was wrong of him," she said, but almost instinctively he detected the lack of conviction in her tone. It was Isabel's great failing that whatever an Amberson did seemed right to her, especially if the Amberson was either her brother George, or her son George. She knew that she should be more severe with the latter now, but severity with him was beyond her power; and the Reverend Malloch Smith had succeeded only in rousing her resentment against himself. Georgie's symmetrical face—altogether an Amberson face—had looked never more beautiful to her. It always looked unusually beautiful when she tried to be severe with him. "You must promise me," she said feebly, "never to use those bad words again."

"I promise not to," he said promptly—and he whispered an immediate codicil under his breath: "Unless I get mad at somebody!" This satisfied a code according to which, in his own sincere belief, he never told lies.

"That's a good boy," she said, and he ran out to the yard, his punishment over. Some admiring friends were gathered there; they had heard of his adventure, knew of the note, and were waiting to see what was going to "happen" to him. They hoped for an account of things, and also that he would allow them to "take turns" riding his pony to the end of the alley and back.

They were really his henchmen: Georgie was a lord among boys. In fact, he was a personage among certain sorts of grown people, and was often fawned upon; the alley negroes delighted in him, chuckled over him, flattered him slavishly. For that matter, he often heard well-dressed people speaking of him admiringly: a group of ladies once gathered about him on the pavement where he was spinning a top. "I *know* this is Georgie!" one exclaimed, and turned to the others with the impressiveness of a showman. "Major Amberson's only grandchild!" The others said, "It *is?*" and made clicking sounds with their mouths; two of them loudly whispering, "*So* handsome!"

Georgie, annoyed because they kept standing upon the circle he had chalked for his top, looked at them coldly and offered a suggestion:

"Oh, go hire a hall!"

As an Amberson, he was already a public character, and the story of his adventure in the Reverend Malloch Smith's front yard became a town topic. Many people glanced at him with great distaste, thereafter, when they chanced to encounter him, which meant nothing to Georgie, because he innocently believed most grown people to be necessarily cross-looking as a normal phenomenon resulting from the adult state; and he failed to comprehend that the distasteful glances had any personal bearing upon himself. If he had perceived such a bearing, he would have been affected only so far, probably, as to mutter, "Riffraff!" Possibly he would have shouted it; and, certainly, most people believed a story that went round the town just after Mrs. Amberson's funeral, when Georgie was eleven. Georgie was reported to have differed with the undertaker about the seating of the family; his indignant voice had become audible: "Well, who *is* the most important person at my own grandmother's funeral?" And later he had projected his head from the window of the foremost mourners' carriage, as the undertaker happened to pass.

"Riffraff!"

There were people—grown people they were—who expressed themselves longingly: they *did* hope to live to see the day, they said, when that boy would get his come-upance! (They used that honest word, so much better than "deserts," and not until many years later to be more clumsily rendered as "what is coming to him.") *Something* was bound to take him down, some day, and they only wanted to *be* there! But Georgie heard nothing of this, and the yearners for his taking down went unsatisfied, while their yearning grew the greater as the happy day of fulfilment was longer and longer postponed. His grandeur was not diminished by the Malloch Smith story; the rather it was increased, and among other children (especially among little girls) there was added to the prestige of his gilded position that diabolical glamour which must inevitably attend a boy who has told a minister to go to hell.

CHAPTER III

Until he reached the age of twelve, Georgie's education was a domestic process; tutors came to the house; and those citizens who yearned for his taking down often said: "Just wait till he has to go to public school; *then* he'll get it!" But at twelve Georgie was sent to a private school in the town, and there came from this small and dependent institution no report, or even rumour, of Georgie's getting anything that he was thought to deserve; therefore the yearning still persisted, though growing gaunt with feeding upon itself. For, although Georgie's pomposities and impudence in the little school were often almost unbearable, the teachers were fascinated by him. They did not like him—he was too arrogant for that—but he kept them in such a state of emotion that they thought more about him than they did about all of the other ten pupils. The emotion he kept them in was usually one resulting from injured self-respect, but sometimes it was dazzled admiration. So far as their conscientious observation went, he "studied" his lessons sparingly; but sometimes, in class, he flashed an admirable answer, with a comprehension not often shown by the pupils they taught; and he passed his examinations easily. In all, without discernible effort, he acquired at this school some rudiments of a liberal education and learned nothing whatever about himself.

The yearners were still yearning when Georgie, at sixteen, was sent away to a great "Prep School." "Now," they said brightly, "he'll get it! He'll find himself among boys just as important in their home towns as he is, and they'll knock the stuffing out of him when he puts on his airs with them! Oh, but that *would* be worth something to see!" They were mistaken, it appeared, for when Georgie returned, a few months later, he still seemed to have the same stuffing. He had been deported by the authorities, the offense being stated as "insolence and profanity"; in fact, he had given the principal of the school instructions almost identical with those formerly objected to by the Reverend Malloch Smith.

But he had not got his come-upance, and those who counted upon it were embittered by his appearance upon the down-town streets driving a dog-cart at a criminal speed, making pedestrians retreat from the crossings, and behaving generally as if he "owned the earth." A disgusted hardware dealer of middle age, one of those who hungered for Georgie's downfall, was thus driven back upon the sidewalk to avoid being run over, and so far forgot himself as to make use of the pet street insult of the year: "Got 'ny *sense*! See here, bub, does your mother know you're out?"

Georgie, without even seeming to look at him, flicked the long lash of his whip dexterously, and a little spurt of dust came from the hardware man's trousers, not far below the waist. He was not made of hardware: he raved, looking for a missile; then, finding none, commanded himself sufficiently to shout after the rapid dog-cart: "Turn down your pants, you would-be dude! Raining in dear ole Lunnon! Git off the earth!"

Georgie gave him no encouragement to think that he was heard. The dog-cart turned the next corner, causing indignation there, likewise, and, having proceeded some distance farther, halted in front of the "Amberson Block"—an old-fashioned four-story brick warren of lawyers' offices, insurance and real-estate offices, with a "drygoods store" occupying the ground floor. Georgie tied his lathered trotter to a telegraph pole, and stood for a moment looking at the building critically: it seemed shabby, and he thought his grandfather ought to replace it with a fourteen-story skyscraper, or even a higher one, such as he had lately seen in New York—when he stopped there for a few days of recreation and rest on his way home from the bereaved school. About the entryway to the stairs were various tin signs, announcing the occupation and location of upper-floor tenants, and Georgie decided to take some of these with him if he should ever go to college. However, he did not stop to collect them at this time, but climbed the worn stairs—there was no elevator—to the fourth floor, went down a dark corridor, and rapped three times upon a door. It was a mysterious door, its upper half, of opaque glass, bearing no sign to state the business or profession of the occupants within; but overhead, upon the lintel, four letters had been smearingly inscribed, partly with purple ink and partly with a soft lead pencil, "F.O.T.A." and upon the plaster wall, above the lintel, there was a drawing dear to male adolescence: a skull and crossbones.

Three raps, similar to Georgie's, sounded from within the room. Georgie then rapped four times; the rapper within the room rapped twice, and Georgie rapped seven times. This ended precautionary measures; and a well-dressed boy of sixteen opened the door; whereupon Georgie entered quickly, and the door was closed behind him. Seven boys of congenial age were seated in a semicircular row of damaged office chairs, facing a platform whereon stood a solemn, red-haired young personage with a table before him. At one end of the room there was a battered sideboard, and upon it were some empty beer bottles, a tobacco can about two-thirds full, with a web of mold over the surface of the tobacco, a dusty cabinet photograph (not inscribed) of Miss Lillian Russell, several withered old pickles, a caseknife, and a half-petrified section of icing-cake on a sooty plate. At the other end of the room were two rickety card-tables and a stand of bookshelves where were displayed under dust four or five small volumes of M. Guy de Maupassant's stories, "Robinson Crusoe," "Sappho," "Mr. Barnes of New York," a work by Giovanni Boccaccio, a Bible, "The Arabian Nights' Entertainment," "Studies of the Human Form Divine," "The Little Minister," and a clutter of monthly magazines and illustrated weeklies of about that crispness one finds in such articles upon a doctor's ante-room table. Upon the wall, above the sideboard, was an old framed lithograph of Miss Della Fox in "Wang"; over the bookshelves there was another lithograph purporting to represent Mr. John L. Sullivan in a boxing costume, and beside it a half-tone reproduction of "A Reading From Homer." The final decoration consisted of damaged papier-maché—a round shield with two battle-axes and two cross-hilted swords, upon the wall over the little platform where stood the red-haired presiding officer. He addressed Georgie in a serious voice:

"Welcome, Friend of the Ace."

"Welcome, Friend of the Ace," Georgie responded, and all of the other boys repeated the words, "Welcome, Friend of the Ace."

"Take your seat in the secret semicircle," said the presiding officer. "We will now proceed to—"

But Georgie was disposed to be informal. He interrupted, turning to the boy who had admitted him: "Look here, Charlie Johnson, what's Fred Kinney doing in the president's chair? That's my place, isn't it? What you men been up to here, anyhow? Didn't you all agree I was to be president just the same, even if I was away at school?"

"Well—" said Charlie Johnson uneasily. "Listen! I didn't have much to do with it. Some of the other members thought that long as you weren't in town or anything, and Fred gave the sideboard, why—"

Mr. Kinney, presiding, held in his hand, in lieu of a gavel, and considered much more impressive, a Civil War relic known as a "horse-pistol." He rapped loudly for order. "All Friends of the Ace will take their seats!" he said sharply. "I'm president of the F.O.T.A. now, George Minafer, and don't you forget it! You and Charlie Johnson sit down, because I was elected perfectly fair, and we're goin' to hold a meeting here."

"Oh, you are, are you?" said George skeptically.

Charlie Johnson thought to mollify him. "Well, didn't we call this meeting just especially because you told us to? You said yourself we ought to have a kind of celebration because you've got back to town, George, and that's what we're here for now, and everything. What do you care about being president? All it amounts to is just calling the roll and—"

The president *de facto* hammered the table. "This meeting will now proceed to—"

"No, it won't," said George, and he advanced to the desk, laughing contemptuously. "Get off that platform."

"This meeting will come to order!" Mr. Kinney commanded fiercely.

"You put down that gavel," said George. "Whose is it, I'd like to know? It belongs to my grandfather, and you quit hammering it that way or you'll break it, and I'll have to knock your head off."

"This meeting will come to order! I was legally elected here, and I'm not going to be bulldozed!"

"All right," said Georgie. "You're president. Now we'll hold another election."

"We will not!" Fred Kinney shouted. "We'll have our reg'lar meeting, and then we'll play euchre a nickel a corner, what we're here for. This meeting will now come to ord—"

Georgie addressed the members. "I'd like to know who got up this thing in the first place," he said. "Who's the founder of the F.O.T.A., if you please? Who got this room rent free? Who got the janitor to let us have most of this furniture? You suppose you could keep this clubroom a minute if I told my grandfather I didn't want it for a literary club any more? I'd like to say a word on how you members been acting, too! When I went away I said I didn't care if you had a *vice*-president or something while I was gone, but here I hardly turned my back and you had to go and elect Fred Kinney president! Well, if that's what you want, you can have it. I was going to have a little celebration down here some night pretty soon, and bring some port wine, like we drink at school in our crowd there, and I *was* going to get my grandfather to give the club an extra room across the hall, and prob'ly I could get my Uncle George to give us his old billiard table, because he's got a new one, and the club could put it in the other room. Well, you got a new president now!" Here Georgie moved toward the door and his tone became plaintive, though undeniably there was disdain beneath his sorrow. "I guess all I better do is—resign!"

And he opened the door, apparently intending to withdraw.

"All in favour of having a new election," Charlie Johnson shouted hastily, "say, 'Aye'!"

"Aye" was said by everyone present except Mr. Kinney, who began a hot protest, but it was immediately smothered.

"All in favour of me being president instead of Fred Kinney," shouted Georgie, "say 'Aye.' The 'Ayes' have it!"

"I resign," said the red-headed boy, gulping as he descended from the platform. "I resign from the club!"

Hot-eyed, he found his hat and departed, jeers echoing after him as he plunged down the corridor. Georgie stepped upon the platform, and took up the emblem of office.

"Ole red-head Fred'll be around next week," said the new chairman. "He'll be around boot-lickin' to get us to take him back in again, but I guess we don't want him: that fellow always was a trouble-maker. We will now proceed with our meeting. Well, fellows, I suppose you want to hear from your president. I don't know that I have much to say, as I have already seen most of you a few times since I got back. I had a good time at the old school, back East, but had a little trouble with the faculty and came on home. My family stood by me as well as I could ask, and I expect to stay right here in the old town until whenever I decide to enter college. Now, I don't suppose there's any more business before the meeting. I guess we might as well play cards. Anybody that's game for a little quarter-limit poker or any limit they say, why I'd like to have 'em sit at the president's card-table."

When the diversions of the Friends of the Ace were concluded for that afternoon, Georgie invited his chief supporter, Mr. Charlie Johnson, to drive home with him to dinner, and as they jingled up National Avenue in the dog-cart, Charlie asked:

"What sort of men did you run up against at that school, George?"

"Best crowd there: finest set of men I ever met."

"How'd you get in with 'em?"

Georgie laughed. "I let them get in with *me*, Charlie," he said in a tone of gentle explanation. "It's vulgar to do any other way. Did I tell you the nickname they gave me—'King'? That was what they called me at that school, 'King Minafer.' "

"How'd they happen to do that?" his friend asked innocently.

"Oh, different things," George answered lightly. "Of course, any of 'em that came from anywhere out in this part the country knew about the family and all that, and so I suppose it was a good deal on account of—oh, on account of the family and the way I do things, most likely."

CHAPTER IV

When Mr. George Amberson Minafer came home for the holidays at Christmastide, in his sophomore year, probably no great change had taken place inside him, but his exterior was visibly altered. Nothing about him encouraged any hope that he had received his comeupance; on the contrary, the yearners for that stroke of justice must yearn even more itchingly: the gilded youth's manner had become polite, but his politeness was of a kind which democratic people found hard to bear. In a word, M. le Duc had returned from the gay life of the capital to show himself for a week among the loyal peasants belonging to the old château, and their quaint habits and costumes afforded him a mild amusement.

Cards were out for a ball in his honour, and this pageant of the tenantry was held in the ballroom of the Amberson Mansion the night after his arrival. It was, as Mrs. Henry Franklin Foster said of Isabel's wedding, "a big Amberson-style thing," though that wise Mrs. Henry Franklin Foster had long ago gone the way of all wisdom, having stepped out of the Midland town, unquestionably into heaven—a long step, but not beyond her powers. She had successors, but no successor; the town having grown too large to confess that it was intellectually led and literarily authorized by one person; and some of these successors were not invited to the ball, for dimensions were now so metropolitan that intellectual leaders and literary authorities loomed in outlying regions unfamiliar to the Ambersons. However, all "old citizens" recognizable as gentry received cards, and of course so did their dancing descendants.

The orchestra and the caterer were brought from away, in the Amberson manner, though this was really a gesture—perhaps one more of habit than of ostentation—for servitors of gaiety as proficient as these importations were nowadays to be found in the town. Even flowers and plants and roped vines were brought from afar—not, however, until the stock of the local florists proved insufficient to obliterate the interior structure of the big house, in the Amberson way. It was the last of the great, long-remembered dances that "everybody talked about"— there were getting to be so many people in town that no later than the next year there were too many for "everybody" to hear of even such a ball as the Ambersons'.

George, white-gloved, with a gardenia in his buttonhole, stood with his mother and the Major, embowered in the big red and gold drawing room downstairs, to "receive" the guests; and, standing thus together, the trio offered a picturesque example of good looks persistent through three generations. The Major, his daughter, and his grandson were of a type all Amberson: tall, straight, and regular, with dark eyes, short noses, good chins; and the grandfather's expression, no less than the grandson's, was one of faintly amused condescension. There was a difference, however. The grandson's unlined young face had nothing to offer except this condescension; the grandfather's had other things to say. It was a handsome, worldly old face, conscious of its importance, but persuasive rather than arrogant, and not without tokens of sufferings withstood. The Major's short white hair was parted in the middle, like his grandson's, and in all he stood as briskly equipped to the fashion as exquisite young George.

Isabel, standing between her father and her son, caused a vague amazement in the mind of the latter. Her age, just under forty, was for George a thought of something as remote as the moons of Jupiter: he could not possibly have conceived such an age ever coming to be his own: five years was the limit of his thinking in time. Five years ago he had been a child not yet fourteen; and those five years were an abyss. Five years hence he would be almost twenty-four; what the girls he knew called "one of the older men." He could imagine himself at twenty-four, but beyond that, his powers staggered and refused the task. He saw little essential difference between thirty-eight and eighty-eight, and his mother was to him not a woman but wholly a mother. He had no perception of her other than as an adjunct to himself, his mother; nor could he imagine her thinking or doing anything—falling in love, walking with a friend, or reading a book—as a woman, and not as his mother. The woman, Isabel, was a stranger to her son; as completely a stranger as if he had never in his life seen her or heard her voice. And it was to-night, while he stood with her, "receiving," that he caught a disquieting glimpse of this stranger whom he thus fleetingly encountered for the first time.

Youth cannot imagine romance apart from youth. That is why the rôles of the heroes and heroines of plays are given by the managers to the most youthful actors they can find among the competent. Both middle-aged people and young people enjoy a play about young lovers; but only middle-aged people will tolerate a play about middle-aged lovers; young people will not come to see such a play, because, for them, middle-aged lovers are a joke—not a very funny one. Therefore, to bring both the middle-aged people and the young people into his house, the manager makes his romance as young as he can. Youth will indeed be served, and its profound instinct is to be not only scornfully amused but vaguely angered by middle-age romance. So, standing beside his mother, George was disturbed by a sudden impression, coming upon him out of nowhere, so far as he could detect, that her eyes were brilliant, that she was graceful and youthful—in a word, that she was romantically lovely.

He had one of those curious moments that seem to have neither a cause nor any connection with actual things. While it lasted, he was disquieted not by thoughts—for he had no definite thoughts—but by a slight emotion like that caused in a dream by the presence of something invisible, soundless, and yet fantastic. There was nothing different or new about his mother, except her new black and silver dress: she was standing there beside him, bending her head a little in her greetings, smiling the same smile she had worn for the half-hour that people had been passing the "receiving" group. Her face was flushed, but the room was warm; and shaking hands with so many people easily accounted for the pretty glow that was upon her. At any time she could have "passed" for twenty-five or twenty-six—a man of fifty would have honestly guessed her to be about thirty but possibly two or three years younger—and though extraordinary in this, she had been extraordinary in it for years. There was nothing in either her looks or her manner to explain George's uncomfortable feeling; and yet it increased, becoming suddenly a vague resentment, as if she had done something unmotherly to him.

The fantastic moment passed; and even while it lasted, he was doing his duty, greeting two pretty girls with whom he had grown up, as people say, and warmly assuring them that he remembered them very well—an assurance which might have surprised them "in anybody but Georgie Minafer!" It seemed unnecessary, since he had spent many hours with them no longer ago than the preceding August. They had with them their parents and an uncle from out of town; and George negligently gave the parents the same assurance he had given the daughters, but murmured another form of greeting to the out-of-town uncle, whom he had never seen before. This person George absently took note of as a "queer-looking duck." Undergraduates had not yet adopted "bird." It was a period previous to that in which a sophomore would have thought of the Sharon girls' uncle as a "queer-looking bird," or, perhaps a "funny-face bird." In George's time, every human male was to be defined, at pleasure, as a "duck"; but "duck" was not spoken with admiring affection, as in its former feminine use to signify a "dear"—on the contrary, "duck" implied the speaker's personal detachment and humorous superiority. An indifferent amusement was what George felt when his mother, with a gentle emphasis, interrupted his interchange of courtesies with the nieces to present him to the queer-looking duck, their uncle. This emphasis of Isabel's, though slight, enabled George to perceive that she considered the queer-looking duck a person of some importance; but it was far from enabling him to understand why. The duck parted his thick and longish black hair on the side; his tie was a forgetful looking thing, and his coat, though it fitted a good enough middle-aged figure, no product of this year, or of last year either. One of his eyebrows was noticeably higher than the other; and there were whimsical lines between them, which gave him an apprehensive expression; but his apprehensions were evidently more humorous than profound, for his prevailing look was that of a genial man of affairs, not much afraid of anything whatever. Nevertheless, observing only his unfashionable hair, his eyebrows, his preoccupied tie and his old coat, the olympic George set him down as a queer-looking duck, and having thus completed his portrait, took no interest in him.

The Sharon girls passed on, taking the queer-looking duck with them, and George became pink with mortification as his mother called his attention to a white-bearded guest waiting to shake his hand. This was George's great-uncle, old John Minafer: it was old John's boast that in spite of his connection by marriage with the Ambersons, he never had worn and never would wear a swaller-tail coat. Members of his family had exerted their influence uselessly—at eighty-nine conservative people seldom form radical new habits, and old John wore his "Sunday suit" of black broadcloth to the Amberson ball. The coat was square, with skirts to the knees; old John called it a "Prince Albert" and was well enough pleased with it, but his great-nephew considered it the next thing to an insult. George's purpose had been to ignore the man, but he had to take his hand for a moment; whereupon old John began to tell George that he was looking well, though there had been a time, during his fourth month, when he was so puny that nobody thought he would live. The great-nephew, in a fury of blushes, dropped old John's hand with some vigour, and seized that of the next person in the line. " 'Member you v'ry well 'ndeed!" he said fiercely.

The large room had filled, and so had the broad hall and the rooms on the other side of the hall, where there were tables for whist. The imported orchestra waited in the ballroom on the third floor, but a local harp, 'cello, violin, and flute were playing airs from "The Fencing Master" in the hall, and people were shouting over the music. Old John Minafer's voice was louder and more penetrating than any other, because he had been troubled with deafness for twenty-five years, heard his own voice but faintly, and liked to hear it. "Smell o' flowers like this always puts me in mind o' funerals," he kept telling his niece, Fanny Minafer, who was with him; and he seemed to get a great deal of satisfaction out of this reminder. His tremulous yet strident voice cut through the voluminous sound that filled the room, and he was heard everywhere: "Always got to think o' funerals when I smell so many flowers!" And, as the pressure of people forced Fanny and himself against the white marble mantelpiece, he pursued this train of cheery thought, shouting, "Right here's where the Major's wife was laid out at *her* funeral. They had her in a good light from that big bow window." He paused to chuckle mournfully. "I s'pose that's where they'll put the Major when *his* time comes."

Presently George's mortification was increased to hear this sawmill droning harshly from the midst of the thickening crowd: "Ain't the dancin' broke out yet, Fanny? Hoopla! Le's push through and go see the young women-folks crack their heels! Start the circus! Hoopse-daisy!" Miss Fanny Minafer, in charge of the lively veteran, was almost as distressed as her nephew George, but she did her duty and managed to get old John through the press and out to the broad stairway, which numbers of young people were now ascending to the ballroom. And here the sawmill voice still rose over all others: "Solid black walnut every inch of it, balustrades and all. Sixty thousand dollars' worth o' carved wood-work in the house! Like water! Spent money like water! Always did! Still do! Like water! God knows where it all comes from!"

He continued the ascent, barking and coughing among the gleaming young heads, white shoulders, jewels, and chiffon, like an old dog slowly swimming up the rapids of a sparkling river; while down below, in the drawing room, George began to recover from the degradation into which this relic of early settler days had dragged him. What restored him completely was a dark-eyed little beauty of nineteen, very knowing in lustrous blue and jet; at sight of this dashing advent in the line of guests before him, George was fully an Amberson again.

"Remember you very well *indeed*!" he said, his graciousness more earnest than any he had heretofore displayed. Isabel heard him and laughed.

"But you don't, George!" she said. "You don't remember her yet, though of course you *will*! Miss Morgan is from out of town, and I'm afraid this is the first time you've ever seen her. You might take her up to the dancing; I think you've pretty well done your duty here."

"Be d'lighted," George responded formally, and offered his arm, not with a flourish, certainly, but with an impressiveness inspired partly by the appearance of the person to whom he offered it, partly by his being the hero of this fête, and partly by his youthfulness—for when manners are new they are apt to be elaborate. The little beauty entrusted her gloved fingers to his coat-sleeve, and they moved away together.

Their progress was necessarily slow, and to George's mind it did not lack stateliness. How could it? Musicians, hired especially for him, were sitting in a grove of palms in the hall and now tenderly playing "Oh, Promise Me" for his pleasuring; dozens and scores of flowers had been brought to life and tended to this hour that they might sweeten the air for him while they died; and the evanescent power that music and floral scents hold over youth stirred his appreciation of strange, beautiful qualities within his own bosom: he seemed to himself to be mysteriously angelic, and about to do something dramatic which would overwhelm the beautiful young stranger upon his arm.

Elderly people and middle-aged people moved away to let him pass with his honoured fair beside him. Worthy middle-class creatures, they seemed, leading dull lives but appreciative of better things when they saw them—and George's bosom was fleetingly touched with a pitying kindness. And since the primordial day when caste or heritage first set one person, in his own esteem, above his fellow-beings, it is to be doubted if anybody ever felt more illustrious, or more negligently grand, than George Amberson Minafer felt at this party.

As he conducted Miss Morgan through the hall, toward the stairway, they passed the open double doors of a card room, where some squadrons of older people were preparing for action, and, leaning gracefully upon the mantelpiece of this room, a tall man, handsome, high-mannered, and sparklingly point-device, held laughing converse with that queer-looking duck, the Sharon girls' uncle. The tall gentleman waved a gracious salutation to George, and Miss Morgan's curiosity was stirred. "Who is that?"

"I didn't catch his name when my mother presented him to me," said George. "You mean the queer-looking duck."

"I mean the aristocratic duck."

"That's my Uncle George. Honourable George Amberson. I thought everybody knew him."

"He looks as though everybody ought to know him," she said. "It seems to run in your family."

If she had any sly intention, it skipped over George harmlessly. "Well, of course, I suppose most everybody does," he admitted—"out in this part of the country especially. Besides, Uncle George is in Congress; the family like to have someone there."

"Why?"

"Well, it's sort of a good thing in one way. For instance, my Uncle Sydney Amberson and his wife, Aunt Amelia, they haven't got much of anything to do with themselves—get bored to death around here, of course. Well, probably Uncle George'll have Uncle Sydney appointed minister or ambassador, or something like that, to Russia or Italy or somewhere, and that'll make it pleasant when any of the rest of the family go travelling, or things like that. I expect to do a good deal of travelling myself when I get out of college."

On the stairway he pointed out this prospective ambassadorial couple, Sydney and Amelia. They were coming down, fronting the ascending tide, and as conspicuous over it as a king and queen in a play. Moreover, as the clear-eyed Miss Morgan remarked, the very least they looked was ambassadorial. Sydney was an Amberson exaggerated, more pompous than gracious; too portly, flushed, starched to a shine, his stately jowl furnished with an Edward the Seventh beard. Amelia, likewise full-bodied, showed glittering blond hair exuberantly dressed; a pink, fat face cold under a white-hot tiara; a solid, cold bosom under a white-hot necklace; great, cold, gloved arms, and the rest of her beautifully upholstered. Amelia was an Amberson born, herself, Sydney's second-cousin: they had no children, and Sydney was without a business or a profession; thus both found a great deal of time to think about the appropriateness of their becoming Excellencies. And as George ascended the broad stairway, they were precisely the aunt and uncle he was most pleased to point out, to a girl from out of town, as his appurtenances in the way of relatives. At sight of them the grandeur of the Amberson family was instantly conspicuous as a permanent thing: it was impossible to doubt that the Ambersons were entrenched, in their nobility and riches, behind polished and glittering barriers which were as solid as they were brilliant, and would last.

CHAPTER V

The hero of the fête, with the dark-eyed little beauty upon his arm, reached the top of the second flight of stairs; and here, beyond a spacious landing, where two proud-like darkies tended a crystalline punch bowl, four wide archways in a rose-vine lattice framed gliding silhouettes of waltzers, already smoothly at it to the castanets of "*La Paloma*." Old John Minafer, evidently surfeited, was in the act of leaving these delights. "D'want 'ny more o' that!" he barked. "Just slidin' around! Call that dancin'? Rather see a jig any day in the world! They ain't very modest, some of 'em. I don't mind *that*, though. Not me!"

Miss Fanny Minafer was no longer in charge of him: he emerged from the ballroom escorted by a middle-aged man of commonplace appearance. The escort had a dry, lined face upon which, not ornamentally but as a matter of course, there grew a business man's short moustache; and his thin neck showed an Adam's apple, but not conspicuously, for there was nothing conspicuous about him. Baldish, dim, quiet, he was an unnoticeable part of this festival, and although there were a dozen or more middle-aged men present, not casually to be distinguished from him in general aspect, he was probably the last person in the big house at whom a stranger would have glanced twice. It did not enter George's mind to mention to Miss Morgan that this was his father, or to say anything whatever about him.

Mr. Minafer shook his son's hand unobtrusively in passing.

"I'll take Uncle John home," he said, in a low voice. "Then I guess

I'll go on home myself—I'm not a great hand at parties, you know. Good-night, George."

George murmured a friendly enough good-night without pausing. Ordinarily he was not ashamed of the Minafers; he seldom thought about them at all, for he belonged, as most American children do, to the mother's family—but he was anxious not to linger with Miss Morgan in the vicinity of old John, whom he felt to be a disgrace.

He pushed brusquely through the fringe of calculating youths who were gathered in the arches, watching for chances to dance only with girls who would soon be taken off their hands, and led his stranger lady out upon the floor. They caught the time instantly, and were away in the waltz.

George danced well, and Miss Morgan seemed to float as part of the music, the very dove itself of "*La Paloma*." They said nothing as they danced; her eyes were cast down all the while—the prettiest gesture for a dancer—and there was left in the universe, for each of them, only their companionship in this waltz; while the faces of the other dancers, swimming by, denoted not people but merely blurs of colour. George became conscious of strange feelings within him: an exaltation of soul, tender, but indefinite, and seemingly located in the upper part of his diaphragm.

The stopping of the music came upon him like the waking to an alarm clock; for instantly six or seven of the calculating persons about the entryways bore down upon Miss Morgan to secure dances. George had to do with one already established as a belle, it seemed.

"Give me the next and the one after that," he said hurriedly, recovering some presence of mind, just as the nearest applicant reached them. "And give me every third one the rest of the evening."

She laughed. "Are you asking?"

"What do you mean, 'asking'?"

"It sounded as though you were just telling me to give you all those dances."

"Well, I want 'em!" George insisted.

"What about all the other girls it's your duty to dance with?"

"They'll have to go without," he said heartlessly; and then, with surprising vehemence: "Here! I want to know: Are you going to give me those—"

"Good gracious!" she laughed. "Yes!"

The applicants flocked round her, urging contracts for what remained, but they did not dislodge George from her side, though he made it evident that they succeeded in annoying him; and presently he extricated her from an accumulating siege—she must have connived in the extrication—and bore her off to sit beside him upon the stairway that led to the musicians' gallery, where they were sufficiently retired, yet had a view of the room.

"How'd all those ducks get to know you so quick?" George inquired, with little enthusiasm.

"Oh, I've been here a week."

"Looks as if you'd been pretty busy!" he said. "Most of those ducks, I don't know what my mother wanted to invite 'em here for."

"Don't you like them?"

"Oh, I used to see something of a few of 'em. I was president of a club we had here, and some of 'em belonged to it, but I don't care much for that sort of thing any more. I really don't see why my mother invited 'em."

"Perhaps it was on account of their parents," Miss Morgan suggested mildly. "Maybe she didn't want to offend their fathers and mothers."

"Oh, hardly! I don't think my mother need worry much about offending anybody in this old town."

"It must be wonderful," said Miss Morgan. "It must be wonderful, Mr. Amberson—Mr. Minafer, I mean."

"What must be wonderful?"

"To be so important as that!"

"*That* isn't 'important,'" George assured her. "Anybody that really is anybody ought to be able to do about as they like in their own town, I should think!"

She looked at him critically from under her shading lashes—but her eyes grew gentler almost at once. In truth, they became more appreciative than critical. George's imperious good looks were altogether manly, yet approached actual beauty as closely as a boy's good looks should dare; and dance-music and flowers have some effect upon nineteen-year-old girls as well as upon eighteen-year-old boys. Miss Morgan turned her eyes slowly from George, and pressed her face among the lilies-of-the-valley and violets of the pretty bouquet she carried, while, from the gallery above, the music of the next dance carolled out merrily in a new two-step. The musicians made the melody gay for the Christmastime with chimes of sleighbells, and the entrance to the shadowed stairway framed the passing flushed and lively dancers, but neither George nor Miss Morgan suggested moving to join the dance.

The stairway was draughty: the steps were narrow and uncomfortable; no older person would have remained in such a place. Moreover, these two young people were strangers to each other; neither had said anything in which the other had discovered the slightest intrinsic interest; there had not arisen between them the beginnings of congeniality, or even of friendliness—but stairways near ballrooms have more to answer for than have moonlit lakes and mountain sunsets. Some day the laws of glamour must be discovered, because they are so important that the world would be wiser now if Sir Isaac Newton had been hit on the head, not by an apple, but by a young lady.

Age, confused by its own long accumulation of follies, is everlastingly inquiring, "What does *she* see in *him?*" as if young love came about through thinking—or through conduct. Age wants to know: "What on earth can they *talk* about?" as if talking had anything to do with April rains! At seventy, one gets up in the morning, finds the air sweet under a bright sun, feels lively; thinks, "I am hearty, today," and plans to go for a drive. At eighteen, one goes to a dance, sits with a stranger on a stairway, feels peculiar, thinks nothing, and becomes incapable of any plan whatever. Miss Morgan and George stayed where they were.

They had agreed to this in silence and without knowing it; certainly without exchanging glances of intelligence—they had exchanged no glances at all. Both sat staring vaguely out into the ballroom, and, for a time, they did not speak. Over their heads the music reached a climax of vivacity: drums, cymbals, triangle, and sleighbells, beating, clashing, tinkling. Here and there were to be seen couples so carried away that, ceasing to move at the decorous, even glide, considered most knowing, they pranced and whirled through the throng, from wall to wall, galloping bounteously in abandon. George suffered a shock of vague surprise when he perceived that his aunt, Fanny Minafer, was the lady-half of one of these wild couples.

Fanny Minafer, who rouged a little, was like fruit which in some climates dries with the bloom on. Her features had remained prettily childlike; so had her figure, and there were times when strangers, seeing her across the street, took her to be about twenty; they were other times when at the same distance they took her to be about sixty, instead of forty, as she was. She had old days and young days; old hours and young hours; old minutes and young minutes; for the change might be that quick. An alteration in her expression, or a difference in the attitude of her head, would cause astonishing indentations to appear—and behold, Fanny was an old lady! But she had been never more childlike than she was to-night as she flew over the floor in the capable arms of the queer-looking duck; for this person was her partner.

The queer-looking duck had been a real dancer in his day, it appeared; and evidently his day was not yet over. In spite of the headlong, gay rapidity with which he bore Miss Fanny about the big room, he danced authoritatively, avoiding without effort the lightest collision with other couples, maintaining sufficient grace throughout his wildest moments, and all the while laughing and talking with his partner. What was most remarkable to George, and a little irritating, this stranger in the Amberson Mansion had no vestige of the air of deference proper to a stranger in such a place: he seemed thoroughly at home. He seemed offensively so, indeed, when, passing the entrance to the gallery stairway, he disengaged his hand from Miss Fanny's for an instant, and not pausing in the dance, waved a laughing salutation more than cordial, then capered lightly out of sight.

George gazed stonily at this manifestation, responding neither by word nor sign. "How's that for a bit of freshness?" he murmured.

"What was?" Miss Morgan asked.

"That queer-looking duck waving his hand at me like that. Except he's the Sharon girls' uncle I don't know him from Adam."

"You don't need to," she said. "He wasn't waving his hand to you: he meant me."

"Oh, he did?" George was not mollified by the explanation. "Everybody seems to mean you! You certainly do seem to've been pretty busy this week you've been here!"

She pressed her bouquet to her face again, and laughed into it, not displeased. She made no other comment, and for another period neither spoke. Meanwhile the music stopped; loud applause insisted upon its renewal; an encore was danced; there was an interlude of voices; and the changing of partners began.

"Well," said George finally, "I must say you don't seem to be much of a prattler. They say it's a great way to get a reputation for being wise, never saying much. Don't you ever talk *any*?"

"When people can understand," she answered.

He had been looking moodily out at the ballroom but he turned to her quickly, at this, saw that her eyes were sunny and content, over the top of her bouquet; and he consented to smile.

"Girls are usually pretty fresh!" he said. "They ought to go to a man's college about a year: they'd get taught a few things about freshness! What you got to do after two o'clock to-morrow afternoon?"

"A whole lot of things. Every minute filled up."

"All right," said George. "The snow's fine for sleighing: I'll come for you in a cutter at ten minutes after two."

"I can't possibly go."

"If you don't," he said, "I'm going to sit in the cutter in front of the gate, wherever you're visiting, all afternoon, and if you try to go out with anybody else he's got to whip me before he gets you." And as she laughed—though she blushed a little, too—he continued, seriously: "If you think I'm not in earnest you're at liberty to make quite a big experiment!"

She laughed again. "I don't think I've often had so large a compliment as that," she said, "especially on such short notice—and yet, I don't think I'll go with you."

"You be ready at ten minutes after two."

"No, I won't."

"Yes, you will!"

"Yes," she said, "I will!" And her partner for the next dance arrived, breathless with searching.

"Don't forget I've got the third from now," George called after her.

"I won't."

"And every third one after that."

"I know!" she called, over her partner's shoulder, and her voice was amused—but meek.

When "the third from now" came, George presented himself before her without any greeting, like a brother, or a mannerless old friend. Neither did she greet him, but moved away with him, concluding, as she went, an exchange of badinage with the preceding partner: she had been talkative enough with him, it appeared. In fact, both George and Miss Morgan talked much more to every one else that evening, than to each other; and they said nothing at all at this time. Both looked preoccupied, as they began to dance, and preserved a gravity of expression to the end of the number. And when "the third one after that" came, they did not dance, but went back to the gallery stairway, seeming to have reached an understanding without any verbal consultation, that this suburb was again the place for them.

"Well," said George, coolly, when they were seated, "what did you say your name was?"

"Morgan."

"Funny name!"

"Everybody else's name always is."

"I didn't mean it was really funny," George explained. "That's just one of my crowd's bits of horsing at college. We always say 'funny name' no matter what it is. I guess we're pretty fresh sometimes; but I knew your name was Morgan because my mother said so downstairs. I meant: what's the rest of it?"

"Lucy."

He was silent.

"Is 'Lucy' a funny name, too?" she inquired.

"No. Lucy's very much all right!" he said, and he went so far as to smile. Even his Aunt Fanny admitted that when George smiled "in a certain way" he was charming.

"Thanks about letting my name be Lucy," she said.

"How old are you?" George asked.

"I don't really know, myself."

"What do you mean: you don't really know yourself?"

"I mean I only know what they tell me. I believe them, of course, but believing isn't really knowing. You believe some certain day is your birthday—at least, I suppose you do—but you don't really know it is because you can't remember."

"Look here!" said George. "Do you always talk like this?"

Miss Lucy Morgan laughed forgivingly, put her young head on one side, like a bird, and responded cheerfully: "I'm willing to learn wisdom. What are you studying in school?"

"College!"

"At the university! Yes. What are you studying there?"

George laughed. "Lot o' useless guff!"

"Then why don't you study some useful guff?"

"What do you mean: 'useful'?"

"Something you'd use later, in your business or profession?"

George waved his hand impatiently. "I don't expect to go into any 'business or profession.' "

"No?"

"Certainly not!" George was emphatic, being sincerely annoyed by a suggestion which showed how utterly she failed to comprehend the kind of person he was.

"Why not?" she asked mildly.

"Just look at 'em!" he said, almost with bitterness, and he made a gesture presumably intended to indicate the business and professional men now dancing within range of vision. "That's a fine career for a man, isn't it! Lawyers, bankers, politicians! What do they get out of life, I'd like to know! What do they ever know about *real* things? Where do they ever *get?*"

He was so earnest that she was surprised and impressed. Evidently he had deep-seated ambitions, for he seemed to speak with actual emotion of these despised things which were so far beneath his planning for the future. She had a vague, momentary vision of Pitt, at twenty-one, prime minister of England; and she spoke, involuntarily in a lowered voice, with deference:

"What do you want to be?" she asked.

George answered promptly.

"A yachtsman," he said.

CHAPTER VI

Having thus, in a word, revealed his ambition for a career above courts, marts, and polling booths, George breathed more deeply than usual, and, turning his face from the lovely companion whom he had just made his confidant, gazed out at the dancers with an expression in which there was both sternness and a contempt for the squalid lives of the unyachted Midlanders before him. However, among them, he marked his mother; and his sombre grandeur relaxed momentarily; a more genial light came into his eyes.

Isabel was dancing with the queer-looking duck; and it was to be noted that the lively gentleman's gait was more sedate than it had been with Miss Fanny Minafer, but not less dexterous and authoritative. He was talking to Isabel as gaily as he had talked to Miss Fanny, though with less laughter, and Isabel listened and answered eagerly: her colour was high and her eyes had a look of delight. She saw George and the beautiful Lucy on the stairway, and nodded to them. George waved his hand vaguely: he had a momentary return of that inexplicable uneasiness and resentment which had troubled him downstairs.

"How lovely your mother is!" Lucy said.

"I think she is," he agreed gently.

"She's the gracefulest woman in that ballroom. She dances like a girl of sixteen."

"Most girls of sixteen," said George, "are bum dancers. Anyhow, I wouldn't dance with one unless I had to."

"Well, you'd better dance with your mother! I never saw anybody lovelier. How wonderfully they dance together!"

"Who?"

"Your mother and—and the queer-looking duck," said Lucy. "I'm going to dance with him pretty soon."

"I don't care—so long as you don't give him one of the numbers that belong to me."

"I'll try to remember," she said, and thoughtfully lifted to her face the bouquet of violets and lilies, a gesture which George noted without approval.

"Look here! Who sent you those flowers you keep makin' such a fuss over?"

"He did."

"Who's 'he'?"

"The queer-looking duck."

George feared no such rival; he laughed loudly. "I s'pose he's some old widower!" he said, the object thus described seeming ignominious enough to a person of eighteen, without additional characterization. "Some old widower!"

Lucy became serious at once. "Yes, he is a widower," she said. "I ought to have told you before; he's my father."

George stopped laughing abruptly. "Well, that's a horse on me. If I'd known he was your father, of course I wouldn't have made fun of him. I'm sorry."

"Nobody could make fun of him," she said quietly.

"Why couldn't they?"

"It wouldn't make him funny: it would only make themselves silly."

Upon this, George had a gleam of intelligence. "Well, I'm not going to make myself silly any more, then; I don't want to take chances like that with *you*. But I thought he was the Sharon girls' uncle. He came with them—"

"Yes," she said, "I'm always late to everything: I wouldn't let them wait for me. We're visiting the Sharons."

"About time I knew that! You forget my being so fresh about your father, will you? Of course he's a distinguished looking man, in a way."

Lucy was still serious. " 'In a way'?" she repeated. "You mean, not in your way, don't you?"

George was perplexed. "How do you mean: not in my way?"

"People pretty often say 'in a way' and 'rather distinguished looking,' or 'rather' so-and-so, or 'rather' anything, to show that *they're* superior, don't they? In New York last month I overheard a climber sort of woman speaking of me as 'little Miss Morgan,' but she didn't mean my height; she meant that she was important. Her husband spoke of a friend of mine as 'little Mr. Pembroke' and 'little Mr. Pembroke' is six-feet-three. This husband and wife were really so terribly unimportant that the only way they knew to pretend to be important was calling people 'little' Miss or Mister so-and-so. It's a kind of snob slang, I think. Of course people don't always say 'rather' or 'in a way' to be superior."

"I should say not! I use both of 'em a great deal myself," said George. "One thing I don't see though: What's the use of a man being six-feet-three? Men that size can't handle themselves as well as a man about five-feet-eleven and a half can. Those long, gangling men, they're nearly always too kind of wormy to be any good in athletics, and they're so awkward they keep falling over chairs or—"

"Mr. Pembroke is in the army," said Lucy primly. "He's extraordinarily graceful."

"In the army? Oh, I suppose he's some old friend of your father's."

"They got on very well," she said, "after I introduced them."

George was a straightforward soul, at least. "See here!" he said. "Are you engaged to anybody?"

"No."

Not wholly mollified, he shrugged his shoulders. "You seem to know a good many people! Do you live in New York?"

"No. We don't live anywhere."

"What you mean: you don't live anywhere?"

"We've lived all over," she answered. "Papa used to live here in this town, but that was before I was born."

"What do you keep moving around so for? Is he a promoter?"

"No. He's an inventor."

"What's he invented?"

"Just lately," said Lucy, "he's been working on a new kind of horseless carriage."

"Well, I'm sorry for him," George said, in no unkindly spirit. "Those things are never going to amount to anything. People aren't going to spend their lives lying on their backs in the road and letting grease drip in their faces. Horseless carriages are pretty much a failure, and your father better not waste his time on 'em."

"Papa'd be so grateful," she returned, "if he could have your advice."

Instantly George's face became flushed. "I don't know that I've done anything to be insulted for!" he said. "I don't see that what I said was particularly fresh."

"No, indeed!"

"Then what do you—"

She laughed gaily. "I don't! And I don't mind your being such a lofty person at all. I think it's ever so interesting—but papa's a great man!"

"Is he?" George decided to be good-natured. "Well, let us hope so. I hope so, I'm sure."

Looking at him keenly, she saw that the magnificent youth was incredibly sincere in this bit of graciousness. He spoke as a tolerant, elderly statesman might speak of a promising young politician; and with her eyes still upon him, Lucy shook her head in gentle wonder. "I'm just beginning to understand," she said.

"Understand what?"

"What it means to be a real Amberson in this town. Papa told me something about it before we came, but I see he didn't say half enough!"

George superbly took this all for tribute. "Did your father say he knew the family before he left here?"

"Yes. I believe he was particularly a friend of your Uncle George; and he didn't say so, but I imagine he must have known your mother very well, too. He wasn't an inventor then; he was a young lawyer. The town was smaller in those days, and I believe he was quite well known."

"I dare say. I've no doubt the family are all very glad to see him back, especially if they used to have him at the house a good deal, as he told you."

"I don't think he meant to boast of it," she said. "He spoke of it quite calmly."

George stared at her for a moment in perplexity, then perceiving that her intention was satirical, "Girls really ought to go to a man's college," he said—"just a month or two, anyhow. It'd take *some* of the freshness out of 'em!"

"I can't believe it," she retorted, as her partner for the next dance arrived. "It would only make them a little politer on the surface— they'd be really just as awful as ever, after you got to know them a few minutes."

"What do you mean: 'after you got to know them a—'"

She was departing to the dance. "Janie and Mary Sharon told me all about what sort of a *little* boy you were," she said, over her shoulder. "You must think it out!"

She took wing away on the breeze of the waltz, and George, having stared gloomily after her for a few moments, postponed filling an engagement, and strolled round the fluctuating outskirts of the dance to where his uncle, George Amberson, stood smilingly watching, under one of the rose-vine arches at the entrance to the room.

"Hello, young namesake," said the uncle. "Why lingers the laggard heel of the dancer? Haven't you got a partner?"

"She's sitting around waiting for me somewhere," said George. "See here: Who is this fellow Morgan that Aunt Fanny Minafer was dancing with a while ago?"

Amberson laughed. "He's a man with a pretty daughter, Georgie. Meseemed you've been spending the evening noticing something of that sort—or do I err?"

"Never mind! What sort is he?"

"I think we'll have to give him a character, Georgie. He's an old friend; used to practise law here—perhaps he had more debts than cases, but he paid 'em all up before he left town. Your question is purely mercenary, I take it: you want to know his true worth before proceeding further with the daughter. I cannot inform you, though I notice signs of considerable prosperity in that becoming dress of hers. However, you never can tell. It is an age when every sacrifice is made for the young, and how your own poor mother managed to provide those genuine pearl studs for you out of her allowance from father, I can't—"

"Oh, dry up!" said the nephew. "I understand this Morgan—"

"Mr. Eugene Morgan," his uncle suggested. "Politeness requires that the young should—"

"I guess the 'young' didn't know much about politeness in your day," George interrupted. "I understand that Mr. Eugene Morgan used to be a great friend of the family."

"Oh, the Minafers?" the uncle inquired, with apparent innocence. "No, I seem to recall that he and your father were not—"

"I mean the Ambersons," George said impatiently. "I understand he was a good deal around the house here."

"What is your objection to that, George?"

"What do you mean: my objection?"

"You seemed to speak with a certain crossness."

"Well," said George, "I meant he seems to feel awfully at home here. The way he was dancing with Aunt Fanny—"

Amberson laughed. "I'm afraid your Aunt Fanny's heart was stirred by ancient recollections, Georgie."

"You mean she used to be silly about him?"

"She wasn't considered singular," said the uncle. "He was—he was popular. Could you bear a question?"

"What do you mean: could I bear—"

"I only wanted to ask: Do you take this same passionate interest in the parents of every girl you dance with? Perhaps it's a new fashion we old bachelors ought to take up. Is it the thing this year to—"

"Oh, go on!" said George, moving away. "I only wanted to know—" He left the sentence unfinished, and crossed the room to where a girl sat waiting for his nobility to find time to fulfil his contract with her for this dance.

"Pardon f' keep' wait," he muttered, as she rose brightly to meet him; and she seemed pleased that he came at all—but George was used to girls' looking radiant when he danced with them, and she had little effect upon him. He danced with her perfunctorily, thinking the while of Mr. Eugene Morgan and his daughter. Strangely enough, his thoughts dwelt more upon the father than the daughter, though George could not possibly have given a reason—even to himself—for this disturbing preponderance.

By a coincidence, though not an odd one, the thoughts and conversation of Mr. Eugene Morgan at this very time were concerned with George Amberson Minafer, rather casually, it is true. Mr. Morgan had retired to a room set apart for smoking, on the second floor, and had found a grizzled gentleman lounging in solitary possession.

" 'Gene Morgan!" this person exclaimed, rising with great heartiness. "I'd heard you were in town—I don't believe you know me!"

"Yes, I do, Fred Kinney!" Mr. Morgan returned with equal friendliness. "Your real face—the one I used to know—it's just underneath the one you're masquerading in to-night. You ought to have changed it more if you wanted a disguise."

"Twenty years!" said Mr. Kinney. "It makes some difference in faces, but more in behaviour!"

"It does so!" his friend agreed with explosive emphasis. "My own behaviour began to be different about that long ago—quite suddenly."

"I remember," said Mr. Kinney sympathetically, "Well, life's odd enough as we look back."

"Probably it's going to be odder still—if we could look forward."

"Probably."

They sat and smoked.

"However," Mr. Morgan remarked presently, "I still dance like an Indian. Don't you?"

"No. I leave that to my boy Fred. He does the dancing for the family."

"I suppose he's upstairs hard at it?"

"No, he's not here." Mr. Kinney glanced toward the open door and lowered his voice. "He wouldn't come. It seems that a couple of years or so ago he had a row with young Georgie Minafer. Fred was president of a literary club they had, and he said this young Georgie got himself elected instead, in an overbearing sort of way. Fred's red-headed, you know—I suppose you remember his mother? You were at the wedding—"

"I remember the wedding," said Mr. Morgan. "And I remember your bachelor dinner—most of it, that is."

"Well, my boy Fred's as red-headed now," Mr. Kinney went on, "as his mother was then, and he's very bitter about his row with Georgie Minafer. He says he'd rather burn his foot off than set it inside any Amberson house or any place else where young Georgie is. Fact is, the boy seemed to have so much feeling over it I had my doubts about coming myself, but my wife said it was all nonsense; we mustn't humour Fred in a grudge over such a little thing, and while she despised that Georgie Minafer, herself, as much as any one else did, she wasn't going to miss a big Amberson show just on account of a boys' rumpus, and so on and so on; and so we came."

"Do people dislike young Minafer generally?"

"I don't know about 'generally.' I guess he gets plenty of toadying; but there's certainly a lot of people that are glad to express their opinions about him."

"What's the matter with him?"

"Too much Amberson, I suppose, for one thing. And for another, his mother just fell down and worshipped him from the day he was born. That's what beats me! I don't have to tell you what Isabel Amberson is, Eugene Morgan. She's got a touch of the Amberson high stuff about her, but you can't get anybody that ever knew her to deny that she's just about the finest woman in the world."

"No," said Eugene Morgan. "You can't get anybody to deny that."

"Then I can't see how she doesn't see the truth about that boy. He thinks he's a little tin god on wheels—and honestly, it makes some people weak and sick just to think about him! Yet that high-spirited, intelligent woman, Isabel Amberson, actually sits and worships him! You can hear it in her voice when she speaks to him or speaks of him. You can see it in her eyes when she looks at him. My Lord! What *does* she see when she looks at him?"

Morgan's odd expression of genial apprehension deepened whimsically, though it denoted no actual apprehension whatever, and cleared away from his face altogether when he smiled; he became surprisingly winning and persuasive when he smiled. He smiled now, after a moment, at this question of his old friend. "She sees something that we don't see," he said.

"What does she see?"

"An angel."

Kinney laughed aloud. "Well, if she sees an angel when she looks at Georgie Minafer, she's a funnier woman than I thought she was!"

"Perhaps she is," said Morgan. "But that's what she sees."

"My Lord! It's easy to see you've only known him an hour or so. In that time have you looked at Georgie and seen an angel?"

"No. All I saw was a remarkably good-looking fool-boy with the pride of Satan and a set of nice new drawing-room manners that he probably couldn't use more than half an hour at a time without busting."

"Then what—"

"Mothers are right," said Morgan. "Do you think this young George is the same sort of creature when he's with his mother that he is when he's bulldozing your boy Fred? Mothers see the angel in us because the angel is there. If it's shown to the mother, the son has got an angel to show, hasn't he? When a son cuts somebody's throat the mother only sees it's possible for a misguided angel to act like a devil—and she's entirely right about that!"

Kinney laughed, and put his hand on his friend's shoulder. "I remember what a fellow you always were to argue," he said. "You mean Georgie Minafer is as much of an angel as any murderer is, and that Georgie's mother is always right."

"I'm afraid she always has been," Morgan said lightly.

The friendly hand remained upon his shoulder. "She was wrong once, old fellow. At least, so it seemed to me."

"No," said Morgan, a little awkwardly. "No—"

Kinney relieved the slight embarrassment that had come upon both of them: he laughed again. "Wait till you know young Georgie a little better," he said. "Something tells me you're going to change your mind about his having an angel to show, if you see anything of him!"

"You mean beauty's in the eye of the beholder, and the angel is all in the eye of the mother. If you were a painter, Fred, you'd paint mothers with angels' eyes holding imps in their laps. Me, I'll stick to the Old Masters and the cherubs."

Mr. Kinney looked at him musingly. "Somebody's eyes must have been pretty angelic," he said, "if they've been persuading you that Georgie Minafer is a cherub!"

"They are," said Morgan heartily. "They're more angelic than ever." And as a new flourish of music sounded overhead he threw away his cigarette, and jumped up briskly. "Good-bye, I've got this dance with her."

"With whom?"

"With Isabel!"

The grizzled Mr. Kinney affected to rub his eyes. "It startles me, your jumping up like that to go and dance with Isabel Amberson! Twenty years seem to have passed—but have they? Tell me, have you danced with poor old Fanny, too, this evening?"

"Twice!"

"My Lord!" Kinney groaned, half in earnest. "Old times starting all over again! My Lord!"

"Old times?" Morgan laughed gaily from the doorway. "Not a bit! There aren't any old times. When times are gone they're not old, they're dead! There aren't any times but new times!"

And he vanished in such a manner that he seemed already to have begun dancing.

Chapter VII

The appearance of Miss Lucy Morgan the next day, as she sat in George's fast cutter, proved so charming that her escort was stricken to soft words instantly, and failed to control a poetic impulse. Her rich little hat was trimmed with black fur; her hair was almost as dark as the fur; a great boa of black fur was about her shoulders; her hands were vanished into a black muff; and George's laprobe was black. "You look like—" he said. "Your face looks like—it looks like a snowflake on a lump of coal. I mean a—a snowflake that would be a rose-leaf, too!"

"Perhaps you'd better look at the reins," she returned. "We almost upset just then."

George declined to heed this advice. "Because there's too much pink in your cheeks for a snowflake," he continued. "What's that fairy story about snow-white and rose-red—"

"We're going pretty fast, Mr. Minafer!"

"Well, you see, I'm only here for two weeks."

"I mean the sleigh!" she explained. "We're not the only people on the street, you know."

"Oh, *they'll* keep out of the way."

"That's very patrician charioteering, but it seems to me a horse like this needs guidance. I'm sure he's going almost twenty miles an hour."

"That's nothing," said George; but he consented to look forward again. "He can trot under three minutes, all right." He laughed. "I suppose your father thinks he can build a horseless carriage to go that fast!"

"They go that fast already, sometimes."

"Yes," said George; "they do—for about a hundred feet! Then they give a yell and burn up."

Evidently she decided not to defend her father's faith in horseless carriages, for she laughed, and said nothing. The cold air was polka-dotted with snowflakes, and trembled to the loud, continuous jingling of sleighbells. Boys and girls, all aglow and panting jets of vapour, darted at the passing sleighs to ride on the runners, or sought to rope their sleds to any vehicle whatever, but the fleetest no more than just touched the flying cutter, though a hundred soggy mittens grasped for it, then reeled and whirled till sometimes the wearers of those daring mittens plunged flat in the snow and lay a-sprawl, reflecting. For this was the holiday time, and all the boys and girls in town were out, most of them on National Avenue.

But there came panting and chugging up that flat thoroughfare a thing which some day was to spoil all their sleigh-time merriment—save for the rashest and most disobedient. It was vaguely like a topless surry, but cumbrous with unwholesome excrescences fore and aft, while underneath were spinning leather belts and something that whirred and howled and seemed to stagger. The ride-stealers made no attempt to fasten their sleds to a contrivance so nonsensical and yet so fearsome. Instead, they gave over their sport and concentrated all their energies in their lungs, so that up and down the street the one cry shrilled increasingly: "Git a hoss! Git a hoss! Git a hoss! Mister, why don't you git a hoss?" But the mahout in charge, sitting solitary on the front seat, was unconcerned—he laughed, and now and then ducked a snowball without losing any of his good-nature. It was Mr. Eugene Morgan who exhibited so cheerful a countenance between the forward visor of a deer-stalker cap and the collar of a fuzzy gray ulster. "Git a hoss!" the children shrieked, and gruffer voices joined them. "Git a hoss! Git a hoss! Git a *hoss!*"

George Minafer was correct thus far: the twelve miles an hour of such a machine would never overtake George's trotter. The cutter was already scurrying between the stone pillars at the entrance to Amberson Addition.

"That's my grandfather's," said George, nodding toward the Amberson Mansion.

"I ought to know that!" Lucy exclaimed. "We stayed there late enough last night: papa and I were almost the last to go. He and your mother and Miss Fanny Minafer got the musicians to play another waltz when everybody else had gone downstairs and the fiddles were being put away in their cases. Papa danced part of it with Miss Minafer and the rest with your mother. Miss Minafer's your aunt, isn't she?"

"Yes; she lives with us. I tease her a good deal."

"What about?"

"Oh, anything handy—whatever's easy to tease an old maid about."

"Doesn't she mind?"

"She usually has sort of a grouch on me," laughed George. "Nothing much. That's our house just beyond grandfather's." He waved a sealskin gauntlet to indicate the house Major Amberson had built for Isabel as a wedding gift. "It's almost the same as grandfather's, only not as large and hasn't got a regular ballroom. We gave the dance, last night, at grandfather's on account of the ballroom, and because I'm the only grandchild, you know. Of course, some day that'll be my house, though I expect my mother will most likely go on living where she does now, with father and Aunt Fanny. I suppose I'll probably build a country house, too—somewhere East, I guess." He stopped speaking, and frowned as they passed a closed carriage and pair. The body of this comfortable vehicle sagged slightly to one side; the paint was old and seamed with hundreds of minute cracks like little rivers on a black map; the coachman, a fat and elderly darky, seemed to drowse upon the box; but the open window afforded the occupants of the cutter a glimpse of a tired, fine old face, a silk hat, a pearl tie, and an astrachan collar, evidently out to take the air.

"There's your grandfather now," said Lucy. "Isn't it?"

George's frown was not relaxed. "Yes, it is; and he ought to give that rat-trap away and sell those old horses. They're a disgrace, all shaggy—not even clipped. I suppose he doesn't notice it—people get awful funny when they get old; they seem to lose their self-respect, sort of."

"He seemed a real Brummell to me," she said.

"Oh, he keeps up about what he *wears,* well enough, but—well, look at that!" He pointed to a statue of Minerva, one of the cast-iron sculptures Major Amberson had set up in opening the Addition years before. Minerva was intact, but a blackish streak descended unpleasantly from her forehead to the point of her straight nose, and a few other streaks were sketched in a repellent dinge upon the folds of her drapery.

"That must be from soot," said Lucy. "There are so many houses around here."

"Anyhow, somebody ought to see that these statues are kept clean. My grandfather owns a good many of these houses, I guess, for renting. Of course, he sold most of the lots—there aren't any vacant ones, and there used to be heaps of 'em when I was a boy. Another thing I don't think he ought to allow: a good many of these people bought big lots and they built houses on 'em; then the price of the land kept getting higher, and they'd sell part of their yards and let the people that bought it build houses on it to live in, till they haven't hardly any of 'em got big, open yards any more, and it's getting all too much built up. The way it used to be, it was like a gentleman's country estate, and that's the way my grandfather ought to keep it. He lets these people take too many liberties: they do anything they want to."

"But how could he stop them?" Lucy asked, surely with reason. "If he sold them the land, it's theirs, isn't it?"

George remained serene in the face of this apparently difficult question. "He ought to have all the trades-people boycott the families that sell part of their yards that way. All he'd have to do would be to tell the trades-people they wouldn't get any more orders from the family if they didn't do it."

"From 'the family'? What family?"

"Our family," said George, unperturbed. "The Ambersons."

"I see!" she murmured, and evidently she did see something that he did not, for, as she lifted her muff to her face, he asked:

"What are you laughing at now?"

"Why?"

"You always seem to have some little secret of your own to get happy over!"

" 'Always'!" she exclaimed. "What a big word, when we only met last night!"

"That's another case of it," he said, with obvious sincerity. "One of the reasons I don't like you—much!—is you've got that way of seeming quietly superior to everybody else."

"I!" she cried. "I have?"

"Oh, you think you keep it sort of confidential to yourself, but it's plain enough! I don't believe in that kind of thing."

"You don't?"

"No," said George emphatically. "Not with *me*! I think the world's like this: there's a few people that their birth and position, and so on, puts them at the top, and they ought to treat each other entirely as equals." His voice betrayed a little emotion as he added, "I wouldn't speak like this to everybody."

"You mean you're confiding your deepest creed—or code, whatever it is—to me?"

"Go on, make fun of it, then!" George said bitterly. "You do think you're terribly clever! It makes me tired!"

"Well, as you don't like my seeming 'quietly superior,' after this I'll be noisily superior," she returned cheerfully. "We aim to please!"

"I had a notion before I came for you to-day that we were going to quarrel," he said.

"No, we won't; it takes two!" She laughed and waved her muff toward a new house, not quite completed, standing in a field upon their right. They had passed beyond Amberson Addition, and were leaving the northern fringes of the town for the open country. "Isn't that a beautiful house!" she exclaimed. "Papa and I call it our Beautiful House."

George was not pleased. "Does it belong to you?"

"Of course not! Papa brought me out here the other day, driving in his machine, and we both loved it. It's so spacious and dignified and plain."

"Yes, it's plain enough!" George grunted.

"Yet it's lovely; the gray-green roof and shutters give just enough colour, with the trees, for the long white walls. It seems to me the finest house I've seen in this part of the country."

George was outraged by an enthusiasm so ignorant—not ten minutes ago they had passed the Amberson Mansion. "Is that a sample of your taste in architecture?" he asked.

"Yes. Why?"

"Because it strikes me you better go somewhere and study the subject a little!"

Lucy looked puzzled. "What makes you have so much feeling about it? Have I offended you?"

" 'Offended' nothing!" George returned brusquely. "Girls usually think they know it all as soon as they've learned to dance and dress and flirt a little. They never know anything about things like architecture, for instance. That house is about as bum a house as any house I ever saw!"

"Why?"

" 'Why?' " George repeated. "Did you ask me 'why?' "

"Yes."

"Well, for one thing—" he paused—"for one thing—well, just look at it! I shouldn't think you'd have to do any more than look at it if you'd ever given any attention to architecture."

"What is the matter with its architecture, Mr. Minafer?"

"Well, it's this way," said George. "It's like this. Well, for instance, that house—well, it was built like a town house." He spoke of it in the past tense, because they had now left it far behind them—a human habit of curious significance. "It was like a house meant for a street in the city. What kind of a house was that for people of any taste to build out here in the country?"

"But papa says it's built that way on purpose. There are a lot of other houses being built in this direction, and papa says the city's coming out this way; and in a year or two that house will be right in town."

"It was a bum house, anyhow," said George crossly. "I don't even know the people that are building it. They say a lot of riffraff come to town every year nowadays and there's other riffraff that have always lived here, and have made a little money, and act as if they owned the place. Uncle Sydney was talking about it yesterday: he says he and some of his friends are organizing a country club, and already some of these riffraff are worming into it—people he never heard of at all! Anyhow, I guess it's pretty clear you don't know a great deal about architecture."

She demonstrated the completeness of her amiability by laughing. "I'll know something about the North Pole before long," she said, "if we keep going much farther in this direction!"

At this he was remorseful. "All right, we'll turn and drive south awhile till you get warmed up again. I expect we have been going against the wind about long enough. Indeed, I'm sorry!"

He said, "Indeed, I'm sorry," in a nice way, and looked very strikingly handsome when he said it, she thought. No doubt it is true that there is more rejoicing in heaven over one sinner repented than over all the saints who consistently remain holy, and the rare, sudden gentlenesses of arrogant people have infinitely more effect than the continual gentleness of gentle people. Arrogance turned gentle melts the heart; and Lucy gave her companion a little sidelong, sunny nod of acknowledgment. George was dazzled by the quick glow of her eyes, and found himself at a loss for something to say.

Having turned about, he kept his horse to a walk, and at this gait the sleighbells tinkled but intermittently. Gleaming wanly through the whitish vapour that kept rising from the trotter's body and flanks, they were like tiny fog-bells, and made the only sounds in a great winter silence. The white road ran between lonesome rail fences; and frozen barnyards beyond the fences showed sometimes a harrow left to rust, with its iron seat half filled with stiffened snow, and sometimes an old dead buggy, its wheels forever set, it seemed, in the solid ice of deep ruts. Chickens scratched the metallic earth with an air of protest, and a masterless ragged colt looked up in sudden horror at the mild tinkle of the passing bells, then blew fierce clouds of steam at the sleigh. The snow no longer fell, and far ahead, in a grayish cloud that lay upon the land, was the town.

Lucy looked at this distant thickening reflection. "When we get this far out we can see there must be quite a little smoke hanging over the town," she said. "I suppose that's because it's growing. As it grows bigger it seems to get ashamed of itself, so it makes this cloud and hides in it. Papa says it used to be a bit nicer when he lived here: he always speaks of it differently—he always has a gentle look, a particular tone of voice, I've noticed. He must have been very fond of it. It must have been a lovely place: everybody must have been so jolly. From the way he talks, you'd think life here then was just one long midsummer serenade. He declares it was always sunshiny, that the air wasn't like the air anywhere else—that, as he remembers it, there always seemed to be gold-dust in the air. I doubt it! I think it doesn't seem to be duller air to him now just on account of having a little soot in it sometimes, but probably because he was twenty years younger then. It seems to me the gold-dust he thinks was here is just his being young that he remembers. I think it was just youth. It *is* pretty pleasant to be young, isn't it?" She laughed absently, then appeared to become wistful. "I wonder if we really do enjoy it as much as we'll look back and think we did! I don't suppose so. Anyhow, for my part I feel as if I must be missing something about it, somehow, because I don't ever seem to be thinking about what's happening at the present moment; I'm always looking forward to something—thinking about things that will happen when I'm older."

"You're a funny girl," George said gently. "But your voice sounds pretty nice when you think and talk along together like that!"

The horse shook himself all over, and the impatient sleighbells made his wish audible. Accordingly, George tightened the reins, and the cutter was off again at a three-minute trot, no despicable rate of speed. It was not long before they were again passing Lucy's Beautiful House, and here George thought fit to put an appendix to his remark. "You're a funny girl, and you know a lot—but I don't believe you know much about architecture!"

Coming toward them, black against the snowy road, was a strange silhouette. It approached moderately and without visible means of progression, so the matter seemed from a distance; but as the cutter shortened the distance, the silhouette was revealed to be Mr. Morgan's horseless carriage, conveying four people atop: Mr. Morgan with George's mother beside him, and, in the rear seat, Miss Fanny Minafer and the Honorable George Amberson. All four seemed to be in the liveliest humour, like high-spirited people upon a new adventure; and Isabel waved her handkerchief dashingly as the cutter flashed by them.

"For the Lord's sake!" George gasped.

"Your mother's a dear," said Lucy. "And she does wear the most bewitching *things*! She looked like a Russian princess, though I doubt if they're that handsome."

George said nothing; he drove on till they had crossed Amberson Addition and reached the stone pillars at the head of National Avenue. There he turned.

"Let's go back and take another look at that old sewing-machine," he said. "It certainly is the weirdest, craziest—"

He left the sentence unfinished, and presently they were again in sight of the old sewing-machine. George shouted mockingly.

Alas! three figures stood in the road, and a pair of legs, with the toes turned up, indicated that a fourth figure lay upon its back in the snow, beneath a horseless carriage that had decided to need a horse.

George became vociferous with laughter, and coming up at his trotter's best gait, snow spraying from runners and every hoof, swerved to the side of the road and shot by, shouting, "Git a hoss! Git a hoss! Git a hoss!"

Three hundred yards away he turned and came back, racing; leaning out as he passed, to wave jeeringly at the group about the disabled machine: "Git a hoss! Git a hoss! Git a—"

The trotter had broken into a gallop, and Lucy cried a warning: "Be careful!" she said. "Look where you're driving! There's a ditch on that side. *Look*—"

George turned too late; the cutter's right runner went into the ditch and snapped off; the little sleigh upset, and, after dragging its occupants some fifteen yards, left them lying together in a bank of snow. Then the vigorous young horse kicked himself free of all annoyances, and disappeared down the road, galloping cheerfully.

Chapter VIII

When George regained some measure of his presence of mind, Miss Lucy Morgan's cheek, snowy and cold, was pressing his nose slightly to one side; his right arm was firmly about her neck; and a monstrous amount of her fur boa seemed to mingle with an equally unplausible quantity of snow in his mouth. He was confused, but conscious of no objection to any of these juxtapositions. She was apparently uninjured, for she sat up, hatless, her hair down, and said mildly:

"Good heavens!"

Though her father had been under his machine when they passed, he was the first to reach them. He threw himself on his knees beside his daughter, but found her already laughing, and was reassured. "They're all right," he called to Isabel, who was running toward them, ahead of her brother and Fanny Minafer. "This snowbank's a feather bed—nothing the matter with them at all. Don't look so pale!"

"Georgie!" she gasped. "*Georgie!*"

Georgie was on his feet, snow all over him.

"Don't make a fuss, mother! Nothing's the matter. That darned silly horse—"

Sudden tears stood in Isabel's eyes. "To see you down underneath—dragging—oh!—" Then with shaking hands she began to brush the snow from him.

"Let me alone," he protested. "You'll ruin your gloves. You're getting snow all over you, and—"

"No, no!" she cried. "You'll catch cold; you mustn't catch cold!" And she continued to brush him.

Amberson had brought Lucy's hat; Miss Fanny acted as lady's-maid; and both victims of the accident were presently restored to about their usual appearance and condition of apparel. In fact, encouraged by the two older gentlemen, the entire party, with one exception, decided that the episode was after all a merry one, and began to laugh about it. But George was glummer than the December twilight now swiftly closing in.

"That darned horse!" he said.

"I wouldn't bother about Pendennis, Georgie," said his uncle. "You can send a man out for what's left of the cutter to-morrow, and Pendennis will gallop straight home to his stable: he'll be there a *long* while before we will, because all we've got to depend on to get us home is Gene Morgan's broken-down chafing-dish yonder."

They were approaching the machine as he spoke, and his friend, again underneath it, heard him. He emerged, smiling. "She'll go," he said.

"What!"

"All aboard!"

He offered his hand to Isabel. She was smiling but still pale, and her eyes, in spite of the smile, kept upon George in a shocked anxiety. Miss Fanny had already mounted to the rear seat, and George, after helping Lucy Morgan to climb up beside his aunt, was following. Isabel saw that his shoes were light things of patent leather, and that snow was clinging to them. She made a little rush toward him, and, as one of his feet rested on the iron step of the machine, in mounting, she began to clean the snow from his shoe with her almost aërial lace handkerchief. "You mustn't catch cold!" she cried.

"Stop that!" George shouted, and furiously withdrew his foot.

"Then stamp the snow off," she begged. "You mustn't ride with wet feet."

"They're not!" George roared, thoroughly outraged. "For heaven's sake get in! You're standing in the snow yourself. Get in!"

Isabel consented, turning to Morgan, whose habitual expression of apprehensiveness was somewhat accentuated. He climbed up after her, George Amberson having gone to the other side. "You're the same Isabel I used to know!" he said in a low voice. "You're a divinely ridiculous woman."

"Am I, Eugene?" she said, not displeased. " 'Divinely' and 'ridiculous' just counterbalance each other, don't they? Plus one and minus one equal nothing; so you mean I'm nothing in particular?"

"No," he answered, tugging at a lever. "That doesn't seem to be precisely what I meant. There!" This exclamation referred to the subterranean machinery, for dismaying sounds came from beneath the floor, and the vehicle plunged, then rolled noisily forward.

"Behold!" George Amberson exclaimed. "She does move! It must be another accident."

" 'Accident'?" Morgan shouted over the din. "No! She breathes, she stirs; she seems to feel a thrill of life along her keel!" And he began to sing "The Star Spangled Banner."

Amberson joined him lustily, and sang on when Morgan stopped. The twilight sky cleared, discovering a round moon already risen; and the musical congressman hailed this bright presence with the complete text and melody of "The Danube River."

His nephew, behind, was gloomy. He had overheard his mother's conversation with the inventor: it seemed curious to him that this Morgan, of whom he had never heard until last night, should be using the name "Isabel" so easily; and George felt that it was not just the thing for his mother to call Morgan "Eugene"; the resentment of the previous night came upon George again. Meanwhile, his mother and Morgan continued their talk; but he could no longer hear what they said; the noise of the car and his uncle's songful mood prevented. He marked how animated Isabel seemed; it was not strange to see his mother so gay, but it was strange that a man not of the family should be the cause of her gaiety. And George sat frowning.

Fanny Minafer had begun to talk to Lucy. "Your father wanted to prove that his horseless carriage would run, even in the snow," she said. "It really does, too."

"Of course!"

"It's so interesting! He's been telling us how he's going to change it. He says he's going to have wheels all made of rubber and blown up with air. I don't understand what he means at all; I should think they'd explode—but Eugene seems to be very confident. He always was confident, though. It seems so like old times to hear him talk!"

She became thoughtful, and Lucy turned to George. "You tried to swing underneath me and break the fall for me when we went over," she said. "I knew you were doing that, and—it was nice of you."

"Wasn't any fall to speak of," he returned brusquely. "Couldn't have hurt either of us."

"Still it was friendly of you—and awfully quick, too. I'll not—I'll not forget it!"

Her voice had a sound of genuineness, very pleasant; and George began to forget his annoyance with her father. This annoyance of his had not been alleviated by the circumstance that neither of the seats of the old sewing-machine was designed for three people, but when his neighbour spoke thus gratefully, he no longer minded the crowding—in fact, it pleased him so much that he began to wish the old sewing-machine would go even slower. And she had spoken no word of blame for his letting that darned horse get the cutter into the ditch. George presently addressed her hurriedly, almost tremulously, speaking close to her ear:

"I forgot to tell you something: you're pretty nice! I thought so the first second I saw you last night. I'll come for you to-night and take you to the Assembly at the Amberson Hotel. You're going, aren't you?"

"Yes, but I'm going with papa and the Sharons. I'll see you there."

"Looks to me as if you were awfully conventional," George grumbled; and his disappointment was deeper than he was willing to let her see—though she probably did see. "Well, we'll dance the cotillion together, anyhow."

"I'm afraid not. I promised Mr. Kinney."

"What!" George's tone was shocked, as at incredible news. "Well, you could break *that* engagement, I guess, if you wanted to! Girls always can get out of things when they want to. Won't you?"

"I don't think so."

"Why not?"

"Because I promised him. Several days ago."

George gulped, and lowered his pride, "I don't—oh, look here! I only want to go to that thing to-night to get to see something of you; and if you don't dance the cotillion with me, how can I? I'll only be here two weeks, and the others have got all the rest of your visit to see you. *Won't* you do it, please?"

"I couldn't."

"See here!" said the stricken George. "If you're going to decline to dance that cotillion with me simply because you've promised a—a—a miserable red-headed outsider like Fred Kinney, why we might as well quit!"

"Quit what?"

"You know perfectly well what I mean," he said huskily.

"I don't."

"Well, you ought to!"

"But I don't at all!"

George, thoroughly hurt, and not a little embittered, expressed himself in a short outburst of laughter: "Well, I ought to have seen it!"

"Seen what?"

"That you might turn out to be a girl who'd like a fellow of the red-headed Kinney sort. I ought to have seen it from the first!"

Lucy bore her disgrace lightly. "Oh, dancing a cotillion with a person doesn't mean that you like him—but I don't see anything in particular the matter with Mr. Kinney. What is?"

"If you don't see anything the matter with him for yourself," George responded, icily, "I don't think pointing it out would help you. You probably wouldn't understand."

"You might try," she suggested. "Of course I'm a stranger here, and if people have done anything wrong or have something unpleasant about them, I wouldn't have any way of knowing it, just at first. If poor Mr. Kinney—"

"I prefer not to discuss it," said George curtly. "He's an enemy of mine."

"Why?"

"I prefer not to discuss it."

"Well, but—"

"I prefer not to discuss it!"

"Very well." She began to hum the air of the song which Mr. George Amberson was now discoursing, "O moon of my delight that knows no wane"—and there was no further conversation on the back seat.

They had entered Amberson Addition, and the moon of Mr. Amberson's delight was overlaid by a slender Gothic filagree; the branches that sprang from the shade trees lining the street. Through the windows of many of the houses rosy lights were flickering; and silver tinsel and evergreen wreaths and brilliant little glass globes of silver and wine colour could be seen, and glimpses were caught of Christmas trees, with people decking them by firelight—reminders that this was Christmas Eve. The ride-stealers had disappeared from the highway, though now and then, over the gasping and howling of the horseless carriage, there came a shrill jeer from some young passer-by upon the sidewalk:

"Mister, fer heaven's sake go an' git a hoss! Git a hoss! *Git* a hoss!"

The contrivance stopped with a heart-shaking jerk before Isabel's house. The gentlemen jumped down, helping Isabel and Fanny to descend; there were friendly leavetakings—and one that was not precisely friendly.

"It's 'au revoir,' till to-night, isn't it?" Lucy asked, laughing.

"Good afternoon!" said George, and he did not wait, as his relatives did, to see the old sewing-machine start briskly down the street, toward the Sharons'; its lighter load consisting now of only Mr. Morgan and his daughter. George went into the house at once.

He found his father reading the evening paper in the library. "Where are your mother and your Aunt Fanny?" Mr. Minafer inquired, not looking up.

"They're coming," said his son; and, casting himself heavily into a chair, stared at the fire.

His prediction was verified a few moments later; the two ladies came in cheerfully, unfastening their fur cloaks. "It's all right, Georgie," said Isabel. "Your Uncle George called to us that Pendennis got home safely. Put your shoes close to the fire, dear, or else go and change them." She went to her husband and patted him lightly on the shoulder, an action which George watched with sombre moodiness. "You might dress before long," she suggested. "We're all going to the Assembly, after dinner, aren't we? Brother George said he'd go with us."

"Look here," said George abruptly. "How about this man Morgan and his old sewing-machine? Doesn't he want to get grandfather to put money into it? Isn't he trying to work Uncle George for that? Isn't that what he's up to?"

It was Miss Fanny who responded. "You little silly!" she cried, with surprising sharpness. "What on earth are you talking about? Eugene Morgan's perfectly able to finance his own inventions these days."

"I'll bet he borrows money of Uncle George," the nephew insisted.

Isabel looked at him in grave perplexity. "Why do you say such a thing, George?" she asked.

"He strikes me as that sort of man," he answered doggedly. "Isn't he, father?"

Minafer set down his paper for the moment. "He was a fairly wild young fellow twenty years ago," he said, glancing at his wife absently. "He was like you in one thing, Georgie; he spent too much money—only he didn't have any mother to get money out of a grandfather for him, so he was usually in debt. But I believe I've heard he's done fairly well of late years. No, I can't say I think he's a swindler, and I doubt if he needs anybody else's money to back his horseless carriage."

"Well, what's he brought the old thing here for, then? People that own elephants don't take their elephants around with 'em when they go visiting. What's he got it here for?"

"I'm sure I don't know," said Mr. Minafer, resuming his paper. "You might ask him."

Isabel laughed and patted her husband's shoulder again. "Aren't you going to dress? Aren't we all going to the dance?"

He groaned faintly. "Aren't your brother and Georgie escorts enough for you and Fanny?"

"Wouldn't you enjoy it at all?"

"You know I don't."

Isabel let her hand remain upon his shoulder a moment longer; she stood behind him, looking into the fire, and George, watching her broodingly, thought there was more colour in her face than the reflection of the flames accounted for. "Well, then," she said indulgently, "stay at home and be happy. We won't urge you if you'd really rather not."

"I really wouldn't," he said contentedly.

Half an hour later, George was passing through the upper hall, in a bath-robe stage of preparation for the evening's gaieties, when he encountered his Aunt Fanny. He stopped her. "Look here!" he said.

"What in the world is the matter with you?" she demanded, regarding him with little amiability. "You look as if you were rehearsing for a villain in a play. Do change your expression!"

His expression gave no sign of yielding to the request; on the contrary, its sombreness deepened. "I suppose you don't know why father doesn't want to go to-night," he said solemnly. "You're his only sister, and yet you don't know!"

"He never wants to go anywhere that I ever heard of," said Fanny. "What *is* the matter with you?"

"He doesn't want to go because he doesn't like this man Morgan."

"Good gracious!" Fanny cried impatiently. "Eugene Morgan isn't in your father's thoughts at all, one way or the other. Why should he be?"

George hesitated. "Well—it strikes me— Look here, what makes you and—and everybody—so excited over him?"

" 'Excited'!" she jeered. "Can't people be glad to see an old friend without silly children like you having to make a to-do about it? I've just been in your mother's room suggesting that she might give a little dinner for them—"

"For who?"

"For *whom*, Georgie! For Mr. Morgan and his daughter."

"Look here!" George said quickly. "Don't do that! Mother mustn't do that. It wouldn't look well."

" 'Wouldn't look well'!" Fanny mocked him; and her suppressed vehemence betrayed a surprising acerbity. "See here, Georgie Minafer, I suggest that you just march straight on into your room and finish your dressing! Sometimes you say things that show you have a pretty mean little mind!"

George was so astounded by this outburst that his indignation was delayed by his curiosity. "Why, what upsets *you* this way?" he inquired.

"I know what you mean," she said, her voice still lowered, but not decreasing in sharpness. "You're trying to insinuate that I'd get your mother to invite Eugene Morgan here on my account because he's a widower!"

"I *am*?" George gasped, nonplussed. "I'm trying to insinuate that you're setting your cap at him and getting mother to help you? Is that what you mean?"

Beyond a doubt that was what Miss Fanny meant. She gave him a white-hot look. "You attend to your own affairs!" she whispered fiercely, and swept away.

George, dumfounded, returned to his room for meditation.

He had lived for years in the same house with his Aunt Fanny, and it now appeared that during all those years he had been thus intimately associating with a total stranger. Never before had he met the passionate lady with whom he had just held a conversation in the hall. So she wanted to get married! And wanted George's mother to help her with this horseless-carriage widower!

"Well, I *will* be shot!" he muttered aloud. "I will—I certainly will be shot!" And he began to laugh. "Lord 'lmighty!"

But presently, at the thought of the horseless-carriage widower's daughter, his grimness returned, and he resolved upon a line of conduct for the evening. He would nod to her carelessly when he first saw her; and, after that, he would notice her no more: he would not dance with her; he would not favour her in the cotillion—he would not go near her!

. . . He descended to dinner upon the third urgent summons of a coloured butler, having spent two hours dressing—and rehearsing.

CHAPTER IX

The Honourable George Amberson was a congressman who led cotillions—the sort of congressman an Amberson would be. He did it negligently, to-night, yet with infallible dexterity, now and then glancing humorously at the spectators, people of his own age. They were seated in a tropical grove at one end of the room whither they had retired at the beginning of the cotillion, which they surrendered entirely to the twenties and the late 'teens. And here, grouped with that stately pair, Sydney and Amelia Amberson, sat Isabel with Fanny, while Eugene Morgan appeared to bestow an amiable devotion impartially upon the three sisters-in-law. Fanny watched his face eagerly, laughing at everything he said; Amelia smiled blandly, but rather because of graciousness than because of interest; while Isabel, looking out at the dancers, rhythmically moved a great fan of blue ostrich feathers, listened to Eugene thoughtfully, yet all the while kept her shining eyes on Georgie.

Georgie had carried out his rehearsed projects with precision. He had given Miss Morgan a nod studied into perfection during his lengthy toilet before dinner. "Oh, yes, I do seem to remember that curious little outsider!" this nod seemed to say. Thereafter, all cognizance of her evaporated: the curious little outsider was permitted no further existence worth the struggle. Nevertheless, she flashed in the corner of his eye too often. He was aware of her dancing demurely, and of her viciously flirtatious habit of never looking up at her partner, but keeping her eyes concealed beneath downcast lashes; and he had over-sufficient consciousness of her between the dances, though it was not possible to see her at these times, even if he had cared to look frankly in her direction—she was invisible in a thicket of young dresscoats. The black thicket moved as she moved, and her location was hatefully apparent, even if he had not heard her voice laughing from the thicket. It was annoying how her voice, though never loud, pursued him. No matter how vociferous were other voices, all about, he seemed unable to prevent himself from constantly recognizing hers. It had a quaver in it, not pathetic—rather humorous than pathetic—a quality which annoyed him to the point of rage, because it was so difficult to get away from. She seemed to be having a "wonderful time!"

An unbearable soreness accumulated in his chest: his dislike of the girl and her conduct increased until he thought of leaving this sickening Assembly and going home to bed. *That* would show her! But just then he heard her laughing, and decided that it wouldn't show her. So he remained.

When the young couples seated themselves in chairs against the walls, round three sides of the room, for the cotillion, George joined a brazen-faced group clustering about the doorway—youths with no partners, yet eligible to be "called out" and favoured. He marked that his uncle placed the infernal Kinney and Miss Morgan, as the leading couple, in the first chairs at the head of the line upon the leader's right; and this disloyalty on the part of Uncle George was inexcusable, for in the family circle the nephew had often expressed his opinion of Fred Kinney. In his bitterness, George uttered a significant monosyllable.

The music flourished; whereupon Mr. Kinney, Miss Morgan, and six of their neighbours rose and waltzed knowingly. Mr. Amberson's whistle blew; then the eight young people went to the favour-table and were given toys and trinkets wherewith to delight the new partners it was now their privilege to select. Around the walls, the seated non-participants in this ceremony looked rather conscious; some chattered, endeavouring not to appear expectant; some tried not to look wistful; and others were frankly solemn. It was a trying moment; and whoever secured a favour, this very first shot, might consider the portents happy for a successful evening.

Holding their twinkling gewgaws in their hands, those about to bestow honour came toward the seated lines, where expressions became feverish. Two of the approaching girls seemed to wander, not finding a predetermined object in sight; and these two were Janie Sharon, and her cousin, Lucy. At this, George Amberson Minafer, conceiving that he had little to anticipate from either, turned a proud back upon the room and affected to converse with his friend, Mr. Charlie Johnson.

The next moment a quick little figure intervened between the two. It was Lucy, gayly offering a silver sleighbell decked with white ribbon.

"I almost couldn't find you!" she cried.

George stared, took her hand, led her forth in silence, danced with her. She seemed content not to talk; but as the whistle blew, signalling that this episode was concluded, and he conducted her to her seat, she lifted the little bell toward him. "You haven't taken your favour. You're supposed to pin it on your coat," she said. "Don't you want it?"

"If you insist!" said George stiffly. And he bowed her into her chair; then turned and walked away, dropping the sleighbell haughtily into his trousers' pocket.

The figure proceeded to its conclusion, and George was given other sleighbells, which he easily consented to wear upon his lapel; but, as the next figure began, he strolled with a bored air to the tropical grove, where sat his elders, and seated himself beside his Uncle Sydney. His mother leaned across Miss Fanny, raising her voice over the music to speak to him.

"Georgie, nobody will be able to see you here. You'll not be favoured. You ought to be where you can dance."

"Don't care to," he returned. "Bore!"

"But you ought—" She stopped and laughed, waving her fan to direct his attention behind him. "Look! Over your shoulder!"

He turned, and discovered Miss Lucy Morgan in the act of offering him a purple toy balloon.

"I found you!" she laughed.

George was startled. "Well—" he said.

"Would you rather 'sit it out'?" Lucy asked quickly, as he did not move. "I don't care to dance if you—"

"No," he said, rising. "It would be better to dance." His tone was solemn, and solemnly he departed with her from the grove. Solemnly he danced with her.

Four times, with not the slightest encouragement, she brought him a favour: four times in succession. When the fourth came, "Look here!" said George huskily. "You going to keep this up all night? What do you mean by it?"

For an instant she seemed confused. "That's what cotillions are for, aren't they?" she murmured.

"What do you mean: what they're for?"

"So that a girl can dance with a person she wants to?"

George's huskiness increased. "Well, do you mean you—you want to dance with me all the time—all evening?"

"Well, this much of it—evidently!" she laughed.

"Is it because you thought I tried to keep you from getting hurt this afternoon when we upset?"

She shook her head.

"Was it because you want to even things up for making me angry—I mean, for hurting my feelings on the way home?"

With her eyes averted—for girls of nineteen can be as shy as boys, sometimes—she said, "Well—you only got angry because I couldn't dance the cotillion with you. I—I didn't feel terribly hurt with you for getting angry about *that*!"

"Was there any other reason? Did my telling you I liked you have anything to do with it?"

She looked up gently, and, as George met her eyes, something exquisitely touching, yet queerly delightful, gave him a catch in the throat. She looked instantly away, and, turning, ran out from the palm grove, where they stood, to the dancing-floor.

"Come on!" she cried. "Let's dance!"

He followed her.

"See here—I—I—" he stammered. "You mean— Do you—"

"No, no!" she laughed. "Let's dance!"

He put his arm about her almost tremulously, and they began to waltz. It was a happy dance for both of them.

———

Christmas day is the children's, but the holidays are youth's dancing-time. The holidays belong to the early twenties and the 'teens, home from school and college. These years possess the holidays for a little while, then possess them only in smiling, wistful memories of holly and twinkling lights and dance-music, and charming faces all aglow. It is the liveliest time in life, the happiest of the irresponsible times in life. Mothers echo its happiness—nothing is like a mother who has a son home from college, except another mother with a son home from college. Bloom does actually come upon these mothers; it is a visible thing; and they run like girls, walk like athletes, laugh like sycophants. Yet they give up their sons to the daughters of other mothers, and find it proud rapture enough to be allowed to sit and watch.

Thus Isabel watched George and Lucy dancing, as together they danced away the holidays of that year into the past.

"They seem to get along better than they did at first, those two children," Fanny Minafer said, sitting beside her at the Sharons' dance, a week after the Assembly. "They seemed to be always having little quarrels of some sort, at first. At least George did: he seemed to be continually pecking at that lovely, dainty, little Lucy, and being cross with her over nothing."

" '*Pecking*'?" Isabel laughed. "What a word to use about Georgie! I think I never knew a more angelically amiable disposition in my life!"

Miss Fanny echoed her sister-in-law's laugh, but it was a rueful echo, and not sweet. "He's amiable to you!" she said. "That's all the side of him you ever happen to see. And why wouldn't he be amiable to anybody that simply fell down and worshipped him every minute of her life? Most of us would!"

"Isn't he worth worshipping? Just look at him! Isn't he *charming* with Lucy! See how hard he ran to get it when she dropped her handkerchief back there."

"Oh, I'm not going to argue with you about George!" said Miss Fanny. "I'm fond enough of him, for that matter. He *can* be charming, and he's certainly stunning *looking*, if only—"

"Let the 'if only' go, dear," Isabel suggested good-naturedly. "Let's talk about that dinner you thought I should—"

"I?" Miss Fanny interrupted quickly. "Didn't you want to give it yourself?"

"Indeed, I did, my dear!" said Isabel heartily. "I only meant that unless you had proposed it, perhaps I wouldn't—"

But here Eugene came for her to dance, and she left the sentence uncompleted. Holiday dances can be happy for youth renewed as well as for youth in bud—and yet it was not with the air of a rival that Miss Fanny watched her brother's wife dancing with the widower. Miss Fanny's eyes narrowed a little, but only as if her mind engaged in a hopeful calculation. She looked pleased.

CHAPTER X

A few days after George's return to the university it became evident that not quite everybody had gazed with complete benevolence upon the various young collegians at their holiday sports. The Sunday edition of the principal morning paper even expressed some bitterness under the heading, "Gilded Youths of the Fin-de-Siècle"—this was considered the knowing phrase of the time, especially for Sunday supplements—and there is no doubt that from certain references in this bit of writing some people drew the conclusion that Mr. George Amberson Minafer had not yet got his come-upance, a postponement still irritating. Undeniably, Fanny Minafer was one of the people who drew this conclusion, for she cut the article out and enclosed it in a letter to her nephew, having written on the border of the clipping, "I wonder whom it can mean!"

George read part of it:

We debate sometimes what is to be the future of this nation when we think that in a few years public affairs may be in the hands of the *fin-de-siècle* gilded youths we see about us during the Christmas holidays. Such foppery, such luxury, such insolence, was surely never practised by the scented, overbearing patricians of the Palatine, even in Rome's most decadent epoch. In all the wild orgy of wastefulness and luxury with which the nineteenth century reaches its close, the gilded youth has been surely the worst symptom. With his airs of young milord, his fast horses, his gold and silver cigarette-cases, his clothes from a New

York tailor, his recklessness of money showered upon him by indulgent mothers or doting grandfathers, he respects nothing and nobody. He is blasé, if you please. Watch him at a social function, how condescendingly he deigns to select a partner for the popular waltz or two-step; how carelessly he shoulders older people out of his way, with what a blank stare he returns the salutation of some old acquaintance whom he may choose in his royal whim to forget! The unpleasant part of all this is that the young women he so condescendingly selects as partners for the dance greet him with seeming rapture, though in their hearts they must feel humiliated by his languid hauteur, and many older people beam upon him almost fawningly if he unbends so far as to throw them a careless, disdainful word!

One wonders what has come over the new generation. Of such as these the Republic was not made. Let us pray that the future of our country is not in the hands of these *fin-de-siècle* gilded youths, but rather in the calloused palms of young men yet unknown, labouring upon the farms of the land. When we compare the young manhood of Abraham Lincoln with the specimens we are now producing, we see too well that it bodes ill for the twentieth century—

George yawned, and tossed the clipping into his waste-basket, wondering why his aunt thought such dull nonsense worth the sending. As for her insinuation, pencilled upon the border, he supposed she meant to joke—a supposition which neither surprised him nor altered his lifelong opinion of her wit.

He read her letter with more interest:

... The dinner your mother gave for the Morgans was a lovely affair. It was last Monday evening, just ten days after you left. It was peculiarly appropriate that your mother should give this dinner, because her brother George, your uncle, was Mr. Morgan's most intimate friend before he left here a number of years ago, and it was a pleasant occasion for the formal announcement of some news which you heard from Lucy Morgan before you returned to college. At least she told me she had told you the night before you left that her father had decided to return here to live. It was appropriate that your mother, herself an old friend, should assemble a representative selection of Mr. Morgan's old friends around him at such a time. He was in great spirits and most entertaining. As your time was so charmingly taken up during your visit home with a *younger member* of his family, you probably overlooked opportunities of hearing him talk, and do not know what an interesting man he can be.

He will soon begin to build his factory here for the manufacture of *automobiles*, which he says is a term he prefers to "horseless carriages." Your Uncle George told me he would like to invest in this factory, as George thinks there is a future for automobiles; perhaps not for general use, but as an interesting novelty, which people with sufficient means would like to own for their amusement and the sake of variety. However, he said Mr. Morgan laughingly declined his offer, as Mr. M. was fully able to finance this venture, though not starting in a very large way. Your uncle said other people are manufacturing automobiles in different parts of the country with success. Your father is not very well, though he is not actually ill, and the doctor tells him he ought not to be so much at his office, as the long years of application indoors with no exercise are beginning to affect him unfavourably, but I believe your father would die if he had to give up his work, which is all that has ever interested him outside of his family. I never could understand it. Mr. Morgan took your mother and me with Lucy to see Modjeska in "Twelfth Night" yesterday evening, and Lucy said she thought the Duke looked rather like you, only much more democratic in his manner. I suppose you will think I have written a great deal about the Morgans in this letter, but thought you would be interested because of your interest in a *younger member* of his family. Hoping that you are finding college still as attractive as ever,

Affectionately,

Aunt Fanny.

George read one sentence in this letter several times. Then he dropped the missive in his waste-basket to join the clipping, and strolled down the corridor of his dormitory to borrow a copy of "Twelfth Night." Having secured one, he returned to his study and refreshed his memory of the play—but received no enlightenment that enabled him to comprehend Lucy's strange remark. However, he found himself impelled in the direction of correspondence, and presently wrote a letter—not a reply to his Aunt Fanny.

Dear Lucy:

No doubt you will be surprised at hearing from me so soon again, especially as this makes two in answer to the one received from you since getting back to the old place. I hear you have been making comments about me at the theatre, that some actor was more democratic in his manners than I am, which I do not understand. You know my theory of life because I explained it to you on our first drive together, when I told you I would not talk to everybody about things I feel like the way I spoke to you of my theory of life. I believe those who are able should have a true theory of life, and I developed my theory of life long, long ago.

Well, here I sit smoking my faithful briar pipe, indulging in the fragrance of my *tabac* as I look out on the campus from my many-paned window, and things are different with me from the way they were way back in Freshman year. I can see now how boyish in many ways I was then. I believe what has changed me as much as anything was my visit home at the time I met you. So I sit here with my faithful briar and dream the old dreams over as it were, dreaming of the waltzes we waltzed together and of that last night before we parted, and you told me the good news you were going to live there, and I would *find my friend waiting for me,* when I get home next summer.

I will be glad my friend *will* be waiting for me. I am not capable of friendship except for the very few, and, looking back over my life, I remember there were times when I doubted if I could feel a great friendship for anybody—especially girls. I do not take a great interest in many people, as you know, for I find most of them shallow. Here in the old place I do not believe in being hail-fellow-well-met with every Tom, Dick, and Harry just because he happens to be a classmate, any more than I do at home, where I have always been careful who I was seen with, largely on account of the family, but also because my disposition ever since my boyhood has been to encourage real intimacy from but the few.

What are you reading now? I have finished both "Henry Esmond" and "The Virginians." I like Thackeray because he is not trashy, and because he writes principally of nice people. My theory of literature is an author who does not indulge in trashiness—writes about people you could introduce into your own home. I agree with my Uncle Sydney, as I once heard him say he did not care to read a book or go to a play about people he would not care to meet at his own dinner table. I believe we should live by certain standards and ideals, as you know from my telling you my theory of life.

Well, a letter is no place for deep discussions, so I will not go into the subject. From several letters from my mother, and one from Aunt Fanny, I hear you are seeing a good deal of the family since I left. I hope sometimes you think of the member who is absent. I got a silver frame for your photograph in New York, and I keep it on my desk. It is the only girl's photograph I ever took the trouble to have framed, though, as I told you frankly, I have had any number of other girls' photographs, yet all were only passing fancies, and oftentimes I have questioned in years past if I was capable of much friendship toward the feminine sex, which I usually found shallow until our own friendship began. When I look at your photograph, I say to myself, "At last, at last here is one that will not prove shallow."

My faithful briar has gone out. I will have to rise and fill it, then once more in the fragrance of My Lady Nicotine, I will sit and dream the old dreams over, and think, too, of the true friend at home awaiting my return in June for the summer vacation.

Friend, this is from your friend,

G.A.M.

George's anticipations were not disappointed. When he came home in June his friend was awaiting him; at least, she was so pleased to see him again that for a few minutes after their first encounter she was a little breathless, and a great deal glowing, and quiet withal. Their sentimental friendship continued, though sometimes he was irritated by her making it less sentimental than he did, and sometimes by what he called her "air of superiority." Her air was usually, in truth, that of a fond but amused older sister; and George did not believe such an attitude was warranted by her eight months of seniority.

Lucy and her father were living at the Amberson Hotel, while Morgan got his small machine-shops built in a western outskirt of the town; and George grumbled about the shabbiness and the old-fashioned look of the hotel, though it was "still the best in the place, of course." He remonstrated with his grandfather, declaring that the whole Amberson Estate would be getting "run-down and out-at-heel, if things weren't taken in hand pretty soon." He urged the general need of rebuilding, renovating, varnishing, and lawsuits. But the Major, declining to hear him out, interrupted querulously, saying that he had enough to bother him without any advice from George; and retired to his library, going so far as to lock the door audibly.

"Second childhood!" George muttered, shaking his head; and he thought sadly that the Major had not long to live. However, this surmise depressed him for only a moment or so. Of course, people couldn't be expected to live forever, and it would be a good thing to have someone in charge of the Estate who wouldn't let it get to looking so rusty that riffraff dared to make fun of it. For George had lately undergone the annoyance of calling upon the Morgans, in the rather stuffy red velours and gilt parlour of their apartment at the hotel, one evening when Mr. Frederick Kinney also was a caller, and Mr. Kinney had not been tactful. In fact, though he adopted a humorous tone of voice, in expressing his sympathy for people who, through the city's poverty in hotels, were obliged to stay at the Amberson, Mr. Kinney's intention was interpreted by the other visitor as not at all humorous, but, on the contrary, personal and offensive.

George rose abruptly, his face the colour of wrath. "Good-night, Miss Morgan. Good-night, Mr. Morgan," he said. "I shall take pleasure in calling at some other time when a more courteous sort of people may be present."

"Look here!" the hot-headed Fred burst out. "Don't you try to make me out a boor, George Minafer! I wasn't hinting anything at you; I simply forgot all about your grandfather owning this old building. Don't you try to put *me* in the light of a boor! I won't—"

But George walked out in the very course of this vehement protest, and it was necessarily left unfinished.

Mr. Kinney remained only a few moments after George's departure; and as the door closed upon him, the distressed Lucy turned to her father. She was plaintively surprised to find him in a condition of immoderate laughter.

"I didn't—I didn't think I could hold out!" he gasped, and, after choking until tears came to his eyes, felt blindly for the chair from which he had risen to wish Mr. Kinney an indistinct good-night. His hand found the arm of the chair; he collapsed feebly, and sat uttering incoherent sounds.

"Papa!"

"It brings things back so!" he managed to explain. "This very Fred Kinney's father and young George's father, Wilbur Minafer, used to do just such things when they were at that age—and, for that matter, so did George Amberson and I, and all the rest of us!" And, in spite of his exhaustion, he began to imitate: " 'Don't you try to put *me* in the light of a boor!' 'I shall take pleasure in calling at some time when a more courteous sort of people—' " He was unable to go on.

There is a mirth for every age, and Lucy failed to comprehend her father's, but tolerated it a little ruefully.

"Papa, I think they were shocking. Weren't they *awful!*"

"Just—just boys!" he moaned, wiping his eyes.

But Lucy could not smile at all; she was beginning to look indignant. "I can forgive that poor Fred Kinney," she said. "He's just blundering—but George—oh, George behaved outrageously!"

"It's a difficult age," her father observed, his calmness somewhat restored. "Girls don't seem to have to pass through it quite as boys do, or their *savoir faire* is instinctive—or something!" And he gave away to a return of his convulsion.

She came and sat upon the arm of his chair. "Papa, *why* should George behave like that?"

"He's sensitive."

"Rather! But why is he? He does anything he likes to, without any regard for what people think. Then why should he mind so furiously when the least little thing reflects upon him, or on anything or anybody connected with him?"

Eugene patted her hand. "That's one of the greatest puzzles of human vanity, dear; and I don't pretend to know the answer. In all my life, the most arrogant people that I've known have been the most sensitive. The people who have done the most in contempt of other people's opinion, and who consider themselves the highest above it, have been the most furious if it went against them. Arrogant and domineering people can't stand the least, lightest, faintest breath of criticism. It just kills them."

"Papa, do you think George is *terribly* arrogant and domineering?"

"Oh, he's still only a boy," said Eugene consolingly. "There's plenty of fine stuff in him—can't help but be, because he's Isabel Amberson's son."

Lucy stroked his hair, which was still almost as dark as her own. "You liked her pretty well once, I guess, papa."

"I do still," he said quietly.

"She's lovely—lovely! Papa—" she paused, then continued—"I wonder sometimes—"

"What?"

"I wonder just how she happened to marry Mr. Minafer."

"Oh, Minafer's all right," said Eugene. "He's a quiet sort of man, but he's a good man and a kind man. He always was, and those things count."

"But in a way—well, I've heard people say there wasn't anything to him at all except business and saving money. Miss Fanny Minafer herself told me that everything George and his mother have of their own—that is, just to spend as they like—she says it has always come from Major Amberson."

"Thrift, Horatio!" said Eugene lightly. "Thrift's an inheritance, and a common enough one here. The people who settled the country *had* to save, so making and saving were taught as virtues, and the people, to the third generation, haven't found out that making and saving are only means to an end. Minafer doesn't believe in money being spent. He believes God made it to be invested and saved."

"But George isn't saving. He's reckless, and even if he is arrogant and conceited and bad-tempered, he's awfully generous."

"Oh, he's an Amberson," said her father. "The Ambersons aren't saving. They're too much the other way, most of them."

"I don't think I should have called George bad-tempered," Lucy said thoughtfully. "No. I don't think he is."

"Only when he's cross about something?" Morgan suggested, with a semblance of sympathetic gravity.

"Yes," she said brightly, not perceiving that his intention was humorous. "All the rest of the time he's really very amiable. Of course, he's much more a perfect *child*, the whole time, than he realizes! He certainly behaved awfully to-night." She jumped up, her indignation returning. "He did, indeed, and it won't do to encourage him in it. I think he'll find me pretty cool—for a week or so!"

Whereupon her father suffered a renewal of his attack of uproarious laughter.

CHAPTER XI

In the matter of coolness, George met Lucy upon her own predetermined ground; in fact, he was there first, and, at their next encounter, proved loftier and more formal than she did. Their estrangement lasted three weeks, and then disappeared without any preliminary treaty: it had worn itself out, and they forgot it.

At times, however, George found other disturbances to the friendship. Lucy was "too much the village belle," he complained; and took a satiric attitude toward his competitors, referring to them as her "local swains and bumpkins," sulking for an afternoon when she reminded him that he, too, was at least "local." She was a belle with older people as well; Isabel and Fanny were continually taking her driving, bringing her home with them to lunch or dinner, and making a hundred little engagements with her, and the Major had taken a great fancy to her, insisting upon her presence and her father's at the Amberson family dinner at the Mansion every Sunday evening. She knew how to flirt with old people, he said, as she sat next him at the table on one of these Sunday occasions; and he had always liked her father, even when Eugene was a "terror" long ago. "Oh, yes, he was!" the Major laughed, when she remonstrated. "He came up here with my son George and some others for a serenade one night, and Eugene stepped into a bass fiddle, and the poor musicians just gave up! I had a pretty half-hour getting my son George upstairs. I remember! It was the last time Eugene ever touched a drop—but he'd touched plenty before that, young lady, and he daren't deny it! Well, well; there's another thing that's changed: hardly anybody drinks nowadays. Perhaps it's just as well, but things used to be livelier. That serenade was just before Isabel was married—and don't you fret, Miss Lucy: your father remembers it well enough!" The old gentleman burst into laughter, and shook his finger at Eugene across the table. "The fact is," the Major went on hilariously, "I believe if Eugene hadn't broken that bass fiddle and given himself away, Isabel would never have taken Wilbur! I shouldn't be surprised if that was about all the reason that Wilbur got her! What do you think, Wilbur?"

"I shouldn't be surprised," said Wilbur placidly. "If your notion is right, I'm glad 'Gene broke the fiddle. He was giving me a hard run!"

The Major always drank three glasses of champagne at his Sunday dinner, and he was finishing the third. "What do *you* say about it, Isabel? By Jove!" he cried, pounding the table. "She's blushing!"

Isabel did blush, but she laughed. "Who wouldn't blush!" she cried, and her sister-in-law came to her assistance.

"The important thing," said Fanny jovially, "is that Wilbur did get her, and not only got her, but kept her!"

Eugene was as pink as Isabel, but he laughed without any sign of embarrassment other than his heightened colour. "There's another important thing—that is, for me," he said. "It's the only thing that makes me forgive that bass viol for getting in my way."

"What is it?" the Major asked.

"Lucy," said Morgan gently.

Isabel gave him a quick glance, all warm approval, and there was a murmur of friendliness round the table.

George was not one of those who joined in this applause. He considered his grandfather's nonsense indelicate, even for second childhood, and he thought that the sooner the subject was dropped the better. However, he had only a slight recurrence of the resentment which had assailed him during the winter at every sign of his mother's interest in Morgan; though he was still ashamed of his aunt sometimes, when it seemed to him that Fanny was almost publicly throwing herself at the widower's head. Fanny and he had one or two arguments in which her fierceness again astonished and amused him.

"You drop your criticisms of your relatives," she bade him, hotly, one day, "and begin thinking a little about your own behaviour! You say people will 'talk' about my—about my merely being pleasant to an old friend! What do I care how they talk? I guess if people are talking about anybody in this family they're talking about the impertinent little snippet that hasn't any respect for anything, and doesn't even know enough to attend to his own affairs!"

" 'Snippet,' Aunt Fanny!" George laughed. "How elegant! And '*little* snippet'—when I'm over five-feet-eleven?"

"I said it!" she snapped, departing. "I don't see how Lucy can stand you!"

"You'd make an amiable stepmother-in-law!" he called after her. "I'll be careful about proposing to Lucy!"

These were but roughish spots in a summer that glided by evenly and quickly enough, for the most part, and, at the end, seemed to fly. On the last night before George went back to be a Junior, his mother asked him confidently if it had not been a happy summer.

He hadn't thought about it, he answered. "Oh, I suppose so. Why?"

"I just thought it would be nice to hear you say so," she said, smiling. "I mean, it's pleasant for people of my age to know that people of your age realize that they're happy."

"People of your age!" he repeated. "You know you don't look precisely like an old woman, mother. Not precisely!"

"No," she said. "And I suppose I feel about as young as you do, inside, but it won't be many years before I must begin to *look* old. It does come!" She sighed, still smiling. "It's seemed to me that it must have been a happy summer for you—a real 'summer of roses and wine'— without the wine, perhaps. 'Gather ye roses while ye may'—or was it primroses? Time does really fly, or perhaps it's more like the sky—and smoke—"

George was puzzled. "What do you mean: time being like the sky and smoke?"

"I mean the things that we have and that we think are so solid— they're like smoke, and time is like the sky that the smoke disappears into. You know how a wreath of smoke goes up from a chimney, and seems all thick and black and busy against the sky, as if it were going to do such important things and last forever, and you see it getting thinner and thinner—and then, in such a little while, it isn't there at all; nothing is left but the sky, and the sky keeps on being just the same forever."

"It strikes me you're getting mixed up," said George cheerfully. "I don't see much resemblance between time and the sky, or between things and smoke-wreaths; but I do see one reason you like Lucy Morgan so much. She talks that same kind of wistful, moony way sometimes—I don't mean to say I mind it in either of you, because I rather like to listen to it, and you've got a very good voice, mother. It's nice to listen to, no matter how much smoke and sky, and so on, you talk. So's Lucy's, for that matter; and I see why you're congenial. She talks that way to her father, too; and he's right there with the same kind of guff. Well, it's all right with *me!*" He laughed, teasingly, and allowed her to retain his hand, which she had fondly seized. "I've got plenty to think about when people drool along!"

She pressed his hand to her cheek, and a tear made a tiny warm streak across one of his knuckles.

"For heaven's sake!" he said. "What's the matter? Isn't everything all right?"

"You're going away!"

"Well, I'm coming back, don't you suppose? Is *that* all that worries you?"

She cheered up, and smiled again, but shook her head. "I never can bear to see you go—that's the most of it. I'm a little bothered about your father, too."

"Why?"

"It seems to me he looks so badly. Everybody thinks so."

"What nonsense!" George laughed. "He's been looking that way all summer. He isn't much different from the way he's looked all his life, that I can see. What's the matter with him?"

"He never talks much about his business to me but I think he's been worrying about some investments he made last year. I think his worry has affected his health."

"What investments?" George demanded. "He hasn't gone into Mr. Morgan's automobile concern, has he?"

"No," Isabel smiled. "The 'automobile concern' is all Eugene's, and it's so small I understand it's taken hardly anything. No; your father has always prided himself on making only the most absolutely safe investments, but two or three years ago he and your Uncle George both put a great deal—pretty much everything they could get together, I think—into the stock of rolling-mills some friends of theirs owned, and I'm afraid the mills haven't been doing well."

"What of that? Father needn't worry. You and I could take care of him the rest of his life on what grandfather—"

"Of course," she agreed. "But your father's always lived so for his business and taken such pride in his sound investments; it's a passion with him. I—"

"Pshaw! *He* needn't worry! You tell him we'll look after him: we'll build him a little stone bank in the backyard, if he busts up, and he can go and put his pennies in it every morning. That'll keep him just as happy as he ever was!" He kissed her. "Good-night, I'm going to tell Lucy good-bye. Don't sit up for me."

She walked to the front gate with him, still holding his hand, and he told her again not to "sit up" for him.

"Yes, I will," she laughed. "You won't be very late."

"Well—it's my last night."

"But I know Lucy, and she knows I want to see you, too, your last night. You'll see: she'll send you home promptly at eleven!"

But she was mistaken: Lucy sent him home promptly at ten.

Chapter XII

Isabel's uneasiness about her husband's health—sometimes reflected in her letters to George during the winter that followed—had not been alleviated when the accredited Senior returned for his next summer vacation, and she confided to him in his room, soon after his arrival, that "something" the doctor had said to her lately had made her more uneasy than ever.

"Still worrying over his rolling-mills investments?" George asked, not seriously impressed.

"I'm afraid it's past that stage from what Dr. Rainey says. His worries only aggravate his condition now. Dr. Rainey says we ought to get him away."

"Well, let's do it, then."

"He won't go."

"He's a man awfully set in his ways; that's true," said George. "I don't think there's anything much the matter with him, though, and he looks just the same to me. Have you seen Lucy lately? How is she?"

"Hasn't she written you?"

"Oh, about once a month," he answered carelessly. "Never says much about herself. How's she look?"

"She looks—pretty!" said Isabel. "I suppose she wrote you they've moved?"

"Yes; I've got her address. She said they were building."

"They did. It's all finished, and they've been in it a month. Lucy is so capable; she keeps house exquisitely. It's small, but oh, such a pretty little house!"

"Well, that's fortunate," George said. "One thing I've always felt they didn't know a great deal about is architecture."

"Don't they?" asked Isabel, surprised. "Anyhow, their house is charming. It's way out beyond the end of Amberson Boulevard; it's quite near that big white house with a gray-green roof somebody built out there a year or so ago. There are any number of houses going up, out that way; and the trolley-line runs within a block of them now, on the next street, and the traction people are laying tracks more than three miles beyond. I suppose you'll be driving out to see Lucy to-morrow."

"I thought—" George hesitated. "I thought perhaps I'd go after dinner this evening."

At this, his mother laughed, not astonished. "It was only my feeble joke about 'to-morrow,' Georgie! I was pretty sure you couldn't wait that long. Did Lucy write you about the factory?"

"No. What factory?"

"The automobile shops. They had rather a dubious time at first, I'm afraid, and some of Eugene's experiments turned out badly, but this spring they've finished eight automobiles and sold them all, and they've got twelve more almost finished, and they're sold already! Eugene's so gay over it!"

"What do his old sewing-machines look like? Like that first one he had when they came here?"

"No, indeed! These have rubber tires blown up with air—pneumatic! And they aren't so high; they're very easy to get into, and the engine's in front—Eugene thinks that's a great improvement. They're very interesting to look at; behind the driver's seat there's a sort of box where four people can sit, with a step and a little door in the rear, and—"

"I know all about it," said George. "I've seen any number like that, East. You can see all you want of 'em, if you stand on Fifth Avenue half an hour, any afternoon. I've seen half-a-dozen go by almost at the same time—within a few minutes, anyhow; and of course electric hansoms are a common sight there any day. I hired one, myself, the last time I was there. How fast do Mr. Morgan's machines go?"

"Much *too* fast! It's very exhilarating—but rather frightening; and they do make a fearful uproar. He says, though, he thinks he sees a way to get around the noisiness in time."

"I don't mind the noise," said George. "Give me a horse, for mine, though, any day. I must get up a race with one of these things: Pendennis'll leave it one mile behind in a two-mile run. How's grandfather?"

"He looks well, but he complains sometimes of his heart: I suppose that's natural at his age—and it's an Amberson trouble." Having mentioned this, she looked anxious instantly. "Did *you* ever feel any weakness there, Georgie?"

"No!" he laughed.

"Are you *sure*, dear?"

"No!" And he laughed again. "Did you?"

"Oh, I think not—at least, the doctor told me he thought my heart was about all right. He said I needn't be alarmed."

"I should think not! Women do seem to be always talking about health: I suppose they haven't got enough else to think of!"

"That must be it," she said gayly. "We're an idle lot!"

George had taken off his coat. "I don't like to hint to a lady," he said, "but I do want to dress before dinner."

"Don't be long; I've got to do a lot of looking at you, dear!" She kissed him and ran away, singing.

But his Aunt Fanny was not so fond; and at the dinner-table there came a spark of liveliness into her eye when George patronizingly asked her what was the news in her own "particular line of sport."

"What do you mean, Georgie?" she asked quietly.

"Oh I mean: What's the news in the fast set generally? You been causing any divorces lately?"

"No," said Fanny, the spark in her eye getting brighter. "I haven't been causing anything."

"Well, what's the gossip? You usually hear pretty much everything that goes on around the nooks and crannies in this town, I hear. What's the last from the gossips' corner, auntie?"

Fanny dropped her eyes, and the spark was concealed, but a movement of her lower lip betokened a tendency to laugh, as she replied, "There hasn't been much gossip lately, except the report that Lucy Morgan and Fred Kinney are engaged—and that's quite old, by this time."

Undeniably, this bit of mischief was entirely successful, for there was a clatter upon George's plate. "What—what do you think you're talking about?" he gasped.

Miss Fanny looked up innocently. "About the report of Lucy Morgan's engagement to Fred Kinney."

George turned dumbly to his mother, and Isabel shook her head reassuringly. "People are always starting rumours," she said. "I haven't paid any attention to this one."

"But you—you've heard it?" he stammered.

"Oh, one hears all sorts of nonsense, dear. I haven't the slightest idea that it's true."

"Then you *have* heard it!"

"I wouldn't let it take my appetite," his father suggested drily. "There are plenty of girls in the world!"

George turned pale.

"Eat your dinner, Georgie," his aunt said sweetly. "Food will do you good. I didn't say I knew this rumour was true. I only said I'd heard it."

"When? When did you hear it!"

"Oh, months ago!" And Fanny found any further postponement of laughter impossible.

"Fanny, you're a hard-hearted creature," Isabel said gently. "You *really* are. Don't pay any attention to her, George. Fred Kinney's only a clerk in his uncle's hardware place: he couldn't marry for ages—even if anybody would accept him!"

George breathed tumultuously. "I don't care anything about 'ages'! What's that got to do with it?" he said, his thoughts appearing to be somewhat disconnected. " 'Ages,' don't mean anything! I only want to know—I want to know— I want—" He stopped.

"What do you want?" his father asked crossly. "Why don't you say it? Don't make such a fuss."

"I'm not—not at all," George declared, pushing his chair back from the table.

"You must finish your dinner, dear," his mother urged. "Don't—"

"I have finished. I've eaten all I want. I don't want any more than I wanted. I don't want—I—" He rose, still incoherent. "I prefer—I want— Please excuse me!"

He left the room, and a moment later the screens outside the open front door were heard to slam.

"Fanny! You shouldn't—"

"Isabel, don't reproach me. He did have plenty of dinner, and I only told the truth: everybody has been saying—"

"But there isn't any truth in it."

"We don't actually know there isn't," Miss Fanny insisted, giggling. "We've never *asked* Lucy."

"I wouldn't ask her anything so absurd!"

"George would," George's father remarked. "That's what he's gone to do."

Mr. Minafer was not mistaken: that was what his son had gone to do. Lucy and her father were just rising from their dinner table when the stirred youth arrived at the front door of the new house. It was a cottage, however, rather than a house; and Lucy had taken a free hand with the architect, achieving results in white and green, outside, and white and blue, inside, to such effect of youth and daintiness that her father complained of "too much springtime!" The whole place, including his own bedroom, was a young damsel's boudoir, he said, so that nowhere could he smoke a cigar without feeling like a ruffian. However, he was smoking when George arrived, and he encouraged George to join him in the pastime, but the caller, whose air was both tense and preoccupied, declined with something like agitation.

"I never smoke—that is, I'm seldom—I mean, no thanks," he said. "I mean not at all. I'd rather not."

"Aren't you well, George?" Eugene asked, looking at him in perplexity. "Have you been overworking at college? You do look rather pa—"

"I don't work," said George. "I mean I don't work. I think, but I don't work. I only work at the end of the term. There isn't much to do."

Eugene's perplexity was little decreased, and a tinkle of the doorbell afforded him obvious relief. "It's my foreman," he said, looking at his watch. "I'll take him out in the yard to talk. This is no place for a foreman." And he departed, leaving the "living room" to Lucy and George. It was a pretty room, white panelled and blue curtained—and no place for a foreman, as Eugene said. There was a grand piano, and Lucy stood leaning back against it, looking intently at George, while her fingers, behind her, absently struck a chord or two. And her dress was the dress for that room, being of blue and white, too; and the high colour in her cheeks was far from interfering with the general harmony of things— George saw with dismay that she was prettier than ever, and naturally he missed the reassurance he might have felt had he been able to guess that Lucy, on her part, was finding him better looking than ever. For, however unusual the scope of George's pride, vanity of beauty was not included; he did not think about his looks.

"What's wrong, George?" she asked softly.

"What do you mean: 'What's wrong?' "

"You're awfully upset about something. Didn't you get though your examination all right?"

"Certainly I did. What makes you think anything's 'wrong' with me?"

"You do look pale, as papa said, and it seemed to me that the way you talked sounded—well, a little confused."

" 'Confused'! I said I didn't care to smoke. What in the world is confused about that?"

"Nothing. But—"

"See here!" George stepped close to her. "Are you glad to see me?"

"You needn't be so fierce about it!" Lucy protested, laughing at his dramatic intensity. "Of course I am! How long have I been looking forward to it?"

"I don't know," he said sharply, abating nothing of his fierceness. "How long have you?"

"Why—ever since you went away!"

"Is that true? Lucy, is that true?"

"You *are* funny!" she said. "Of course it's true. Do tell me what's the matter with you, George!"

"I will!" he exclaimed. "I was a boy when I saw you last. I see that now, though I didn't then. Well, I'm not a boy any longer. I'm a man, and a man has a right to demand a totally different treatment."

"Why has he?"

"What?"

"I don't seem to be able to understand you at all, George. Why shouldn't a boy be treated just as well as a man?"

George seemed to find himself at a loss. "Why shouldn't— Well, he shouldn't, because a man has a right to certain explanations."

"What explanations?"

"Whether he's been made a toy of!" George almost shouted. "*That's* what I want to know!"

Lucy shook her head despairingly. "You *are* the queerest person! You say you're a man now, but you talk more like a boy than ever. What *does* make you so excited?"

" 'Excited'!" he stormed. "Do you dare to stand there and call me 'excited'? I tell you, I never have been more calm or calmer in my life! I don't know that a person needs to be called 'excited' because he demands explanations that are his simple due!"

"What in the world do you want me to explain?"

"Your conduct with Fred *Kinney!*" George shouted.

Lucy uttered a sudden cry of laughter; she was delighted. "It's been awful!" she said. "I don't know that I ever heard of worse misbehaviour!

Papa and I have been twice to dinner with his family, and I've been three times to church with Fred—and once to the circus! I don't know when they'll be here to arrest me!"

"Stop that!" George commanded fiercely. "I want to know just one thing, and I mean to know it, too!"

"Whether I enjoyed the circus?"

"I want to know if you're engaged to him!"

"No!" she cried, and lifting her face close to his for the shortest instant possible, she gave him a look half merry, half defiant, but all fond. It was an adorable look.

"Lucy!" he said huskily.

But she turned quickly from him, and ran to the other end of the room. He followed awkwardly, stammering:

"Lucy, I want—I want to ask you. Will you—will you—will you be engaged to *me?"*

She stood at a window, seeming to look out into the summer darkness, her back to him.

"Will you, Lucy?"

"No," she murmured, just audibly.

"Why not?"

"I'm older than you."

"Eight months!"

"You're too young."

"Is that—" he said, gulping—"is that the only reason you won't?"

She did not answer.

As she stood, persistently staring out of the window, with her back to him, she did not see how humble his attitude had become; but his voice was low, and it shook so that she could have no doubt of his emotion. "Lucy, please forgive me for making such a row," he said, thus gently. "I've been—I've been terribly upset—terribly! You know how I feel about you, and always have felt about you. I've shown it in every single thing I've done since the first time I met you, and I know you know it. Don't you?"

Still she did not move or speak.

"Is the only reason you won't be engaged to me you think I'm too young, Lucy?"

"It's—it's reason enough," she said faintly.

At that he caught one of her hands, and she turned to him: there were tears in her eyes, tears which he did not understand at all.

"Lucy, you little dear!" he cried. "I *knew* you—"

"No, no!" she said, and she pushed him away, withdrawing her hand. "George, let's not talk of solemn things."

" 'Solemn things'! Like what?"

"Like—being engaged."

But George had become altogether jubilant, and he laughed triumphantly. "Good gracious, *that* isn't solemn!"

"It is, too!" she said, wiping her eyes. "It's too solemn for us."

"No, it isn't! I—"

"Let's sit down and be sensible, dear," she said. "You sit over there—"

"I will if you'll call me 'dear' again."

"No," she said. "I'll only call you that once again this summer—the night before you go away."

"That will have to do, then," he laughed, "so long as I know we're engaged."

"But we're not!" she protested. "And we never will be, if you don't promise not to speak of it again until—until I tell you to!"

"I won't promise that," said the happy George. "I'll only promise not to speak of it till the next time you call me 'dear'; and you've promised to call me that the night before I leave for my senior year."

"Oh, but I didn't!" she said earnestly, then hesitated. "Did I?"

"Didn't you?"

"I don't think I meant it," she murmured, her wet lashes flickering above troubled eyes.

"I know *one* thing about you," he said gayly, his triumph increasing. "You never went back on anything you said, yet, and I'm not afraid of this being the first time!"

"But we mustn't let—" she faltered; then went on tremulously, "George, we've got on so well together, we won't let this make a difference between us, will we?" And she joined in his laughter.

"It will all depend on what you tell me the night before I go away. You agree we're going to settle things then, don't you, Lucy?"

"I don't promise."

"Yes, you do! Don't you?"

"Well—"

Chapter XIII

That night George began a jubilant warfare upon his Aunt Fanny, opening the campaign upon his return home at about eleven o'clock. Fanny had retired, and was presumably asleep, but George, on the way to his own room, paused before her door, and serenaded her in a full baritone;

> "As I walk along the Boy de Balong
>   With my independent air,
>   The people all declare,
>   'He must be a millionaire!'
> Oh, you hear them sigh, and wish to die,
>   And see them wink the other eye
> At the man that broke the bank at Monte Carlo!"

Isabel came from George's room, where she had been reading, waiting for him. "I'm afraid you'll disturb your father, dear. I wish you'd sing more, though—in the daytime! You have a splendid voice."

"Good-night, old lady!"

"I thought perhaps I— Didn't you want me to come in with you and talk a little?"

"Not to-night. You go to bed. Good-night, old lady!"

He kissed her hilariously, entered his room with a skip, closed his door noisily; and then he could be heard tossing things about, loudly humming "The Man that Broke the Bank at Monte Carlo."

Smiling, his mother knelt outside his door to pray; then, with her

"Amen," pressed her lips to the bronze door-knob; and went silently to her own apartment.

. . . After breakfasting in bed, George spent the next morning at his grandfather's and did not encounter his Aunt Fanny until lunch, when she seemed to be ready for him.

"Thank you so much for the serenade, George!" she said. "Your poor father tells me he'd just got to sleep for the first time in two nights, but after your kind attentions he lay awake the rest of last night."

"Perfectly true," Mr. Minafer said grimly.

"Of course, I didn't know, sir," George hastened to assure him. "I'm awfully sorry. But Aunt Fanny was so gloomy and excited before I went out, last evening, I thought she needed cheering up."

"*I!*" Fanny jeered. "*I* was gloomy? *I* was excited? You mean about that engagement?"

"Yes. Weren't you? I thought I heard you worrying over somebody's being engaged. Didn't I hear you say you'd heard Mr. Eugene Morgan was engaged to marry some pretty little seventeen-year-old girl?"

Fanny was stung, but she made a brave effort. "Did you ask Lucy?" she said, her voice almost refusing the teasing laugh she tried to make it utter. "Did you ask her when Fred Kinney and she—"

"Yes. *That* story wasn't true. But the other one—" Here he stared at Fanny, and then affected dismay. "Why, what's the matter with your face, Aunt Fanny? It seems agitated!"

" 'Agitated'!" Fanny said disdainfully, but her voice undeniably lacked steadiness. " 'Agitated'!"

"Oh, come!" Mr. Minafer interposed. "Let's have a little peace!"

"I'm willing," said George. "*I* don't want to see poor Aunt Fanny all stirred up over a rumour I just this minute invented myself. She's so excitable—about certain subjects—it's hard to control her." He turned to his mother. "What's the matter with grandfather?"

"Didn't you see him this morning?" Isabel asked.

"Yes. He was glad to see me, and all that, but he seemed pretty fidgety. Has he been having trouble with his heart again?"

"Not lately. No."

"Well, he's not himself. I tried to talk to him about the estate; it's disgraceful—it really is—the way things are looking. He wouldn't listen, and he seemed upset. What's he upset over?"

Isabel looked serious; however, it was her husband who suggested gloomily, "I suppose the Major's bothered about this Sydney and Amelia business, most likely."

"What Sydney and Amelia business?" George asked.

"Your mother can tell you, if she wants to," Minafer said. "It's not my side of the family, so I keep off."

"It's rather disagreeable for all of us, Georgie," Isabel began. "You see, your Uncle Sydney wanted a diplomatic position, and he thought brother George, being in Congress, could arrange it. George did get him the offer of a South American ministry, but Sydney wanted a European ambassadorship, and he got quite indignant with poor George for thinking he'd take anything smaller—and he believes George didn't work hard enough for him. George had done his best, of course, and now he's out of Congress, and won't run again—so there's Sydney's idea of a big diplomatic position gone for good. Well, Sydney and your Aunt Amelia are terribly disappointed, and they say they've been thinking for years that this town isn't really fit to live in—'for a gentleman,' Sydney says—and it *is* getting rather big and dirty. So they've sold their house and decided to go abroad to live permanently; there's a villa near Florence they've often talked of buying. And they want father to let them have their share of the estate now, instead of waiting for him to leave it to them in his will."

"Well, I suppose that's fair enough," George said. "That is, in case he intended to leave them a certain amount in his will."

"Of course that's understood, Georgie. Father explained his will to us long ago; a third to them, and a third to brother George, and a third to us."

Her son made a simple calculation in his mind. Uncle George was a bachelor, and probably would never marry; Sydney and Amelia were childless. The Major's only grandchild appeared to remain the eventual heir of the entire property, no matter if the Major did turn over to Sydney a third of it now. And George had a fragmentary vision of himself, in mourning, arriving to take possession of a historic Florentine villa—he saw himself walking up a cypress-bordered path, with ancient carven stone balustrades in the distance, and servants in mourning livery greeting the new signore. "Well, I suppose it's grandfather's own affair. He can do it or not, just as he likes. I don't see why he'd mind much."

"He seemed rather confused and pained about it," Isabel said. "I think they oughtn't to urge it. George says that the estate won't stand taking out the third that Sydney wants, and that Sydney and Amelia are behaving like a couple of pigs." She laughed, continuing, "Of course *I* don't know whether they are or not: I never have understood any more about business myself than a little pig would! But I'm on George's side, whether he's right or wrong; I always was from the time we were children: and Sydney and Amelia are hurt with me about it, I'm afraid. They've stopped speaking to George entirely. Poor father! Family rows at his time of life."

George became thoughtful. If Sydney and Amelia were behaving like pigs, things might not be so simple as at first they seemed to be. Uncle Sydney and Aunt Amelia might live an *awful* long while, he thought; and besides, people didn't always leave their fortunes to relatives. Sydney might die first, leaving everything to his widow, and some curly-haired Italian adventurer might get round her, over there in Florence; she might be fool enough to marry again—or even adopt somebody!

He became more and more thoughtful, forgetting entirely a plan he had formed for the continued teasing of his Aunt Fanny; and, an hour after lunch, he strolled over to his grandfather's, intending to apply for further information, as a party rightfully interested.

He did not carry out this intention, however. Going into the big house by a side entrance, he was informed that the Major was upstairs in his bedroom, that his sons Sydney and George were both with him, and that a serious argument was in progress. "You kin stan' right in de middle dat big sta'y-way," said Old Sam, the ancient negro, who was his informant, "an' you kin heah all you a-mind to wivout goin' on up no fudda. Mist' Sydney an' Mist' Jawge talkin' louduh'n I evuh heah nobody ca'y on in nish heah house! Quollin', honey, big quollin'!"

"All right," said George shortly. "You go on back to your own part of the house, and don't make any talk. Hear me?"

"Yessuh, yessuh," Sam chuckled, as he shuffled away. "Plenty talkin' wivout Sam! Yessuh!"

George went to the foot of the great stairway. He could hear angry voices overhead—those of his two uncles—and a plaintive murmur, as if the Major tried to keep the peace.

Such sounds were far from encouraging to callers, and George decided not to go upstairs until this interview was over. His decision was the result of no timidity, nor of a too sensitive delicacy. What he felt was, that if he interrupted the scene in his grandfather's room, just at this time, one of the three gentlemen engaging in it might speak to him in a peremptory manner (in the heat of the moment) and George saw no reason for exposing his dignity to such mischances. Therefore he turned from the stairway, and going quietly into the library, picked up a magazine—but he did not open it, for his attention was instantly arrested by his Aunt Amelia's voice, speaking in the next room. The door was open and George heard her distinctly.

"Isabel does? *Isabel!*" she exclaimed, her tone high and shrewish. "You needn't tell me anything about Isabel Minafer, I guess, my dear old Frank Bronson! I know her a little better than you do, don't you think?"

George heard the voice of Mr. Bronson replying—a voice familiar to him as that of his grandfather's attorney-in-chief and chief intimate as well. He was a contemporary of the Major's, being over seventy, and they had been through three years of the War in the same regiment. Amelia addressed him now, with an effect of angry mockery, as "my dear old Frank Bronson"; but that (without the mockery) was how the Amberson family almost always spoke of him: "dear old Frank Bronson." He was a hale, thin old man, six feet three inches tall, and without a stoop.

"I doubt your knowing Isabel," he said stiffly. "You speak of her as you do because she sides with her brother George, instead of with you and Sydney."

"Poot!" Aunt Amelia was evidently in a passion. "You know what's been going on over there, well enough, Frank Bronson!"

"I don't even know what you're talking about."

"Oh, you don't? You don't know that Isabel takes George's side simply because he's Eugene Morgan's best friend?"

"It seems to me you're talking pure nonsense," said Bronson sharply. "Not impure nonsense, I hope!"

Amelia became shrill. "I thought you were a man of the world: don't tell me you're blind! For nearly two years Isabel's been pretending to chaperone Fanny Minafer with Eugene, and all the time she's been dragging that poor fool Fanny around to chaperone *her* and Eugene! Under the circumstances, she knows people will get to thinking Fanny's a pretty slim kind of chaperone, and Isabel wants to please George because she thinks there'll be less talk if she can keep her own brother around, seeming to approve. 'Talk'! She'd better look out! The whole town will be talking, the first thing she knows! She—"

Amelia stopped, and stared at the doorway in a panic, for her nephew stood there.

She kept her eyes upon his white face for a few strained moments, then, regaining her nerve, looked away and shrugged her shoulders.

"You weren't intended to hear what I've been saying, George," she said quietly. "But since you seem to—"

"Yes, I did."

"So!" She shrugged her shoulders again. "After all, I don't know but it's just as well, in the long run."

He walked up to where she sat. "You—you—" he said thickly. "It seems—it seems to me you're—you're pretty common!"

Amelia tried to give the impression of an unconcerned person laughing with complete indifference, but the sounds she produced were disjointed and uneasy. She fanned herself, looking out of the open window near her. "Of course, if you want to make more trouble in the family than we've already got, George, with your eavesdropping, you can go and repeat—"

Old Bronson had risen from his chair in great distress. "Your aunt was talking nonsense because she's piqued over a business matter, George," he said. "She doesn't mean what she said, and neither she nor any one else gives the slightest credit to such foolishness—no one in the world!"

George gulped, and wet lines shone suddenly along his lower eyelids. "They—they'd better not!" he said, then stalked out of the room, and out of the house. He stamped fiercely across the stone slabs of the front porch, descended the steps, and halted abruptly, blinking in the strong sunshine.

In front of his own gate, beyond the Major's broad lawn, his mother was just getting into her victoria, where sat already his Aunt Fanny and Lucy Morgan. It was a summer fashion-picture: the three ladies charmingly dressed, delicate parasols aloft; the lines of the victoria graceful as those of a violin; the trim pair of bays in glistening harness picked out with silver, and the serious black driver whom Isabel, being an Amberson, dared even in that town to put into a black livery coat, boots, white breeches, and cockaded hat. They jingled smartly away, and, seeing George standing on the Major's lawn, Lucy waved, and Isabel threw him a kiss.

But George shuddered, pretending not to see them, and stooped as if searching for something lost in the grass, protracting that posture until the victoria was out of hearing. And ten minutes later, George Amberson, somewhat in the semblance of an angry person plunging out of the Mansion, found a pale nephew waiting to accost him.

"I haven't time to talk, Georgie."

"Yes, you have. You'd better!"

"What's the matter, then?"

His namesake drew him away from the vicinity of the house. "I want to tell you something I just heard Aunt Amelia say, in there."

"I don't want to hear it," said Amberson. "I've been hearing entirely too much of what 'Aunt Amelia' says, lately."

"She says my mother's on your side about this division of the property because you're Eugene Morgan's best friend."

"What in the name of heaven has that got to do with your mother's being on my side?"

"She said—" George paused to swallow. "She said—" He faltered.

"You look sick," said his uncle, and laughed shortly. "If it's because of anything Amelia's been saying, I don't blame you! What else did she say?"

George swallowed again, as with nausea, but under his uncle's encouragement he was able to be explicit. "She said my mother wanted you to be friendly to her about Eugene Morgan. She said my mother had been using Aunt Fanny as a chaperone."

Amberson emitted a laugh of disgust. "It's wonderful what tommy-rot a woman in a state of spite can think of! I suppose you don't doubt that Amelia Amberson created this specimen of tommy-rot herself?"

"I know she did."

"Then what's the matter?"

"She said—" George faltered again. "She said—she implied people were—were talking about it."

"Of all the damn nonsense!" his uncle exclaimed.

George looked at him haggardly. "You're sure they're not?"

"Rubbish! Your mother's on my side about this division because she knows Sydney's a pig and always has been a pig, and so has his spiteful wife. I'm trying to keep them from getting the better of your mother as well as from getting the better of me, don't you suppose? Well, they're in a rage because Sydney always could do what he liked with father unless your mother interfered, and they know I got Isabel to ask him not to do what they wanted. They're keeping up the fight and they're sore—and Amelia's a woman who always says any damn thing that comes into her head! That's all there is to it."

"But she said," George persisted wretchedly; "she said there was *talk*. She said—"

"Look here, young fellow!" Amberson laughed good-naturedly. "There probably *is* some harmless talk about the way your Aunt Fanny goes after poor Eugene, and I've no doubt I've abetted it myself. People can't help being amused by a thing like that. Fanny was always languishing at him, twenty-odd years ago, before he left here. Well, we can't blame the poor thing if she's got her hopes up again, and I don't know that I blame her, myself, for using your mother the way she does."

"How do you mean?"

Amberson put his hand on George's shoulder. "You like to tease Fanny," he said, "but I wouldn't tease her about this, if I were you. Fanny hasn't got much in her life. You know, Georgie, just being an aunt isn't really the great career it may sometimes appear to you! In fact, I don't know of anything much that Fanny *has* got, except her feeling about Eugene. She's always had it—and what's funny to us is pretty much life-and-death to her, I suspect. Now, I'll not deny that Eugene Morgan is attracted to your mother. He is; and that's another case of 'always was'; but I know him, and he's a knight, George—a crazy one, perhaps, if you've read 'Don Quixote.' And I think your mother likes him better than she likes any man outside her own family, and that he interests her more than anybody else—and 'always has.' And that's all there is to it, except—"

"Except what?" George asked quickly, as he paused.

"Except that I suspect—" Amberson chuckled, and began over: "I'll tell you in confidence. I think Fanny's a fairly tricky customer, for such an innocent old girl! There isn't any real harm in her, but she's a great diplomatist—lots of cards up her lace sleeves, Georgie! By the way, did you ever notice how proud she is of her arms? Always flashing 'em at poor Eugene!" And he stopped to laugh again.

"I don't see anything confidential about that," George complained. "I thought—"

"Wait a minute! My idea is—don't forget it's a confidential one, but I'm devilish right about it, young Georgie!—it's this: Fanny uses your mother for a decoy duck. She does everything in the world she can to keep your mother's friendship with Eugene going, because she thinks that's what keeps Eugene about the place, so to speak. Fanny's always with your mother, you see; and whenever he sees Isabel he sees Fanny. Fanny thinks he'll get used to the idea of her being around, and some day her chance may come! You see, she's probably afraid—perhaps she even knows, poor thing!—that she wouldn't get to see much of Eugene if it weren't for Isabel's being such a friend of his. There! D'you see?"

"Well—I suppose so." George's brow was still dark, however. "If you're sure whatever talk there is, is about Aunt Fanny. If that's so—"

"Don't be an ass," his uncle advised him lightly, moving away. "I'm off for a week's fishing to forget that woman in there, and her pig of a husband." (His gesture toward the Mansion indicated Mr. and Mrs. Sydney Amberson.) "I recommend a like course to you, if you're silly enough to pay any attention to such rubbishings! Good-bye!"

. . . George was partially reassured, but still troubled: a word haunted him like the recollection of a nightmare. *"Talk!"*

He stood looking at the houses across the street from the Mansion; and though the sunshine was bright upon them, they seemed mysteriously threatening. He had always despised them, except the largest of them, which was the home of his henchman, Charlie Johnson. The Johnsons had originally owned a lot three hundred feet wide, but they had sold all of it except the meagre frontage before the house itself, and five houses were now crowded into the space where one used to squire it so spaciously. Up and down the street, the same transformation had taken place: every big, comfortable old brick house now had two or three smaller frame neighbours crowding up to it on each side, cheap-looking neighbours, most of them needing paint and not clean—and yet, though they were cheap looking, they had cost as much to build as the big brick houses, whose former ample yards they occupied. Only where George stood was there left a sward as of yore; the great, level, green lawn that served for both the Major's house and his daughter's. This serene domain—unbroken, except for the two gravelled carriage-drives—alone remained as it had been during the early glories of the Amberson Addition.

George stared at the ugly houses opposite, and hated them more than ever; but he shivered. Perhaps the riffraff living in those houses sat at the windows to watch their betters; perhaps they dared to gossip—

He uttered an exclamation, and walked rapidly toward his own front gate. The victoria had returned with Miss Fanny alone; she jumped out briskly and the victoria waited.

"Where's mother?" George asked sharply, as he met her.

"At Lucy's. I only came back to get some embroidery, because we found the sun too hot for driving. I'm in a hurry."

But, going into the house with her, he detained her when she would have hastened upstairs.

"I haven't time to talk now, Georgie; I'm going right back. I promised your mother—"

"You listen!" said George.

"What on earth—"

He repeated what Amelia had said. This time, however, he spoke coldly, and without the emotion he had exhibited during the recital to his uncle: Fanny was the one who showed agitation during this interview, for she grew fiery red, and her eyes dilated. "What on earth do you want to bring such trash to *me* for?" she demanded, breathing fast.

"I merely wished to know two things: whether it is your duty or mine to speak to father of what Aunt Amelia—"

Fanny stamped her foot. "You little fool!" she cried. "You *awful* little fool!"

"I decline—"

"Decline, my hat! Your father's a sick man, and you—"

"He doesn't seem so to me."

"Well, he does to me! And you want to go troubling him with an Amberson family row! It's just what that cat would *love* you to do!"

"Well, I—"

"Tell your father if you like! It will only make him a little sicker to think he's got a son silly enough to listen to such craziness!"

"Then you're *sure* there isn't any talk?"

Fanny disdained a reply in words. She made a hissing sound of utter contempt and snapped her fingers. Then she asked scornfully: "What's the other thing you wanted to know?"

George's pallor increased. "Whether it mightn't be better, under the circumstances," he said, "if this family were not so intimate with the Morgan family—at least for a time. It might be better—"

Fanny stared at him incredulously. "You mean you'd quit seeing Lucy?"

"I hadn't thought of that side of it, but if such a thing were necessary on account of talk about my mother, I—I—" He hesitated unhappily. "I suggested that if all of us—for a time—perhaps only for a time—it might be better if—"

"See here," she interrupted. "We'll settle this nonsense right now. If Eugene Morgan comes to this house, for instance, to see *me*, your mother can't get up and leave the place the minute he gets here, can she? What do you want her to do: insult him? Or perhaps you'd prefer she'd insult Lucy? That would do just as well. What is it you're up to, anyhow? Do you really love your Aunt Amelia so much that you want to please her? Or do you really hate your Aunt *Fanny* so much that you want to—that you want to—"

She choked and sought for her handkerchief; suddenly she began to cry.

"Oh, see here," George said. "I don't hate you, Aunt Fanny. That's silly. I don't—"

"You do! You *do*! You want to—you want to destroy the only thing— that I—that I ever—" And, unable to continue, she became inaudible in her handkerchief.

George felt remorseful, and his own troubles were lightened: all at once it became clear to him that he had been worrying about nothing. He perceived that his Aunt Amelia was indeed an old cat, and that to give her scandalous meanderings another thought would be the height of folly. By no means insusceptible to such pathos as that now exposed before him, he did not lack pity for Fanny, whose almost spoken confession was lamentable; and he was granted the vision to understand that his mother also pitied Fanny infinitely more than he did. This seemed to explain everything.

He patted the unhappy lady awkwardly upon her shoulder. "There, there!" he said. "I didn't mean anything. Of course the only thing to do about Aunt Amelia is to pay no attention to her. It's all right, Aunt Fanny. Don't cry. I feel a lot better now, myself. Come on; I'll drive back there with you. It's all over, and nothing's the matter. Can't you cheer up?"

Fanny cheered up; and presently the customarily hostile aunt and nephew were driving out Amberson Boulevard amiably together in the hot sunshine.

CHAPTER XIV

"*Almost*" was Lucy's last word on the last night of George's vacation—that vital evening which she had half consented to agree upon for "settling things" between them. "Almost engaged," she meant. And George, discontented with the "almost," but contented that she seemed glad to wear a sapphire locket with a tiny photograph of George Amberson Minafer inside it, found himself wonderful in a new world at the final instant of their parting. For, after declining to let him kiss her "good-bye," as if his desire for such a ceremony were the most preposterous absurdity in the world, she had leaned suddenly close to him and left upon his cheek the veriest feather from a fairy's wing.

She wrote him a month later:

No. It must keep on being almost.

Isn't almost pretty pleasant? You know well enough that I care for you. I did from the first minute I saw you, and I'm pretty sure you knew it—I'm afraid you did. I'm afraid you always knew it. I'm not conventional and cautious about being engaged, as you say I am, dear. (I always read over the "dears" in your letters a time or two, as you say you do in mine—only I read all of your letters a time or two!) But it's such a solemn thing it scares me. It means a good deal to a lot of people besides you and me, and that scares me, too. You write that I take your feeling for me "too lightly" and that I "take the whole affair too lightly." Isn't that odd! Because to myself I seem to take it as something so much more solemn than you do. I shouldn't be a bit surprised to find myself an old lady, some day, still thinking of you—while you'd be away and away with somebody else perhaps, and me forgotten ages ago! "Lucy Morgan," you'd say, when you saw my obituary. "Lucy Morgan? Let me see: I seem to remember the name. Didn't I know some Lucy Morgan or other, once upon a time?" Then you'd shake your big white head and stroke your long white beard—you'd have such a distinguished long white beard! and you'd say, "No. I don't seem to remember any Lucy Morgan; I wonder what made me think I did?" And poor me! I'd be deep in the ground, wondering if you'd heard about it and what you were saying! Good-bye for to-day. Don't work too hard—dear!

George immediately seized pen and paper, plaintively but vigorously requesting Lucy not to imagine him with a beard, distinguished or otherwise, even in the extremities of age. Then, after inscribing his protest in the matter of this visioned beard, he concluded his missive in a tone mollified to tenderness, and proceeded to read a letter from his mother which had reached him simultaneously with Lucy's. Isabel wrote from Asheville, where she had just arrived with her husband.

I think your father looks better already, darling, though we've been here only a few hours. It may be we've found just the place to build him up. The doctors said they hoped it would prove to be, and if it is, it would be worth the long struggle we had with him to get him to give up and come. Poor dear man, he was so blue, not about his health but about giving up the worries down at his office and forgetting them for a time—if he only will forget them! It took the pressure of the family and all his best friends, to get him to come—but father and brother George and Fanny and Eugene Morgan all kept at him so constantly that he just had to give in. I'm afraid that in my anxiety to get him to do what the doctors wanted him to, I wasn't able to back up brother George as I should in his difficulty with Sydney and Amelia. I'm so sorry! George is more upset than I've ever seen him—they've got what they wanted, and they're sailing before long, I hear, to live in Florence. Father said he couldn't stand the constant persuading—I'm afraid the word he used was "nagging." I can't understand people behaving like that. George says they may be Ambersons, but they're vulgar! I'm afraid I almost agree with him. At least, I think they were inconsiderate. But I don't see why I'm unburdening myself of all this to you, poor darling! We'll have forgotten all about it long before you come home for the holidays, and it should mean little or nothing to you, anyway. Forget that I've been so foolish!

Your father is waiting for me to take a walk with him—that's a splendid sign, because he hasn't felt he could walk much, at home, lately. I mustn't keep him waiting. Be careful to wear your mackintosh and rubbers in rainy weather, and, as soon as it begins to get colder, your ulster. Wish you could see your father now. Looks *so* much better! We plan to stay six weeks if the place agrees with him. It does really seem to already! He's just called in the door to say he's waiting. Don't smoke too much, darling boy.

Devotedly, your mother
Isabel.

But she did not keep her husband there for the six weeks she anticipated. She did not keep him anywhere that long. Three weeks after writing this letter, she telegraphed suddenly to George that they were leaving for home at once; and four days later, when he and a friend came whistling into his study, from lunch at the club, he found another telegram upon his desk.

He read it twice before he comprehended its import.

Papa left us at ten this morning, dearest.

Mother.

The friend saw the change in his face. "Not bad news?"

George lifted utterly dumfounded eyes from the yellow paper.

"My father," he said weakly. "She says—she says he's *dead*. I've got to go home."

... His Uncle George and the Major met him at the station when he arrived—the first time the Major had ever come to meet his grandson. The old gentleman sat in his closed carriage (which still needed paint) at the entrance to the station, but he got out and advanced to grasp George's hand tremulously, when the latter appeared. "Poor fellow!" he said, and patted him repeatedly upon the shoulder. "Poor fellow! Poor Georgie!"

George had not yet come to a full realization of his loss: so far, his condition was merely dazed; and as the Major continued to pat him, murmuring "Poor fellow!" over and over, George was seized by an almost irresistible impulse to tell his grandfather that he was not a poodle. But he said "Thanks," in a low voice, and got into the carriage, his two relatives following with deferential sympathy. He noticed that the Major's tremulousness did not disappear, as they drove up the street, and that he seemed much feebler than during the summer. Principally, however, George was concerned with his own emotion, or rather, with his lack of emotion; and the anxious sympathy of his grandfather and his uncle made him feel hypocritical. He was not grief-stricken; but he felt that he ought to be, and, with a secret shame, concealed his callousness beneath an affectation of solemnity.

But when he was taken into the room where lay what was left of Wilbur Minafer, George had no longer to pretend; his grief was sufficient. It needed only the sight of that forever inert semblance of the quiet man who had been always so quiet a part of his son's life—so quiet a part that George had seldom been consciously aware that his father was indeed a part of his life. As the figure lay there, its very quietness was what was most lifelike; and suddenly it struck George hard. And in that unexpected, racking grief of his son, Wilbur Minafer became more vividly George's father than he had ever been in life.

When George left the room, his arm was about his black-robed mother, his shoulders were still shaken with sobs. He leaned upon his mother; she gently comforted him; and presently he recovered his composure and became self-conscious enough to wonder if he had not been making an unmanly display of himself. "I'm all right again, mother," he said awkwardly. "Don't worry about me: you'd better go lie down, or something; you look pretty pale."

Isabel did look pretty pale, but not ghastly pale, as Fanny did. Fanny's grief was overwhelming; she stayed in her room, and George did not see her until the next day, a few minutes before the funeral, when her haggard face appalled him. But by this time he was quite himself again, and during the short service in the cemetery his thoughts even wandered so far as to permit him a feeling of regret not directly connected with his father. Beyond the open flower-walled grave was a mound where new grass grew; and here lay his great-uncle, old John Minafer, who had died the previous autumn; and beyond this were the graves of George's grandfather and grandmother Minafer, and of his grandfather Minafer's second wife, and her three sons, George's half-uncles, who had been drowned together in a canoe accident when George was a child—Fanny was the last of the family. Next beyond was the Amberson family lot, where lay the Major's wife and their sons Henry and Milton, uncles whom George dimly remembered; and beside them lay Isabel's older sister, his Aunt Estelle, who had died in her girlhood, long before George was born. The Minafer monument was a granite block, with the name chiselled upon its one polished side, and the Amberson monument was a white marble shaft, taller than any other in that neighbourhood. But farther on there was a newer section of the cemetery, an addition which had been thrown open to occupancy only a few years before, after dexterous modern treatment by a landscape specialist. There were some large new mausoleums here, and shafts taller than the Ambersons', as well as a number of monuments of some sculptural pretentiousness; and altogether the new section appeared to be a more fashionable and important quarter than that older one which contained the Amberson and Minafer lots. This was what caused George's regret, during the moment or two when his mind strayed from his father and the reading of the service.

—

. . . On the train, going back to college, ten days later, this regret (though it was as much an annoyance as a regret) recurred to his mind, and a feeling developed within him that the new quarter of the cemetery was in bad taste—not architecturally or sculpturally perhaps, but in presumption: it seemed to flaunt a kind of parvenu ignorance, as if it were actually pleased to be unaware that all the aristocratic and really important families were buried in the old section.

The annoyance gave way before a recollection of the sweet mournfulness of his mother's face, as she had said good-bye to him at the station, and of how lovely she looked in her mourning. He thought of Lucy, whom he had seen only twice, and he could not help feeling that in these quiet interviews he had appeared to her as tinged with heroism—she had shown, rather than said, how brave she thought him in his sorrow. But what came most vividly to George's mind, during these retrospections, was the despairing face of his Aunt Fanny. Again and again he thought of it; he could not avoid its haunting. And for days, after he got back to college, the stricken likeness of Fanny would appear before him unexpectedly, and without a cause that he could trace in his immediately previous thoughts. Her grief had been so silent, yet it had so amazed him.

George felt more and more compassion for this ancient antagonist of his, and he wrote to his mother about her:

I'm afraid poor Aunt Fanny might think now father's gone we won't want her to live with us any longer and because I always teased her so much she might think I'd be for turning her out. I don't know where on earth she'd go or what she could live on if we did do something like this,

CHAPTER XV

Isabel did more for Fanny than telling her to cheer up. Everything that Fanny inherited from her father, old Aleck Minafer, had been invested in Wilbur's business; and Wilbur's business, after a period of illness corresponding in dates to the illness of Wilbur's body, had died just before Wilbur did. George Amberson and Fanny were both "wiped out to a miracle of precision," as Amberson said. They "owned not a penny and owed not a penny," he continued, explaining his phrase. "It's like the moment just before drowning: you're not under water and you're not out of it. All you know is that you're not dead yet."

He spoke philosophically, having his "prospects" from his father to fall back upon; but Fanny had neither "prospects" nor philosophy. However, a legal survey of Wilbur's estate revealed the fact that his life insurance was left clear of the wreck; and Isabel, with the cheerful consent of her son, promptly turned this salvage over to her sister-in-law. Invested, it would yield something better than nine hundred dollars a year, and thus she was assured of becoming neither a pauper nor a dependent, but proved to be, as Amberson said, adding his efforts to the cheering up of Fanny, "an heiress, after all, in spite of rolling mills and the devil." She was unable to smile, and he continued his humane gayeties. "See what a wonderfully desirable income nine hundred dollars is, Fanny: a bachelor, to be in your class, must have exactly forty-nine thousand one hundred a year. Then, you see, all you need to do, in order to have fifty thousand a year, is to be a little encouraging when some bachelor in your class begins to show by his haberdashery what he wants you to think about him!"

She looked at him wanly, murmured a desolate response—she had "sewing to do"—and left the room; while Amberson shook his head ruefully at his sister. "I've often thought that humour was not my forte," he sighed. "Lord! She doesn't 'cheer up' much!"

———

The collegian did not return to his home for the holidays. Instead, Isabel joined him, and they went South for the two weeks. She was proud of her stalwart, good-looking son at the hotel where they stayed, and it was meat and drink to her when she saw how people stared at him in the lobby and on the big verandas—indeed, her vanity in him was so dominant that she was unaware of their staring at her with more interest and an admiration friendlier than George evoked. Happy to have him to herself for this fortnight, she loved to walk with him, leaning upon his arm, to read with him, to watch the sea with him—perhaps most of all she liked to enter the big dining room with him.

Yet both of them felt constantly the difference between this Christmastime and other Christmastimes of theirs—in all, it was a sorrowful holiday. But when Isabel came East for George's commencement, in June, she brought Lucy with her—and things began to seem different, especially when George Amberson arrived with Lucy's father on Class Day. Eugene had been in New York, on business; Amberson easily persuaded him to this outing; and they made a cheerful party of it, with the new graduate of course the hero and centre of it all.

His uncle was a fellow alumnus. "Yonder was where I roomed when I was here," he said, pointing out one of the university buildings to Eugene. "I don't know whether George would let my admirers place a tablet to mark the spot, or not. He owns all these buildings now, you know."

"Didn't you, when you were here? Like uncle, like nephew."

"Don't tell George you think he's like me. Just at this time we should be careful of the young gentleman's feelings."

"Yes," said Eugene. "If we weren't he mightn't let us exist at all."

"I'm sure I didn't have it so badly at his age," Amberson said reflectively, as they strolled on through the commencement crowd. "For one thing, I had brothers and sisters, and my mother didn't just sit at my feet as George's does; and I wasn't an only grandchild, either. Father's always spoiled Georgie a lot more than he did any of his own children."

Eugene laughed. "You need only three things to explain all that's good and bad about Georgie."

"Three?"

"He's Isabel's only child. He's an Amberson. He's a boy."

"Well, Mister Bones, of these three things which are the good ones and which are the bad ones?"

"All of them," said Eugene.

It happened that just then they came in sight of the subject of their discourse. George was walking under the elms with Lucy, swinging a stick and pointing out to her various objects and localities which had attained historical value during the last four years. The two older men marked his gestures, careless and graceful; they observed his attitude, unconsciously noble, his easy proprietorship of the ground beneath his feet and round about, of the branches overhead, of the old buildings beyond, and of Lucy.

"I don't know," Eugene said, smiling whimsically. "I don't know. When I spoke of his being a human being—I don't know. Perhaps it's more like deity."

"I wonder if I *was* like that!" Amberson groaned. "You don't suppose every Amberson has had to go through it, do you?"

"Don't worry! At least half of it is a combination of youth, good looks, and college; and even the noblest Ambersons get over their nobility and come to be people in time. It takes more than time, though."

"I should say it *did* take more than time!" his friend agreed, shaking a rueful head.

Then they walked over to join the loveliest Amberson, whom neither time nor trouble seemed to have touched. She stood alone, thoughtful under the great trees, chaperoning George and Lucy at a distance; but, seeing the two friends approaching, she came to meet them.

"It's charming, isn't it!" she said, moving her black-gloved hand to indicate the summery dressed crowd strolling about them, or clustering in groups, each with its own hero. "They seem so eager and so confident, all these boys—it's touching. But of course youth doesn't know it's touching."

Amberson coughed. "No, it doesn't seem to take itself as pathetic, precisely! Eugene and I were just speaking of something like that. Do you know what I think whenever I see these smooth, triumphal young faces? I always think: '*Oh*, how you're going to catch it'!"

"George!"

"Oh, yes," he said. "Life's most ingenious: it's got a special walloping for every mother's son of 'em!"

"Maybe," said Isabel, troubled—"maybe some of the mothers can take the walloping for them."

"Not one!" her brother assured her, with emphasis. "Not any more than she can take on her own face the lines that are bound to come on her son's. I suppose you know that all these young faces have got to get lines on 'em?"

"Maybe they won't," she said, smiling wistfully. "Maybe times will change, and nobody will have to wear lines."

"Times have changed like that for only one person that I know," Eugene said. And as Isabel looked inquiring, he laughed, and she saw that she was the "only one person." His implication was justified, moreover, and she knew it. She blushed charmingly.

"Which is it puts the lines on the faces?" Amberson asked. "Is it age or trouble? Of course we can't decide that wisdom does it—we must be polite to Isabel."

"I'll tell you what puts the lines there," Eugene said. "Age puts some, and trouble puts some, and work puts some, but the deepest are carved by lack of faith. The serenest brow is the one that believes the most."

"In what?" Isabel asked gently.

"In everything!"

She looked at him inquiringly, and he laughed as he had a moment before, when she looked at him that way. "Oh, yes, you do!" he said.

She continued to look at him inquiringly a moment or two longer, and there was an unconscious earnestness in her glance, something trustful as well as inquiring, as if she knew that whatever he meant it was all right. Then her eyes drooped thoughtfully, and she seemed to address some inquiries to herself. She looked up suddenly. "Why, I believe," she said, in a tone of surprise, "I believe I do!"

And at that both men laughed. "Isabel!" her brother exclaimed. "You're a foolish person! There are times when you look exactly fourteen years old!"

But this reminded her of her real affair in that part of the world. "Good gracious!" she said. "Where have the children got to? We must take Lucy pretty soon, so that George can go and sit with the Class. We must catch up with them."

She took her brother's arm, and the three moved on, looking about them in the crowd.

"Curious," Amberson remarked, as they did not immediately discover the young people they sought. "Even in such a concourse one would think we couldn't fail to see the proprietor."

"Several hundred proprietors to-day," Eugene suggested.

"No; they're only proprietors of the university," said George's uncle. "We're looking for the proprietor of the universe."

"There he is!" cried Isabel fondly, not minding this satire at all. "And doesn't he look it!"

Her escorts were still laughing at her when they joined the proprietor of the universe and his pretty friend, and though both Amberson and Eugene declined to explain the cause of their mirth, even upon Lucy's urgent request, the portents of the day were amiable, and the five made a happy party—that is to say, four of them made a happy audience for the fifth, and the mood of this fifth was gracious and cheerful.

George took no conspicuous part in either the academic or the social celebrations of his class; he seemed to regard both sets of exercises with a tolerant amusement, his own "crowd" "not going in much for either of those sorts of things," as he explained to Lucy. What his crowd had gone in for remained ambiguous; some negligent testimony indicating that, except for an astonishing reliability which they all seemed to have attained in matters relating to musical comedy, they had not gone in for anything. Certainly the question one of them put to Lucy, in response to investigations of hers, seemed to point that way: "Don't you think," he said, "really, don't you think that being things is rather better than doing things?"

He said "rahthuh bettuh" for "rather better," and seemed to do it deliberately, with perfect knowledge of what he was doing. Later, Lucy mocked him to George, and George refused to smile: he somewhat inclined to such pronunciations, himself. This inclination was one of the things that he had acquired in the four years.

What else he had acquired, it might have puzzled him to state, had anybody asked him and required a direct reply within a reasonable space of time. He had learned how to pass examinations by "cramming"; that is, in three or four days and nights he could get into his head enough of a selected fragment of some scientific or philosophical or literary or linguistic subject to reply plausibly to six questions out of ten. He could retain the information necessary for such a feat just long enough to give a successful performance; then it would evaporate utterly from his brain, and leave him undisturbed. George, like his "crowd," not only preferred "being things" to "doing things," but had contented himself with four years of "being things" as a preparation for going on "being things." And when Lucy rather shyly pressed him for his friend's probable definition of the "things" it seemed so superior and beautiful to be, George raised his eyebrows slightly, meaning that she should have understood without explanation; but he did explain: "Oh, family and all that—being a gentleman, I suppose."

Lucy gave the horizon a long look, but offered no comment.

Chapter XVI

"Aunt Fanny doesn't look much better," George said to his mother, a few minutes after their arrival, on the night they got home. He stood with a towel in her doorway, concluding some sketchy ablutions before going downstairs to a supper which Fanny was hastily preparing for them. Isabel had not telegraphed; Fanny was taken by surprise when they drove up in a station cab at eleven o'clock; and George instantly demanded "a little decent food." (Some criticisms of his had publicly disturbed the composure of the dining-car steward four hours previously.) "I never saw anybody take things so hard as she seems to," he observed, his voice muffled by the towel. "Doesn't she get over it at all? I thought she'd feel better when we turned over the insurance to her—gave it to her absolutely, without any strings to it. She looks about a thousand years old!"

"She looks quite girlish, sometimes, though," his mother said.

"Has she looked that way much since father—"

"Not so much," Isabel said thoughtfully. "But she will, as time goes on."

"Time'll have to hurry, then, it seems to me," George observed, returning to his own room.

When they went down to the dining room, he pronounced acceptable the salmon salad, cold beef, cheese, and cake which Fanny made ready for them without disturbing the servants. The journey had fatigued Isabel, she ate nothing, but sat to observe with tired pleasure the manifestations of her son's appetite, meanwhile giving her sister-in-law a brief summary of the events of commencement. But presently she kissed them both good-night—taking care to kiss George lightly upon the side of his head, so as not to disturb his eating—and left aunt and nephew alone together.

"It never was becoming to her to look pale," Fanny said absently, a few moments after Isabel's departure.

"Wha'd you say, Aunt Fanny?"

"Nothing. I suppose your mother's been being pretty gay? Going a lot?"

"How could she?" George asked cheerfully. "In mourning, of course all she could do was just sit around and look on. That's all Lucy could do either, for the matter of that."

"I suppose so," his aunt assented. "How did Lucy get home?"

George regarded her with astonishment. "Why, on the train with the rest of us, of course."

"I didn't mean that," Fanny explained. "I meant from the station. Did you drive out to their house with her before you came here?"

"No. She drove home with her father, of course."

"Oh, I see. So Eugene came to the station to meet you."

" 'To meet us'?" George echoed, renewing his attack upon the salmon salad. "How could he?"

"I don't know what you mean," Fanny said drearily, in the desolate voice that had become her habit. "I haven't seen him while your mother's been away."

"Naturally," said George. "He's been East himself."

At this Fanny's drooping eyelids opened wide.

"Did you *see* him?"

"Well, naturally, since he made the trip home with us!"

"He did?" she said sharply. "He's been with you all the time?"

"No; only on the train and the last three days before we left. Uncle George got him to come."

Fanny's eyelids drooped again, and she sat silent until George pushed back his chair and lit a cigarette, declaring his satisfaction with what she had provided. "You're a fine housekeeper," he said benevolently. "You know how to make things look dainty as well as taste the right way. I don't believe you'd stay single very long if some of the bachelors and widowers around town could just once see—"

She did not hear him. "It's a little odd," she said.

"What's odd?"

"Your mother's not mentioning that Mr. Morgan had been with you."

"Didn't think of it, I suppose," said George carelessly; and, his benevolent mood increasing, he conceived the idea that a little harmless rallying might serve to elevate his aunt's drooping spirits. "I'll tell you something, in confidence," he said solemnly.

She looked up, startled. "What?"

"Well, it struck me that Mr. Morgan was looking pretty absentminded, most of the time; and he certainly is dressing better than he used to. Uncle George told me he heard that the automobile factory had been doing quite well—won a race, too! I shouldn't be a bit surprised if all the young fellow had been waiting for was to know he had an assured income before he proposed."

"What 'young fellow'?"

"This young fellow Morgan," laughed George. "Honestly, Aunt Fanny, I shouldn't be a bit surprised to have him request an interview with me any day, and declare that his intentions are honourable, and ask my permission to pay his addresses to you. What had I better tell him?"

Fanny burst into tears.

"Good heavens!" George cried. "I was only teasing. I didn't mean—"

"Let me alone," she said lifelessly; and, continuing to weep, rose and began to clear away the dishes.

"Please, Aunt Fanny—"

"Just let me alone."

George was distressed. "I didn't mean anything, Aunt Fanny! I didn't know you'd got so sensitive as all that."

"You'd better go up to bed," she said desolately, going on with her work and her weeping.

"Anyhow," he insisted, "do let these things wait. Let the servants 'tend to the table in the morning."

"No."

"But, why not?"

"Just let me alone."

"Oh, Lord!" George groaned, going to the door. There he turned. "See here, Aunt Fanny, there's not a bit of use your bothering about those dishes to-night. What's the use of a butler and three maids if—"

"Just let me alone."

He obeyed, and could still hear a pathetic sniffing from the dining room as he went up the stairs.

"By George!" he grunted, as he reached his own room; and his thought was that living with a person so sensitive to kindly raillery might prove lugubrious. He whistled, long and low, then went to the window and looked through the darkness to the great silhouette of his grandfather's house. Lights were burning over there, upstairs; probably his newly arrived uncle was engaged in talk with the Major.

George's glance lowered, resting casually upon the indistinct ground, and he beheld some vague shapes, unfamiliar to him. Formless heaps, they seemed; but, without much curiosity, he supposed that sewer connections or water pipes might be out of order, making necessary some excavations. He hoped the work would not take long; he hated to see that sweep of lawn made unsightly by trenches and lines of dirt, even temporarily. Not greatly disturbed, however, he pulled down the shade, yawned, and began to undress, leaving further investigation for the morning.

But in the morning he had forgotten all about it, and raised his shade, to let in the light, without even glancing toward the ground. Not until he had finished dressing did he look forth from his window, and then his glance was casual. The next instant his attitude became electric, and he gave utterance to a bellow of dismay. He ran from his room, plunged down the stairs, out of the front door, and, upon a nearer view of the destroyed lawn, began to release profanity upon the breezeless summer air, which remained unaffected. Between his mother's house and his grandfather's, excavations for the cellars of five new houses were in process, each within a few feet of its neighbour. Foundations of brick were being laid; everywhere were piles of brick and stacked lumber, and sand heaps and mortar beds.

It was Sunday, and so the workmen implicated in these defacings were denied what unquestionably they would have considered a treat; but as the fanatic orator continued the monologue, a gentleman in flannels emerged upward from one of the excavations, and regarded him contemplatively.

"Obtaining any relief, nephew?" he inquired with some interest. "You must have learned quite a number of those expressions in childhood—it's so long since I'd heard them I fancied they were obsolete."

"Who wouldn't swear?" George demanded hotly. "In the name of God, what does grandfather mean, doing such things?"

"My private opinion is," said Amberson gravely, "he desires to increase his income by building these houses to rent."

"Well, in the name of God, can't he increase his income any other way but this?"

"In the name of God, it would appear he couldn't."

"It's beastly! It's a damn degradation! It's a crime!"

"I don't know about its being a crime," said his uncle, stepping over some planks to join him. "It might be a mistake, though. Your mother said not to tell you until we got home, so as not to spoil commencement for you. She rather feared you'd be upset."

"Upset! Oh, my Lord, I should think I *would* be upset! He's in his second childhood. What did you let him *do* it for, in the name of—"

"Make it in the name of heaven this time, George; it's Sunday. Well, I thought, myself, it was a mistake."

"I should say so!"

"Yes," said Amberson. "I wanted him to put up an apartment building instead of these houses."

"An apartment building! *Here?*"

"Yes; that was my idea."

George struck his hands together despairingly. "An apartment house! Oh, my Lord!"

"Don't worry! Your grandfather wouldn't listen to me, but he'll wish he had, some day. He says that people aren't going to live in miserable little flats when they can get a whole house with some grass in front and plenty of backyard behind. He sticks it out that apartment houses will never do in a town of this type, and when I pointed out to him that a dozen or so of 'em already *are* doing, he claimed it was just the novelty, and that they'd all be empty as soon as people got used to 'em. So he's putting up these houses."

"Is he getting miserly in his old age?"

"Hardly! Look what he gave Sydney and Amelia!"

"I don't mean he's a miser, of course," said George. "Heaven knows he's liberal enough with mother and me; but why on earth didn't he *sell* something or other rather than do a thing like this?"

"As a matter of fact," Amberson returned coolly, "I believe he *has* sold something or other, from time to time."

"Well, in heaven's name," George cried, "what did he do it for?"

"To get money," his uncle mildly replied. "That's my deduction."

"I suppose you're joking—or trying to!"

"That's the best way to look at it," Amberson said amiably. "Take the whole thing as a joke—and in the meantime, if you haven't had your breakfast—"

"I haven't!"

"Then if I were you I'd go in and get some. And"—he paused, becoming serious—"and if I were you I wouldn't say anything to your grandfather about this."

"I don't think I could trust myself to speak to him about it," said George. "I want to treat him respectfully, because he *is* my grandfather, but I don't believe I could if I talked to him about such a thing as this!"

And with a gesture of despair, plainly signifying that all too soon after leaving bright college years behind him he had entered into the full tragedy of life, George turned bitterly upon his heel and went into the house for his breakfast.

His uncle, with his head whimsically upon one side, gazed after him not altogether unsympathetically, then descended again into the excavation whence he had lately emerged. Being a philosopher he was not surprised, that afternoon, in the course of a drive he took in the old carriage with the Major, when George was encountered upon the highway, flashing along in his runabout with Lucy beside him and Pendennis doing better than three minutes.

"He seems to have recovered," Amberson remarked: "Looks in the highest good spirits."

"I beg your pardon."

"Your grandson," Amberson explained. "He was inclined to melancholy this morning, but seemed jolly enough just now when they passed us."

"What was he melancholy about? Not getting remorseful about all the money he's spent at college, was he?" The Major chuckled feebly, but with sufficient grimness. "I wonder what he thinks I'm made of," he concluded querulously.

"Gold," his son suggested, adding gently, "And he's right about part of you, father."

"What part?"

"Your heart."

The Major laughed ruefully. "I suppose that may account for how heavy it feels, sometimes, nowadays. This town seems to be rolling right over that old heart you mentioned, George—rolling over it and burying it under! When I think of those devilish workmen digging up my lawn, yelling around my house—"

"Never mind, father. Don't think of it. When things are a nuisance it's a good idea not to keep remembering 'em."

"I *try* not to," the old gentleman murmured. "I try to keep remembering that I won't be remembering anything very long." And, somehow convinced that this thought was a mirthful one, he laughed loudly, and slapped his knee. "Not so very long now, my boy!" he chuckled, continuing to echo his own amusement. "Not so very long. Not so very long!"

Chapter XVII

Young George paid his respects to his grandfather the following morning, having been occupied with various affairs and engagements on Sunday until after the Major's bedtime; and topics concerned with building or excavations were not introduced into the conversation, which was a cheerful one until George lightly mentioned some new plans of his. He was a skillful driver, as the Major knew, and he spoke of his desire to extend his proficiency in this art: in fact, he entertained the ambition to drive a four-in-hand. However, as the Major said nothing, and merely sat still, looking surprised, George went on to say that he did not propose to "go in for coaching just at the start"; he thought it would be better to begin with a tandem. He was sure Pendennis could be trained to work as a leader; and all that one needed to buy at present, he said, would be "comparatively inexpensive—a new trap, and the harness, of course, and a good bay to match Pendennis." He did not care for a special groom; one of the stablemen would do.

At this point the Major decided to speak. "You say one of the stablemen would do?" he inquired, his widened eyes remaining fixed upon his grandson. "That's lucky, because one's all there is, just at present, George. Old fat Tom does it all. Didn't you notice, when you took Pendennis out, yesterday?"

"Oh, that will be all right, sir. My mother can lend me her man."

"Can she?" The old gentleman smiled faintly. "I wonder—" He paused.

"What, sir?"

"Whether you mightn't care to go to law-school somewhere perhaps. I'd be glad to set aside a sum that would see you through."

This senile divergence from the topic in hand surprised George painfully. "I have no interest whatever in the law," he said. "I don't care for it, and the idea of being a professional man has never appealed to me. None of the family has ever gone in for that sort of thing, to my knowledge, and I don't care to be the first. I was speaking of driving a tandem—"

"I know you were," the Major said quietly.

George looked hurt. "I beg your pardon. Of course if the idea doesn't appeal to you—" And he rose to go.

The Major ran a tremulous hand through his hair, sighing deeply. "I—I don't like to refuse you anything, Georgie," he said. "I don't know that I often have refused you whatever you wanted—in reason—"

"You've always been more than generous, sir," George interrupted quickly. "And if the idea of a tandem doesn't appeal to you, why—of course—" And he waved his hand, heroically dismissing the tandem.

The Major's distress became obvious. "Georgie, I'd like to, but—but I've an idea tandems are dangerous to drive, and your mother might be anxious. She—"

"No, sir; I think not. She felt it would be rather a good thing—help to keep me out in the open air. But if perhaps your finances—"

"Oh, it isn't that so much," the old gentleman said hurriedly. "I wasn't thinking of that altogether." He laughed uncomfortably. "I guess we could still afford a new horse or two, if need be—"

"I thought you said—"

The Major waved his hand airily. "Oh, a few retrenchments where things were useless: nothing gained by a raft of idle darkies in the stable—nor by a lot of extra land that might as well be put to work for us in rentals. And if you want this thing so very much—"

"It's not important enough to bother about, really, of course."

"Well, let's wait till autumn then," said the Major in a tone of relief. "We'll see about it in the autumn, if you're still in the mind for it then. That will be a great deal better. You remind me of it, along in September—or October. We'll see what can be done." He rubbed his hands cheerfully. "We'll see what can be done about it then, Georgie. We'll see."

And George, in reporting this conversation to his mother, was ruefully humorous. "In fact, the old boy cheered up so much," he told her, "you'd have thought he'd got a real load off his mind. He seemed to think he'd fixed *me* up perfectly, and that I was just as good as driving a tandem around his library right that minute! Of course I know he's anything but miserly; still I can't help thinking he must be salting a lot of money away. I know prices are higher than they used to be, but he doesn't spend within thousands of what he used to, and *we* certainly can't be spending more than we always have spent. Where does it all go to? Uncle George told me grandfather had sold some pieces of property, and it looks a little queer. If he's really 'property poor,' of course we ought to be more saving than we are, and help him out. *I* don't mind giving up a tandem if it seems a little too expensive just now. I'm perfectly willing to live quietly till he gets his bank balance where he wants it. But I have a faint suspicion, not that he's getting miserly—not that at all—but that old age has begun to make him timid about money. There's no doubt about it, he's getting a little queer: he can't keep his mind on a subject long. Right in the middle of talking about one thing he'll wander off to something else; and I shouldn't be surprised if he turned out to be a lot better off than any of us guess. It's entirely possible that whatever he's sold just went into government bonds, or even his safety deposit box. There was a friend of mine in college had an old uncle like that: made the whole family think he was poor as dirt—and then left seven millions. People get terribly queer as they get old, sometimes, and grandfather certainly doesn't act the way he used to. He seems to be a totally different man. For instance, he said he thought tandem driving might be dangerous—"

"Did he?" Isabel asked quickly. "Then I'm glad he doesn't want you to have one. I didn't dream—"

"But it's not. There isn't the slightest—"

Isabel had a bright idea. "Georgie! Instead of a tandem wouldn't it interest you to get one of Eugene's automobiles?"

"I don't think so. They're fast enough, of course. In fact, running one of those things is getting to be quite on the cards for sport, and people go all over the country in 'em. But they're dirty things, and they keep getting out of order, so that you're always lying down on your back in the mud, and—"

"Oh, no," she interrupted eagerly. "Haven't you noticed? You don't see nearly so many people doing that nowadays as you did two or three years ago, and, when you do, Eugene says it's apt to be one of the older patterns. The way they make them now, you can get at most of the machinery from the top. I do think you'd be interested, dear."

George remained indifferent. "Possibly—but I hardly think so. I know a lot of good people are really taking them up, but still—"

" 'But still' what?" she said as he paused.

"But still—well, I suppose I'm a little old-fashioned and fastidious, but I'm afraid being a sort of engine driver never will appeal to me, mother. It's exciting, and I'd like that part of it, but still it doesn't seem to me precisely the thing a gentleman ought to do. Too much overalls and monkey-wrenches and grease!"

"But Eugene says people are hiring mechanics to do all that sort of thing for them. They're beginning to have them just the way they have coachmen; and he says it's developing into quite a profession."

"I know that, mother, of course; but I've seen some of these mechanics, and they're not very satisfactory. For one thing, most of them only pretend to understand the machinery and they let people break down a hundred miles from nowhere, so that about all these fellows are good for is to hunt up a farmer and hire a horse to pull the automobile. And friends of mine at college that've had a good deal of experience tell me the mechanics who do understand the engines have no training at all as servants. They're awful! They say anything they like, and usually speak to members of the family as 'Say!' No, I believe I'd rather wait for September and a tandem, mother."

Nevertheless, George sometimes consented to sit in an automobile, while waiting for September, and he frequently went driving in one of Eugene's cars with Lucy and her father. He even allowed himself to be escorted with his mother and Fanny through the growing factory, which was now, as the foreman of the paint shop informed the visitors, "turning out a car and a quarter a day." George had seldom been more excessively bored, but his mother showed a lively interest in everything, wishing to have all the machinery explained to her. It was Lucy who did most of the explaining, while her father looked on and laughed at the mistakes she made, and Fanny remained in the background with George, exhibiting a bleakness that overmatched his boredom.

From the factory Eugene took them to lunch at a new restaurant, just opened in the town, a place which surprised Isabel with its metropolitan air, and, though George made fun of it to her, in a whisper, she offered everything the tribute of pleased exclamations; and her gayety helped Eugene's to make the little occasion almost a festive one.

George's ennui disappeared in spite of himself, and he laughed to see his mother in such spirits. "I didn't know mineral waters could go to a person's head," he said. "Or perhaps it's this place. It might pay to have a new restaurant opened somewhere in town every time you get the blues."

Fanny turned to him with a wan smile. "Oh, *she* doesn't 'get the blues,' George!" Then she added, as if fearing her remark might be thought unpleasantly significant, "I never knew a person of a more even disposition. I wish I could be like that!" And though the tone of this afterthought was not so enthusiastic as she tried to make it, she succeeded in producing a fairly amiable effect.

"No," Isabel said, reverting to George's remark, and overlooking Fanny's. "What makes me laugh so much at nothing is Eugene's factory. Wouldn't anybody be delighted to see an old friend take an idea out of the air like that—an idea that most people laughed at him for— wouldn't any old friend of his be happy to see how he'd made his idea into such a splendid, humming thing as that factory—all shiny steel, clicking and buzzing away, and with all those workmen, such *muscled* looking men and yet so intelligent looking?"

"Hear! Hear!" George applauded. "We seem to have a lady orator among us. I hope the waiters won't mind."

Isabel laughed, not discouraged. "It's beautiful to see such a thing," she said. "It makes us all happy, dear old Eugene!"

And with a brave gesture she stretched out her hand to him across the small table. He took it quickly, giving her a look in which his laughter tried to remain, but vanished before a gratitude threatening to become emotional in spite of him. Isabel, however, turned instantly to Fanny. "Give him your hand, Fanny," she said gayly; and, as Fanny mechanically obeyed, "There!" Isabel cried. "If brother George were here, Eugene would have his three oldest and best friends congratulating him all at once. We know what brother George thinks about it, though. It's just beautiful, Eugene!"

Probably if her brother George had been with them at the little table, he would have made known what he thought about herself, for it must inevitably have struck him that she was in the midst of one of those "times" when she looked "exactly fourteen years old." Lucy served as a proxy for Amberson, perhaps, when she leaned toward George and whispered: "Did you *ever* see anything so lovely?"

"As what?" George inquired, not because he misunderstood, but because he wished to prolong the pleasant neighbourliness of whispering.

"As your mother! Think of her doing that! She's a darling! And papa"—here she imperfectly repressed a tendency to laugh—"papa looks as if he were either going to explode or utter loud sobs!"

Eugene commanded his features, however, and they resumed their customary apprehensiveness. "I used to write verse," he said—"if you remember—"

"Yes," Isabel interrupted gently. "I remember."

"I don't recall that I've written any for twenty years or so," he continued. "But I'm almost thinking I could do it again, to thank you for making a factory visit into such a kind celebration."

"Gracious!" Lucy whispered, giggling. "Aren't they sentimental!"

"People that age always are," George returned. "They get sentimental over anything at all. Factories or restaurants, it doesn't matter what!"

And both of them were seized with fits of laughter which they managed to cover under the general movement of departure, as Isabel had risen to go.

Outside, upon the crowded street, George helped Lucy into his runabout, and drove off, waving triumphantly, and laughing at Eugene who was struggling with the engine of his car, in the tonneau of which Isabel and Fanny had established themselves. "Looks like a hand-organ man grinding away for pennies," said George, as the runabout turned the corner and into National Avenue. "I'll still take a horse, any day."

He was not so cocksure, half an hour later, on an open road, when a siren whistle wailed behind him, and before the sound had died away, Eugene's car, coming from behind with what seemed fairly like one long leap, went by the runabout and dwindled almost instantaneously in perspective, with a lace handkerchief in a black-gloved hand fluttering sweet derision as it was swept onward into minuteness—a mere white speck—and then out of sight.

George was undoubtedly impressed. "Your father does know how to drive some," the dashing exhibition forced him to admit. "Of course Pendennis isn't as young as he was, and I don't care to push him too hard. I wouldn't mind handling one of those machines on the road like that, myself, if that was all there was to it—no cranking to do, or fooling with the engine. Well, I enjoyed part of that lunch quite a lot, Lucy."

"The salad?"

"No. Your whispering to me."

"Blarney!"

George made no response, but checked Pendennis to a walk. Whereupon Lucy protested quickly: "Oh, don't!"

"Why? Do you want him to trot his legs off?"

"No, but—"

" 'No, but'—what?"

She spoke with apparent gravity: "I know when you make him walk it's so you can give all your attention to—to proposing to me again!"

And as she turned a face of exaggerated colour to him, "By the Lord, but you're a little witch!" George cried.

"George, *do* let Pendennis trot again!"

"I won't!"

She clucked to the horse. "Get up, Pendennis! Trot! Go on! Commence!"

Pendennis paid no attention; she meant nothing to him, and George laughed at her fondly. "You *are* the prettiest thing in this world, Lucy!" he exclaimed. "When I see you in winter, in furs, with your cheeks red, I think you're prettiest then, but when I see you in summer, in a straw hat and a shirtwaist and a duck skirt and white gloves and those little silver buckled slippers, and your rose-coloured parasol, and your cheeks not red but with a kind of pinky glow about them, then I see I must have been wrong about the winter! When are you going to drop the 'almost' and say we're really engaged?"

"Oh, not for *years*! So there's the answer, and let's trot again."

But George was persistent; moreover, he had become serious during the last minute or two. "I want to know," he said. "I really mean it."

"Let's don't be serious, George," she begged him hopefully. "Let's talk of something pleasant."

He was a little offended. "Then it isn't pleasant for you to know that I want to marry you?"

At this she became as serious as he could have asked; she looked down, and her lip quivered like that of a child about to cry. Suddenly she put her hand upon one of his for just an instant, and then withdrew it.

"Lucy!" he said huskily. "Dear, what's the matter? You look as if you were going to cry. You always do that," he went on plaintively, "whenever I can get you to talk about marrying me."

"I know it," she murmured.

"Well, why do you?"

Her eyelids flickered, and then she looked up at him with a sad gravity, tears seeming just at the poise. "One reason's because I have a feeling that it's never going to be."

"Why?"

"It's just a feeling."

"You haven't any reason or—"

"It's just a feeling."

"Well, if that's all," George said, reassured, and laughing confidently, "I guess I won't be very much troubled!" But at once he became serious again, adopting the tone of argument. "Lucy, how is anything ever going to get a *chance* to come of it, so long as you keep sticking to 'almost'? Doesn't it strike you as unreasonable to have a 'feeling' that we'll never be married, when what principally stands between us is the fact that you won't be really engaged to me? That does seem pretty absurd! Don't you *care* enough about me to marry me?"

She looked down again, pathetically troubled. "Yes."

"Won't you always care that much about me?"

"I'm—yes—I'm afraid so, George. I never do change much about anything."

"Well, then, why in the world won't you drop the 'almost'?"

Her distress increased. "Everything is—everything—"

"What about 'everything'?"

"Everything is so—so unsettled."

And at that he uttered an exclamation of impatience. "If you aren't the queerest girl! *What* is 'unsettled'?"

"Well, for one thing," she said, able to smile at his vehemence, "you haven't settled on anything to do. At least, if you have you've never spoken of it."

As she spoke, she gave him the quickest possible side glance of hopeful scrutiny; then looked away, not happily. Surprise and displeasure were intentionally visible upon the countenance of her companion; and he permitted a significant period of silence to elapse before making any response. "Lucy," he said, finally, with cold dignity, "I should like to ask you a few questions."

"Yes?"

"The first is: Haven't you perfectly well understood that I don't mean to go into business or adopt a profession?"

"I wasn't quite sure," she said gently. "I really didn't know—quite."

"Then of course it's time I did tell you. I never have been able to see any occasion for a man's going into trade, or being a lawyer, or any of those things if his position and family were such that he didn't need to. You know, yourself, there are a lot of people in the East—in the South, too, for that matter—that don't think we've got any particular family or position or culture in this part of the country. I've met plenty of that kind of provincial snobs myself, and they're pretty galling. There were one or two men in my crowd at college, their families had lived on their income for three generations, and they never dreamed there was anybody in their class out here. I had to show them a thing or two, right at the start, and I guess they won't forget it! Well, I think it's time all their sort found out that three generations *can* mean just as much out here as anywhere else. That's the way I feel about it, and let me tell you I feel it pretty deeply!"

"But what *are* you going to do, George?" she cried.

George's earnestness surpassed hers; he had become flushed and his breathing was emotional. As he confessed, with simple genuineness, he did feel what he was saying "pretty deeply"; and in truth his state approached the tremulous. "I expect to live an honourable life," he said. "I expect to contribute my share to charities, and to take part in—in movements."

"What kind?"

"Whatever appeals to me," he said.

Lucy looked at him with grieved wonder. "But you really don't mean to have any regular business or profession at *all*?"

"I certainly do not!" George returned promptly and emphatically.

"I was afraid so," she said in a low voice.

George continued to breathe deeply throughout another protracted interval of silence. Then he said, "I should like to revert to the questions I was asking you, if you don't mind."

"No, George. I think we'd better—"

"Your father is a business man—"

"He's a mechanical genius," Lucy interrupted quickly. "Of course he's both. And he was a lawyer once—he's done all sorts of things."

"Very well. I merely wished to ask if it's his influence that makes you think I ought to 'do' something?"

Lucy frowned slightly. "Why, I suppose almost everything I think or say must be owing to his influence in one way or another. We haven't had anybody but each other for so many years, and we always think about alike, so of course—"

"I see!" And George's brow darkened with resentment. "So that's it, is it? It's your father's idea that I ought to go into business and that you oughtn't to be engaged to me until I do."

Lucy gave a start, her denial was so quick. "No! I've never once spoken to him about it. Never!"

George looked at her keenly, and he jumped to a conclusion not far from the truth. "But you know without talking to him that it's the way he does feel about it? I see."

She nodded gravely. "Yes."

George's brow grew darker still. "Do you think I'd be much of a man," he said, slowly, "if I let any other man dictate to me my own way of life?"

"George! Who's 'dictating' your—"

"It seems to me it amounts to that!" he returned.

"Oh, *no*! I only know how papa thinks about things. He's never, never spoken unkindly, or 'dictatingly' of you." She lifted her hand in protest, and her face was so touching in its distress that for the moment George forgot his anger. He seized that small, troubled hand.

"Lucy," he said huskily. "Don't you know that I love you?"

"Yes—I do."

"Don't you love me?"

"Yes—I do."

"Then what does it matter what your father thinks about my doing something or not doing anything? He has his way, and I have mine. I don't believe in the whole world scrubbing dishes and selling potatoes and trying law cases. Why, look at your father's best friend, my Uncle George Amberson—he's never done anything in his life, and—"

"Oh, yes, he has," she interrupted. "He was in politics."

"Well, I'm glad he's out," George said. "Politics is a dirty business for a gentleman, and Uncle George would tell you that himself. Lucy, let's not talk any more about it. Let me tell mother when I get home that we're engaged. Won't you, dear?"

She shook her head.

"Is it because—"

For a fleeting instant she touched to her cheek the hand that held hers. "No," she said, and gave him a sudden little look of renewed gayety. "Let's let it stay 'almost.' "

"Because your father—"

"Oh, because it's better!"

George's voice shook. "Isn't it your father?"

"It's his ideals I'm thinking of—yes."

George dropped her hand abruptly and anger narrowed his eyes. "I know what you mean," he said. "I dare say I don't care for your father's ideals any more than he does for mine!"

He tightened the reins, Pendennis quickening eagerly to the trot; and when George jumped out of the runabout before Lucy's gate, and assisted her to descend, the silence in which they parted was the same that had begun when Pendennis began to trot.

CHAPTER XVIII

That evening, after dinner, George sat with his mother and his Aunt Fanny upon the veranda. In former summers, when they sat outdoors in the evening, they had customarily used an open terrace at the side of the house, looking toward the Major's, but that more private retreat now afforded too blank and abrupt a view of the nearest of the new houses; so, without consultation, they had abandoned it for the Romanesque stone structure in front, an oppressive place.

Its oppression seemed congenial to George; he sat upon the copestone of the stone parapet, his back against a stone pilaster; his attitude not comfortable, but rigid, and his silence not comfortable, either, but heavy. However, to the eyes of his mother and his aunt, who occupied wicker chairs at a little distance, he was almost indistinguishable except for the stiff white shield of his evening frontage.

"It's so nice of you always to dress in the evening, George," his mother said, her glance resting upon this surface. "Your Uncle George always used to, and so did father, for years; but they both stopped quite a long time ago. Unless there's some special occasion, it seems to me we don't see it done any more, except on the stage and in the magazines."

He made no response, and Isabel, after waiting a little while, as if she expected one, appeared to acquiesce in his mood for silence, and turned her head to gaze thoughtfully out at the street.

There, in the highway, the evening life of the Midland city had begun. A rising moon was bright upon the tops of the shade trees, where their branches met overhead, arching across the street, but only filtered splashings of moonlight reached the block pavement below; and through this darkness flashed the firefly lights of silent bicycles gliding by in pairs and trios—or sometimes a dozen at a time might come, and not so silent, striking their little bells; the riders' voices calling and laughing; while now and then a pair of invisible experts would pass, playing mandolin and guitar as if handle-bars were of no account in the world—their music would come swiftly, and then too swiftly die away. Surreys rumbled lightly by, with the plod-plod of honest old horses, and frequently there was the glitter of whizzing spokes from a runabout or a sporting buggy, and the sharp, decisive hoof-beats of a trotter. Then, like a cowboy shooting up a peaceful camp, a frantic devil would hurtle out of the distance, bellowing, exhaust racketing like a machine gun gone amuck—and at these horrid sounds the surreys and buggies would hug the curbstone, and the bicycles scatter to cover, cursing; while children rushed from the sidewalks to drag pet dogs from the street. The thing would roar by, leaving a long wake of turbulence; then the indignant street would quiet down for a few minutes—till another came.

"There are a great many more than there used to be," Miss Fanny observed, in her lifeless voice, as the lull fell after one of these visitations. "Eugene is right about that; there seem to be at least three or four times as many as there were last summer, and you never hear the ragamuffins shouting 'Get a horse!' nowadays; but I think he may be mistaken about their going on increasing after this. I don't believe we'll see so many next summer as we do now."

"Why?" asked Isabel.

"Because I've begun to agree with George about their being more a fad than anything else, and I think it must be the height of the fad just now. You know how roller-skating came in—everybody in the world seemed to be crowding to the rinks—and now only a few children use rollers for getting to school. Besides, people won't permit the automobiles to be used. Really, I think they'll make laws against them. You see how they spoil the bicycling and the driving; people just seem to hate them! They'll never stand it—never in the world! Of course I'd be sorry to see such a thing happen to Eugene, but I shouldn't be really surprised to see a law passed forbidding the sale of automobiles, just the way there is with concealed weapons."

"Fanny!" exclaimed her sister-in-law. "You're not in earnest?"

"I am, though!"

Isabel's sweet-toned laugh came out of the dusk where she sat. "Then you didn't mean it when you told Eugene you'd enjoyed the drive this afternoon?"

"I didn't say it so very enthusiastically, did I?"

"Perhaps not, but he certainly thought he'd pleased you."

"I don't think I gave him any right to think he'd pleased me," Fanny said slowly.

"Why not? Why shouldn't you, Fanny?"

Fanny did not reply at once, and when she did, her voice was almost inaudible, but much more reproachful than plaintive. "I hardly think I'd want any one to get the notion he'd pleased me just now. It hardly seems time, yet—to me."

Isabel made no response, and for a time the only sound upon the dark veranda was the creaking of the wicker rocking-chair in which Fanny sat—a creaking which seemed to denote content and placidity on the part of the chair's occupant, though at this juncture a series of human shrieks could have been little more eloquent of emotional disturbance. However, the creaking gave its hearer one great advantage: it could be ignored.

"Have you given up smoking, George?" Isabel asked presently.

"No."

"I hoped perhaps you had, because you've not smoked since dinner. We shan't mind if you care to."

"No, thanks."

There was silence again, except for the creaking of the rocking-chair; then a low, clear whistle, singularly musical, was heard softly rendering an old air from "Fra Diavolo." The creaking stopped.

"Is that you, George?" Fanny asked abruptly.

"Is that me what?"

"Whistling 'On Yonder Rock Reclining'?"

"It's I," said Isabel.

"Oh," Fanny said dryly.

"Does it disturb you?"

"Not at all. I had an idea George was depressed about something, and merely wondered if he could be making such a cheerful sound." And Fanny resumed her creaking.

"Is she right, George?" his mother asked quickly, leaning forward in her chair to peer at him through the dusk. "You didn't eat a very hearty dinner, but I thought it was probably because of the warm weather. Are you troubled about anything?"

"*No!*" he said angrily.

"That's good. I thought we had such a nice day, didn't you?"

"I suppose so," he muttered, and, satisfied, she leaned back in her chair; but "Fra Diavolo" was not revived. After a time she rose, went to the steps, and stood for several minutes looking across the street. Then her laughter was faintly heard.

"Are you laughing about something?" Fanny inquired.

"Pardon?" Isabel did not turn, but continued her observation of what had interested her upon the opposite side of the street.

"I asked: Were you laughing at something?"

"Yes, I was!" And she laughed again. "It's that funny, fat old Mrs. Johnson. She has a habit of sitting at her bedroom window with a pair of opera-glasses."

"Really!"

"Really. You can see the window through the place that was left when we had the dead walnut tree cut down. She looks up and down the street, but mostly at father's and over here. Sometimes she forgets to put out the light in her room, and there she is, spying away for all the world to see!"

However, Fanny made no effort to observe this spectacle, but continued her creaking. "I've always thought her a very good woman," she said primly.

"So she is," Isabel agreed. "She's a good, friendly old thing, a little too intimate in her manner, sometimes, and if her poor old opera-glasses afford her the quiet happiness of knowing what sort of young man our new cook is walking out with, I'm the last to begrudge it to her! Don't you want to come and look at her, George?"

"What? I beg your pardon. I hadn't noticed what you were talking about."

"It's nothing," she laughed. "Only a funny old lady—and she's gone now. I'm going, too—at least, I'm going indoors to read. It's cooler in the house, but the heat's really not bad anywhere, since nightfall. Summer's dying. How quickly it goes, once it begins to die."

When she had gone into the house, Fanny stopped rocking, and, leaning forward, drew her black gauze wrap about her shoulders and shivered. "Isn't it queer," she said drearily, "how your mother can use such words?"

"What words are you talking about?" George asked.

"Words like 'die' and 'dying.' I don't see how she can bear to use them so soon after your poor father—" She shivered again.

"It's almost a year," George said absently, and he added: "It seems to me you're using them yourself."

"I? Never!"

"Yes, you did."

"When?"

"Just this minute."

"Oh!" said Fanny. "You mean when I repeated what *she* said? That's hardly the same thing, George."

He was not enough interested to argue the point. "I don't think you'll convince anybody that mother's unfeeling," he said indifferently.

"I'm not trying to convince anybody. I mean merely that in my opinion—well, perhaps it may be just as wise for me to keep my opinions to myself."

She paused expectantly, but her possible anticipation that George would urge her to discard wisdom and reveal her opinion was not fulfilled. His back was toward her, and he occupied himself with opinions of his own about other matters. Fanny may have felt some disappointment as she rose to withdraw.

However, at the last moment she halted with her hand upon the latch of the screen door.

"There's *one* thing I hope," she said. "I hope at least she won't leave off her full mourning on the *very* anniversary of Wilbur's death!"

The light door clanged behind her, and the sound annoyed her nephew. He had no idea why she thus used inoffensive wood and wire to dramatize her departure from the veranda, the impression remaining with him being that she was critical of his mother upon some point of funeral millinery. Throughout the desultory conversation he had been profoundly concerned with his own disturbing affairs, and now was preoccupied with a dialogue taking place (in his mind) between himself and Miss Lucy Morgan. As he beheld the vision, Lucy had just thrown herself at his feet. "George, you *must* forgive me!" she cried. "Papa was utterly wrong! I have told him so, and the truth is that I have come to rather dislike him as you do, and as you always have, in your heart of hearts. George, I understand you: thy people shall be my people and thy gods my gods. George, won't you take me back?"

"Lucy, are you *sure* you understand me?" And in the darkness George's bodily lips moved in unison with those which uttered the words in his imaginary rendering of this scene. An eavesdropper, concealed behind the column, could have heard the whispered word "sure," the emphasis put upon it in the vision was so poignant. "You say you understand me, but are you *sure?*"

Weeping, her head bowed almost to her waist, the ethereal Lucy made reply: "*Oh,* so sure! I will never listen to father's opinions again. I do not even care if I never see him again!"

"Then I pardon you," he said gently.

This softened mood lasted for several moments—until he realized that it had been brought about by processes strikingly lacking in substance. Abruptly he swung his feet down from the copestone to the floor of the veranda. "Pardon nothing!" No meek Lucy had thrown herself in remorse at his feet; and now he pictured her as she probably really was at this moment: sitting on the white steps of her own front porch in the moonlight, with red-headed Fred Kinney and silly Charlie Johnson and four or five others—all of them laughing, most likely, and some idiot playing the guitar!

George spoke aloud: "Riffraff!"

And because of an impish but all too natural reaction of the mind, he could see Lucy with much greater distinctness in this vision than in his former pleasing one. For a moment she was miraculously real before him, every line and colour of her. He saw the moonlight shimmering in the chiffon of her skirt, brightest on her crossed knee and the tip of her slipper; saw the blue curve of the characteristic shadow behind her, as she leaned back against the white step; saw the watery twinkling of sequins in the gauze wrap over her white shoulders as she moved, and the faint, symmetrical lights in her black hair—and not one alluring, exasperating twentieth-of-an-inch of her laughing profile was spared him as she seemed to turn to the infernal Kinney—

"Riffraff!" And George began furiously to pace the stone floor. "Riffraff!" By this hard term—a favourite with him since childhood's scornful hour—he meant to indicate, not Lucy, but the young gentlemen who, in his vision, surrounded her. "Riffraff!" he said again, aloud, and again:

"Riffraff!"

At that moment, as it happened, Lucy was playing chess with her father; and her heart, though not remorseful, was as heavy as George could have wished. But she did not let Eugene see that she was troubled, and he was pleased when he won three games of her. Usually she beat him.

CHAPTER XIX

George went driving the next afternoon alone, and, encountering Lucy and her father on the road, in one of Morgan's cars, lifted his hat, but nowise relaxed his formal countenance as they passed. Eugene waved a cordial hand quickly returned to the steering-wheel; but Lucy only nodded gravely and smiled no more than George did. Nor did she accompany Eugene to the Major's for dinner, the following Sunday evening, though both were bidden to attend that feast, which was already reduced in numbers and gayety by the absence of George Amberson. Eugene explained to his host that Lucy had gone away to visit a school-friend.

The information, delivered in the library, just before old Sam's appearance to announce dinner, set Miss Minafer in quite a flutter. "Why, George!" she said, turning to her nephew. "How does it happen you didn't tell us?" And with both hands opening, as if to express her innocence of some conspiracy, she exclaimed to the others, "He's never said one word to us about Lucy's planning to go away!"

"Probably afraid to," the Major suggested. "Didn't know but he might break down and cry if he tried to speak of it!" He clapped his grandson on the shoulder, inquiring jocularly, "That it, Georgie?"

Georgie made no reply, but he was red enough to justify the Major's developing a chuckle into laughter; though Miss Fanny, observing her nephew keenly, got an impression that this fiery blush was in truth more fiery than tender. She caught a glint in his eye less like confusion than resentment, and saw a dilation of his nostrils which might have indicated not so much a sweet agitation as an inaudible snort. Fanny had never been lacking in curiosity, and, since her brother's death, this quality was more than ever alert. The fact that George had spent all the evenings of the past week at home had not been lost upon her, nor had she failed to ascertain, by diplomatic inquiries, that since the day of the visit to Eugene's shops George had gone driving alone.

At the dinner-table she continued to observe him, sidelong; and toward the conclusion of the meal she was not startled by an episode which brought discomfort to the others. After the arrival of coffee the Major was rallying Eugene upon some rival automobile shops lately built in a suburb, and already promising to flourish.

"I suppose they'll either drive you out of the business," said the old gentleman, "or else the two of you'll drive all the rest of us off the streets."

"If we do, we'll even things up by making the streets five or ten times as long as they are now," Eugene returned.

"How do you propose to do that?"

"It isn't the distance from the center of a town that counts," said Eugene; "it's the time it takes to get there. This town's already spreading; bicycles and trolleys have been doing their share, but the automobile is going to carry city streets clear out to the county line."

The Major was skeptical. "Dream on, fair son!" he said. "It's lucky for us that you're only dreaming; because if people go to moving that far, real estate values in the old residence part of town are going to be stretched pretty thin."

"I'm afraid so," Eugene assented. "Unless you keep things so bright and clean that the old section will stay more attractive than the new ones."

"Not very likely! How are things going to be kept 'bright and clean' with soft coal and our kind of city government?"

"They aren't," Eugene replied quickly. "There's no hope of it, and already the boarding-house is marching up National Avenue. There are two in the next block below here, and there are a dozen in the half-mile below that. My relatives, the Sharons, have sold their house and are building in the country—at least, they call it 'the country.' It will be city in two or three years."

"Good gracious!" the Major exclaimed, affecting dismay. "So your little shops are going to ruin all your old friends, Eugene!"

"Unless my old friends take warning in time, or abolish smoke and get a new kind of city government. I should say the best chance is to take warning."

"Well, well!" the Major laughed. "You have enough faith in miracles, Eugene—granting that trolleys and bicycles and automobiles are miracles. So you think they're to change the face of the land, do you?"

"They're already doing it, Major; and it can't be stopped. Automobiles—"

At this point he was interrupted. George was the interrupter. He had said nothing since entering the dining room, but now he spoke in a loud and peremptory voice, using the tone of one in authority who checks idle prattle and settles a matter forever.

"Automobiles are a useless nuisance," he said.

There fell a moment's silence.

Isabel gazed incredulously at George, colour slowly heightening upon her cheeks and temples, while Fanny watched him with a quick eagerness, her eyes alert and bright. But Eugene seemed merely quizzical, as if not taking this brusquerie to himself. The Major was seriously disturbed.

"What did you say, George?" he asked, though George had spoken but too distinctly.

"I said all automobiles were a nuisance," George answered, repeating not only the words but the tone in which he had uttered them. And he added, "They'll never amount to anything but a nuisance. They had no business to be invented."

The Major frowned. "Of course you forget that Mr. Morgan makes them, and also did his share in inventing them. If you weren't so thoughtless he might think you rather offensive."

"That would be too bad," said George coolly. "I don't think I could survive it."

Again there was a silence, while the Major stared at his grandson, aghast. But Eugene began to laugh cheerfully.

"I'm not sure he's wrong about automobiles," he said. "With all their speed forward they may be a step backward in civilization—that is, in spiritual civilization. It may be that they will not add to the beauty of the world, nor to the life of men's souls. I am not sure. But automobiles have come, and they bring a greater change in our life than most of us suspect. They are here, and almost all outward things are going to be different because of what they bring. They are going to alter war, and they are going to alter peace. I think men's minds are going to be changed in subtle ways because of automobiles; just how, though, I could hardly guess. But you can't have the immense outward changes that they will cause without some inward ones, and it may be that George is right, and that the spiritual alteration will be bad for us. Perhaps, ten or twenty years from now, if we can see the inward change in men by that time, I shouldn't be able to defend the gasoline engine, but would have to agree with him that automobiles 'had no business to be invented.'" He laughed good-naturedly, and looking at his watch, apologized for having an engagement which made his departure necessary when he would so much prefer to linger. Then he shook hands with the Major, and bade Isabel, George, and Fanny a cheerful goodnight—a collective farewell cordially addressed to all three of them together—and left them at the table.

Isabel turned wondering, hurt eyes upon her son. "George, dear!" she said. "What *did* you mean?"

"Just what I said," he returned, lighting one of the Major's cigars, and his manner was imperturbable enough to warrant the definition (sometimes merited by imperturbability) of stubbornness.

Isabel's hand, pale and slender, upon the tablecloth, touched one of the fine silver candlesticks aimlessly: the fingers were seen to tremble. "Oh, he was hurt!" she murmured.

"I don't see why he should be," George said. "I didn't say anything about *him*. He didn't seem to me to be hurt—seemed perfectly cheerful. What made you think he was hurt?"

"I know him!" was all of her reply, half whispered.

The Major stared hard at George from under his white eyebrows. "You didn't mean '*him*,' you say, George? I suppose if we had a clergyman as a guest here you'd expect him not to be offended, and to understand that your remarks were neither personal nor untactful, if you said the church was a nuisance and ought never to have been invented. By Jove, but you're a puzzle!"

"In what way, may I ask, sir?"

"We seem to have a new kind of young people these days," the old gentleman returned, shaking his head. "It's a new style of courting a pretty girl, certainly, for a young fellow to go deliberately out of his way to try and make an enemy of her father by attacking his business! By Jove! That's a new way to win a woman!"

George flushed angrily and seemed about to offer a retort, but held his breath for a moment; and then held his peace. It was Isabel who responded to the Major. "Oh, no!" she said. "Eugene would never be any-body's enemy—he couldn't!—and last of all Georgie's. I'm afraid he was hurt, but I don't fear his not having understood that George spoke without thinking of what he was saying—I mean, without realizing its bearing on Eugene."

Again George seemed upon the point of speech, and again controlled the impulse. He thrust his hands in his pockets, leaned back in his chair, and smoked, staring inflexibly at the ceiling.

"Well, well," said his grandfather, rising. "It wasn't a very successful little dinner!"

Thereupon he offered his arm to his daughter, who took it fondly, and they left the room, Isabel assuring him that all his little dinners were pleasant and that this one was no exception.

George did not move, and Fanny, following the other two, came round the table, and paused close beside his chair; but George remained posed in his great imperturbability, cigar between teeth, eyes upon ceiling, and paid no attention to her. Fanny waited until the sound of Isabel's and the Major's voices became inaudible in the hall. Then she said quickly, and in a low voice so eager that it was unsteady:

"George, you've struck *just* the treatment to adopt: you're doing the right thing!"

She hurried out, scurrying after the others with a faint rustling of her black skirts, leaving George mystified but incurious. He did not understand why she should bestow her approbation upon him in the matter, and cared so little whether she did or not that he spared himself even the trouble of being puzzled about it.

In truth, however, he was neither so comfortable nor so imperturbable as he appeared. He felt some gratification: he had done a little to put the man in his place—that man whose influence upon his daughter was precisely the same thing as a contemptuous criticism of George Amberson Minafer, and of George Amberson Minafer's "ideals of life." Lucy's going away without a word was intended, he supposed, as a bit of punishment. Well, he wasn't the sort of man that people were allowed to punish: he could demonstrate that to them— since they started it!

It appeared to him as almost a kind of insolence, this abrupt departure—not even telephoning! Probably she wondered how he would take it; she even might have supposed he would show some betraying chagrin when he heard of it.

He had no idea that this was just what he had shown; and he was satisfied with his evening's performance. Nevertheless, he was not comfortable in his mind; though he could not have explained his inward perturbations, for he was convinced, without any confirmation from his Aunt Fanny, that he had done "just the right thing."

Chapter XX

Isabel came to George's door that night, and when she had kissed him good-night she remained in the open doorway with her hand upon his shoulder and her eyes thoughtfully lowered, so that her wish to say something more than good-night was evident. Not less obvious was her perplexity about the manner of saying it; and George, divining her thought, amiably made an opening for her.

"Well, old lady," he said indulgently, "you needn't look so worried. I won't be tactless with Morgan again. After this I'll just keep out of his way."

Isabel looked up, searching his face with the fond puzzlement which her eyes sometimes showed when they rested upon him; then she glanced down the hall toward Fanny's room, and, after another moment of hesitation, came quickly in, and closed the door.

"Dear," she said, "I wish you'd tell me something: Why don't you like Eugene?"

"Oh, I like him well enough," George returned, with a short laugh, as he sat down and began to unlace his shoes. "I like him well enough—in his place."

"No, dear," she said hurriedly. "I've had a feeling from the very first that you didn't really like him—that you really never liked him. Sometimes you've seemed to be friendly with him, and you'd laugh with him over something in a jolly, companionable way, and I'd think I was wrong, and that you really did like him, after all; but to-night I'm sure my other feeling was the right one: you don't like him. I can't understand it, dear; I don't see what can be the matter."

"Nothing's the matter."

This easy declaration naturally failed to carry great weight, and Isabel went on, in her troubled voice, "It seems so queer, especially when you feel as you do about his daughter."

At this, George stopped unlacing his shoes abruptly, and sat up. "How do I feel about his daughter?" he demanded.

"Well, it's seemed—as if—as if—" Isabel began timidly. "It did seem— At least, you haven't looked at any other girl, ever since they came here, and—and certainly you've seemed very much interested in her. Certainly you've been very great *friends?*"

"Well, what of that?"

"It's only that I'm like your grandfather: I can't see how you could be so much interested in a girl and—and not feel very pleasantly toward her father."

"Well, I'll tell you something," George said slowly; and a frown of concentration could be seen upon his brow, as from a profound effort at self-examination. "I haven't ever thought much on that particular point, but I admit there may be a little something in what you say. The truth is, I don't believe I've ever thought of the two together, exactly— at least, not until lately. I've always thought of Lucy just as Lucy, and of Morgan just as Morgan. I've always thought of her as a person herself, not as anybody's daughter. I don't see what's very extraordinary about that. You've probably got plenty of friends, for instance, that don't care much about your son—"

"No, indeed!" she protested quickly. "And if I knew anybody who felt like that, I wouldn't—"

"Never mind," he interrupted. "I'll try to explain a little more. If I have a friend, I don't see that it's incumbent upon me to like that friend's relatives. If I didn't like them, and pretended to, I'd be a hypocrite. If that friend likes me and wants to stay my friend he'll have to stand my not liking his relatives, or else he can quit. I decline to be a hypocrite about it; that's all. Now, suppose I have certain ideas or ideals which I have chosen for the regulation of my own conduct in life. Suppose some friend of mine has a relative with ideals directly the opposite of mine, and my friend believes more in the relative's ideals than in mine: Do you think I ought to give up my own just to please a person who's taken up ideals that I really despise?"

"No, dear; of course people can't give up their ideals; but I don't see what this has to do with dear little Lucy and—"

"I didn't say it had anything to do with them," he interrupted. "I was merely putting a case to show how a person would be justified in being a friend of one member of a family, and feeling anything but friendly toward another. I don't say, though, that I feel unfriendly to Mr. Morgan. I don't say that I feel friendly to him, and I don't say that I feel unfriendly; but if you really think that I was rude to him to-night—"

"Just thoughtless, dear. You didn't see that what you said to-night—"

"Well, I'll not say anything of that sort again where he can hear it. There, isn't that enough?"

This question, delivered with large indulgence, met with no response; for Isabel, still searching his face with her troubled and perplexed gaze, seemed not to have heard it. On that account, George repeated it, and rising, went to her and patted her reassuringly upon the shoulder. "There, old lady, you needn't fear my tactlessness will worry you again. I can't quite promise to like people I don't care about one way or another, but you can be sure I'll be careful, after this, not to let them see it. It's all right, and you'd better toddle along to bed, because I want to undress."

"But, George," she said earnestly, "you *would* like him, if you'd just let yourself. You say you don't dislike him. Why don't you like him? I can't understand at all. *What* is it that you don't—"

"There, there!" he said. "It's all right, and you toddle along."

"But, George—"

"Now, now! I really do want to get into bed. Good-night, old lady."

"Good-night, dear. But—"

"Let's not talk of it any more," he said. "It's all right, and nothing in the world to worry about. So good-night, old lady. I'll be polite enough to him, never fear—if we happen to be thrown together. So *good*-night!"

"But, George, dear—"

"I'm going to bed, old lady; so good-night."

Thus the interview closed perforce. She kissed him again before going slowly to her own room, her perplexity evidently not dispersed; but the subject was not renewed between them the next day or subsequently. Nor did Fanny make any allusion to the cryptic approbation she had bestowed upon her nephew after the Major's "not very successful little dinner"; though she annoyed George by looking at him oftener and longer than he cared to be looked at by an aunt. He could not glance her way, it seemed, without finding her red-rimmed eyes fixed upon him eagerly, with an alert and hopeful calculation in them which he declared would send a nervous man into fits. For thus, one day, he broke out, in protest:

"It would!" he repeated vehemently. "Given time it would—straight into fits! What do you find the matter with me? Is my tie *always* slipping up behind? Can't you look at something else? My Lord! We'd better buy a cat for you to stare at, Aunt Fanny! A cat could stand it, maybe. What in the name of goodness do you expect to *see?*"

But Fanny laughed good-naturedly, and was not offended. "It's more as if I expected *you* to see something, isn't it?" she said quietly, still laughing.

"Now, what do you mean by that?"

"Never mind!"

"All right, I don't. But for heaven's sake stare at somebody else awhile. Try it on the housemaid!"

"Well, well," Fanny said indulgently, and then chose to be more obscure in her meaning than ever, for she adopted a tone of deep sympathy for her final remark, as she left him: "I don't wonder you're nervous these days, poor boy!"

And George indignantly supposed that she referred to the ordeal of Lucy's continued absence. During this period he successfully avoided contact with Lucy's father, though Eugene came frequently to the house, and spent several evenings with Isabel and Fanny; and sometimes persuaded them and the Major to go for an afternoon's motoring. He did not, however, come again to the Major's Sunday evening dinner, even when George Amberson returned. Sunday evening was the time, he explained, for going over the week's work with his factory managers.

———

. . . When Lucy came home the autumn was far enough advanced to smell of burning leaves, and for the annual editorials, in the papers, on the purple haze, the golden branches, the ruddy fruit, and the pleasure of long tramps in the brown forest. George had not heard of her arrival, and he met her, on the afternoon following that event, at the Sharons', where he had gone in the secret hope that he might hear something about her. Janie Sharon had just begun to tell him that she heard Lucy was expected home soon, after having "a perfectly gorgeous time"—information which George received with no responsive enthusiasm—when Lucy came demurely in, a proper little autumn figure in green and brown.

Her cheeks were flushed, and her dark eyes were bright indeed; evidences, as George supposed, of the excitement incidental to the perfectly gorgeous time just concluded; though Janie and Mary Sharon both thought they were the effect of Lucy's having seen George's runabout in front of the house as she came in. George took on colour, himself, as he rose and nodded indifferently; and the hot suffusion to which he became subject extended its area to include his neck and ears. Nothing could have made him much more indignant than his consciousness of these symptoms of the icy indifference which it was his purpose not only to show but to feel.

She kissed her cousins, gave George her hand, said "How d'you do," and took a chair beside Janie with a composure which augmented George's indignation.

"How d'you do," he said. "I trust that ah—I trust—I do trust—"

He stopped, for it seemed to him that the word "trust" sounded idiotic. Then, to cover his awkwardness, he coughed, and even to his own rosy ears his cough was ostentatiously a false one. Whereupon, seeking to be plausible, he coughed again, and instantly hated himself: the sound he made was an atrocity. Meanwhile, Lucy sat silent, and the two Sharon girls leaned forward, staring at him with strained eyes, their lips tightly compressed; and both were but too easily diagnosed as subject to an agitation which threatened their self-control. He began again.

"I tr—I hope you have had a—a pleasant time. I tr—I hope you are well. I hope you are extremely—I hope extremely—extremely—" And again he stopped in the midst of his floundering, not knowing how to progress beyond "extremely," and unable to understand why the infernal word kept getting into his mouth.

"I beg your pardon?" Lucy said.

George was never more furious; he felt that he was "making a spectacle of himself"; and no young gentleman in the world was more loath than George Amberson Minafer to look a figure of fun. And while he stood there, undeniably such a figure, with Janie and Mary Sharon threatening to burst at any moment, if laughter were longer denied them, Lucy sat looking at him with her eyebrows delicately lifted in casual, polite inquiry. Her own complete composure was what most galled him.

"Nothing of the slightest importance!" he managed to say. "I was just leaving. *Good* afternoon!" And with long strides he reached the door, and hastened through the hall; but before he closed the front door he heard from Janie and Mary Sharon the outburst of wild, irrepressible emotion which his performance had inspired.

He drove home in a tumultuous mood, and almost ran down two ladies who were engaged in absorbing conversation at a crossing. They were his Aunt Fanny and the stout Mrs. Johnson; a jerk of the reins at the last instant saved them by a few inches; but their conversation was so interesting that they were unaware of their danger, and did not notice the runabout, nor how close it came to them. George was so furious with himself and with the girl whose unexpected coming into a room could make him look such a fool, that it might have soothed him a little if he had actually run over the two absorbed ladies without injuring them beyond repair. At least, he said to himself that he wished he had; it might have taken his mind off of himself for a few minutes. For, in truth, to be ridiculous (and know it) was one of several things that George was unable to endure. He was savage.

He drove into the Major's stable too fast, the sagacious Pendennis saving himself from going through a partition by a swerve which splintered a shaft of the runabout and almost threw the driver to the floor. George swore, and then swore again at the fat old darkey, Tom, for giggling at his swearing.

"Hoopee!" said old Tom. "Mus' been some white lady use Mist' Jawge mighty bad! White lady say, 'No, suh, I ain' go'n out ridin' 'ith Mist' Jawge no mo'!' Mist' Jawge drive in. 'Dam de dam worl'! Dam de dam hoss! Dam de dam nigga'! Dam de dam dam!' Hoopee!"

"That'll do!" George said sternly.

"Yessuh!"

George strode from the stable, crossed the Major's back yard, then passed behind the new houses, on his way home. These structures were now approaching completion, but still in a state of rawness hideous to George—though, for that matter, they were never to be anything except hideous to him. Behind them, stray planks, bricks, refuse of plaster and lath, shingles, straw, empty barrels, strips of twisted tin and broken tiles were strewn everywhere over the dried and pitted gray mud where once the suave lawn had lain like a green lake around those stately islands, the two Amberson houses. And George's state of mind was not improved by his present view of this repulsive area, nor by his sensations when he kicked an uptilted shingle only to discover that what uptilted it was a brickbat on the other side of it. After that, the whole world seemed to be one solid conspiracy of malevolence.

In this temper he emerged from behind the house nearest to his own, and, glancing toward the street, saw his mother standing with Eugene Morgan upon the cement path that led to the front gate. She was bareheaded, and Eugene held his hat and stick in his hand; evidently he had been calling upon her, and she had come from the house with him, continuing their conversation and delaying their parting.

They had paused in their slow walk from the front door to the gate, yet still stood side by side, their shoulders almost touching, as though neither Isabel nor Eugene quite realized that their feet had ceased to bear them forward; and they were not looking at each other, but at some indefinite point before them, as people do who consider together thoughtfully and in harmony. The conversation was evidently serious; his head was bent, and Isabel's lifted left hand rested against her cheek; but all the significances of their thoughtful attitude denoted companionableness and a shared understanding. Yet, a stranger, passing, would not have thought them married: somewhere about Eugene, not quite to be located, there was a romantic gravity; and Isabel, tall and graceful, with high colour and absorbed eyes, was visibly no wife walking down to the gate with her husband.

George stared at them. A hot dislike struck him at the sight of Eugene; and a vague revulsion, like a strange, unpleasant taste in his mouth, came over him as he looked at his mother: her manner was eloquent of so much thought about her companion and of such reliance upon him. And the picture the two thus made was a vivid one indeed, to George, whose angry eyes, for some reason, fixed themselves most intently upon Isabel's lifted hand, upon the white ruffle at her wrist, bordering the graceful black sleeve, and upon the little indentations in her cheek where the tips of her fingers rested. She should not have worn white at her wrist, or at the throat either, George felt; and then, strangely, his resentment concentrated upon those tiny indentations at the tips of her fingers—actual changes, however slight and fleeting, in his mother's face, made because of Mr. Eugene Morgan. For the moment, it seemed to George that Morgan might have claimed the ownership of a face that changed for him. It was as if he owned Isabel.

The two began to walk on toward the gate, where they stopped again, turning to face each other, and Isabel's glance, passing Eugene, fell upon George. Instantly she smiled and waved her hand to him;

CHAPTER XXI

He went to his room, threw off his coat, waistcoat, collar, and tie, letting them lie where they chanced to fall, and then, having violently enveloped himself in a black velvet dressing-gown, continued this action by lying down with a vehemence that brought a wheeze of protest from his bed. His repose was only a momentary semblance, however, for it lasted no longer than the time it took him to groan "Riffraff!" between his teeth. Then he sat up, swung his feet to the floor, rose, and began to pace up and down the large room.

He had just been consciously rude to his mother for the first time in his life; for, with all his riding down of populace and riffraff, he had never before been either deliberately or impulsively disregardful of her. When he had hurt her it had been accidental; and his remorse for such an accident was always adequate compensation—and more—to Isabel. But now he had done a rough thing to her; and he did not repent; the rather he was the more irritated with her. And when he heard her presently go by his door with a light step, singing cheerfully to herself as she went to her room, he perceived that she had mistaken his intention altogether, or, indeed, had failed to perceive that he had any intention at all. Evidently she had concluded that he refused to speak to her and Morgan out of sheer absent-mindedness, supposing him so immersed in some preoccupation that he had not seen them or heard her calling to him. Therefore there was nothing of which to repent, even if he had been so minded; and probably Eugene himself was unaware that any disapproval had recently been expressed.

George snorted. What sort of a dreamy loon did they take him to be?

There came a delicate, eager tapping at his door, not done with a knuckle but with the tip of a fingernail, which was instantly clarified to George's mind's eye as plainly as if he saw it: the long and polished white-mooned pink shield on the end of his Aunt Fanny's right forefinger. But George was in no mood for human communications, and even when things went well he had little pleasure in Fanny's society. Therefore it is not surprising that at the sound of her tapping, instead of bidding her enter, he immediately crossed the room with the intention of locking the door to keep her out.

Fanny was too eager, and, opening the door before he reached it, came quickly in, and closed it behind her. She was in a street dress and a black hat, with a black umbrella in her black-gloved hand—for Fanny's heavy mourning, at least, was nowhere tempered with a glimpse of white, though the anniversary of Wilbur's death had passed. An infinitesimal perspiration gleamed upon her pale skin; she breathed fast, as if she had run up the stairs; and excitement was sharp in her widened eyes. Her look was that of a person who had just seen something extraordinary or heard thrilling news.

"Now, what on earth do *you* want?" her chilling nephew demanded.

"George," she said hurriedly, "I saw what you did when you wouldn't speak to them. I was sitting with Mrs. Johnson at her front window, across the street, and I saw it all."

"Well, what of it?"

"You did right!" Fanny said with a vehemence not the less spirited because she suppressed her voice almost to a whisper. "You did exactly right! You're behaving splendidly about the whole thing, and I want to tell you I know your father would thank you if he could see what you're doing."

"My Lord!" George broke out at her. "You make me dizzy! For heaven's sake quit the mysterious detective business—at least do quit it around me! Go and try it on somebody else, if you like; but *I* don't want to hear it!"

She began to tremble, regarding him with a fixed gaze. "You don't care to hear then," she said huskily, "that I approve of what you're doing?"

"Certainly not! Since I haven't the faintest idea what you think I'm 'doing,' naturally I don't care whether you approve of it or not. All I'd like, if you please, is to be alone. I'm not giving a tea here, this afternoon, if you'll permit me to mention it!"

Fanny's gaze wavered; she began to blink; then suddenly she sank into a chair and wept silently, but with a terrible desolation.

"Oh, for the Lord's sake!" he moaned. "What in the world is wrong with you?"

"You're always picking on me," she quavered wretchedly, her voice indistinct with the wetness that bubbled into it from her tears. "You do—you always pick on me! You've always done it—always—ever since you were a little boy! Whenever anything goes wrong with you, you take it out on me! You do! You always—"

George flung to heaven a gesture of despair; it seemed to him the last straw that Fanny should have chosen this particular time to come and sob in his room over his mistreatment of her!

"Oh, my Lord!" he whispered; then, with a great effort, addressed her in a reasonable tone: "Look here, Aunt Fanny; I don't see what you're making all this fuss about. Of course I know I've teased you sometimes, but—"

" '*Teased*' me?" she wailed. " '*Teased*' me! Oh, it does seem too hard, sometimes—this mean old life of mine does seem too hard! I don't think I *can* stand it! Honestly, I don't think I can! I came in here just to show you I sympathized with you—just to say something *pleasant* to you, and you treat me as if I were—oh, no, you *wouldn't* treat a servant the way you treat me! You wouldn't treat anybody in the world like this except old Fanny! 'Old Fanny' you say. 'It's nobody but old Fanny, so I'll kick her—nobody will resent it. I'll kick her all I want to!' You do! That's how you think of me—I know it! And you're right: I haven't got anything in the world, since my brother died—nobody—nothing—nothing!"

"Oh my *Lord*!" George groaned.

Fanny spread out her small, soaked handkerchief, and shook it in the air to dry it a little, crying as damply and as wretchedly during this operation as before—a sight which gave George a curious shock to add to his other agitations, it seemed so strange. "I ought not to have come," she went on, "because I might have known it would only give you an excuse to pick on me again! I'm sorry enough I came, I can tell you! I didn't mean to speak of it again to you, at all; and I wouldn't have, but I saw how you treated them, and I guess I got excited about it, and couldn't help following the impulse—but I'll know better next time, I can tell you! I'll keep my mouth shut as I meant to, and as I would have, if I hadn't got excited and if I hadn't felt sorry for you. But what does it matter to anybody if I'm sorry for them? I'm only old Fanny!"

"Oh, good gracious! How *can* it matter to me who's sorry for me when I don't know what they're sorry about!"

"You're so proud," she quavered, "and so hard! I *tell* you I didn't mean to speak of it to you, and I never, never in the world would have *told* you about it, nor have made the faintest reference to it, if I hadn't seen that somebody else had told you, or you'd found out for yourself some way. I—"

In despair of her intelligence, and in some doubt of his own, George struck the palms of his hands together. "Somebody else had told me what? I'd found *what* out for myself?"

"How people are talking about your mother."

Except for the incidental teariness of her voice, her tone was casual, as though she mentioned a subject previously discussed and understood; for Fanny had no doubt that George had only pretended to be mystified because, in his pride, he would not in words admit that he knew what he knew.

"What did you say?" he asked incredulously.

"Of course *I* understood what you were doing," Fanny went on, drying her handkerchief again. "It puzzled other people when you began to be rude to Eugene, because they couldn't see how you could treat him as you did when you were so interested in Lucy. But I remembered how you came to me, that other time when there was so much talk about Isabel; and I knew you'd give Lucy up in a minute, if it came to a question of your mother's reputation, because you said then that—"

"Look here," George interrupted in a shaking voice. "Look here, I'd like—" He stopped, unable to go on, his agitation was so great. His chest heaved as from hard running, and his complexion, pallid at first, had become mottled; fiery splotches appearing at his temples and cheeks. "What do you mean by telling me—telling me there's talk about—about—" He gulped, and began again: "What do you mean by using such words as 'reputation'? What do you mean, speaking of a 'question' of my—my mother's reputation?"

Fanny looked up at him woefully over the handkerchief which she now applied to her reddened nose. "God knows I'm sorry for you, George," she murmured. "I wanted to say so, but it's only old Fanny, so whatever she says—even when it's sympathy—pick on her for it! Hammer her!" She sobbed. "Hammer her! It's only poor old lonely Fanny!"

"You look here!" George said harshly. "When I spoke to my Uncle George after that rotten thing I heard Aunt Amelia say about my mother, he said if there was any gossip it was about *you*! He said people might be laughing about the way you ran after Morgan, but that was all."

Fanny lifted her hands, clenched them, and struck them upon her knees. "Yes; it's always Fanny!" she sobbed. "Ridiculous old Fanny—always, always!"

"You listen!" George said. "After I'd talked to Uncle George I saw *you;* and you said I had a mean little mind for thinking there might be truth in what Aunt Amelia said about people talking. You denied it. And that wasn't the only time; you'd attacked me before then, because I intimated that Morgan might be coming here too often. You made me believe that mother let him come entirely on your account, and *now* you say—"

"I think he did," Fanny interrupted desolately. "I think he did come as much to see me as anything—for a *while* it looked like it. Anyhow, he liked to dance with me. He danced with me as much as he danced with her, and he acted as if he came on my account at least as much as he did on hers. He *did* act a good deal that way—and if Wilbur hadn't died—"

"You told me there *wasn't* any talk."

"I didn't think there was much, then," Fanny protested. "*I* didn't know how much there was."

"What!"

"People don't come and tell such things to a person's family, you know. You don't suppose anybody was going to say to George Amberson that his sister was getting herself talked about, do you? Or that they were going to say much to *me?*"

"You told me," said George, fiercely, "that mother never saw him except when she was chaperoning you."

"They weren't much alone together, then," Fanny returned. "Hardly ever, before Wilbur died. But you don't suppose *that* stops people from talking, do you? Your father never went anywhere, and people saw Eugene with her everywhere she went—and though I was with them people just thought"—she choked—"they just thought I didn't count! 'Only old Fanny Minafer,' I suppose they'd say! Besides, everybody knew that he'd been engaged to her—"

"What's that?" George cried.

"Everybody knows it. Don't you remember your grandfather speaking of it at the Sunday dinner one night?"

"He didn't say they were engaged or—"

"Well, they were! Everybody knows it; and she broke it off on account of that serenade when Eugene didn't know what he was doing. He drank when he was a young man, and she wouldn't stand it, but everybody in this town knows that Isabel has never really cared for any other man in her life! Poor Wilbur! He was the only soul alive that didn't know it!"

Nightmare had descended upon the unfortunate George; he leaned back against the foot-board of his bed, gazing wildly at his aunt. "I believe I'm going crazy," he said. "You mean when you told me there wasn't any talk, you told me a falsehood?"

"No!" Fanny gasped.

"You did!"

"I tell you I didn't know how much talk there *was,* and it wouldn't have amounted to much if Wilbur had lived." And Fanny completed this with a fatal admission: "I didn't want you to interfere."

George overlooked the admission; his mind was not now occupied with analysis. "What do you mean," he asked, "when you say that if father had lived, the talk wouldn't have amounted to anything?"

"Things might have been—they might have been different."

"You mean Morgan might have married *you?*"

Fanny gulped. "No. Because I don't know that I'd have accepted him." She had ceased to weep, and now she sat up stiffly. "I certainly didn't care enough about him to marry him; I wouldn't have let myself care that much until he showed that he wished to marry me. I'm not that sort of person!" The poor lady paid her vanity this piteous little tribute. "What I mean is, if Wilbur hadn't died, people wouldn't have had it proved before their very *eyes* that what they'd been talking about was true!"

"You say—you say that people believe—" George shuddered, then forced himself to continue, in a sick voice: "They believe my mother is—is in love with that man?"

"Of course!"

"And because he comes here—and they see her with him driving—and all that—they think they were right when they said she was in—in love with him before—before my father died?"

She looked at him gravely with her eyes now dry between their reddened lids. "Why, George," she said, gently, "don't *you* know that's what they say? You *must* know that everybody in town thinks they're going to be married very soon."

George uttered an incoherent cry; and sections of him appeared to writhe. He was upon the verge of actual nausea.

"You know it!" Fanny cried, getting up. "You don't think I'd have spoken of it to you unless I was sure you knew it?" Her voice was wholly genuine, as it had been throughout the wretched interview: Fanny's sincerity was unquestionable. "George, *I* wouldn't have told you, if you didn't know. What other reason could you have for treating Eugene as you did, or for refusing to speak to them like that, a while ago in the yard? Somebody *must* have told you?"

"Who told *you*?" he said.

"What?"

"Who told you there was talk? Where *is* this talk? Where does it come from? Who does it?"

"Why, I suppose pretty much everybody," she said. "I know it must be pretty general."

"Who said so?"

"What?"

George stepped close to her. "You say people don't speak to a person of gossip about that person's family. Well, how did you hear it, then? How did you get hold of it? Answer me!"

Fanny looked thoughtful. "Well, of course nobody not one's most intimate friends would speak to them about such things, and then only in the kindest, most considerate way."

"Who's spoken of it to you in any way at all?" George demanded.

"Why—" Fanny hesitated.

"You answer me!"

"I hardly think it would be fair to give names."

"Look here," said George. "One of your most intimate friends is that mother of Charlie Johnson's, for instance. Has *she* ever mentioned this to you? You say everybody is talking. Is she one?"

"Oh, she may have intimated—"

"I'm asking you: Has she ever spoken of it to you?"

"She's a very kind, discreet woman, George; but she may have intimated—"

George had a sudden intuition, as there flickered into his mind the picture of a street-crossing and two absorbed ladies almost run down by a fast horse. "You and she have been talking about it to-day!" he cried. "You were talking about it with her not two hours ago. Do you deny it?"

"I—"

"Do you deny it?"

"No!"

"All right," said George. "That's enough!"

She caught at his arm as he turned away. "What are you going to do, George?"

"I'll not talk about it, now," he said heavily. "I think you've done a good deal for one day, Aunt Fanny!"

And Fanny, seeing the passion in his face, began to be alarmed. She tried to retain possession of the black velvet sleeve which her fingers had clutched, and he suffered her to do so, but used this leverage to urge her to the door. "George, you know I'm sorry for you, whether you care or not," she whimpered. "I never in the world would have spoken of it, if I hadn't thought you knew all about it. I wouldn't have—"

But he had opened the door with his free hand. "Never mind!" he said, and she was obliged to pass out into the hall, the door closing quickly behind her.

CHAPTER XXII

George took off his dressing-gown and put on a collar and a tie, his fingers shaking so that the tie was not his usual success; then he picked up his coat and waistcoat, and left the room while still in process of donning them, fastening the buttons as he ran down the front stairs to the door. It was not until he reached the middle of the street that he realized that he had forgotten his hat; and he paused for an irresolute moment, during which his eye wandered, for no reason, to the Fountain of Neptune. This cast-iron replica of too elaborate sculpture stood at the next corner, where the Major had placed it when the Addition was laid out so long ago. The street corners had been shaped to conform with the great octagonal basin, which was no great inconvenience for horse-drawn vehicles, but a nuisance to speeding automobiles; and, even as George looked, one of the latter, coming too fast, saved itself only by a dangerous skid as it rounded the fountain. This skid was to George's liking, though he would have been more pleased to see the car go over, for he was wishing grief and destruction, just then, upon all the automobiles in the world.

His eyes rested a second or two longer upon the Fountain of Neptune, not an enlivening sight even in the shielding haze of autumn twilight. For more than a year no water had run in the fountain: the connections had been broken, and the Major was evasive about restorations, even when reminded by his grandson that a dry fountain is as gay as a dry fish. Soot streaks and a thousand pits gave Neptune the distinction, at least, of leprosy, which the mermaids associated with him had been consistent in catching; and his trident had been so deeply affected as to drop its prongs. Altogether, this heavy work of heavy art, smoked dry, hugely scabbed, cracked, and crumbling, was a dismal sight to the distracted eye of George Amberson Minafer, and its present condition of craziness may have added a mite to his own. His own was sufficient, with no additions, however, as he stood looking at the Johnsons' house and those houses on both sides of it—that row of riffraff dwellings he had thought so damnable, the day when he stood in his grandfather's yard, staring at them, after hearing what his Aunt Amelia said of the "talk" about his mother.

He decided that he needed no hat for the sort of call he intended to make, and went forward hurriedly. Mrs. Johnson was at home, the Irish girl who came to the door informed him, and he was left to await the lady, in a room like an elegant well—the Johnsons' "reception room": floor space, nothing to mention; walls, blue calcimined; ceiling, twelve feet from the floor; inside shutters and gray lace curtains; five gilt chairs, a brocaded sofa, soiled, and an inlaid walnut table, supporting two tall alabaster vases; a palm, with two leaves, dying in a corner.

Mrs. Johnson came in, breathing noticeably; and her round head, smoothly but economically decorated with the hair of an honest woman, seemed to be lingering far in the background of the Alpine bosom which took precedence of the rest of her everywhere; but when she was all in the room, it was to be seen that her breathing was the result of hospitable haste to greet the visitor, and her hand, not so dry as Neptune's Fountain, suggested that she had paused for only the briefest ablutions. George accepted this cold, damp lump mechanically.

"Mr. Amberson—I mean Mr. Minafer!" she exclaimed. "I'm really delighted: I understood you asked for me. Mr. Johnson's out of the city, but Charlie's downtown and I'm looking for him at any minute, now, and he'll be so pleased that you—"

"I didn't want to see Charlie," George said. "I want—"

"Do sit down," the hospitable lady urged him, seating herself upon the sofa. "Do sit down."

"No, I thank you. I wish—"

"Surely you're not going to run away again, when you've just come. Do sit down, Mr. Minafer. I hope you're all well at your house and at the dear old Major's, too. He's looking—"

"Mrs. Johnson" George said, in a strained loud voice which arrested her attention immediately, so that she was abruptly silent, leaving her surprised mouth open. She had already been concealing some astonishment at this unexampled visit, however, and the condition of George's ordinarily smooth hair (for he had overlooked more than his hat) had not alleviated her perplexity. "Mrs. Johnson," he said, "I have come to ask you a few questions which I would like you to answer, if you please."

She became grave at once. "Certainly, Mr. Minafer. Anything I can—"

He interrupted sternly, yet his voice shook in spite of its sternness. "You were talking with my Aunt Fanny about my mother this afternoon."

At this Mrs. Johnson uttered an involuntary gasp, but she recovered herself. "Then I'm sure our conversation was a very pleasant one, if we were talking of your mother, because—"

Again he interrupted. "My aunt has told me what the conversation virtually was, and I don't mean to waste any time, Mrs. Johnson. You were talking about a—" George's shoulders suddenly heaved uncontrollably; but he went fiercely on: "You were discussing a scandal that involved my mother's name."

"Mr. Minafer!"

"Isn't that the truth?"

"I don't feel called upon to answer, Mr. Minafer," she said with visible agitation. "I do not consider that you have any right—"

"My aunt told me you repeated this scandal to her."

"I don't think your aunt can have said that," Mrs. Johnson returned sharply. "I did not repeat a scandal of any kind to your aunt and I think you are mistaken in saying she told you I did. We may have discussed some matters that have been a topic of comment about town—"

"Yes!" George cried. "I think you may have! That's what I'm here about, and what I intend to—"

"Don't tell *me* what you intend, please," Mrs. Johnson interrupted crisply. "And I should prefer that you would not make your voice quite so loud in this house, which I happen to own. Your aunt may have told you—though I think it would have been very unwise in her if she did, and not very considerate of *me*—she may have told you that we discussed some such topic as I have mentioned, and possibly that would have been true. If I talked it over with her, you may be sure I spoke in the most charitable spirit, and without sharing in other people's disposition to put an evil interpretation on what *may* be nothing more than unfortunate appearances and—"

"My God!" said George. "I can't stand this!"

"You have the option of dropping the subject," Mrs. Johnson suggested tartly, and she added: "Or of leaving the house."

"I'll do that soon enough, but first I mean to know—"

"I am perfectly willing to tell you anything you wish if you will remember to ask it quietly. I'll also take the liberty of reminding you that I had a perfect right to discuss the subject with your aunt. Other people may be less considerate in not confining their discussion of it, as I have, to charitable views expressed only to a member of the family. Other people—"

"Other people!" the unhappy George repeated viciously. "That's what I want to know about—these other people!"

"I beg your pardon."

"I want to ask you about them. You say you know of other people who talk about this."

"I presume they do."

"How many?"

"What?"

"I want to know how many other people talk about it?"

"Dear, dear!" she protested. "How should I know that?"

"Haven't you heard anybody mention it?"

"I presume so."

"Well, how *many* have you heard?"

Mrs. Johnson was becoming more annoyed than apprehensive, and she showed it. "Really, this isn't a court-room," she said. "And I'm not a defendant in a libel-suit, either!"

The unfortunate young man lost what remained of his balance. "You may be!" he cried. "I intend to know just who's dared to say these things, if I have to force my way into every house in town, and I'm going to make them take every word of it back! I mean to know the name of every slanderer that's spoken of this matter to you and of every tattler you've passed it on to yourself. I mean to know—"

"You'll know *something* pretty quick!" she said, rising with difficulty; and her voice was thick with the sense of insult. "You'll know that you're out in the street. Please to leave my house!"

George stiffened sharply. Then he bowed, and strode out of the door.

Three minutes later, dishevelled and perspiring, but cold all over, he burst into his Uncle George's room at the Major's without knocking. Amberson was dressing.

"Good gracious, Georgie!" he exclaimed. "What's up?"

"I've just come from Mrs. Johnson's—across the street," George panted.

"You have your own tastes!" was Amberson's comment. "But curious as they are, you ought to do something better with your hair, and button your waistcoat to the right buttons—even for Mrs. Johnson! What were you doing over there?"

"She told me to leave the house," George said desperately. "I went there because Aunt Fanny told me the whole town was talking about my mother and that man Morgan—that they say my mother is going to marry him and that proves she was too fond of him before my father died—she said this Mrs. Johnson was one that talked about it, and I went to her to ask who were the others."

Amberson's jaw fell in dismay. "Don't tell me you did that!" he said, in a low voice; and then, seeing that it was true, "Oh, now you *have* done it!"

Chapter XXIII

I've 'done it'?" George cried. "What do you mean: I've done it? And what have I done?"

Amberson had collapsed into an easy chair beside his dressing-table, the white evening tie he had been about to put on dangling from his hand, which had fallen limply on the arm of the chair. The tie dropped to the floor before he replied; and the hand that had held it was lifted to stroke his graying hair reflectively. "By Jove!" he muttered. "That *is* too bad!"

George folded his arms bitterly. "Will you kindly answer my question? What have I done that wasn't honourable and right? Do you think these riffraff can go about bandying my mother's name—"

"They can now," said Amberson. "I don't know if they could before, but they certainly can now!"

"What do you mean by that?"

His uncle sighed profoundly, picked up his tie, and, preoccupied with despondency, twisted the strip of white lawn till it became unwearable. Meanwhile, he tried to enlighten his nephew. "Gossip is never fatal, Georgie," he said, "until it is denied. Gossip goes on about every human being alive and about all the dead that are alive enough to be remembered, and yet almost never does any harm until some defender makes a controversy. Gossip's a nasty thing, but it's sickly, and if people of good intentions will let it entirely alone, it will die, ninety-nine times out of a hundred."

"See here," George said: "I didn't come to listen to any generalizing dose of philosophy! I ask you—"

"You asked me what you've done, and I'm telling you." Amberson gave him a melancholy smile, continuing: "Suffer me to do it in my own way. Fanny says there's been talk about your mother, and that Mrs. Johnson does some of it. I don't know, because naturally nobody would come to me with such stuff or mention it before me; but it's presumably true—I suppose it is. I've seen Fanny with Mrs. Johnson quite a lot; and that old lady is a notorious gossip, and that's why she ordered you out of her house when you pinned her down that she'd been gossiping. I have a suspicion Mrs. Johnson has been quite a comfort to Fanny in their long talks; but she'll probably quit speaking to her over this, because Fanny told you. I suppose it's true that the 'whole town,' a lot of others, that is, do share in the gossip. In this town, naturally, anything about any Amberson has always been a stone dropped into the centre of a pond, and a lie would send the ripples as far as a truth would. I've been on a steamer when the story went all over the boat, the second day out, that the prettiest girl on board didn't have any ears; and you can take it as a rule that when a woman's past thirty-five the prettier her hair is, the more certain you are to meet somebody with reliable information that it's a wig. You can be sure that for many years there's been more gossip in this place about the Ambersons than about any other family. I dare say it isn't so much so now as it used to be, because the town got too big long ago, but it's the truth that the more prominent you are the more gossip there is about you, and the more people would like to pull you down. Well, they can't do it as long as you refuse to know what gossip there is about you. But the minute you notice it, it's got you! I'm not speaking of certain kinds of slander that sometimes people have got to take to the courts; I'm talking of the wretched buzzing the Mrs. Johnsons do—the thing you seem to have such a horror of—people 'talking'—the kind of thing that has assailed your mother. People who have repeated a slander either get ashamed or forget it, if they're let alone. Challenge them, and in self-defense they believe everything they've said: they'd rather believe you a sinner than believe themselves liars, naturally. Submit to gossip and you kill it; fight it and you make it strong. People will forget almost any slander except one that's been fought."

"Is that all?" George asked.

"I suppose so," his uncle murmured sadly.

"Well, then, may I ask what you'd have done, in my place?"

"I'm not sure, Georgie. When I was your age I was like you in many ways, especially in not being very cool-headed, so I can't say. Youth can't be trusted for much, except asserting itself and fighting and making love."

"Indeed!" George snorted. "May I ask what you think I *ought* to have done?"

"Nothing."

" 'Nothing'?" George echoed, mocking bitterly. "I suppose you think I mean to let my mother's good name—"

"Your mother's good name!" Amberson cut him off impatiently. "Nobody has a good name in a bad mouth. Nobody has a good name in a silly mouth, either. Well, your mother's name was in some silly mouths, and all you've done was to go and have a scene with the worst old woman gossip in the town—a scene that's going to make her into a partisan against your mother, whereas she was a mere prattler before. Don't you suppose she'll be all over town with this to-morrow? To-morrow? Why, she'll have her telephone going to-night as long as any of her friends are up! People that never heard anything about this are going to hear it all now, with embellishments. And she'll see to it that everybody who's hinted anything about poor Isabel will know that you're on the warpath; and that will put them on the defensive and make them vicious. The story will grow as it spreads and—"

George unfolded his arms to strike his right fist into his left palm. "But do you suppose I'm going to tolerate such things?" he shouted. "What do you suppose *I'll* be doing?"

"Nothing helpful."

"Oh, you think so, do you?"

"You can do absolutely nothing," said Amberson. "Nothing of any use. The more you do the more harm you'll do."

"You'll see! I'm going to stop this thing if I have to force my way into every house on National Avenue and Amberson Boulevard!"

His uncle laughed rather sourly, but made no other comment.

"Well, what do *you* propose to do?" George demanded. "Do you propose to sit there—"

"Yes."

"—and let this riffraff bandy my mother's good name back and forth among them? Is that what *you* propose to do?"

"It's all I *can* do," Amberson returned. "It's all any of us can do now:

just sit still and hope that the thing may die down in time, in spite of your stirring up that awful old woman."

George drew a long breath, then advanced and stood close before his uncle. "Didn't you understand me when I told you that people are saying my mother means to marry this man?"

"Yes, I understood you."

"You say that my going over there has made matters worse," George went on. "How about it if such a—such an unspeakable marriage did take place? Do you think *that* would make people believe they'd been wrong in saying—you know what they say."

"No," said Amberson deliberately; "I don't believe it would. There'd be more badness in the bad mouths and more silliness in the silly mouths, I dare say. But it wouldn't hurt Isabel and Eugene, if they never heard of it; and if they did hear of it, then they could take their choice between placating gossip or living for their own happiness. If they have decided to marry—"

George almost staggered. "Good God!" he gasped. "You speak of it calmly!"

Amberson looked up at him inquiringly. "Why shouldn't they marry if they want to?" he asked. "It's their own affair."

"Why shouldn't they?" George echoed. "Why shouldn't they?"

"Yes. Why shouldn't they? I don't see anything precisely monstrous about two people getting married when they're both free and care about each other. What's the matter with their marrying?"

"It *would* be monstrous!" George shouted. "Monstrous even if *this* horrible thing hadn't happened, but *now* in the face of *this*—oh, that you can sit there and even speak of it! Your own sister! O God! Oh—" He became incoherent, swinging away from Amberson and making for the door, wildly gesturing.

"For heaven's sake, don't be so theatrical!" said his uncle, and then, seeing that George was leaving the room: "Come back here. You mustn't speak to your mother of this!"

"Don't 'tend to," George said indistinctly; and he plunged out into the big dimly lit hall. He passed his grandfather's room on the way to the stairs; and the Major was visible within, his white head brightly illuminated by a lamp, as he bent low over a ledger upon his roll-top desk. He did not look up, and his grandson strode by the door, not really conscious of the old figure stooping at its tremulous work with long additions and subtractions that refused to balance as they used to. George went home and got a hat and overcoat without seeing either his mother or Fanny. Then he left word that he would be out for dinner, and hurried away from the house.

He walked the dark streets of Amberson Addition for an hour, then went downtown and got coffee at a restaurant. After that he walked through the lighted parts of the town until ten o'clock, when he turned north and came back to the purlieus of the Addition. He strode through the length and breadth of it again, his hat pulled down over his forehead, his overcoat collar turned up behind. He walked fiercely, though his feet ached, but by and by he turned homeward, and, when he reached the Major's, went in and sat upon the steps of the huge stone veranda in front—an obscure figure in that lonely and repellent place. All lights were out at the Major's, and finally, after twelve, he saw his mother's window darken at home.

He waited half an hour longer, then crossed the front yards of the new houses and let himself noiselessly in the front door. The light in the hall had been left burning, and another in his own room, as he discovered when he got there. He locked the door quickly and without noise, but his fingers were still upon the key when there was a quick footfall in the hall outside.

"Georgie, dear?"

He went to the other end of the room before replying.

"Yes?"

"I'd been wondering where you were, dear."

"Had you?"

There was a pause; then she said timidly: "Wherever it was, I hope you had a pleasant evening."

After a silence, "Thank you," he said, without expression.

Another silence followed before she spoke again.

"You wouldn't care to be kissed good-night, I suppose?" And with a little flurry of placative laughter, she added: "At your age, of course!"

"I'm going to bed, now," he said. "Good-night."

Another silence seemed blanker than those which had preceded it, and finally her voice came—it was blank, too.

"Good-night."

———

. . . After he was in bed his thoughts became more tumultuous than ever; while among all the inchoate and fragmentary sketches of this dreadful day, now rising before him, the clearest was of his uncle collapsed in a big chair with a white tie dangling from his hand; and one conviction, following upon that picture, became definite in George's mind: that his Uncle George Amberson was a hopeless dreamer from whom no help need be expected, an amiable imbecile lacking in normal impulses, and wholly useless in a struggle which required honour to be defended by a man of action.

Then would return a vision of Mrs. Johnson's furious round head, set behind her great bosom like the sun far sunk on the horizon of a mountain plateau—and her crackling, asthmatic voice . . . "Without sharing in other people's disposition to put an evil interpretation on what *may* be nothing more than unfortunate appearances." . . . "Other people may be less considerate in not confining their discussion of it, as I have, to charitable views." . . . "You'll know *something* pretty quick! You'll know you're out in the street." . . . And then George would get up again—and again—and pace the floor in his bare feet.

That was what the tormented young man was doing when daylight came gauntly in at his window—pacing the floor, rubbing his head in his hands, and muttering:

"It can't be true: this can't be happening to *me!*"

Chapter XXIV

Breakfast was brought to him in his room, as usual; but he did not make his normal healthy raid upon the dainty tray: the food remained untouched, and he sustained himself upon coffee—four cups of it, which left nothing of value inside the glistening little percolator. During this process he heard his mother being summoned to the telephone in the hall, not far from his door, and then her voice responding: "Yes? Oh, it's you! . . . Indeed I should! . . . Of course. . . . Then I'll expect you about three . . . Yes. . . . Good-bye till then." A few minutes later he heard her speaking to someone beneath his window and, looking out, saw her directing the removal of plants from a small garden bed to the Major's conservatory for the winter. There was an air of briskness about her; as she turned away to go into the house, she laughed gaily with the Major's gardener over something he said, and this unconcerned cheerfulness of her was terrible to her son.

He went to his desk, and, searching the jumbled contents of a drawer, brought forth a large, unframed photograph of his father, upon which he gazed long and piteously, till at last hot tears stood in his eyes. It was strange how the inconsequent face of Wilbur seemed to increase in high significance during this belated interview between father and son; and how it seemed to take on a reproachful nobility—and yet, under the circumstances, nothing could have been more natural than that George, having paid but the slightest attention to his father in life, should begin to deify him, now that he was dead. "Poor, poor father!"

the son whispered brokenly. "Poor man, I'm glad you didn't know!"

He wrapped the picture in a sheet of newspaper, put it under his arm, and, leaving the house hurriedly and stealthily, went downtown to the shop of a silversmith, where he spent sixty dollars on a resplendently festooned silver frame for the picture. Having lunched upon more coffee, he returned to the house at two o'clock, carrying the framed photograph with him, and placed it upon the centre-table in the library, the room most used by Isabel and Fanny and himself. Then he went to a front window of the long "reception room," and sat looking out through the lace curtains.

The house was quiet, though once or twice he heard his mother and Fanny moving about upstairs, and a ripple of song in the voice of Isabel—a fragment from the romantic ballad of Lord Bateman.

> "Lord Bateman was a noble lord,
> A noble lord of high degree;
> And he sailed West and he sailed East,
> Far countries for to see. . . ."

The words became indistinct; the air was hummed absently; the humming shifted to a whistle, then drifted out of hearing, and the place was still again.

George looked often at his watch, but his vigil did not last an hour. At ten minutes of three, peering through the curtain, he saw an automobile stop in front of the house and Eugene Morgan jump lightly down from it. The car was of a new pattern, low and long, with an ample seat in the tonneau, facing forward; and a professional driver sat at the wheel, a strange figure in leather, goggled out of all personality and seemingly part of the mechanism.

Eugene himself, as he came up the cement path to the house, was a figure of the new era which was in time to be so disastrous to stiff hats and skirted coats; and his appearance afforded a debonair contrast to that of the queer-looking duck capering at the Amberson Ball in an old dress coat, and next day chugging up National Avenue through the snow in his nightmare of a sewing-machine. Eugene, this afternoon, was richly in the new outdoor mode: his motoring coat was soft gray fur; his cap and gloves were of gray suede; and though Lucy's hand may have shown itself in the selection of these high garnitures, he wore them easily, even with a becoming hint of jauntiness. Some change might be seen in his face, too, for a successful man is seldom to be mistaken, especially if his temper be genial. Eugene had begun to look like a millionaire.

But above everything else, what was most evident about him, as he came up the path, was his confidence in the happiness promised by his present errand; the anticipation in his eyes could have been read by a stranger. His look at the door of Isabel's house was the look of a man who is quite certain that the next moment will reveal something ineffably charming, inexpressibly dear.

. . . When the bell rang, George waited at the entrance of the "reception room" until a housemaid came through the hall on her way to answer the summons.

"You needn't mind, Mary," he told her. "I'll see who it is and what they want. Probably it's only a pedlar."

"Thank you, sir, Mister George," said Mary; and returned to the rear of the house.

George went slowly to the front door, and halted, regarding the misty silhouette of the caller upon the ornamental frosted glass. After a minute of waiting, this silhouette changed outline so that an arm could be distinguished—an arm outstretched toward the bell, as if the gentleman outside doubted whether or not it had sounded, and were minded to try again. But before the gesture was completed George abruptly threw open the door, and stepped squarely upon the middle of the threshold.

A slight change shadowed the face of Eugene; his look of happy anticipation gave way to something formal and polite. "How do you do, George," he said. "Mrs. Minafer expects to go driving with me, I believe—if you'll be so kind as to send her word that I'm here."

George made not the slightest movement.

"No," he said.

Eugene was incredulous, even when his second glance revealed how hot of eye was the haggard young man before him. "I beg your pardon. I said—"

"I heard you," said George. "You said you had an engagement with my mother, and I told you, No!"

Eugene gave him a steady look, and then he asked quietly: "What is the—the difficulty?"

George kept his own voice quiet enough, but that did not mitigate the vibrant fury of it. "My mother will have no interest in knowing that you came for her to-day," he said. "Or any other day!"

Eugene continued to look at him with a scrutiny in which began to gleam a profound anger, none the less powerful because it was so quiet. "I am afraid I do not understand you."

"I doubt if I could make it much plainer," George said, raising his voice slightly, "but I'll try. You're not wanted in this house, Mr. Morgan, now or at any other time. Perhaps you'll understand—this!"

And with the last word he closed the door in Eugene's face.

Then, not moving away, he stood just inside the door, and noted that the misty silhouette remained upon the frosted glass for several moments, as if the forbidden gentleman debated in his mind what course to pursue. "Let him ring again!" George thought grimly. "Or try the side door—or the kitchen!"

But Eugene made no further attempt; the silhouette disappeared; footsteps could be heard withdrawing across the floor of the veranda; and George, returning to the window in the "reception room," was rewarded by the sight of an automobile manufacturer in baffled retreat, with all his wooing furs and fineries mocking him. Eugene got into his car slowly, not looking back at the house which had just taught him such a lesson; and it was easily visible—even from a window seventy feet distant—that he was not the same light suitor who had jumped so gallantly from the car only a few minutes earlier. Observing the heaviness of his movements as he climbed into the tonneau, George indulged in a sickish throat rumble which bore a distant cousinship to mirth.

The car was quicker than its owner; it shot away as soon as he had sunk into his seat; and George, having watched its impetuous disappearance from his field of vision, ceased to haunt the window. He went to the library, and, seating himself beside the table whereon he had placed the photograph of his father, picked up a book, and pretended to be engaged in reading it.

Presently Isabel's buoyant step was heard descending the stairs, and her low, sweet whistling, renewing the air of "Lord Bateman." She came into the library, still whistling thoughtfully, a fur coat over her arm, ready to put on, and two veils round her small black hat, her right hand engaged in buttoning the glove upon her left; and, as the large room contained too many pieces of heavy furniture, and the inside shutters excluded most of the light of day, she did not at once perceive George's presence. Instead, she went to the bay window at the end of the room, which afforded a view of the street, and glanced out expectantly; then bent her attention upon her glove; after that, looked out toward the street again, ceased to whistle, and turned toward the interior of the room.

"Why, Georgie!"

She came, leaned over from behind him, and there was a faint, exquisite odour as from distant apple-blossoms as she kissed his cheek. "Dear, I waited lunch almost an hour for you, but you didn't come! Did you lunch out somewhere?"

"Yes." He did not look up from the book.

"Did you have plenty to eat?"

"Yes."

"Are you sure? Wouldn't you like to have Maggie get you something now in the dining room? Or they could bring it to you here, if you think it would be cosier. Shan't I—"

"No."

A tinkling bell was audible, and she moved to the doorway into the hall. "I'm going out driving, dear. I—" She interrupted herself to address the housemaid, who was passing through the hall: "I think it's Mr. Morgan, Mary. Tell him I'll be there at once."

"Yes, ma'am."

Mary returned. " 'Twas a pedlar, ma'am."

"Another one?" Isabel said, surprised. "I thought you said it was a pedlar when the bell rang a little while ago."

"Mister George said it was, ma'am; he went to the door," Mary informed her, disappearing.

"There seem to be a great many of them," Isabel mused. "What did yours want to sell, George?"

"He didn't say."

"You must have cut him off short!" she laughed; and then, still standing in the doorway, she noticed the big silver frame upon the table beside him. "Gracious, Georgie!" she exclaimed. "You *have* been investing!" and as she came across the room for a closer view, "Is it—is it Lucy?" She asked half timidly, half archly. But the next instant she saw whose likeness was thus set forth in elegiac splendour—and she was silent, except for a long, just-audible *"Oh!"*

He neither looked up nor moved.

"That was nice of you, Georgie," she said, in a low voice presently. "I ought to have had it framed, myself, when I gave it to you."

He said nothing, and, standing beside him, she put her hand gently upon his shoulder, then as gently withdrew it, and went out of the room. But she did not go upstairs; he heard the faint rustle of her dress in the hall, and then the sound of her footsteps in the "reception room." After a time, silence succeeded even these slight tokens of her presence; whereupon George rose and went warily into the hall, taking care to make no noise, and he obtained an oblique view of her through the open double doors of the "reception room." She was sitting in the chair which he had occupied so long; and she was looking out of the window expectantly—a little troubled.

He went back to the library, waited an interminable half hour, then returned noiselessly to the same position in the hall, where he could see her. She was still sitting patiently by the window.

Waiting for that man, was she? Well, it might be quite a long wait! And the grim George silently ascended the stairs to his own room, and began to pace his suffering floor.

CHAPTER XXV

He left his door open, however, and when he heard the front door-bell ring, by and by, he went half way down the stairs and stood to listen. He was not much afraid that Morgan would return, but he wished to make sure.

Mary appeared in the hall below him, but, after a glance toward the front of the house, turned back, and withdrew. Evidently Isabel had gone to the door. Then a murmur was heard, and George Amberson's voice, quick and serious: "I want to talk to you, Isabel" . . . and another murmur; then Isabel and her brother passed the foot of the broad, dark stairway, but did not look up, and remained unconscious of the watchful presence above them. Isabel still carried her cloak upon her arm, but Amberson had taken her hand, and retained it; and as he led her silently into the library there was something about her attitude, and the pose of her slightly bent head, that was both startled and meek. Thus they quickly disappeared from George's sight, hand in hand; and Amberson at once closed the massive double doors of the library.

For a time all that George could hear was the indistinct sound of his uncle's voice: what he was saying could not be surmised, though the troubled brotherliness of his tone was evident. He seemed to be explaining something at considerable length, and there were moments when he paused, and George guessed that his mother was speaking, but her voice must have been very low, for it was entirely inaudible to him.

Suddenly he did hear her. Through the heavy doors her outcry came, clear and loud:

"Oh, *no!*"

It was a cry of protest, as if something her brother told her must be untrue, or, if it were true, the fact he stated must be undone; and it was a sound of sheer pain.

Another sound of pain, close to George, followed it; this was a vehement sniffling which broke out just above him, and, looking up, he saw Fanny Minafer on the landing, leaning over the banisters and applying her handkerchief to her eyes and nose.

"I can guess what *that* was about," she whispered huskily. "He's just told her what you did to Eugene!"

George gave her a dark look over his shoulder. "You go on back to your room!" he said; and he began to descend the stairs; but Fanny, guessing his purpose, rushed down and caught his arm, detaining him.

"You're not going in *there?*" she whispered huskily. "You don't—"

"Let go of me!"

But she clung to him savagely. "No, you don't, Georgie Minafer! You'll keep away from there! You will!"

"You let go of—"

"I won't! You come back here! You'll come upstairs and let them alone; that's what you'll do!" And with such passionate determination did she clutch and tug, never losing a grip of him somewhere, though George tried as much as he could, without hurting her, to wrench away—with such utter forgetfulness of her maiden dignity did she assault him, that she forced him, stumbling upward, to the landing.

"Of all the ridiculous—" he began furiously; but she spared one hand from its grasp of his sleeve and clapped it over his mouth.

"Hush up!" Never for an instant in this grotesque struggle did Fanny raise her voice above a husky whisper. "Hush up! It's indecent—like squabbling outside the door of an operating-room! Go on to the top of the stairs—go on!"

And when George had most unwillingly obeyed, she planted herself in his way, on the top step. "There!" she said. "The idea of your going in there now! I never heard of such a thing!" And with the sudden departure of the nervous vigour she had shown so amazingly, she began to cry again. "I was an *awful* fool! I thought you knew what was going on or I never, never would have done it. Do you suppose I *dreamed* you'd go making everything into such a tragedy? Do you?"

"I don't care what you dreamed," George muttered.

But Fanny went on, always taking care to keep her voice from getting too loud, in spite of her most grievous agitation. "Do you dream I thought you'd go making such a fool of yourself at Mrs. Johnson's? Oh, I saw her this morning! She wouldn't talk to me, but I met George Amberson on my way back, and he told me what you'd done over there! And do you dream I thought you'd do what you've done here this afternoon to Eugene? Oh, I knew that, too! I was looking out of the front bedroom window, and I saw him drive up, and then go away again, and I knew you'd been to the door. Of course he went to George Amberson about it, and that's why George is here. He's got to tell Isabel the whole thing now, and you wanted to go in there interfering—God knows what! You stay here and let her brother tell her; he's got some consideration for her!"

"I suppose you think I haven't!" George said, challenging her, and at that Fanny laughed witheringly.

"You! Considerate of anybody!"

"I'm considerate of her good name!" he said hotly. "It seems to me that's about the first thing to be considerate of, in being considerate of a person! And look here: it strikes me you're taking a pretty different tack from what you did yesterday afternoon!"

Fanny wrung her hands. "I did a terrible thing!" she lamented. "Now that it's done and too late, I know what it *was*! I didn't have sense enough just to let things go on. I didn't have any business to interfere, and I didn't *mean* to interfere—I only wanted to talk, and let out a little! I did think you already knew everything I told you. I did! And I'd rather have cut my hand off than stir you up to doing what you *have* done! I was just suffering so that I wanted to let out a little—I didn't mean any real harm. But now I *see* what's happened—oh, I was a fool! I hadn't any business interfering. Eugene never would have looked at me, anyhow, and, oh, why couldn't I have seen that before! He never came here a single time in his life except on her account, never! And I might have let them alone, because he wouldn't have looked at me even if he'd never seen Isabel. And they haven't done any harm: she made Wilbur happy, and she was a true wife to him as long as he lived. It wasn't a crime for her to care for Eugene all the time; she certainly never *told* him she did—and she gave me every chance in the world! She left us alone together every time she could—even since Wilbur died—but what was the use? And here I go, not doing myself a bit of good by it, and just"—Fanny wrung her hands again—"just ruining them!"

"I suppose you mean I'm doing that," George said bitterly.

"Yes, I do!" she sobbed, and drooped upon the stairway railing, exhausted.

"On the contrary, I mean to save my mother from a calamity."

Fanny looked at him wanly, in a tired despair; then she stepped by him and went slowly to her own door, where she paused and beckoned to him.

"What do you want?"

"Just come here a minute."

"What for?" he asked impatiently.

"I just wanted to say something to you."

"Well, for heaven's sake, say it! There's nobody to hear." Nevertheless, after a moment, as she beckoned him again, he went to her, profoundly annoyed. "Well, what is it?"

"George," she said in a low voice, "I think you ought to be told something. If I were you, I'd let my mother alone."

"Oh, my Lord!" he groaned. "I'm doing these things *for* her, not against her!"

A mildness had come upon Fanny, and she had controlled her weeping. She shook her head gently. "No, I'd let her alone if I were you. I don't think she's very well, George."

"She! I never saw a healthier person in my life."

"No. She doesn't let anybody know, but she goes to the doctor regularly."

"Women are always going to doctors regularly."

"No. He told her to."

George was not impressed. "It's nothing at all; she spoke of it to me years ago—some kind of family failing. She said grandfather had it, too; and look at him! Hasn't proved very serious with him! You act as if I'd done something wrong in sending that man about his business, and as if I were going to persecute my mother, instead of protecting her. By Jove, it's sickening! *You* told me how all the riffraff in town were busy with her name, and then the minute I lift my hand to protect her, you begin to attack me and—"

"*Sh!*" Fanny checked him, laying her hand on his arm. "Your uncle is going."

The library doors were heard opening, and a moment later there came the sound of the front door closing.

George moved toward the head of the stairs, then stood listening; but the house was silent.

Fanny made a slight noise with her lips to attract his attention, and, when he glanced toward her, shook her head at him urgently. "Let her alone," she whispered. "She's down there by herself. Don't go down. Let her alone."

She moved a few steps toward him and halted, her face pallid and awestruck, and then both stood listening for anything that might break the silence downstairs. No sound came to them; that poignant silence was continued throughout long, long minutes, while the two listeners stood there under its mysterious spell; and in its plaintive eloquence— speaking, as it did, of the figure alone in the big, dark library, where dead Wilbur's new silver frame gleamed in the dimness—there was something that checked even George.

Above the aunt and nephew, as they kept this strange vigil, there was a triple window of stained glass, to illumine the landing and upper reaches of the stairway. Figures in blue and amber garments posed gracefully in panels, conceived by some craftsman of the Eighties to represent Love and Purity and Beauty, and these figures, leaded to un- alterable attitudes, were little more motionless than the two human be- ings upon whom fell the mottled faint light of the window. The colours were growing dull; evening was coming on.

Fanny Minafer broke the long silence with a sound from her throat, a stifled gasp; and with that great companion of hers, her handkerchief, retired softly to the loneliness of her own chamber. After she had gone George looked about him bleakly, then on tiptoe crossed the hall and went into his own room, which was filled with twilight. Still tiptoeing, though he could not have said why, he went across the room and sat down heavily in a chair facing the window. Outside there was nothing but the darkening air and the wall of the nearest of the new houses. He had not slept at all, the night before, and he had eaten nothing since the preceding day at lunch, but he felt neither drowsiness nor hunger. His set determination filled him, kept him but too wide awake, and his gaze at the grayness beyond the window was wide-eyed and bitter.

Darkness had closed in when there was a step in the room behind him. Then someone knelt beside the chair, two arms went round him with infinite compassion, a gentle head rested against his shoulder, and there came the faint scent as of apple-blossoms far away.

"You mustn't be troubled, darling," his mother whispered.

"Now, mother—"

"Wait, dearest," she said; and though he stood stone cold, she lifted her arms, put them round him again, and pressed her cheek lightly to his. "Oh, you do look so troubled, poor dear! One thing you couldn't doubt, beloved boy: you know I could never care for anything in the world as I care for you—never, never!"

"Now, mother—"

She released him, and stepped back. "Just a moment more, dearest. I want you to read this first. We can get at things better." She pressed into his hand the envelope she had brought with her, and as he opened it, and began to read the long enclosure, she walked slowly to the other end of the room; then stood there, with her back to him, and her head drooping a little, until he had finished.

The sheets of paper were covered with Eugene's handwriting.

George Amberson will bring you this, dear Isabel. He is waiting while I write. He and I have talked things over, and before he gives this to you he will tell you what has happened. Of course I'm rather confused, and haven't had time to think matters out very definitely, and yet I believe I should have been better prepared for what took place today—I ought to have known it was coming, because I have understood for quite a long time that young George was getting to dislike me more and more. Somehow, I've never been able to get his friendship; he's always had a latent distrust of me—or something like distrust—and perhaps that's made me sometimes a little awkward and diffident with him. I think it may be he felt from the first that I cared a great deal about you, and he naturally resented it. I think perhaps he felt this even during all the time when I was so careful—at least I thought I was—not to show, even to you, how immensely I did care. And he may have feared that you were thinking too much about me—even when you weren't and only liked me as an old friend. It's perfectly comprehensible to me, also, that at his age one gets excited about gossip. Dear Isabel, what I'm trying to get at, in my confused way, is that you and I don't care about this nonsensical gossip, ourselves, at all. Yesterday I thought the time had come when I could ask you to marry me, and you were dear enough to tell me "some time it might come to that." Well, you and I, left to ourselves, and knowing what we have been and what we are, we'd pay as much attention to "talk" as we would to any other kind of old cats' mewing! We'd not be very apt to let such things keep us from the plenty of life we have left to us for making up to ourselves for old unhappinesses and mistakes. But now we're faced with—not the slander and not our own fear of it, because we haven't any, but someone else's fear of it—your son's. And, oh, dearest woman in the world, I know what your son is to you, and it frightens me! Let me explain a little: I don't think he'll change—at twenty-one or twenty-two so many things appear solid and permanent and terrible which forty sees are nothing but disappearing miasma. Forty can't *tell* twenty about this; that's the pity of it! Twenty can find out only by getting to be forty. And so we come to this, dear: Will you live your own life your way, or George's way? I'm going a little further, because it would be fatal not to be wholly frank now. George will act toward you only as your long worship of him, your sacrifices—all the unseen little ones every day since he was born—will make him act. Dear, it breaks my heart for you, but what you have to oppose now is the history of your own selfless and perfect motherhood. I remember saying once that what you worshipped in your son was the angel you saw in him—and I still believe that is true of every mother. But in a mother's worship she may not see that the Will in her son should not always be offered incense along with the angel. I grow sick with fear for you—for both you and me—when I think how the Will against us two has grown strong through the love you have given the angel—and how long your own sweet Will has served that other. Are you strong enough, Isabel? Can you make the fight? I promise you that if you will take heart for it, you will find so quickly that it has all amounted to nothing. You shall have happiness, and, in a little while, *only* happiness. You need only to write me a line— I can't come to your house—and tell me where you will meet me. We will come back in a month, and the angel in your son will bring him to you; I promise it. What is good in him will grow so fine, once you have beaten the turbulent Will—but it must be beaten!

Your brother, that good friend, is waiting with such patience; I should not keep him longer—and I am saying too much for wisdom, I fear. But, oh, my dear, won't you be strong—such a little short strength it would need! Don't strike my life down twice, dear—this time I've not deserved it.

Eugene.

Concluding this missive, George tossed it abruptly from him so that one sheet fell upon his bed and the others upon the floor; and at the faint noise of their falling Isabel came, and, kneeling, began to gather them up.

"Did you read it, dear?"

George's face was pale no longer, but pink with fury. "Yes, I did."

"All of it?" she asked gently, as she rose.

"Certainly!"

She did not look at him, but kept her eyes downcast upon the letter in her hands, tremulously rearranging the sheets in order as she spoke—and though she smiled, her smile was as tremulous as her hands. Nervousness and an irresistible timidity possessed her. "I—I wanted to say, George," she faltered. "I felt that if—if some day it *should* happen—I mean, if you came to feel differently about it, and Eugene and I—that is if we found that it seemed the most sensible thing to do—I was afraid you might think it would be a little queer about—Lucy. I mean if—if she were your step-sister. Of course, she'd not be even legally related to you, and if you—if you cared for her—"

Thus far she got stumblingly with what she wanted to say, while George watched her with a gaze that grew harder and hotter; but here he cut her off. "I have already given up all idea of Lucy," he said. "Naturally, I couldn't have treated her father as I deliberately did treat him—I could hardly have done that and expected his daughter ever to speak to me again."

Isabel gave a quick cry of compassion, but he allowed her no opportunity to speak. "You needn't think I'm making any particular sacrifice," he said sharply, "though I would, quickly enough, if I thought it necessary in a matter of honour like this. I *was* interested in her, and I could even say I did care for her; but she proved pretty satisfactorily that she cared little enough about me! She went away right in the midst of a—of a difference of opinion we were having; she didn't even let me know she was going, and never wrote a line to me, and then came back telling everybody she'd had 'a perfectly gorgeous time'! That's quite enough for me. I'm not precisely the sort to arrange for that kind of thing to be done to me more than once! The truth is, we're not congenial and we'd found that much out, at least, before she left. We should never have been happy; she was 'superior' all the time, and critical of me—not very pleasant, that! I was disappointed in her, and I might as well say it. I don't think she has the very deepest nature in the world, and—"

But Isabel put her hand timidly on his arm. "Georgie, dear, this is only a quarrel: all young people have them before they get adjusted, and you mustn't let—"

"If you please!" he said emphatically, moving back from her. "This isn't that kind. It's all over, and I don't care to speak of it again. It's settled. Don't you understand?"

"But, dear—"

"No. I want to talk to you about this letter of her father's."

"Yes, dear, that's why—"

"It's simply the most offensive piece of writing that I've ever held in my hands!"

She stepped back from him, startled. "But, dear, I thought—"

"I can't understand your even showing me such a thing!" he cried. "How *did* you happen to bring it to me?"

"Your uncle thought I'd better. He thought it was the simplest thing to do, and he said that he'd suggested it to Eugene, and Eugene had agreed. They thought—"

"Yes!" George said bitterly. "I should like to hear what they thought!"

"They thought it would be the most straightforward thing."

George drew a long breath. "Well, what do *you* think, mother?"

"I thought it would be the simplest and most straightforward thing; I thought they were right."

"Very well! We'll agree it was simple and straightforward. Now, what do you think of that letter itself?"

She hesitated, looking away. "I—of course I don't agree with him in the way he speaks of you, dear—except about the angel! I don't agree with some of the things he implies. You've always been unselfish— nobody knows that better than your mother. When Fanny was left with nothing, you were so quick and generous to give up what really should have come to you, and—"

"And yet," George broke in, "you see what he implies about me. Don't you think, really, that this was a pretty insulting letter for that man to be asking you to hand your son?"

"Oh, no!" she cried. "You can see how fair he means to be, and he didn't ask for me to give it to you. It was brother George who—"

"Never mind that, now! You say he tries to be fair, and yet do you suppose it ever occurs to him that I'm doing my simple duty? That I'm doing what my *father* would do if he were alive? That I'm doing what my father would ask me to do if he could speak from his grave out yonder? Do you suppose it ever occurs to that man for one minute that I'm *protecting* my mother?" George raised his voice, advancing upon the helpless lady fiercely; and she could only bend her head before him. "He talks about my 'Will'—how it must be beaten down; yes, and he asks my *mother* to do that little thing to please him! What for? *Why* does he want me 'beaten' by my mother? Because I'm trying to protect her name! He's got my mother's name bandied up and down the streets of this town till I can't *step* in those streets without wondering what every soul I meet is thinking of me and of my family, and now he wants you to marry him so that every gossip in town will say 'There! What did I tell you? I guess *that* proves it's true!' You can't get away from it; that's exactly what they'd say, and this man pretends he cares for you, and yet asks you to marry him and give them the *right* to say it. He says he and you don't care what they say, but I know better! He may not care— probably he's that kind—but you do. There never was an Amberson yet that would let the Amberson name go trailing in the dust like that! It's the proudest name in this town and it's going to stay the proudest; and I tell you that's the deepest thing in my nature—not that I'd expect Eugene Morgan to understand—the very deepest thing in my nature is to protect that name, and to fight for it to the last breath when danger threatens it, as it does now—through my mother!" He turned from her, striding up and down and tossing his arms about, in a tumult of gesture. "I can't believe it of you, that you'd *think* of such a sacrilege! That's what it would be—sacrilege! When he talks about your unselfishness toward me, he's right—you have been unselfish and you have been a perfect mother. But what about him? Is it unselfish of him to want you to throw away your good name just to please him? That's all he asks of you—and to quit being my mother! Do you think I can believe you *really* care for him? I don't! You are my mother and you're an Amberson—and I believe you're too proud! You're too proud to care for a man who could write such a letter as that!" He stopped, faced her, and spoke with more self-control: "Well, what are you going to do about it, mother?"

George was right about his mother's being proud. And even when she laughed with a negro gardener, or even those few times in her life when people saw her weep, Isabel had a proud look—something that was independent and graceful and strong. But she did not have it now: she leaned against the wall, beside his dressing-table, and seemed beset with humility and with weakness. Her head drooped.

"What answer are you going to make to such a letter?" George demanded, like a judge on the bench.

"I—I don't quite know, dear," she murmured.

"You don't?" he cried. "You—"

"Wait," she begged him. "I'm so—confused."

"I want to know what you're going to write him. Do you think if you did what he wants you to I could bear to stay another day in this town, mother? Do you think I could ever bear even to see you again if you married him? I'd want to, but you surely know I just—couldn't!"

She made a futile gesture, and seemed to breathe with difficulty. "I—I wasn't—quite sure," she faltered, "about—about its being wise for us to be married—even before knowing how you feel about it. I wasn't even sure it was quite fair to—to Eugene. I have—I seem to have that family trouble—like father's—that I spoke to you about once." She managed a deprecatory little dry laugh. "Not that it amounts to much, but I wasn't at all sure that it would be fair to him. Marrying doesn't mean so much, after all—not at my age. It's enough to know that—that people think of you—and to see them. I thought we were all—oh, pretty happy the way things were, and I don't think it would mean giving up a great deal for him or me, either, if we just went on as we have been. I—I see him almost every day, and—"

"Mother!" George's voice was loud and stern. "Do you think you could go on seeing him after *this*!"

She had been talking helplessly enough before; her tone was little more broken now. "Not—not even—see him?"

"How could you?" George cried. "Mother, it seems to me that if he ever set foot in this house again—oh! I can't speak of it! *Could* you see him, knowing what talk it makes every time he turns into this street, and knowing what that means to me! Oh, I *don't* understand all this—I don't! If you'd told me, a year ago, that such things were going to happen, I'd have thought you were insane—and now I believe *I* am!"

Then, after a preliminary gesture of despair, as though he meant harm to the ceiling, he flung himself heavily, face downward, upon the bed. His anguish was none the less real for its vehemence; and the stricken lady came to him instantly and bent over him, once more enfolding him in her arms. She said nothing, but suddenly her tears fell upon his head; she saw them, and seemed to be startled.

"Oh, this won't do!" she said. "I've never let you see me cry before, except when your father died. I mustn't!"

And she ran from the room.

. . . A little while after she had gone, George rose and began solemnly to dress for dinner. At one stage of these conscientious proceedings he put on, temporarily, his long black velvet dressing-gown, and, happening to catch sight in his pier glass of the picturesque and mediæval figure thus presented, he paused to regard it; and something profoundly theatrical in his nature came to the surface.

His lips moved; he whispered, half-aloud, some famous fragments:

> " 'Tis not alone my inky cloak, good mother,
>   Nor customary suits of solemn black . . ."

For, in truth, the mirrored princely image, with hair dishevelled on the white brow, and the long tragic fall of black velvet from the shoulders, had brought about (in his thought, at least) some comparisons of his own times, so out of joint, with those of that other gentle prince and heir whose widowed mother was minded to marry again.

> "But I have that within which passeth show;
>   These but the trappings and the suits of Woe."

Not less like Hamlet did he feel and look as he sat gauntly at the dinner table with Fanny to partake of a meal throughout which neither spoke. Isabel had sent word "not to wait" for her, an injunction it was as well they obeyed, for she did not come at all. But with the renewal of sustenance furnished to his system, some relaxation must have occurred within the high-strung George. Dinner was not quite finished when, without warning, sleep hit him hard. His burning eyes could no longer restrain the lids above them; his head sagged beyond control; and he got to his feet, and went lurching upstairs, yawning with exhaustion. From the door of his room, which he closed mechanically, with his eyes shut, he went blindly to his bed, fell upon it soddenly, and slept—with his face full upturned to the light.

. . . It was after midnight when he woke, and the room was dark. He had not dreamed, but he woke with the sense that somebody or something had been with him while he slept—somebody or something infinitely compassionate; somebody or something infinitely protective, that would let him come to no harm and to no grief.

He got up, and pressed the light on. Pinned to the cover of his dressing-table was a square envelope, with the words, "For you, dear," written in pencil upon it. But the message inside was in ink, a little smudged here and there.

> I have been out to the mail-box, darling, with a letter I've written to Eugene, and he'll have it in the morning. It would be unfair not to let him know at once, and my decision could not change if I waited. It would always be the same. I think it is a little better for me to write to you, like this, instead of waiting till you wake up and then telling you, because I'm foolish and might cry again, and I took a vow once, long

ago, that you should never see me cry. Not that I'll feel like crying when we talk things over to-morrow. I'll be "all right and fine" (as you say so often) by that time—don't fear. I think what makes me most ready to cry now is the thought of the terrible suffering in your poor face, and the unhappy knowledge that it is I, your mother, who put it there. It shall never come again! I love you better than anything and everything else on earth. God gave you to me—and oh! how thankful I have been every day of my life for that sacred gift—and nothing can ever come between me and God's gift. I cannot hurt you, and I cannot let you stay hurt as you have been—not another instant after you wake up, my darling boy! It is beyond my power. And Eugene was right—I know you couldn't change about this. Your suffering shows how deep-seated the feeling is within you. So I've written him just about what I think you would like me to—though I told him I would always be fond of him and always his best friend, and I hoped his dearest friend. He'll understand about not seeing him. He'll understand that, though I didn't say it in so many words. You mustn't trouble about that—he'll understand. Good-night, my darling, my beloved, my beloved! You mustn't be troubled. I think I shouldn't mind anything very much so long as I have you "all to myself"—as people say—to make up for your long years away from me at college. We'll talk of what's best to do in the morning, shan't we? And for all this pain you'll forgive your loving and devoted mother.

Isabel.

CHAPTER XXVII

Having finished some errands downtown, the next afternoon, George Amberson Minafer was walking up National Avenue on his homeward way when he saw in the distance, coming toward him, upon the same side of the street, the figure of a young lady—a figure just under the middle height, comely indeed, and to be mistaken for none other in the world—even at two hundred yards. To his sharp discomfiture his heart immediately forced upon him the consciousness of its acceleration; a sudden warmth about his neck made him aware that he had turned red, and then, departing, left him pale. For a panicky moment he thought of facing about in actual flight; he had little doubt that Lucy would meet him with no token of recognition, and all at once this probability struck him as unendurable. And if she did not speak, was it the proper part of chivalry to lift his hat and take the cut bareheaded? Or should the finer gentleman acquiesce in the lady's desire for no further acquaintance, and pass her with stony mien and eyes constrained forward? George was a young man badly flustered.

But the girl approaching him was unaware of his trepidation, being perhaps somewhat preoccupied with her own. She saw only that he was pale, and that his eyes were darkly circled. But here he was advantaged with her, for the finest touch to his good looks was given by this toning down; neither pallor nor dark circles detracting from them, but rather adding to them a melancholy favour of distinction. George had retained his mourning, a tribute completed down to the final details of black gloves and a polished ebony cane (which he would have been pained to name otherwise than as a "walking-stick") and in the aura of this sombre elegance his straight figure and drawn face were not without a tristful and appealing dignity.

In everything outward he was cause enough for a girl's cheek to flush, her heart to beat faster, and her eyes to warm with the soft light that came into Lucy's now, whether she would or no. If his spirit had been what his looks proclaimed it, she would have rejoiced to let the light glow forth which now shone in spite of her. For a long time, thinking of that spirit of his, and what she felt it should be, she had a persistent sense: "It must be there!" but she had determined to believe this folly no longer. Nevertheless, when she met him at the Sharons', she had been far less calm than she seemed.

People speaking casually of Lucy were apt to define her as "a little beauty," a definition short of the mark. She was "a little beauty," but an independent, masterful, self-reliant little American, of whom her father's earlier gipsyings and her own sturdiness had made a woman ever since she was fifteen. But though she was the mistress of her own ways and no slave to any lamp save that of her own conscience, she had a weakness: she had fallen in love with George Amberson Minafer at first sight, and no matter how she disciplined herself, she had never been able to climb out. The thing had happened to her; that was all. George had looked just the way she had always wanted someone to look—the riskiest of all the moonshine ambushes wherein tricky romance snares credulous young love. But what was fatal to Lucy was that this thing having happened to her, she could not change it. No matter what she discovered in George's nature she was unable to take away what she had given him; and though she could think differently about him, she could not feel differently about him, for she was one of those too faithful victims of glamour. When she managed to keep the picture of George away from her mind's eye, she did well enough; but when she let him become visible, she could not choose but love what she disdained. She was a little angel who had fallen in love with high-handed Lucifer; quite an experience, and not apt to be soon succeeded by any falling in love with a tamer party—and the unhappy truth was that George did make better men seem tame. But though she was a victim, she was a heroic one, anything but helpless.

As they drew nearer, George tried to prepare himself to meet her with some remnants of aplomb. He decided that he would keep on looking straight ahead, and lift his hand toward his hat at the very last moment when it would be possible for her to see him out of the corner of her eye: then when she thought it over later, she would not be sure whether he had saluted her or merely rubbed his forehead. And there was the added benefit that any third person who might chance to look from a window, or from a passing carriage, would not think that he was receiving a snub, because he did not intend to lift his hat, but, timing the gesture properly, would in fact actually rub his forehead. These were the hasty plans which occupied his thoughts until he was within about fifty feet of her—when he ceased to have either plans or thoughts. He had kept his eyes from looking full at her until then, and as he saw her, thus close at hand, and coming nearer, a regret that was dumfounding took possession of him. For the first time he had the sense of having lost something of overwhelming importance.

Lucy did not keep to the right, but came straight to meet him, smiling, and with her hand offered to him.

"Why—you—" he stammered, as he took it. "Haven't you—" What he meant to say was, "Haven't you heard?"

"Haven't I what?" she asked; and he saw that Eugene had not yet told her.

"Nothing!" he gasped. "May I—may I turn and walk with you a little way?"

"Yes, indeed!" she said cordially.

He would not have altered what had been done: he was satisfied with all that—satisfied that it was right, and that his own course was right. But he began to perceive a striking inaccuracy in some remarks he had made to his mother. Now when he had put matters in such shape that even by the relinquishment of his "ideals of life" he could not have Lucy, knew that he could never have her, and knew that when Eugene told her the history of yesterday he could not have a glance or word even friendly from her—now when he must in good truth "give up all idea of Lucy," he was amazed that he could have used such words as "no particular sacrifice," and believed them when he said them! She had looked never in his life so bewitchingly pretty as she did to-day; and as he walked beside her he was sure that she was the most exquisite thing in the world.

"Lucy," he said huskily, "I want to tell you something. Something that matters."

"I hope it's a lively something then," she said; and laughed. "Papa's been so glum to-day he's scarcely spoken to me. Your Uncle George Amberson came to see him an hour ago and they shut themselves up in the library, and your uncle looked as glum as papa. I'd be glad if you'll tell me a funny story, George."

"Well, it may seem one to you," he said bitterly. "Just to begin with: when you went away you didn't let me know; not even a word—not a line—"

Her manner persisted in being inconsequent. "Why, no," she said. "I just trotted off for some visits."

"Well, at least you might have—"

"Why, no," she said again briskly. "Don't you remember, George? We'd had a grand quarrel, and didn't speak to each other all the way home from a long, long drive! So, as we couldn't play together like good children, of course it was plain that we oughtn't to play at all."

" 'Play'!" he cried.

"Yes. What I mean is that we'd come to the point where it was time to quit playing—well, what we were playing."

"At being lovers, you mean, don't you?"

"Something like that," she said lightly. "For us two, playing at being lovers was just the same as playing at cross-purposes. I had all the purposes, and that gave you all the crossness: things weren't getting along at all. It was absurd!"

"Well, have it your own way," he said. "It needn't have been absurd."

"No, it couldn't help but be!" she informed him cheerfully. "The way I am and the way you are, it couldn't ever be anything else. So what was the use?"

"I don't know," he sighed, and his sigh was abysmal. "But what I wanted to tell you is this: when you went away, you didn't let me know and didn't care how or when I heard it, but I'm not like that with you. This time, *I'm* going away. That's what I wanted to tell you. I'm going away to-morrow night—indefinitely."

She nodded sunnily. "That's nice for you. I hope you'll have ever so jolly a time, George."

"I don't expect to have a particularly 'jolly time.' "

"Well, then," she laughed, "if I were you I don't think I'd go."

It seemed impossible to impress this distracting creature, to make her serious. "Lucy," he said desperately, "this is our last walk together."

"Evidently!" she said. "If you're going away to-morrow night."

"Lucy—this may be the last time I'll see you—ever—ever in my life."

At that she looked at him quickly, across her shoulder, but she smiled as brightly as before, and with the same cordial inconsequence: "Oh, I can hardly think that!" she said. "And of course I'd be awfully sorry to think it. You're not moving away, are you, to live?"

"No."

"And even if you were, of course you'd be coming back to visit your relatives every now and then."

"I don't know when I'm coming back. Mother and I are starting tomorrow night for a trip around the world."

At this she did look thoughtful. "Your mother is going with you?"

"Good heavens!" he groaned. "Lucy, doesn't it make any difference to you that *I* am going?"

At this her cordial smile instantly appeared again. "Yes, of course," she said. "I'm sure I'll miss you ever so much. Are you to be gone long?"

He stared at her wanly. "I told you indefinitely," he said. "We've made no plans—at all—for coming back."

"That does sound like a long trip!" she exclaimed admiringly. "Do you plan to be travelling all the time, or will you stay in some one place the greater part of it? I think it would be lovely to—"

"Lucy!"

He halted; and she stopped with him. They had come to a corner at the edge of the "business section" of the city, and people were everywhere about them, brushing against them, sometimes, in passing.

"I can't stand this," George said, in a low voice. "I'm just about ready to go in this drug-store here, and ask the clerk for something to keep me from dying in my tracks! It's quite a shock, you see, Lucy!"

"What is?"

"To find out certainly, at last, how deeply you've cared for me! To see how much difference this makes to you! By Jove, I *have* mattered to you!"

Her cordial smile was tempered now with good-nature. "George!" She laughed indulgently. "Surely you don't want me to do pathos on a downtown corner!"

"*You* wouldn't 'do pathos' anywhere!"

"Well—don't you think pathos is generally rather foozling?"

"I can't stand this any longer," he said. "I can't! Good-bye, Lucy!" He took her hand. "It's good-bye—I think it's good-bye for good, Lucy!"

"Good-bye! I do hope you'll have the most splendid trip." She gave his hand a cordial little grip, then released it lightly. "Give my love to your mother. Good-bye!"

He turned heavily away, and a moment later glanced back over his shoulder. She had not gone on, but stood watching him, that same casual, cordial smile on her face to the very last; and now, as he looked back, she emphasized her friendly unconcern by waving her small hand to him cheerily, though perhaps with the slightest hint of preoccupation, as if she had begun to think of the errand that brought her downtown.

In his mind, George had already explained her to his own poignant dissatisfaction—some blond pup, probably, whom she had met during that "perfectly gorgeous time!" And he strode savagely onward, not looking back again.

But Lucy remained where she was until he was out of sight. Then she went slowly into the drugstore which had struck George as a possible source of stimulant for himself.

"Please let me have a few drops of aromatic spirits of ammonia in a glass of water," she said, with the utmost composure.

"Yes, *ma'am!*" said the impressionable clerk, who had been looking at her through the display window as she stood on the corner.

But a moment later, as he turned from the shelves of glass jars against the wall, with the potion she had asked for in his hand, he uttered an exclamation: "For goshes' sake, Miss!" And, describing this adventure to his fellow-boarders, that evening, "Sagged pretty near to the counter, she was," he said. " 'F I hadn't been a bright, quick, ready-for-anything young fella she'd 'a' flummixed plum! I was watchin' her out the window—talkin' to some young s'iety fella, and she was all right then. She was all right when she come in the store, too. Yes, sir; the prettiest girl that ever walked in our place and took one good look at me. I reckon it must be the truth what some you town wags say about my face!"

Chapter XXVIII

At that hour the heroine of the susceptible clerk's romance was engaged in brightening the rosy little coal fire under the white mantelpiece in her pretty white-and-blue boudoir. Four photographs all framed in decorous plain silver went to the anthracite's fierce destruction—frames and all—and three packets of letters and notes in a charming Florentine treasure-box of painted wood; nor was the box, any more than the silver frames, spared this rousing finish. Thrown heartily upon live coal, the fine wood sparkled forth in stars, then burst into an alarming blaze which scorched the white mantelpiece, but Lucy stood and looked on without moving.

It was not Eugene who told her what had happened at Isabel's door. When she got home, she found Fanny Minafer waiting for her—a secret excursion of Fanny's for the purpose, presumably, of "letting out" again; because that was what she did. She told Lucy everything (except her own lamentable part in the production of the recent miseries) and concluded with a tribute to George: "The worst of it is, he thinks he's been such a hero, and Isabel does, too, and that makes him more than twice as awful. It's been the same all his life: everything he did was noble and perfect. He had a domineering nature to begin with, and she let it go on, and fostered it till it absolutely ruled her. I never saw a plainer case of a person's fault making them pay for having it! She goes about, overseeing the packing and praising George and pretending to be perfectly cheerful about what he's making her do and about the dreadful things he's done. She pretends he did such a fine thing—so manly and protective—going to Mrs. Johnson. And so heroic—doing what his 'principles' made him—even though he knew what it would cost him with you! And all the while it's almost killing her—what he said to your father! She's always been lofty enough, so to speak, and had the greatest idea of the Ambersons being superior to the rest of the world, and all that, but rudeness, or anything like a 'scene,' or any bad manners—they always just made her sick! But she could never see what George's manners were—oh, it's been a terrible adulation!... It's going to be a task for me, living in that big house, all alone: you must come and see me—I mean after they've gone, of course. I'll go crazy if I don't see something of people. I'm sure you'll come as often as you can. I know you too well to think you'll be sensitive about coming there, or being reminded of George. Thank heaven you're too well-balanced," Miss Fanny concluded, with a profound fervour, "you're too well-balanced to let anything affect you deeply about that—that monkey!"

The four photographs and the painted Florentine box went to their cremation within the same hour that Miss Fanny spoke; and a little later Lucy called her father in, as he passed her door, and pointed to the blackened area on the underside of the mantelpiece, and to the burnt heap upon the coal, where some metallic shapes still retained outline. She flung her arms about his neck in passionate sympathy, telling him that she knew what had happened to him; and presently he began to comfort her and managed an embarrassed laugh.

"Well, well—" he said. "I was too old for such foolishness to be getting into my head, anyhow."

"No, no!" she sobbed. "And if you knew how I despise myself for—for ever having thought one instant about—oh, Miss Fanny called him the right name: that *monkey*! He is!"

"There, I think I agree with you," Eugene said grimly, and in his eyes there was a steady light of anger that was to last. "Yes, I think I agree with you about *that*!"

"There's only one thing to do with such a person," she said vehemently. "That's to put him out of our thoughts forever—*forever*!"

And yet, the next day, at six o'clock, which was the hour, Fanny had told her, when George and his mother were to leave upon their long journey, Lucy touched that scorched place on her mantel with her hand just as the little clock above it struck. Then, after this odd, unconscious gesture, she went to a window and stood between the curtains, looking out into the cold November dusk; and in spite of every reasoning and reasonable power within her, a pain of loneliness struck through her heart. The dim street below her window, the dark houses across the way, the vague air itself—all looked empty, and cold and (most of all) uninteresting. Something more sombre than November dusk took the colour from them and gave them that air of desertion.

The light of her fire, flickering up behind her, showed suddenly a flying group of tiny snowflakes nearing the window-pane; and for an instant she felt the sensation of being dragged through a snowdrift under a broken cutter, with a boy's arms about her—an arrogant, handsome, too-conquering boy, who nevertheless did his best to get hurt himself, keeping her from any possible harm.

She shook the picture out of her eyes indignantly, then came and sat before her fire, and looked long and long at the blackened mantelpiece. She did not have the mantelpiece repainted—and, since she did not, might as well have kept his photographs. One forgets what made the scar upon his hand but not what made the scar upon his wall.

She played no *marche funebre* upon her piano, even though Chopin's romantic lamentation was then at the top of nine-tenths of the music-racks in the country, American youth having recently discovered the distinguished congeniality between itself and this deathless bit of deathly gloom. She did not even play "Robin Adair"; she played "Bedelia" and all the new cake-walks, for she was her father's housekeeper, and rightly looked upon the office as being the same as that of his heart-keeper. Therefore it was her affair to keep both house and heart in what state of cheerfulness might be contrived. She made him "go out" more than ever; made him take her to all the gayeties of that winter, declining to go herself unless he took her, and, though Eugene danced no more, and quoted Shakespeare to prove all lightfoot caperings beneath the dignity of his age, she broke his resolution for him at the New Year's Eve "Assembly" and half coaxed, half dragged him forth upon the floor, and made him dance the New Year in with her.

. . . New faces appeared at the dances of the winter; new faces had been appearing everywhere, for that matter, and familiar ones were disappearing, merged in the increasing crowd, or gone forever and missed a little and not long; for the town was growing and changing as it never had grown and changed before.

It was heaving up in the middle incredibly; it was spreading incredibly; and as it heaved and spread, it befouled itself and darkened its sky. Its boundary was mere shapelessness on the run; a raw, new house would appear on a country road; four or five others would presently be built at intervals between it and the outskirts of the town; the country road would turn into an asphalt street with a brick-faced drugstore and a frame grocery at a corner; then bungalows and six-room cottages would swiftly speckle the open green spaces—and a farm had become a suburb, which would immediately shoot out other suburbs into the country, on one side, and, on the other, join itself solidly to the city. You drove between pleasant fields and woodland groves one spring day; and in the autumn, passing over the same ground, you were warned off the tracks by an interurban trolley-car's gonging, and beheld, beyond cement sidewalks just dry, new house-owners busy "moving in." Gasoline and electricity were performing the miracles Eugene had predicted.

But the great change was in the citizenry itself. What was left of the patriotic old-stock generation that had fought the Civil War, and subsequently controlled politics, had become venerable and was little heeded. The descendants of the pioneers and early settlers were merging into the new crowd, becoming part of it, little to be distinguished from it. What happened to Boston and to Broadway happened in degree to the Midland city; the old stock became less and less typical, and of the grown people who called the place home, less than a third had been born in it. There was a German quarter; there was a Jewish quarter; there was a negro quarter—square miles of it—called "Bucktown"; there were many Irish neighbourhoods; and there were large settlements of Italians, and of Hungarians, and of Rumanians, and of Servians and other Balkan peoples. But not the emigrants, themselves, were the almost dominant type on the streets downtown. That type was the emigrant's prosperous offspring: descendant of the emigrations of the Seventies and Eighties and Nineties, those great folk-journeyings in search not so directly of freedom and democracy as of more money for the same labour. A new Midlander—in fact, a new American—was beginning dimly to emerge.

A new spirit of citizenship had already sharply defined itself. It was idealistic, and its ideals were expressed in the new kind of young men in business downtown. They were optimists—optimists to the point of belligerence—their motto being "Boost! Don't Knock!" And they were hustlers, believing in hustling and in honesty because both paid. They loved their city and worked for it with a plutonic energy which was always ardently vocal. They were viciously governed, but they sometimes went so far as to struggle for better government on account of the helpful effect of good government on the price of real estate and "betterment" generally; the politicians could not go too far with them, and knew it. The idealists planned and strove and shouted that their city should become a better, better, and better city—and what they meant, when they used the word "better," was "more prosperous," and the core of their idealism was this: "The more prosperous my beloved city, the more prosperous beloved I!" They had one supreme theory: that the perfect beauty and happiness of cities and of human life was to be brought about by more factories; they had a mania for factories; there was nothing they would not do to cajole a factory away from another city; and they were never more piteously embittered than when another city cajoled one away from them.

What they meant by Prosperity was credit at the bank; but in exchange for this credit they got nothing that was not dirty, and, therefore, to a sane mind, valueless; since whatever was cleaned was dirty again before the cleaning was half done. For, as the town grew, it grew dirty with an incredible completeness. The idealists put up magnificent business buildings and boasted of them, but the buildings were begrimed before they were finished. They boasted of their libraries, of their monuments and statues; and poured soot on them. They boasted of their schools, but the schools were dirty, like the children within them. This was not the fault of the children or their mothers. It was the fault of the idealists, who said: "The more dirt, the more prosperity." They drew patriotic, optimistic breaths of the flying powdered filth of the streets, and took the foul and heavy smoke with gusto into the profundities of their lungs. "Boost! Don't knock!" they said. And every year or so they boomed a great Clean-Up Week, when everybody was supposed to get rid of the tin cans in his backyard.

They were happiest when the tearing down and building up were most riotous, and when new factory districts were thundering into life. In truth, the city came to be like the body of a great dirty man, skinned, to show his busy works, yet wearing a few barbaric ornaments; and such a figure carved, coloured, and discoloured, and set up in the market-place, would have done well enough as the god of the new people. Such a god they had indeed made in their own image, as all peoples make the god they truly serve; though of course certain of the idealists went to church on Sunday, and there knelt to Another, considered to be impractical in business. But while the Growing went on, this god of their market-place was their true god, their familiar and spirit-control. They did not know that they were his helplessly obedient slaves, nor could they ever hope to realize their serfdom (as the first step toward becoming free men) until they should make the strange and hard discovery that matter should serve man's spirit.

"Prosperity" meant good credit at the bank, black lungs, and housewives' Purgatory. The women fought the dirt all they could; but if they let the air into their houses they let in the dirt. It shortened their lives, and kept them from the happiness of ever seeing anything white. And thus, as the city grew, the time came when Lucy, after a hard struggle, had to give up her blue-and-white curtains and her white walls. Indoors, she put everything into dull gray and brown, and outside had the little house painted the dark green nearest to black. Then she knew, of course, that everything was as dirty as ever, but was a little less distressed because it no longer looked so dirty as it was.

These were bad times for Amberson Addition. This quarter, already old, lay within a mile of the centre of the town, but business moved in other directions; and the Addition's share of Prosperity was only the smoke and dirt, with the bank credit left out. The owners of the original big houses sold them, or rented them to boarding-house keepers, and the tenants of the multitude of small houses moved "farther out" (where the smoke was thinner) or into apartment houses, which were built by dozens now. Cheaper tenants took their places, and the rents were lower and lower, and the houses shabbier and shabbier—for all these shabby houses, burning soft coal, did their best to help in the destruction of their own value. They helped to make the quarter so dingy and the air so foul to breathe that no one would live there who had money enough to get "farther out" where there were glimpses of ungrayed sky and breaths of cleaner winds. And with the coming of the new speed, "farther out" was now as close to business as the Addition had been in the days of its prosperity. Distances had ceased to matter.

The five new houses, built so closely where had been the fine lawn of the Amberson Mansion, did not look new. When they were a year old they looked as old as they would ever look; and two of them were vacant, having never been rented, for the Major's mistake about apartment houses had been a disastrous one. "He guessed wrong," George Amberson said. "He guessed wrong at just the wrong time! Housekeeping in a house is harder than in an apartment; and where the smoke and dirt are as thick as they are in the Addition, women can't stand it. People were crazy for apartments—too bad he couldn't have seen it in time. Poor man! he digs away at his ledgers by his old gas drop-light lamp almost every night—he still refuses to let the Mansion be torn up for wiring, you know. But he had one painful satisfaction this spring: he got his taxes lowered!"

Amberson laughed ruefully, and Fanny Minafer asked how the Major could have managed such an economy. They were sitting upon the veranda at Isabel's one evening during the third summer of the absence of their nephew and his mother; and the conversation had turned toward Amberson finances.

"I said it was a '*painful* satisfaction,' Fanny," he explained. "The property has gone down in value, and they assessed it lower than they did fifteen years ago."

"But farther out—"

"Oh, yes, 'farther out'! Prices are magnificent 'farther out,' and farther in, too! We just happen to be the wrong spot, that's all. Not that I don't think something could be done if father would let me have a hand; but he won't. He can't, I suppose I ought to say. He's 'always done his own figuring,' he says; and it's his lifelong habit to keep his affairs, and even his books, to himself, and just hand us out the money. Heaven knows he's done enough of that!"

He sighed; and both were silent, looking out at the long flares of the constantly passing automobile headlights, shifting in vast geometric demonstrations against the darkness. Now and then a bicycle wound its nervous way among these portents, or, at long intervals, a surrey or buggy plodded forlornly by.

"There seem to be so many ways of making money nowadays," Fanny said thoughtfully. "Every day I hear of a new fortune some person has got hold of, one way or another—nearly always it's somebody you never heard of. It doesn't seem all to be in just making motor cars; I hear there's a great deal in manufacturing these things that motor cars use—new inventions particularly. I met dear old Frank Bronson the other day, and he told me—"

"Oh, yes, even dear old Frank's got the fever," Amberson laughed. "He's as wild as any of them. He told me about this invention he's gone into, too. 'Millions in it!' Some new electric headlight better than anything yet—'every car in America can't *help* but have 'em,' and all that. He's putting half he's laid by into it, and the fact is, he almost talked me into getting father to 'finance me' enough for me to go into it. Poor father! he's financed me before! I suppose he would again if I had the heart to ask him; and this seems to be a good thing, though probably old Frank is a *little* too sanguine. At any rate, I've been thinking it over."

"So have I," Fanny admitted. "He seemed to be certain it would pay twenty-five per cent. the first year, and enormously more after that; and I'm only getting four on my little principal. People *are* making such enormous fortunes out of everything to do with motor cars, it does seem as if—" She paused. "Well, I told him I'd think it over seriously."

"We may turn out to be partners and millionaires then," Amberson laughed. "I thought I'd ask Eugene's advice."

"I wish you would," said Fanny. "He probably knows exactly how much profit there would be in this."

Eugene's advice was to "go slow": he thought electric lights for automobiles were "coming—*some* day," but probably not until certain difficulties could be overcome. Altogether, he was discouraging, but by this time his two friends "had the fever" as thoroughly as old Frank Bronson himself had it; for they had been with Bronson to see the light working beautifully in a machine shop. They were already enthusiastic, and after asking Eugene's opinion they argued with him, telling him how they had seen with their own eyes that the difficulties he mentioned *had* been overcome. "Perfectly!" Fanny cried. "And if it worked in the shop it's bound to work any place else, isn't it?"

He would not agree that it was "bound to"—yet, being pressed, was driven to admit that "it *might*," and, retiring from what was developing into an oratorical contest, repeated a warning about not "putting too much into it."

George Amberson also laid stress on this caution later, though the Major had "financed him" again, and he was "going in." "You must be careful to leave yourself a 'margin of safety,' Fanny," he said. "I'm confident that is a pretty conservative investment of its kind, and all the chances are with us, but you must be careful to leave yourself enough to fall back on, in case anything *should* go wrong."

Fanny deceived him. In the impossible event of "anything going wrong" she would have enough left to "live on," she declared, and laughed excitedly, for she was having the best time that had come to her since Wilbur's death. Like so many women for whom money has always been provided without their understanding how, she was prepared to be a thorough and irresponsible plunger.

Amberson, in his wearier way, shared her excitement, and in the winter, when the exploiting company had been formed, and he brought Fanny her importantly engraved shares of stock, he reverted to his prediction of possibilities, made when they first spoke of the new light.

"We seem to be partners, all right," he laughed. "Now let's go ahead and be millionaires before Isabel and young George come home."

"When they come home!" she echoed sorrowfully—and it was a phrase which found an evasive echo in Isabel's letters. In these letters Isabel was always planning pleasant things that she and Fanny and the Major and George and "brother George" would do—when she and her son came home. "They'll find things pretty changed, I'm afraid," Fanny said. "If they ever do come home!"

———

Amberson went over, the next summer, and joined his sister and nephew in Paris, where they were living. "Isabel does want to come home," he told Fanny gravely, on the day of his return, in October. "She's wanted to for a long while—and she ought to come while she can stand the journey—" And he amplified this statement, leaving Fanny looking startled and solemn when Lucy came by to drive him out to dinner at the new house Eugene had just completed.

This was no white-and-blue cottage, but a great Georgian picture in brick, five miles north of Amberson Addition, with four acres of its own hedged land between it and its next neighbour; and Amberson laughed wistfully as they turned in between the stone and brick gate pillars, and rolled up the crushed stone driveway. "I wonder, Lucy, if history's going on forever repeating itself," he said. "I wonder if this town's going on building up things and rolling over them, as poor father once said it was rolling over his poor old heart. It looks like it: here's the Amberson Mansion again, only it's Georgian instead of nondescript Romanesque; but it's just the same Amberson Mansion that my father built long before you were born. The only difference is that it's your father who's built this one now. It's all the same, in the long run."

Lucy did not quite understand, but she laughed as a friend should, and, taking his arm, showed him through vasty rooms where ivory-panelled walls and trim window hangings were reflected dimly in dark, rugless floors, and the sparse furniture showed that Lucy had been "collecting" with a long purse. "By Jove!" he said. "You *have* been going it! Fanny tells me you had a great 'house-warming' dance, and you keep right on being the belle of the ball, not any softer-hearted than you used to be. Fred Kinney's father says you've refused Fred so often that he got engaged to Janie Sharon just to prove that someone would have him in spite of his hair. Well, the material world do move, and you've got the new kind of house it moves into nowadays—if it has the new price! And even the grand old expanses of plate glass we used to be so proud of at the other Amberson Mansion—they've gone, too, with the crowded heavy gold and red stuff. Curious! *We've* still got the plate glass windows, though all we can see out of 'em is the smoke and the old Johnson house, which is a counter-jumper's boarding-house now, while you've got a view, and you cut it all up into little panes. Well, you're pretty refreshingly out of the smoke up here."

"Yes, for a while," Lucy laughed. "Until it comes and we have to move out farther."

"No, you'll stay here," he assured her. "It will be somebody else who'll move out farther."

He continued to talk of the house after Eugene arrived, and gave them no account of his journey until they had retired from the dinner table to Eugene's library, a gray and shadowy room, where their coffee was brought. Then, equipped with a cigar, which seemed to occupy his attention, Amberson spoke in a casual tone of his sister and her son.

"I found Isabel as well as usual," he said, "only I'm afraid 'as usual' isn't particularly well. Sydney and Amelia had been up to Paris in the spring, but she hadn't seen them. Somebody told her they were there, it seems. They'd left Florence and were living in Rome; Amelia's become a Catholic and is said to give great sums to charity and to go about with the gentry in consequence, but Sydney's ailing and lives in a wheel-chair most of the time. It struck me Isabel ought to be doing the same thing."

He paused, bestowing minute care upon the removal of the little band from his cigar; and as he seemed to have concluded his narrative, Eugene spoke out of the shadow beyond a heavily shaded lamp: "What do you mean by that?" he asked quietly.

"Oh, she's cheerful enough," said Amberson, still not looking at either his young hostess or her father. "At least," he added, "she manages to seem so. I'm afraid she hasn't been really well for several years. She isn't stout you know—she hasn't changed in looks much—and she seems rather alarmingly short of breath for a slender person. Father's been that way for years, of course; but never nearly so much as Isabel is now. Of course she makes nothing of it, but it seemed rather serious to me when I noticed she had to stop and rest twice to get up the one short flight of stairs in their two-floor apartment. I told her I thought she ought to make George let her come home."

" 'Let her'?" Eugene repeated, in a low voice. "Does she want to?"

"She doesn't urge it. George seems to like the life there—in his grand, gloomy, and peculiar way; and of course she'll never change about being proud of him and all that—he's quite a swell. But in spite of anything she said, rather than because, I know she does indeed want to come. She'd like to be with father, of course; and I think she's—well, she intimated one day that she feared it might even happen that she wouldn't get to see him again. At the time I thought she referred to his age and feebleness, but on the boat, coming home, I remembered the little look of wistfulness, yet of resignation, with which she said it, and it struck me all at once that I'd been mistaken: I saw she was really thinking of her own state of health."

"I see," Eugene said, his voice even lower than it had been before. "And you say he won't 'let' her come home?"

Amberson laughed, but still continued to be interested in his cigar. "Oh, I don't think he uses force! He's very gentle with her. I doubt if the subject is mentioned between them, and yet—and yet, knowing my interesting nephew as you do, wouldn't you think that was about the way to put it?"

"Knowing him as I do—yes," said Eugene slowly. "Yes, I should think that was about the way to put it."

A murmur out of the shadows beyond him—a faint sound, musical and feminine, yet expressive of a notable intensity—seemed to indicate that Lucy was of the same opinion.

Chapter XXIX

"Let her" was correct; but the time came—and it came in the spring of the next year—when it was no longer a question of George's letting his mother come home. He had to bring her, and to bring her quickly if she was to see her father again; and Amberson had been right: her danger of never seeing him again lay not in the Major's feebleness of heart but in her own. As it was, George telegraphed his uncle to have a wheeled chair at the station, for the journey had been disastrous, and to this hybrid vehicle, placed close to the car platform, her son carried her in his arms when she arrived. She was unable to speak, but patted her brother's and Fanny's hands and looked "very sweet," Fanny found the desperate courage to tell her. She was lifted from the chair into a carriage, and seemed a little stronger as they drove home; for once she took her hand from George's, and waved it feebly toward the carriage window.

"Changed," she whispered. "So changed."

"You mean the town," Amberson said. "You mean the old place is changed, don't you, dear?"

She smiled and moved her lips: "Yes."

"It'll change to a happier place, old dear," he said, "now that you're back in it, and going to get well again."

But she only looked at him wistfully, her eyes a little frightened.

When the carriage stopped, her son carried her into the house, and up the stairs to her own room, where a nurse was waiting; and he came out a moment later, as the doctor went in. At the end of the hall a stricken group was clustered: Amberson, and Fanny, and the Major. George, deathly pale and speechless, took his grandfather's hand, but the old gentleman did not seem to notice his action.

"When are they going to let me see my daughter?" he asked querulously. "They told me to keep out of the way while they carried her in, because it might upset her. I wish they'd let me go in and speak to my daughter. I think she wants to see me."

He was right—presently the doctor came out and beckoned to him; and the Major shuffled forward, leaning on a shaking cane; his figure, after all its years of proud soldierliness, had grown stooping at last, and his untrimmed white hair straggled over the back of his collar. He looked old—old and divested of the world—as he crept toward his daughter's room. Her voice was stronger, for the waiting group heard a low cry of tenderness and welcome as the old man reached the open doorway. Then the door was closed.

Fanny touched her nephew's arm. "George, you must need something to eat—I know she'd want you to. I've had things ready: I knew she'd want me to. You'd better go down to the dining room: there's plenty on the table, waiting for you. She'd want you to eat something."

He turned a ghastly face to her, it was so panic-stricken. "I don't want anything to *eat!*" he said savagely. And he began to pace the floor, taking care not to go near Isabel's door, and that his footsteps were muffled by the long, thick hall rug. After a while he went to where Amberson, with folded arms and bowed head, had seated himself near the front window. "Uncle George," he said hoarsely. "I didn't—"

"Well?"

"Oh, my God, I didn't think this thing the matter with her could ever be serious! I—" He gasped. "When that doctor I had meet us at the boat—" He could not go on.

Amberson only nodded his head, and did not otherwise change his attitude.

. . . Isabel lived through the night. At eleven o'clock Fanny came timidly to George in his room. "Eugene is here," she whispered. "He's downstairs. He wants—" She gulped. "He wants to know if he can't *see* her. I didn't know what to say. I said I'd see. I didn't know—the doctor said—"

"The doctor said we 'must keep her peaceful,' " George said sharply. "Do you think that man's coming would be very soothing? My God! if

it hadn't been for him this mightn't have happened: we could have gone
on living here quietly, and—why, it would be like taking a stranger into
her room! She hasn't even spoken of him more than twice in all the
time we've been away. Doesn't he know how *sick* she is? You tell him the
doctor said she had to be quiet and peaceful. That's what he did say,
isn't it?"

Fanny acquiesced tearfully. "I'll tell him. I'll tell him the doctor said
she was to be kept very quiet. I—I didn't know—" And she pottered
out.

An hour later the nurse appeared in George's doorway; she came
noiselessly, and his back was toward her; but he jumped as if he had
been shot, and his jaw fell, he so feared what she was going to say.

"She wants to see you."

The terrified mouth shut with a click; and he nodded and followed
her; but she remained outside his mother's room while he went in.

Isabel's eyes were closed, and she did not open them or move her
head, but she smiled and edged her hand toward him as he sat on a stool
beside the bed. He took that slender, cold hand, and put it to his cheek.

"Darling, did you—get something to eat?" She could only whisper,
slowly and with difficulty. It was as if Isabel herself were far away, and
only able to signal what she wanted to say.

"Yes, mother."

"All you—needed?"

"Yes, mother."

She did not speak again for a time; then, "Are you sure you didn't—
didn't catch cold—coming home?"

"I'm all right, mother."

"That's good. It's sweet—it's sweet—"

"What is, mother darling?"

"To feel—my hand on your cheek. I—I *can* feel it."

But this frightened him horribly—that she seemed so glad she
could feel it, like a child proud of some miraculous seeming thing ac-
complished. It frightened him so that he could not speak, and he feared
that she would know how he trembled; but she was unaware, and again
was silent. Finally she spoke again:

"I wonder if—if Eugene and Lucy know that we've come—home."

"I'm sure they do."

"Has he—asked about me?"

"Yes, he was here."

"Has he—gone?"

"Yes, mother."

She sighed faintly. "I'd like—"

"What, mother?"

"I'd like to have—seen him." It was just audible, this little regretful murmur. Several minutes passed before there was another. "Just—just once," she whispered, and then was still.

She seemed to have fallen asleep, and George moved to go, but a faint pressure upon his fingers detained him, and he remained, with her hand still pressed against his cheek. After a while he made sure she was asleep, and moved again, to let the nurse come in, and this time there was no pressure of the fingers to keep him. She was not asleep, but, thinking that if he went he might get some rest, and be better prepared for what she knew was coming, she commanded those longing fingers of hers—and let him go.

He found the doctor standing with the nurse in the hall; and, telling them that his mother was drowsing now, George went back to his own room, where he was startled to find his grandfather lying on the bed, and his uncle leaning against the wall. They had gone home two hours before, and he did not know they had returned.

"The doctor thought we'd better come over," Amberson said, then was silent, and George, shaking violently, sat down on the edge of the bed. His shaking continued, and from time to time he wiped heavy sweat from his forehead.

The hours passed, and sometimes the old man upon the bed would snore a little, stop suddenly, and move as if to rise, but George Amberson would set a hand upon his shoulder, and murmur a reassuring word or two. Now and then, either uncle or nephew would tiptoe into the hall and look toward Isabel's room, then come tiptoeing back, the other watching him haggardly.

Once George gasped defiantly: "That doctor in New York said she *might* get better! Don't you know he did? Don't you know he said she might?"

Amberson made no answer.

Dawn had been murking through the smoky windows, growing stronger for half an hour, when both men started violently at a sound in the hall; and the Major sat up on the bed, unchecked. It was the voice of the nurse speaking to Fanny Minafer, and the next moment, Fanny appeared in the doorway, making contorted efforts to speak.

Amberson said weakly: "Does she want us—to come in?"

But Fanny found her voice, and uttered a long, loud cry. She threw her arms about George, and sobbed in an agony of loss and compassion:

"She loved you!" she wailed. "She loved you! She loved you! Oh, how she did love you!"

Isabel had just left them.

Chapter XXX

Major Amberson remained dry-eyed through the time that followed: he knew that this separation from his daughter would be short; that the separation which had preceded it was the long one. He worked at his ledgers no more under his old gas drop-light, but would sit all evening staring into the fire, in his bedroom, and not speaking unless someone asked him a question. He seemed almost unaware of what went on around him, and those who were with him thought him dazed by Isabel's death, guessing that he was lost in reminiscences and vague dreams. "Probably his mind is full of pictures of his youth, or the Civil War, and the days when he and mother were young married people and all of us children were jolly little things—and the city was a small town with one cobbled street and the others just dirt roads with board sidewalks." This was George Amberson's conjecture, and the others agreed; but they were mistaken. The Major was engaged in the profoundest thinking of his life. No business plans which had ever absorbed him could compare in momentousness with the plans that absorbed him now, for he had to plan how to enter the unknown country where he was not even sure of being recognized as an Amberson—not sure of anything, except that Isabel would help him if she could. His absorption produced the outward effect of reverie, but of course it was not. The Major was occupied with the first really important matter that had taken his attention since he came home invalided, after the Gettysburg campaign, and went into business; and he realized that everything which had worried him or delighted him during this lifetime between then and to-day—all his buying and building and trading and banking—that it all was trifling and waste beside what concerned him now.

He seldom went out of his room, and often left untouched the meals they brought to him there; and this neglect caused them to shake their heads mournfully, again mistaking for dazedness the profound concentration of his mind. Meanwhile, the life of the little bereft group still forlornly centering upon him began to pick up again, as life will, and to emerge from its own period of dazedness. It was not Isabel's father but her son who was really dazed.

A month after her death he walked abruptly into Fanny's room, one night, and found her at her desk, eagerly adding columns of figures with which she had covered several sheets of paper. This mathematical computation was concerned with her future income to be produced by the electric headlight, now just placed on the general market; but Fanny was ashamed to be discovered doing anything except mourning, and hastily pushed the sheets aside, even as she looked over her shoulder to greet her hollow-eyed visitor.

"George! You startled me."

"I beg your pardon for not knocking," he said huskily. "I didn't think."

She turned in her chair and looked at him solicitously. "Sit down, George, won't you?"

"No. I just wanted—"

"I could hear you walking up and down in your room," said Fanny. "You were doing it ever since dinner, and it seems to me you're at it almost every evening. I don't believe it's good for you—and I know it would worry your mother terribly if she—" Fanny hesitated.

"See here," George said, breathing fast, "I want to tell you once more that what I did was right. How could I have done anything else but what I did do?"

"About what, George?"

"About everything!" he exclaimed; and he became vehement. "I did the right thing, I tell you! In heaven's name, I'd like to know what else there was for anybody in my position to do! It would have been a dreadful thing for me to just let matters go on and not interfere—it would have been terrible! What else on earth was there *for* me to do? I *had* to stop that talk, didn't I? Could a son do less than I did? Didn't it *cost* me something to do it? Lucy and I'd had a quarrel, but that would have come round in time—and it meant the end forever when I turned her father back from our door. I knew what it meant, yet I went ahead and did it because I knew it had to be done if the talk was to be stopped. I took mother away for the same reason. I knew that would help to stop it. And she was happy over there—she was perfectly happy. I tell you, I think she had a happy life, and that's my only consolation. She didn't live to be old; she was still beautiful and young looking, and I feel she'd rather have gone before she got old. She'd had a good husband, and all the comfort and luxury that anybody could have—and how could it be called anything but a happy life? She was always cheerful, and when I think of her I can always see her laughing—I can always hear that pretty laugh of hers. When I can keep my mind off of the trip home, and that last night, I *always* think of her gay and laughing. So how on earth *could* she have had anything but a happy life? People that aren't happy don't look cheerful all the time, do they? They look unhappy if they *are* unhappy; that's how they look! See here"—he faced her challengingly—"do *you* deny that I did the right thing?"

"Oh, I don't pretend to judge," Fanny said soothingly, for his voice and gesture both partook of wildness. "I know you think you did, George."

" 'Think I did'!" he echoed violently. "My God in heaven!" And he began to walk up and down the floor. "What else *was* there to do? What *choice* did I have? Was there any other way of stopping the talk?" He stopped, close in front of her, gesticulating, his voice harsh and loud: "Don't you hear me? I'm asking you: Was there any other way on earth of protecting her from the talk?"

Miss Fanny looked away. "It died down before long, I think," she said nervously.

"*That* shows I was right, doesn't it?" he cried. "If I hadn't acted as I did, that slanderous old Johnson woman would have kept on with her slanders—she'd *still* be—"

"No," Fanny interrupted. "She's dead. She dropped dead with apoplexy one day about six weeks after you left. I didn't mention it in my letters because I didn't want—I thought—"

"Well, the *other* people would have kept on, then. *They'd* have—"

"I don't know," said Fanny, still averting her troubled eyes. "Things are so changed here, George. The other people you speak of—one hardly knows what's become of them. Of course not a great many were doing the talking, and they—well, some of them are dead, and some might as well be—you never see them any more—and the rest, whoever they were, are probably so mixed in with the crowds of new people that seem never even to have heard of *us*—and I'm sure we certainly never heard of *them*—and people seem to forget things so soon—they seem to forget anything. You can't imagine how things have changed here!"

George gulped painfully before he could speak. "You—you mean to sit there and tell me that if I'd just let things go on— Oh!" He swung away, walking the floor again. "I tell you I did the only right thing! If you don't think so, why in the name of heaven can't you say what *else* I should have done? It's easy enough to criticize, but the person who criticizes a man ought at least to tell him what *else* he should have done! You think I was wrong!"

"I'm not saying so," she said.

"You did at the time!" he cried. "You said enough then, I think! Well, what have you to say now, if you're so sure I was wrong?"

"Nothing, George."

"It's only because you're afraid to!" he said, and he went on with a sudden bitter divination: "You're reproaching yourself with what *you* had to do with all that; and you're trying to make up for it by doing and saying what you think mother would want you to, and you think I couldn't stand it if I got to thinking I might have done differently. Oh, I know! That's exactly what's in your mind: you *do* think I was wrong! So does Uncle George. I challenged him about it the other day, and he answered just as you're answering—evaded, and tried to be gentle! I don't care to be handled with gloves! I tell you I was right, and I don't need any coddling by people that think I wasn't! And I suppose you believe I was wrong not to let Morgan see her that last night when he came here, and she—she was dying. If you do, why in the name of God did you come and ask *me*? *You* could have taken him in! She *did* want to see him. She—"

Miss Fanny looked startled. "You think—"

"She told me so!" And the tortured young man choked. "She said— 'just once.' She said 'I'd like to have seen him—just once!' She meant— to tell him good-bye! *That's* what she meant! And you put this on me, too; you put this responsibility on me! But I tell you, and I told Uncle George, that the responsibility isn't *all* mine! If you were so sure I was wrong all the time—when I took her away, and when I turned Morgan out—if you were so sure, what did you let me do it for? You and Uncle George were grown people, both of you, weren't you? You were older than I, and if you were so sure you were *wiser* than I, why did you just stand around with your hands hanging down, and let me go ahead? You could have stopped it if it was wrong, couldn't you?"

Fanny shook her head. "No, George," she said slowly. "Nobody could have stopped you. You were too strong, and—"

"And what?" he demanded loudly.

"And she loved you—too well."

George stared at her hard, then his lower lip began to move convulsively, and he set his teeth upon it but could not check its frantic twitching.

He ran out of the room.

She sat still, listening. He had plunged into his mother's room, but no sound came to Fanny's ears after the sharp closing of the door; and presently she rose and stepped out into the hall—but could hear nothing. The heavy black walnut door of Isabel's room, as Fanny's troubled eyes remained fixed upon it, seemed to become darker and vaguer; the polished wood took the distant ceiling light, at the end of the hall, in dim reflections which became mysterious; and to Fanny's disturbed mind the single sharp point of light on the bronze door-knob was like a continuous sharp cry in the stillness of night. What interview was sealed away from human eye and ear within the lonely darkness on the other side of that door—in that darkness where Isabel's own special chairs were, and her own special books, and the two great walnut wardrobes filled with her dresses and wraps? What tragic argument might be there vainly striving to confute the gentle dead? "In God's name, what else could I have done?" For his mother's immutable silence was surely answering him as Isabel in life would never have answered him, and he was beginning to understand how eloquent the dead can be. They cannot stop their eloquence, no matter how they have loved the living: they cannot choose. And so, no matter in what agony George should cry out, "What else could I have done?" and to the end of his life no matter how often he made that wild appeal, Isabel was doomed to answer him with the wistful, faint murmur:

"I'd like to have—seen him. Just—just once."

A cheerful darkey went by the house, loudly and tunelessly whistling some broken thoughts upon women, fried food and gin; then a group of high-school boys, returning homeward after important initiations, were heard skylarking along the sidewalk, rattling sticks on the fences, squawking hoarsely, and even attempting to sing in the shocking new voices of uncompleted adolescence. For no reason, and just as a poultry yard falls into causeless agitation, they stopped in front of the house, and for half an hour produced the effect of a noisy multitude in full riot.

To the woman standing upstairs in the hall, this was almost unbearable; and she felt that she would have to go down and call to them to stop; but she was too timid, and after a time went back to her room, and sat at her desk again. She left the door open, and frequently glanced out into the hall, but gradually became once more absorbed in the figures which represented her prospective income from her great plunge in electric lights for automobiles. She did not hear George return to his own room.

. . . A superstitious person might have thought it unfortunate that her partner in this speculative industry (as in Wilbur's disastrous rolling-mills) was that charming but too haphazardous man of the world, George Amberson. He was one of those optimists who believe that if you put money into a great many enterprises one of them is sure to turn out a fortune, and therefore, in order to find the lucky one, it is only necessary to go into a large enough number of them. Altogether gallant in spirit, and beautifully game under catastrophe, he had gone into a great many, and the unanimity of their "bad luck," as he called it, gave him one claim to be a distinguished person, if he had no other. In business he was ill fated with a consistency which made him, in that alone, a remarkable man; and he declared, with some earnestness, that there was no accounting for it except by the fact that there had been so much good luck in his family before he was born that something had to balance it.

"You ought to have thought of my record and stayed out," he told Fanny, one day the next spring, when the affairs of the headlight company had begun to look discouraging. "I feel the old familiar sinking that's attended all my previous efforts to prove myself a business genius. I think it must be something like the feeling an aeronaut has when his balloon bursts, and, looking down, he sees below him the old home farm where he used to live—I mean the feeling he'd have just before he flattened out in that same old clay barnyard. Things do look bleak, and I'm only glad you didn't go into this confounded thing to the extent I did."

Miss Fanny grew pink. "But it *must* go right!" she protested. "We saw with our own eyes how perfectly it worked in the shop. The light was so bright no one could face it, and so there *can't* be any reason for it not to work. It simply—"

"Oh, you're right about that," Amberson said. "It certainly was a perfect thing—in the shop! The only thing *we* didn't know was how fast an automobile had to go to keep the light going. It appears that this was a matter of some importance."

"Well, how fast *does* one have to—"

"To keep the light from going entirely out," he informed her with elaborate deliberation, "it is computed by those enthusiasts who have bought our product—and subsequently returned it to us and got their money back—they compute that a motor car must maintain a speed of twenty-five miles an hour, or else there won't be any light at all. To make the illumination bright enough to be noticed by an approaching automobile, they state the speed must be more than thirty miles an hour. At thirty-five, objects in the path of the light begin to become visible; at forty they are revealed distinctly; and at fifty and above we have a real headlight. Unfortunately many people don't care to drive that fast at all times after dusk, especially in the traffic, or where policemen are likely to become objectionable."

"But think of that test on the road when we—"

"That test was lovely," he admitted. "The inventor made us happy with his oratory, and you and Frank Bronson and I went whirling through the night at a speed that thrilled us. It was an intoxicating sensation: we were intoxicated by the lights, the lights and the music. We must never forget that drive, with the cool wind kissing our cheeks and the road lit up for miles ahead. We must never forget it—and we never shall. It cost—"

"But something's got to be done."

"It has, indeed! *My* something would seem to be leaving my watch at my uncle's. Luckily, you—"

The pink of Fanny's cheeks became deeper. "But isn't that man going to *do* anything to remedy it? Can't he try to—"

"He can try," said Amberson. "He *is* trying, in fact. I've sat in the shop watching him try for several beautiful afternoons, while outside the windows all Nature was fragrant with spring and smoke. He hums ragtime to himself as he tries, and I think his mind is wandering to something else less tedious—to some new invention in which he'd take more interest."

"But you mustn't let him," she cried. "You must *make* him keep on trying!"

"Oh, yes. He understands that's what I sit there for. I'll keep sitting!"

However, in spite of the time he spent sitting in the shop, worrying the inventor of the fractious light, Amberson found opportunity to worry himself about another matter of business. This was the settlement of Isabel's estate.

"It's curious about the deed to her house," he said to his nephew. "You're absolutely sure it wasn't among her papers?"

"Mother didn't have any papers," George told him. "None at all. All she ever had to do with business was to deposit the cheques grandfather gave her and then write her own cheques against them."

"The deed to the house was never recorded," Amberson said thoughtfully. "I've been over to the courthouse to see. I asked father if he never gave her one, and he didn't seem able to understand me at first. Then he finally said he thought he must have given her a deed long ago; but he wasn't sure. I rather think he never did. I think it would be just as well to get him to execute one now in your favour. I'll speak to him about it."

George sighed. "I don't think I'd bother him about it: the house is mine, and you and I understand that it is. That's enough for me, and there isn't likely to be much trouble between you and me when we come to settling poor grandfather's estate. I've just been with him, and I think it would only confuse him for you to speak to him about it again. I notice he seems distressed if anybody tries to get his attention—he's a long way off, somewhere, and he likes to stay that way. I think—I think mother wouldn't want us to bother him about it; I'm sure she'd tell us to let him alone. He looks so white and queer."

Amberson shook his head. "Not much whiter and queerer than you do, young fellow! You'd better begin to get some air and exercise and quit hanging about in the house all day. I won't bother him any more than I can help; but I'll have the deed made out ready for his signature."

"I wouldn't bother him at all. I don't see—"

"You might see," said his uncle uneasily. "The estate is just about as involved and mixed-up as an estate can well get, to the best of my knowledge; and I haven't helped it any by what he let me have for this infernal headlight scheme which has finally gone trolloping forever to where the woodbine twineth. Leaves me flat, and poor old Frank Bronson just half flat, and Fanny—well, thank heaven! I kept her from going in so deep that it would leave *her* flat. It's rough on her as it is, I suspect. You ought to have that deed."

"No. Don't bother him."

"I'll bother him as little as possible. I'll wait till some day when he seems to brighten up a little."

But Amberson waited too long. The Major had already taken eleven months since his daughter's death to think important things out. He had got as far with them as he could, and there was nothing to detain him longer in the world. One evening his grandson sat with him—the Major seemed to like best to have young George with him, so far as they were able to guess his preferences—and the old gentleman made a queer gesture: he slapped his knee as if he had made a sudden discovery, or else remembered that he had forgotten something.

George looked at him with an air of inquiry, but said nothing. He had grown to be almost as silent as his grandfather. However, the Major spoke without being questioned.

"It must be in the sun," he said. "There wasn't anything here but the sun in the first place, and the earth came out of the sun, and we came out of the earth. So, whatever we are, we must have been in the sun. We go back to the earth we came out of, so the earth will go back to the sun that it came out of. And time means nothing—nothing at all—so in a little while we'll all be back in the sun together. I wish—"

He moved his hand uncertainly as if reaching for something, and George jumped up. "Did you want anything, grandfather?"

"What?"

"Would you like a glass of water?"

"No—no. No; I don't want anything." The reaching hand dropped back upon the arm of his chair, and he relapsed into silence; but a few minutes later he finished the sentence he had begun:

"I wish—somebody could tell me!"

The next day he had a slight cold, but he seemed annoyed when his son suggested calling the doctor, and Amberson let him have his own way so far, in fact, that after he had got up and dressed, the following morning, he was all alone when he went away to find out what he hadn't been able to think out—all those things he had wished "somebody" would tell him.

Old Sam, shuffling in with the breakfast tray, found the Major in his accustomed easy-chair by the fireplace—and yet even the old darkey could see instantly that the Major was not there.

Chapter XXXI

When the great Amberson Estate went into court for settlement, "there wasn't any," George Amberson said—that is, when the settlement was concluded there was no estate. "I guessed it," Amberson went on. "As an expert on prosperity, my career is disreputable, but as a prophet of calamity I deserve a testimonial banquet." He reproached himself bitterly for not having long ago discovered that his father had never given Isabel a deed to her house. "And those pigs, Sydney and Amelia!" he added, for this was another thing he was bitter about. "They won't do anything. I'm sorry I gave them the opportunity of making a polished refusal. Amelia's letter was about half in Italian; she couldn't remember enough ways of saying no in English. One has to live quite a long while to realize there *are* people like that! The estate was badly crippled, even before they took out their 'third,' and the 'third' they took was the only good part of the rotten apple. Well, I didn't ask them for restitution on my own account, and at least it will save *you* some trouble, young George. Never waste any time writing to them; you mustn't count on them."

"I don't," George said quietly. "I don't count on anything."

"Oh, we'll not feel that things are quite desperate," Amberson laughed, but not with great cheerfulness. "We'll survive, Georgie—*you* will, especially. For my part I'm a little too old and too accustomed to fall back on somebody else for supplies to start a big fight with life: I'll be content with just surviving, and I can do it on an eighteen-hundred-dollar-a-year consulship. An ex-congressman can always be pretty sure of getting some such job, and I hear from Washington the matter's about settled. I'll live pleasantly enough with a pitcher of ice under a palm tree, and black folks to wait on me—that part of it will be like home—and I'll manage to send you fifty dollars every now and then, after I once get settled. So much for me! But you—of course you've had a poor training for making your own way, but you're only a boy after all, and the stuff of the old stock is in you. It'll come out and do something. I'll never forgive myself about that deed: it would have given you something substantial to start with. Still, you have a little tiny bit, and you'll have a little tiny salary, too; and of course your Aunt Fanny's here, and she's got something you can fall back on if you get *too* pinched, until I can begin to send you a dribble now and then."

George's "little tiny bit" was six hundred dollars which had come to him from the sale of his mother's furniture; and the "little tiny salary" was eight dollars a week which old Frank Bronson was to pay him for services as a clerk and student-at-law. Old Frank would have offered more to the Major's grandson, but since the death of that best of clients and his own experience with automobile headlights, he was not certain of being able to pay more and at the same time settle his own small bills for board and lodging. George had accepted haughtily, and thereby removed a burden from his uncle's mind.

Amberson himself, however, had not even a "tiny bit"; though he got his consular appointment; and to take him to his post he found it necessary to borrow two hundred of his nephew's six hundred dollars. "It makes me sick, George," he said. "But I'd better get there and get that salary started. Of course Eugene would do anything in the world, and the fact is he wanted to, but I felt that—ah—under the circumstances—"

"Never!" George exclaimed, growing red. "I can't imagine one of the family—" He paused, not finding it necessary to explain that "the family" shouldn't turn a man from the door and then accept favours from him. "I wish you'd take more."

Amberson declined. "One thing I'll say for you, young George; you haven't a stingy bone in your body. That's the Amberson stock in you—and I like it!"

He added something to this praise of his nephew on the day he left for Washington. He was not to return, but to set forth from the capital on the long journey to his post. George went with him to the station, and their farewell was lengthened by the train's being several minutes late.

"I may not see you again, Georgie," Amberson said; and his voice was a little husky as he set a kind hand on the young man's shoulder. "It's quite probable that from this time on we'll only know each other by letter—until you're notified as my next of kin that there's an old valise to be forwarded to you, and perhaps some dusty curios from the consulate mantelpiece. Well, it's an odd way for us to be saying good-bye: one wouldn't have thought it, even a few years ago, but here we are, two gentlemen of elegant appearance in a state of bustitude. We can't ever tell what will happen at all, can we? Once I stood where we're standing now, to say good-bye to a pretty girl—only it was in the old station before this was built, and we called it the 'dépôt.' She'd been visiting your mother, before Isabel was married, and I was wild about her, and she admitted she didn't mind that. In fact, we decided we couldn't live without each other, and we were to be married. But she had to go abroad first with her father, and when we came to say good-bye we knew we wouldn't see each other again for almost a year. I thought I couldn't live through it—and she stood here crying. Well, I don't even know where she lives now, or if she *is* living—and I only happen to think of her sometimes when I'm here at the station waiting for a train. If she ever thinks of me she probably imagines I'm still dancing in the ballroom at the Amberson Mansion, and she probably thinks of the Mansion as still beautiful—still the finest house in town. Life and money both behave like loose quicksilver in a nest of cracks. And when they're gone we can't tell where—or what the devil we did with 'em! But I believe I'll say now—while there isn't much time left for either of us to get embarrassed about it—I believe I'll say that I've always been fond of you, Georgie, but I can't say that I always liked you. Sometimes I've felt you were distinctly *not* an acquired taste. Until lately, one had to be fond of you just *naturally*—this isn't very 'tactful,' of course—for if he didn't, well, he wouldn't! We all spoiled you terribly when you were a little boy and let you grow up *en prince*—and I must say you took to it! But you've received a pretty heavy jolt, and I had enough of your disposition, myself, at your age, to understand a little of what cocksure youth has to go through inside when it finds that it *can* make terrible mistakes. Poor old fellow! You get both kinds of jolts together, spiritual and material—and you've taken them pretty quietly and—well, with my train coming into the shed, you'll forgive me for saying that there have been times when I thought you ought to be hanged—but I've always been fond of you, and now I *like* you! And just for a last word: there may be somebody else in this town who's always felt about you like that—fond of you, I mean, no matter how much it seemed you ought to be hanged. You might try— Hello, I must run. I'll send back the money as fast as they pay me—so, good-bye and God bless you, Georgie!"

He passed through the gates, waved his hat cheerily from the other side of the iron screen, and was lost from sight in the hurrying crowd. And as he disappeared, an unexpected poignant loneliness fell upon his nephew so heavily and so suddenly that he had no energy to recoil from the shock. It seemed to him that the last fragment of his familiar world had disappeared, leaving him all alone forever.

He walked homeward slowly through what appeared to be the strange streets of a strange city; and, as a matter of fact, the city was strange to him. He had seen little of it during his years in college, and then had followed the long absence and his tragic return. Since that he had been "scarcely outdoors at all," as Fanny complained, warning him that his health would suffer, and he had been downtown only in a closed carriage. He had not realized the great change.

The streets were thunderous; a vast energy heaved under the universal coating of dinginess. George walked through the begrimed crowds of hurrying strangers and saw no face that he remembered. Great numbers of the faces were even of a kind he did not remember ever to have seen; they were partly like the old type that his boyhood knew, and partly like types he knew abroad. He saw German eyes with American wrinkles at their corners; he saw Irish eyes and Neapolitan eyes, Roman eyes, Tuscan eyes, eyes of Lombardy, of Savoy, Hungarian eyes, Balkan eyes, Scandinavian eyes—all with a queer American look in them. He saw Jews who had been German Jews, Jews who had been Russian Jews, Jews who had been Polish Jews but were no longer German or Russian or Polish Jews. All the people were soiled by the smoke-mist through which they hurried, under the heavy sky that hung close upon the new skyscrapers; and nearly all seemed harried by something impending, though here and there a woman with bundles would be laughing to a companion about some adventure of the department stores, or perhaps an escape from the charging traffic of the streets—and not infrequently a girl, or a free-and-easy young matron, found time to throw an encouraging look to George.

He took no note of these, and, leaving the crowded sidewalks, turned north into National Avenue, and presently reached the quieter but no less begrimed region of smaller shops and old-fashioned houses. Those latter had been the homes of his boyhood playmates; old friends of his grandfather had lived here;—in this alley he had fought with two boys at the same time, and whipped them; in that front yard he had been successfully teased into temporary insanity by a Sunday-school class of pinky little girls. On that sagging porch a laughing woman had fed him and other boys with doughnuts and gingerbread; yonder he saw the staggered relics of the iron picket fence he had made his white pony jump, on a dare, and in the shabby, stone-faced house behind the fence he had gone to children's parties, and, when he was a little older he had danced there often, and fallen in love with Mary Sharon, and kissed her, apparently by force, under the stairs in the hall. The double front doors, of meaninglessly carved walnut, once so glossily varnished, had been painted smoke gray, but the smoke grime showed repulsively, even on the smoke gray; and over the doors a smoked sign proclaimed the place to be a "Stag Hotel."

Other houses had become boarding-houses too genteel for signs, but many were franker, some offering "board by the day, week or meal," and some, more laconic, contenting themselves with the label: "Rooms." One, having torn out part of an old stone-trimmed bay window for purposes of commercial display, showed forth two suspended petticoats and a pair of oyster-coloured flannel trousers to prove the claims of its black-and-gilt sign: "French Cleaning and Dye House." Its next neighbour also sported a remodelled front and permitted no doubt that its mission in life was to attend cosily upon death: "J. M. Rolsener. Caskets. The Funeral Home." And beyond that, a plain old honest four-square gray-painted brick house was flamboyantly decorated with a great gilt scroll on the railing of the old-fashioned veranda: "Mutual Benev't Order Cavaliers and Dames of Purity." This was the old Minafer house.

George passed it without perceptibly wincing; in fact, he held his head up, and except for his gravity of countenance and the prison pallor he had acquired by too constantly remaining indoors, there was little to warn an acquaintance that he was not precisely the same George Amberson Minafer known aforetime. He was still so magnificent, indeed, that there came to his ears a waft of comment from a passing automobile. This was a fearsome red car, glittering in brass, with half-a-dozen young people in it whose motorism had reached an extreme manifestation in dress. The ladies of this party were favourably affected at sight of the pedestrian upon the sidewalk, and, as the machine was moving slowly, and close to the curb, they had time to observe him in detail, which they did with a frankness not pleasing to the object of their attentions. "One sees so many nice-looking people one doesn't know nowadays," said the youngest of the young ladies. "This old town of ours is really getting enormous. I shouldn't mind knowing who he is."

"*I* don't know," the youth beside her said, loudly enough to be heard at a considerable distance. "I don't know who he is, but from his looks I know who he thinks he is: he thinks he's the Grand Duke Cuthbert!" There was a burst of tittering as the car gathered speed and rolled away, with the girl continuing to look back until her scandalized companions forced her to turn by pulling her hood over her face. She made an impression upon George, so deep a one, in fact, that he unconsciously put his emotion into a muttered word:

"Riffraff!"

This was the last "walk home" he was ever to take by the route he was now following: up National Avenue to Amberson Addition and the two big old houses at the foot of Amberson Boulevard; for tonight would be the last night that he and Fanny were to spend in the house which the Major had forgotten to deed to Isabel. To-morrow they were to "move out," and George was to begin his work in Bronson's office. He had not come to this collapse without a fierce struggle—but the struggle was inward, and the rolling world was not agitated by it, and rolled calmly on. For of all the "ideals of life" which the world, in its rolling, inconsiderately flattens out to nothingness, the least likely to retain a profile is that ideal which depends upon inheriting money. George Amberson, in spite of his record of failures in business, had spoken shrewdly when he realized at last that money, like life, was "like quicksilver in a nest of cracks." And his nephew had the awakening experience of seeing the great Amberson Estate vanishing into such a nest—in a twinkling, it seemed, now that it was indeed so utterly vanished.

His uncle had suggested that he might write to college friends; perhaps they could help him to something better than the prospect offered by Bronson's office; but George flushed and shook his head, without explaining. In that small and quietly superior "crowd" of his he had too emphatically supported the ideal of being rather than doing. He could not appeal to one of its members now to help him to a job. Besides, they were not precisely the warmest-hearted crew in the world, and he had long ago dropped the last affectation of a correspondence with any of them. He was as aloof from any survival of intimacy with his boyhood friends in the city, and, in truth, had lost track of most of them. "The

Friends of the Ace," once bound by oath to succour one another in peril or poverty, were long ago dispersed; one or two had died; one or two had gone to live elsewhere; the others were disappeared into the smoky bigness of the heavy city. Of the brethren, there remained within his present cognizance only his old enemy, the red-haired Kinney, now married to Janie Sharon, and Charlie Johnson, who, out of deference to his mother's memory, had passed the Amberson Mansion one day, when George stood upon the front steps, and, looking in fiercely, had looked away with continued fierceness—his only token of recognition.

... On this last homeward walk of his, when George reached the entrance to Amberson Addition—that is, when he came to where the entrance had formerly been—he gave a little start, and halted for a moment to stare. This was the first time he had noticed that the stone pillars, marking the entrance, had been removed. Then he realized that for a long time he had been conscious of a queerness about this corner without being aware of what made the difference. National Avenue met Amberson Boulevard here at an obtuse angle, and the removal of the pillars made the Boulevard seem a cross-street of no overpowering importance—certainly it did not seem to be a boulevard!

At the next corner Neptune's Fountain remained, and one could still determine with accuracy what its designer's intentions had been. It stood in sore need of just one last kindness; and if the thing had possessed any friends they would have done that doleful shovelling after dark.

George did not let his eyes linger upon the relic; nor did he look steadfastly at the Amberson Mansion. Massive as the old house was, it managed to look gaunt: its windows stared with the skull emptiness of all windows in empty houses that are to be lived in no more. Of course the rowdy boys of the neighbourhood had been at work: many of these haggard windows were broken; the front door stood ajar, forced open; and idiot salacity, in white chalk, was smeared everywhere upon the pillars and stonework of the verandas.

George walked by the Mansion hurriedly, and came home to his mother's house for the last time.

Emptiness was there, too, and the closing of the door resounded through bare rooms; for downstairs there was no furniture in the house except a kitchen table in the dining room, which Fanny had kept "for dinner," she said, though as she was to cook and serve that meal herself George had his doubts about her name for it. Upstairs, she had retained her own furniture, and George had been living in his mother's room, having sent everything from his own to the auction. Isabel's room was still as it had been, but the furniture would be moved with Fanny's to new quarters in the morning. Fanny had made plans for her nephew as well as herself; she had found a "three-room kitchenette apartment" in an apartment house where several old friends of hers had established themselves—elderly widows of citizens once "prominent" and other retired gentry. People used their own "kitchenettes" for breakfast and lunch, but there was a table-d'hôte arrangement for dinner on the ground floor; and after dinner bridge was played all evening, an attraction powerful with Fanny. She had "made all the arrangements," she reported, and nervously appealed for approval, asking if she hadn't shown herself "pretty practical" in such matters. George acquiesced absent-mindedly, not thinking of what she said and not realizing to what it committed him.

He began to realize it now, as he wandered about the dismantled house; he was far from sure that he was willing to go and live in a "three-room apartment" with Fanny and eat breakfast and lunch with her (prepared by herself in the "kitchenette") and dinner at the table d'hôte in "such a pretty Colonial dining room" (so Fanny described it) at a little round table they would have all to themselves in the midst of a dozen little round tables which other relics of disrupted families would have all to themselves. For the first time, now that the change was imminent, George began to develop before his mind's eye pictures of what he was in for; and they appalled him. He decided that such a life verged upon the sheerly unbearable, and that after all there were some things left that he just couldn't stand. So he made up his mind to speak to his aunt about it at "dinner," and tell her that he preferred to ask Bronson to let him put a sofa-bed, a trunk, and a folding rubber bathtub behind a screen in the dark rear room of the office. George felt that this would be infinitely more tolerable; and he could eat at restaurants, especially as about all he ever wanted nowadays was coffee.

But at "dinner" he decided to put off telling Fanny of his plan until later: she was so nervous, and so distressed about the failure of her efforts with sweetbreads and macaroni; and she was so eager in her talk of how comfortable they would be "by this time to-morrow night." She fluttered on, her nervousness increasing, saying how "nice" it would be for him, when he came from work in the evenings, to be among "nice people—people who know who we *are*," and to have a pleasant game of bridge with "people who are really old friends of the family."

When they stopped probing among the scorched fragments she had set forth, George lingered downstairs, waiting for a better opportunity to introduce his own subject, but when he heard dismaying sounds from the kitchen he gave up. There was a crash, then a shower of crashes; falling tin clamoured to be heard above the shattering of porcelain; and over all rose Fanny's wail of lamentation for the treasures saved from the sale, but now lost forever to the "kitchenette." Fanny was nervous indeed; so nervous that she could not trust her hands.

For a moment George thought she might have been injured, but, before he reached the kitchen, he heard her sweeping at the fragments, and turned back. He put off speaking to Fanny until morning.

Things more insistent than his vague plans for a sofa-bed in Bronson's office had possession of his mind as he went upstairs, moving his hand slowly along the smooth walnut railing of the balustrade. Half way to the landing he stopped, turned, and stood looking down at the heavy doors masking the black emptiness that had been the library. Here he had stood on what he now knew was the worst day of his life; here he had stood when his mother passed through that doorway, hand-in-hand with her brother, to learn what her son had done.

He went on more heavily, more slowly; and, more heavily and slowly still, entered Isabel's room and shut the door. He did not come forth again, and bade Fanny good-night through the closed door when she stopped outside it later.

"I've put all the lights out, George," she said. "Everything's all right."

"Very well," he called. "Good-night."

She did not go. "I'm sure we're going to enjoy the new little home, George," she said timidly. "I'll try hard to make things nice for you, and the people really are lovely. You mustn't feel as if things are altogether gloomy, George. I know everything's going to turn out all right. You're young and strong and you have a good mind and I'm sure—" she hesitated—"I'm sure your mother's watching over you, Georgie. Good-night, dear."

"Good-night, Aunt Fanny."

His voice had a strangled sound in spite of him; but she seemed not to notice it, and he heard her go to her own room and lock herself in with bolt and key against burglars. She had said the one thing she should not have said just then: "I'm sure your mother's watching over you, Georgie." She had meant to be kind, but it destroyed his last chance for sleep that night. He would have slept little if she had not said it, but since she had said it, he did not sleep at all. For he knew that it was true—if it *could* be true—and that his mother, if she still lived in spirit, would be weeping on the other side of the wall of silence, weeping and seeking for some gate to let her through so that she could come and "watch over him."

He felt that if there were such gates they were surely barred: they were like those awful library doors downstairs, which had shut her in to begin the suffering to which he had consigned her.

The room was still Isabel's. Nothing had been changed: even the photographs of George, of the Major, and of "brother George" still stood on her dressing-table, and in a drawer of her desk was an old picture of Eugene and Lucy, taken together, which George had found, but had slowly closed away again from sight, not touching it. To-morrow everything would be gone; and he had heard there was not long to wait before the house itself would be demolished. The very space which to-night was still Isabel's room would be cut into new shapes by new walls and floors and ceilings; yet the room would always live, for it could not die out of George's memory. It would live as long as he did, and it would always be murmurous with a tragic, wistful whispering.

And if space itself can be haunted, as memory is haunted, then some time, when the space that was Isabel's room came to be made into the small bedrooms and "kitchenettes" already designed as its destiny, that space might well be haunted and the new occupants come to feel that some seemingly causeless depression hung about it—a wraith of the passion that filled it throughout the last night that George Minafer spent there.

Whatever remnants of the old high-handed arrogance were still within him, he did penance for his deepest sin that night—and it may be that to this day some impressionable, overworked woman in a "kitchenette," after turning out the light, will seem to see a young man kneeling in the darkness, shaking convulsively, and, with arms outstretched through the wall, clutching at the covers of a shadowy bed. It may seem to her that she hears the faint cry, over and over:

"Mother, forgive me! *God,* forgive me!"

CHAPTER XXXII

At least, it may be claimed for George that his last night in the house where he had been born was not occupied with his own disheartening future, but with sorrow for what sacrifices his pride and youth had demanded of others. And early in the morning he came downstairs and tried to help Fanny make coffee on the kitchen range.

"There was something I wanted to say to you last night, Aunt Fanny," he said, as she finally discovered that an amber fluid, more like tea than coffee, was as near ready to be taken into the human system as it would ever be. "I think I'd better do it now."

She set the coffee-pot back upon the stove with a little crash, and, looking at him in a desperate anxiety, began to twist her dainty apron between her fingers without any consciousness of what she was doing.

"Why—why—" she stammered; but she knew what he was going to say, and that was why she had been more and more nervous. "Hadn't—perhaps—perhaps we'd better get the—the things moved to the little new home first, George. Let's—"

He interrupted quietly, though at her phrase, "the little new home," his pungent impulse was to utter one loud shout and run. "It was about this new place that I wanted to speak. I've been thinking it over, and I've decided. I want you to take all the things from mother's room and use them and keep them for me, and I'm sure the little apartment will be just what you like; and with the extra bedroom probably you could find some woman friend to come and live there, and share the expense with you. But I've decided on another arrangement for myself, and so I'm not going with you. I don't suppose you'll mind much, and I don't see why you *should* mind—particularly, that is. I'm not very lively company these days, or any days, for that matter. I can't imagine you, or any one else, being much attached to me, so—"

He stopped in amazement: no chair had been left in the kitchen, but Fanny gave a despairing glance around her, in search of one, then sank abruptly, and sat flat upon the floor.

"You're going to leave me in the lurch!" she gasped.

"What on earth—" George sprang to her. "Get up, Aunt Fanny!"

"I can't. I'm too weak. Let me alone, George!" And as he released the wrist he had seized to help her, she repeated the dismal prophecy which for days she had been matching against her hopes: "You're going to leave me—in the lurch!"

"Why no, Aunt Fanny!" he protested. "At first I'd have been something of a burden on you. I'm to get eight dollars a week; about thirty-two a month. The rent's thirty-six dollars a month, and the table d'hôte dinner runs up to over twenty-two dollars apiece, so with my half of the rent—eighteen dollars—I'd have less than nothing left out of my salary to pay my share of the groceries for all the breakfasts and luncheons. You see you'd not only be doing all the housework and cooking, but you'd be paying more of the expenses than I would."

She stared at him with such a forlorn blankness as he had never seen. "I'd be paying—" she said feebly. "I'd be paying—"

"Certainly you would. You'd be using more of your money than—"

"My money!" Fanny's chin drooped upon her thin chest, and she laughed miserably. "I've got twenty-eight dollars. That's all."

"You mean until the interest is due again?"

"I mean that's all," Fanny said. "I mean that's all there is. There won't be any more interest because there isn't any principal."

"Why, you told—"

She shook her head. "No. I haven't told you anything."

"Then it was Uncle George. *He* told me you had enough to fall back on. That's just what he said: 'to fall back on.' He said you'd lost more than you should, in the headlight company, but he'd insisted that you should hold out enough to live on, and you'd very wisely followed his advice."

"I know," she said weakly. "I told him so. He didn't know, or else he'd forgotten, how much Wilbur's insurance amounted to, and I—oh, it seemed such a sure way to make a real fortune out of a little—and I thought I could do something for *you*, George, if you ever came to need it—and it all looked so bright I just thought I'd put it all in. I did—every cent except my last interest payment—and it's gone."

"Good Lord!" George began to pace up and down the worn planks of the bare floor. "Why on earth did you wait till now to tell such a thing as this?"

"I *couldn't* tell till I had to," she said piteously. "I couldn't till George Amberson went away. He couldn't do anything to help, anyhow, and I just didn't want him to talk to me about it—he's been at me so much about not putting more in than I could afford to lose, and said he considered he had my—my word I *wasn't* putting more than that in it. So I thought: What was the use? What was the use of going over it all with him and having him reproach me, and probably reproach himself? It wouldn't do any good—not any good on earth." She got out her lace handkerchief and began to cry. "Nothing does any good, I guess, in this old world! Oh, how tired of this old world I am! I didn't know *what* to do. I just tried to go ahead and be as practical as I could, and arrange *some* way for us to live. Oh, I knew you didn't want me, George! You always teased me and berated me whenever you had a chance from the time you were a little boy—you did *so*! Later, you've tried to be kinder to me, but you don't want me around—oh, I can see *that* much! You don't suppose I want to thrust myself on you, do you? It isn't very pleasant to be thrusting yourself on a person you know doesn't want you—but I knew you oughtn't to be left all alone in the world; it isn't good. I knew your mother'd want me to watch over you and try to have *something* like a home for you—I know she'd want me to do what I tried to do!" Fanny's tears were bitter now, and her voice, hoarse and wet, was tragically sincere. "I tried—I tried to be practical—to look after your interests—to make things as nice for you as I could—I walked my heels down looking for a place for us to live—I walked and walked over this town—I didn't ride one block on a street-car—I wouldn't use five cents no matter how tired I— Oh!" She sobbed uncontrollably. "Oh! and now—you don't want—you want—you want to leave me in the lurch! You—"

George stopped walking. "In God's name, Aunt Fanny," he said, "quit spreading out your handkerchief and drying it and then getting it all wet again! I mean stop crying! Do! And for heaven's sake, get up. Don't sit there with your back against the boiler and—"

"It's not hot," Fanny sniffled. "It's cold; the plumbers disconnected it. I wouldn't mind if they hadn't. *I* wouldn't mind if it burned me, George."

"Oh, my *Lord!*" He went to her, and lifted her. "For God's sake, get up! Come, let's take the coffee into the other room, and see what's to be done."

He got her to her feet; she leaned upon him, already somewhat comforted, and, with his arm about her, he conducted her to the dining room and seated her in one of the two kitchen chairs which had been placed at the rough table. "There!" he said, "get over it!" Then he brought the coffee-pot, some lumps of sugar in a tin pan, and, finding that all the coffee-cups were broken, set water glasses upon the table, and poured some of the pale coffee into them. By this time Fanny's spirits had revived appreciably: she looked up with a plaintive eagerness. "I *had* bought all my fall clothes, George," she said; "and I paid every bill I owed. I don't owe a cent for clothes, George."

"That's good," he said wanly, and he had a moment of physical dizziness that decided him to sit down quickly. For an instant it seemed to him that he was not Fanny's nephew, but married to her. He passed his pale hand over his paler forehead. "Well, let's see where we stand," he said feebly. "Let's see if we can afford this place you've selected."

Fanny continued to brighten. "I'm sure it's the most practical plan we could possibly have worked out, George—and it *is* a comfort to be among nice people. I think we'll both enjoy it, because the truth is we've been keeping too much to ourselves for a long while. It isn't good for people."

"I was thinking about the money, Aunt Fanny. You see—"

"I'm sure we can manage it," she interrupted quickly. "There really isn't a cheaper place in town that we could actually live in and be—" Here she interrupted herself. "Oh! There's one *great* economy I forgot to tell you, and it's especially an economy for you, because you're always too generous about such things: they don't allow any tipping. They have signs that prohibit it."

"That's good," he said grimly. "But the rent is thirty-six dollars a month; the dinner is twenty-two and a half for each of us, and we've got to have some provision for other food. We won't need any clothes for a year, perhaps—"

"Oh, longer!" she exclaimed. "So you see—"

"I see that forty-five and thirty-six make eighty-one," he said. "At the lowest, we need a hundred dollars a month—and I'm going to make thirty-two."

"I thought of that, George," she said confidently, "and I'm sure it will be all right. You'll be earning a great deal more than that very soon."

"I don't see any prospect of it—not till I'm admitted to the bar, and that will be two years at the earliest."

Fanny's confidence was not shaken. "I know *you'll* be getting on faster than—"

" 'Faster'?" George echoed gravely. "We've got to have more than that to start with."

"Well, there's the six hundred dollars from the sale. Six hundred and twelve dollars it was."

"It isn't six hundred and twelve now," said George. "It's about one hundred and sixty."

Fanny showed a momentary dismay. "Why, how—"

"I lent Uncle George two hundred; I gave fifty apiece to old Sam and those two other old darkies that worked for grandfather so long, and ten to each of the servants here—"

"And you gave me thirty-six," she said thoughtfully, "for the first month's rent, in advance."

"Did I? I'd forgotten. Well, with about a hundred and sixty in bank and our expenses a hundred a month, it doesn't seem as if this new place—"

"Still," she interrupted, "we *have* paid the first month's rent in advance, and it does seem to be the most practical—"

George rose. "See here, Aunt Fanny," he said decisively. "You stay here and look after the moving. Old Frank doesn't expect me until afternoon, this first day, but I'll go and see him now."

. . . It was early, and old Frank, just established at his big, flat-topped desk, was surprised when his prospective assistant and pupil walked in. He was pleased, as well as surprised, however, and rose, offering a cordial old hand. "The real flare!" he said. "The real flare for the law. That's right! Couldn't wait till afternoon to begin! I'm delighted that you—"

"I wanted to say—" George began, but his patron cut him off.

"Wait just a minute, my boy. I've prepared a little speech of welcome, and even though you're five hours ahead of time, I mean to deliver it. First of all, your grandfather was my old war-comrade and my best client; for years I prospered through my connection with his business, and his grandson is welcome in my office and to my best efforts in his behalf. But I want to confess, Georgie, that during your earlier youth I may have had some slight feeling of—well, prejudice, not altogether in your favour; but whatever slight feeling it was, it began to vanish on that afternoon, a good while ago, when you stood up to your Aunt Amelia Amberson as you did in the Major's library, and talked to her as a man and a gentleman should. I saw then what good stuff was in you—and I always wanted to mention it. If my prejudice hadn't altogether vanished after that, the last vestiges disappeared during these trying times that have come upon you this past year, when I have been a witness to the depth of feeling you've shown and your quiet consideration for your grandfather and for everyone else around you. I just want to add that I think you'll find an honest pleasure now in industry and frugality that wouldn't have come to you in a more frivolous career. The law is a jealous mistress and a stern mistress, but a—"

George had stood before him in great and increasing embarrassment; and he was unable to allow the address to proceed to its conclusion.

"I can't do it!" he burst out. "I can't take her for my mistress."

"What?"

"I've come to tell you, I've got to find something that's quicker. I can't—"

Old Frank got a little red. "Let's sit down," he said. "What's the trouble?"

George told him.

The old gentleman listened sympathetically, only murmuring: "Well, well!" from time to time, and nodding acquiescence.

"You see she's set her mind on this apartment," George explained. "She's got some old cronies there, and I guess she's been looking forward to the games of bridge and the kind of harmless gossip that goes on in such places. Really, it's a life she'd like better than anything else—better than that she's lived at home, I really believe. It struck me she's just about got to have it, and after all she could hardly have anything less."

"This comes pretty heavily upon me, you know," said old Frank. "I got her into that headlight company, and she fooled me about her resources as much as she did your Uncle George. I was never your father's adviser, if you remember, and when the insurance was turned over to her some other lawyer arranged it—probably your father's. But it comes pretty heavily on me, and I feel a certain responsibility."

"Not at all. I'm taking the responsibility." And George smiled with one corner of his mouth. "She's not *your* aunt, you know, sir."

"Well, I'm unable to see, even if she's yours, that a young man is morally called upon to give up a career at the law to provide his aunt with a favourable opportunity to play bridge whist!"

"No," George agreed. "But I haven't begun my 'career at the law' so it can't be said I'm making any considerable sacrifice. I'll tell you how it is, sir." He flushed, and, looking out of the streaked and smoky window beside which he was sitting, spoke with difficulty. "I feel as if—as if perhaps I had one or two pretty important things in my life to make up for. Well, I can't. I can't make them up to—to whom I would. It's struck me that, as I couldn't, I might be a little decent to somebody else, perhaps—if I could manage it! I never have been particularly decent to poor old Aunt Fanny."

"Oh, I don't know: I shouldn't say that. A little youthful teasing—I doubt if she's minded so much. She felt your father's death terrifically, of course, but it seems to me she's had a fairly comfortable life—up to now—if she was disposed to take it that way."

"But 'up to now' is the important thing," George said. "Now is now—and you see I can't wait two years to be admitted to the bar and begin to practice. I've got to start in at something else that pays from the start, and that's what I've come to you about. I have an idea, you see."

"Well, I'm glad of that!" said old Frank, smiling. "I can't think of anything just at this minute that pays from the start."

"I only know of one thing, myself."

"What is it?"

George flushed again, but managed to laugh at his own embarrassment. "I suppose I'm about as ignorant of business as anybody in the world," he said. "But I've heard they pay very high wages to people in dangerous trades; I've always heard they did, and I'm sure it must be true. I mean people that handle touchy chemicals or high explosives—men in dynamite factories, or who take things of that sort about the country in wagons, and shoot oil wells. I thought I'd see if you couldn't tell me something more about it, or else introduce me to someone who could, and then I thought I'd see if I couldn't get something of the kind to do as soon as possible. My nerves are good; I'm muscular, and I've got a steady hand; it seemed to me that this was about the only line of work in the world that I'm fitted for. I wanted to get started to-day if I could."

Old Frank gave him a long stare. At first this scrutiny was sharply incredulous; then it was grave; finally it developed into a threat of overwhelming laughter; a forked vein in his forehead became more visible and his eyes seemed about to protrude.

But he controlled his impulse; and, rising, took up his hat and overcoat. "All right," he said. "If you'll promise not to get blown up, I'll go with you to see if we can find the job." Then, meaning what he said, but amazed that he did mean it, he added: "You certainly are the most practical young man I ever met!"

Chapter XXXIII

They found the job. It needed an apprenticeship of only six weeks, during which period George was to receive fifteen dollars a week; after that he would get twenty-eight. This settled the apartment question, and Fanny was presently established in a greater contentment than she had known for a long time. Early every morning she made something she called (and believed to be) coffee for George, and he was gallant enough not to undeceive her. She lunched alone in her "kitchenette," for George's place of employment was ten miles out of town on an interurban trolley-line, and he seldom returned before seven. Fanny found partners for bridge by two o'clock almost every afternoon, and she played until about six. Then she got George's "dinner clothes" out for him—he maintained this habit—and she changed her own dress. When he arrived he usually denied that he was tired, though he sometimes looked tired, particularly during the first few months; and he explained to her frequently—looking bored enough with her insistence—that his work was "fairly light, and fairly congenial, too." Fanny had the foggiest idea of what it was, though she noticed that it roughened his hands and stained them. "Something in those new chemical works," she explained to casual inquirers. It was not more definite in her own mind.

Respect for George undoubtedly increased within her, however, and she told him she'd always had a feeling he might "turn out to be a mechanical genius, or something." George assented with a nod, as the easiest course open to him. He did not take a hand at bridge after dinner: his provisions for Fanny's happiness refused to extend that far, and at the table d'hôte he was a rather discouraging boarder. He was considered "affected" and absurdly "up-stage" by the one or two young men, and the three or four young women, who enlivened the elderly retreat; and was possibly less popular there than he had been elsewhere during his life, though he was now nothing worse than a coldly polite young man who kept to himself. After dinner he would escort his aunt from the table in some state (not wholly unaccompanied by a leerish wink or two from the wags of the place) and he would leave her at the door of the communal parlours and card rooms, with a formality in his bow of farewell which afforded an amusing contrast to Fanny's always voluble protests. (She never failed to urge loudly that he really *must* come and play, just this once, and not go hiding from everybody in his room *every* evening like this!) At least some of the other inhabitants found the contrast amusing, for sometimes, as he departed stiffly toward the elevator, leaving her still entreating in the doorway (though with one eye already on her table, to see that it was not seized) a titter would follow him which he was no doubt meant to hear. He did not care whether they laughed or not.

And once, as he passed the one or two young men of the place entertaining the three or four young women, who were elbowing and jerking on a settee in the lobby, he heard a voice inquiring quickly, as he passed:

"What makes people tired?"

"Work?"

"No."

"Well, what's the answer?"

Then, with an intentional outbreak of mirth, the answer was given by two loudly whispering voices together:

"A stuck-up boarder!"

George didn't care.

On Sunday mornings Fanny went to church and George took long walks. He explored the new city, and found it hideous, especially in the early spring, before the leaves of the shade trees were out. Then the town was fagged with the long winter and blacked with the heavier smoke that had been held close to the earth by the smoke-fog it bred. Everything was damply streaked with the soot: the walls of the houses, inside and out, the gray curtains at the windows, the windows themselves, the dirty cement and unswept asphalt underfoot, the very sky overhead. Throughout this murky season he continued his explorations, never seeing a face he knew—for, on Sunday, those whom he remembered, or who might remember him, were not apt to be found within the limits of the town, but were congenially occupied with the new outdoor life which had come to be the mode since his boyhood. He and Fanny were pretty thoroughly buried away within the bigness of the city.

One of his Sunday walks, that spring, he made into a sour pilgrimage. It was a misty morning of belated snow slush, and suited him to a perfection of miserableness, as he stood before the great dripping department store which now occupied the big plot of ground where once had stood both the Amberson Hotel and the Amberson Opera House. From there he drifted to the old "Amberson Block," but this was fallen into a back-water; business had stagnated here. The old structure had not been replaced, but a cavernous entryway for trucks had been torn in its front, and upon the cornice, where the old separate metal letters had spelt "Amberson Block," there was a long billboard sign: "Doogan Storage."

To spare himself nothing, he went out National Avenue and saw the piles of slush-covered wreckage where the Mansion and his mother's house had been, and where the Major's ill-fated five "new" houses had stood; for these were down, too, to make room for the great tenement already shaped in unending lines of foundation. But the Fountain of Neptune was gone at last—and George was glad that it was!

He turned away from the devastated site, thinking bitterly that the only Amberson mark still left upon the town was the name of the boulevard—Amberson Boulevard. But he had reckoned without the city council of the new order, and by an unpleasant coincidence, while the thought was still in his mind, his eye fell upon a metal oblong sign upon the lamppost at the corner. There were two of these little signs upon the lamp-post, at an obtuse angle to each other, one to give passers-by the name of National Avenue, the other to acquaint them with Amberson Boulevard. But the one upon which should have been stencilled "Amberson Boulevard" exhibited the words "Tenth Street."

George stared at it hard. Then he walked quickly along the boulevard to the next corner and looked at the little sign there. "Tenth Street."

It had begun to rain, but George stood unheeding, staring at the little sign. "Damn them!" he said finally, and, turning up his coat-collar, plodded back through the soggy streets toward "home."

The utilitarian impudence of the city authorities put a thought into

his mind. A week earlier he had happened to stroll into the large parlour of the apartment house, finding it empty, and on the centre-table
he noticed a large, red-bound, gilt-edged book, newly printed, bearing
the title: "A Civic History," and beneath the title, the rubric, "Biogra-
phies of the 500 Most Prominent Citizens and Families in the History
of the City." He had glanced at it absently, merely noticing the title
and sub-title, and wandered out of the room, thinking of other things
and feeling no curiosity about the book. But he had thought of it several times since with a faint, vague uneasiness; and now when he entered the lobby he walked directly into the parlour where he had seen
the book. The room was empty, as it always was on Sunday mornings,
and the flamboyant volume was still upon the table—evidently a fix-
ture as a sort of local Almanach de Gotha, or Burke, for the enlightenment of tenants and boarders.

He opened it, finding a few painful steel engravings of placid, chin-
bearded faces, some of which he remembered dimly; but much more
numerous, and also more unfamiliar to him, were the pictures of neat,
aggressive men, with clipped short hair and clipped short moustaches—
almost all of them strangers to him. He delayed not long with these, but
turned to the index where the names of the five hundred Most Prominent Citizens and Families in the History of the City were arranged in
alphabetical order, and ran his finger down the column of *A*'s:

Abbett	Ambrose
Abbott	Ambuhl
Abrams	Anderson
Adams	Andrews
Adams	Appenbasch
Adler	Archer
Akers	Arszman
Albertsmeyer	Ashcraft
Alexander	Austin
Allen	Avey

George's eyes remained for some time fixed on the thin space between the names "Allen" and "Ambrose." Then he closed the book quietly, and went up to his own room, agreeing with the elevator boy, on
the way, that it was getting to be a mighty nasty wet and windy day
outside.

The elevator boy noticed nothing unusual about him and neither did Fanny, when she came in from church with her hat ruined, an hour later. And yet something had happened—a thing which, years ago, had been the eagerest hope of many, many good citizens of the town. They had thought of it, longed for it, hoping acutely that they might live to see the day when it would come to pass. And now it had happened at last: Georgie Minafer had got his come-upance.

He had got it three times filled and running over. The city had rolled over his heart, burying it under, as it rolled over the Major's and buried it under. The city had rolled over the Ambersons and buried them under to the last vestige; and it mattered little that George guessed easily enough that most of the five hundred Most Prominent had paid something substantial "to defray the cost of steel engraving, etc."—the Five Hundred had heaved the final shovelful of soot upon that heap of obscurity wherein the Ambersons were lost forever from sight and history. "Quicksilver in a nest of cracks!"

Georgie Minafer had got his come-upance, but the people who had so longed for it were not there to see it, and they never knew it. Those who were still living had forgotten all about it and all about him.

CHAPTER XXXIV

There was one border section of the city which George never explored in his Sunday morning excursions. This was far out to the north where lay the new Elysian Fields of the millionaires, though he once went as far in that direction as the white house which Lucy had so admired long ago—her "Beautiful House." George looked at it briefly and turned back, rumbling with an interior laugh of some grimness. The house was white no longer; nothing could be white which the town had reached, and the town reached far beyond the beautiful white house now. The owners had given up and painted it a despairing chocolate, suitable to the freight-yard life it was called upon to endure.

George did not again risk going even so far as that, in the direction of the millionaires, although their settlement began at least two miles farther out. His thought of Lucy and her father was more a sensation than a thought, and may be compared to that of a convicted cashier beset by recollections of the bank he had pillaged—there are some thoughts to which one closes the mind. George had seen Eugene only once since their calamitous encounter. They had passed on opposite sides of the street, downtown; each had been aware of the other, and each had been aware that the other was aware of him, and yet each kept his eyes straight forward, and neither had shown a perceptible alteration of countenance. It seemed to George that he felt emanating from the outwardly imperturbable person of his mother's old friend a hate that was like a hot wind.

At his mother's funeral and at the Major's he had been conscious that Eugene was there: though he had afterward no recollection of seeing him, and, while certain of his presence, was uncertain how he knew of it. Fanny had not told him, for she understood George well enough not to speak to him of Eugene or Lucy. Nowadays Fanny almost never saw either of them and seldom thought of them—so sly is the way of time with life. She was passing middle age, when old intensities and longings grow thin and flatten out, as Fanny herself was thinning and flattening out; and she was settling down contentedly to her apartment house intimacies. She was precisely suited by the table-d'hôte life, with its bridge, its variable alliances and shifting feuds, and the long whisperings of elderly ladies at corridor corners—those eager but suppressed conversations, all sibilance, of which the elevator boy declared he heard the words "*she said*" a million times and the word "*she,*" five million. The apartment house suited Fanny and swallowed her.

The city was so big, now, that people disappeared into it unnoticed, and the disappearance of Fanny and her nephew was not exceptional. People no longer knew their neighbours as a matter of course; one lived for years next door to strangers—that sharpest of all the changes since the old days—and a friend would lose sight of a friend for a year, and not know it.

One May day George thought he had a glimpse of Lucy. He was not certain, but he was sufficiently disturbed, in spite of his uncertainty. A promotion in his work now frequently took him out of town for a week, or longer, and it was upon his return from one of these absences that he had the strange experience. He had walked home from the station, and as he turned the corner which brought him in sight of the apartment house entrance, though two blocks distant from it, he saw a charming little figure come out, get into a shiny landaulet automobile, and drive away. Even at that distance no one could have any doubt that the little figure was charming; and the height, the quickness and decision of motion, even the swift gesture of a white glove toward the chauffeur—all were characteristic of Lucy. George was instantly subjected to a shock of indefinable nature, yet definitely a shock: he did not know what he felt—but he knew that he felt. Heat surged over him: probably he would not have come face to face with her if the restoration of all the ancient Amberson magnificence could have been his reward. He went on slowly, his knees shaky.

But he found Fanny not at home; she had been out all afternoon; and there was no record of any caller—and he began to wonder, then to doubt if the small lady he had seen in the distance was Lucy. It might as well have been, he said to himself—since any one who looked like her could give him "a jolt like that!"

Lucy had not left a card. She never left one when she called on Fanny; though she did not give her reasons a quite definite form in her own mind. She came seldom; this was but the third time that year, and, when she did come, George was not mentioned, either by her hostess or by herself—an oddity contrived between the two ladies without either of them realizing how odd it was. For, naturally, while Fanny was with Lucy, Fanny thought of George, and what time Lucy had George's aunt before her eyes she could not well avoid the thought of him. Consequently, both looked absent-minded as they talked, and each often gave a wrong answer which the other consistently failed to notice.

At other times Lucy's thoughts of George were anything but continuous, and weeks went by when he was not consciously in her mind at all. Her life was a busy one: she had the big house "to keep up"; she had a garden to keep up, too, a large and beautiful garden; she represented her father as a director for half a dozen public charity organizations, and did private charity work of her own, being a proxy mother of several large families; and she had "danced down," as she said, groups from eight or nine classes of new graduates returned from the universities, without marrying any of them, but she still danced—and still did not marry.

Her father, observing this circumstance happily, yet with some hypocritical concern, spoke of it to her one day as they stood in her garden. "I suppose I'd want to shoot him," he said, with attempted lightness. "But I mustn't be an old pig. I'd build you a beautiful house close by—just over yonder."

"No, no! That would be like—" she began impulsively; then checked herself. George Amberson's comparison of the Georgian house to the Amberson Mansion had come into her mind, and she thought that another new house, built close by for her, would be like the house the Major built for Isabel.

"Like what?"

"Nothing." She looked serious, and when he reverted to his idea of "some day" grudgingly surrendering her up to a suitor, she invented a legend. "Did you ever hear the Indian name for that little grove of beech trees on the other side of the house?" she asked him.

"No—and you never did either!" he laughed.

"Don't be so sure! I read a great deal more than I used to—getting ready for my bookish days when I'll have to do something solid in the evenings and won't be asked to dance any more, even by the very youngest boys who think it's a sporting event to dance with the oldest of the 'older girls.' The name of the grove was 'Loma-Nashah' and it means 'They-Couldn't-Help-It.' "

"Doesn't sound like it."

"Indian names don't. There was a bad Indian chief lived in the grove before the white settlers came. He was the worst Indian that ever lived, and his name was—it was 'Vendonah.' That means 'Rides-Down-Everything.' "

"What?"

"His name was Vendonah, the same thing as Rides-Down-Everything."

"I see," said Eugene thoughtfully. He gave her a quick look and then fixed his eyes upon the end of the garden path. "Go on."

"Vendonah was an unspeakable case," Lucy continued. "He was so proud that he wore iron shoes, and he walked over people's faces with them. He was always killing people that way, and so at last the tribe decided that it wasn't a good enough excuse for him that he was young and inexperienced—he'd have to go. They took him down to the river, and put him in a canoe, and pushed him out for shore; and then they ran along the bank and wouldn't let him land, until at last the current carried the canoe out into the middle, and then on down to the ocean, and he never got back. They didn't want him back, of course, and if he'd been able to manage it, they'd have put him in another canoe and shoved him out into the river again. But still, they didn't elect another chief in his place. Other tribes thought that was curious, and wondered about it a lot, but finally they came to the conclusion that the beech grove people were afraid a new chief might turn out to be a bad Indian, too, and wear iron shoes like Vendonah. But they were wrong, because the real reason was that the tribe had led such an exciting life under Vendonah that they couldn't settle down to anything tamer. He was awful, but he always kept things happening—terrible things, of course. They hated him, but they weren't able to discover any other warrior that they wanted to make chief in his place. I suppose it was a little like drinking a glass of too strong wine and then trying to take the taste out of your mouth with barley water. They couldn't help feeling that way."

"I see," said Eugene. "So that's why they named the place 'They-Couldn't-Help-It'!"

"It must have been."

"And so you're going to stay here in your garden," he said musingly. "You think it's better to keep on walking these sunshiny gravel paths between your flower-beds, and growing to look like a pensive garden lady in a Victorian engraving."

"I suppose I'm like the tribe that lived here, papa. I had too much unpleasant excitement. It was unpleasant—but it was excitement. I don't want any more; in fact, I don't want anything but you."

"You don't?" He looked at her keenly, and she laughed and shook her head; but he seemed perplexed, rather doubtful. "What was the name of the grove?" he asked. "The Indian name, I mean."

"Mola-Haha."

"No, it wasn't; that wasn't the name you said."

"I've forgotten."

"I see you have," he said, his look of perplexity remaining. "Perhaps you remember the chief's name better."

She shook her head again. "I don't!"

At this he laughed, but not very heartily, and walked slowly to the house, leaving her bending over a rose-bush, and a shade more pensive than the most pensive garden lady in any Victorian engraving.... Next day, it happened that this same "Vendonah" or "Rides-Down-Everything" became the subject of a chance conversation between Eugene and his old friend Kinney, father of the fire-topped Fred. The two gentlemen found themselves smoking in neighbouring leather chairs beside a broad window at the club, after lunch.

Mr. Kinney had remarked that he expected to get his family established at the seashore by the Fourth of July, and, following a train of thought, he paused and chuckled. "Fourth of July reminds me," he said. "Have you heard what that Georgie Minafer is doing?"

"No, I haven't," said Eugene, and his friend failed to notice the crispness of the utterance.

"Well, sir," Kinney chuckled again, "it beats the devil! My boy Fred told me about it yesterday. He's a friend of this young Henry Akers, son of F. P. Akers of the Akers Chemical Company. It seems this young Akers asked Fred if he knew a fellow named Minafer, because he knew Fred had always lived here, and young Akers had heard some way that Minafer used to be an old family name here, and was sort of curious about it. Well, sir, you remember this young Georgie sort of disappeared, after his grandfather's death, and nobody seemed to know much what had become of him—though I did hear, once or twice, that he was still around somewhere. Well, sir, he's working for the Akers Chemical Company, out at their plant on the Thomasville Road."

He paused, seeming to reserve something to be delivered only upon inquiry, and Eugene offered him the expected question, but only after a cold glance through the nose-glasses he had lately found it necessary to adopt. "What does he do?"

Kinney laughed and slapped the arm of his chair. "He's a nitro-glycerin expert!"

He was gratified to see that Eugene was surprised, if not, indeed, a little startled.

"He's what?"

"He's an expert on nitro-glycerin. Doesn't that beat the devil! Yes, sir! Young Akers told Fred that this George Minafer had worked like a houn'-dog ever since he got started out at the works. They have a special plant for nitro-glycerin, way off from the main plant, o' course—in the woods somewhere—and George Minafer's been working there, and lately they put him in charge of it. He oversees shooting oil-wells, too, and shoots 'em himself, sometimes. They aren't allowed to carry it on the railroads, you know—have to team it. Young Akers says George rides around over the bumpy roads, sitting on as much as three hundred quarts of nitroglycerin! My Lord! Talk about romantic tumbles! If he gets blown sky-high some day he won't have a bigger drop, when he comes down, than he's already had! Don't it beat the devil! Young Akers said he's got all the nerve there is in the world. Well, he always did have plenty of *that*—from the time he used to ride around here on his white pony and fight all the Irish boys in Can-Town, with his long curls all handy to be pulled out. Akers says he gets a fair salary, and I should think he ought to! Seems to me I've heard the average life in that sort of work is somewhere around four years, and agents don't write any insurance at all for nitro-glycerin experts. Hardly!"

"No," said Eugene. "I suppose not."

Kinney rose to go. "Well, it's a pretty funny thing—pretty odd, I mean—and I suppose it would be pass-around-the-hat for old Fanny Minafer if he blew up. Fred told me that they're living in some apartment house, and said Georgie supports her. He was going to study law, but couldn't earn enough that way to take care of Fanny, so he gave it up. Fred's wife told him all this. Says Fanny doesn't do anything but play bridge these days. Got to playing too high for awhile and lost more than she wanted to tell Georgie about, and borrowed a little from old Frank Bronson. Paid him back, though. Don't know how Fred's wife heard it. Women do hear the darndest things!"

"They do," Eugene agreed.

"I thought you'd probably heard about it—thought most likely Fred's wife might have said something to your daughter, especially as they're cousins."

"I think not."

"Well, I'm off to the store," said Mr. Kinney briskly; yet he lingered. "I suppose we'll all have to club in and keep old Fanny out of the poorhouse if he does blow up. From all I heard it's usually only a question of time. They say she hasn't got anything else to depend on."

"I suppose not."

"Well—I wondered—" Kinney hesitated. "I was wondering why you hadn't thought of finding something around your works for him. They say he's an all-fired worker and he certainly does seem to have hid some decent stuff in him under all his damfoolishness. And you used to be such a tremendous friend of the family—I thought perhaps you—of course I know he's a queer lot—I know he's—"

"Yes, I think he is," said Eugene. "No. I haven't anything to offer him."

"I suppose not," Kinney returned thoughtfully, as he went out. "I don't know that I would myself. Well, we'll probably see his name in the papers some day if he stays with that job!"

... However, the nitro-glycerin expert of whom they spoke did not get into the papers as a consequence of being blown up, although his daily life was certainly a continuous exposure to that risk. Destiny has a constant passion for the incongruous, and it was George's lot to manipulate wholesale quantities of terrific and volatile explosives in safety, and to be laid low by an accident so commonplace and inconsequent that it was a comedy. Fate had reserved for him the final insult of riding him down under the wheels of one of those juggernauts at which he had once shouted "Git a hoss!" Nevertheless, Fate's ironic choice for Georgie's undoing was not a big and swift and momentous car, such as Eugene manufactured; it was a specimen of the hustling little type that was flooding the country, the cheapest, commonest, hardiest little car ever made.

The accident took place upon a Sunday morning, on a downtown crossing, with the streets almost empty, and no reason in the world for such a thing to happen. He had gone out for his Sunday morning walk, and he was thinking of an automobile at the very moment when the little car struck him; he was thinking of a shiny landaulet and a charming figure stepping into it, and of the quick gesture of a white glove toward the chauffeur, motioning him to go on. George heard a shout but did not look up, for he could not imagine anybody's shouting at him, and he was too engrossed in the question "Was it Lucy?" He could not decide, and his lack of decision in this matter probably superinduced a lack of decision in another, more pressingly vital. At the second and louder shout he did look up; and the car was almost on him; but he could not make up his mind if the charming little figure he had seen was Lucy's and he could not make up his mind whether to go backward or forward: these questions became entangled in his mind. Then, still not being able to decide which of two ways to go, he tried to go both—and the little car ran him down. It was not moving very rapidly, but it went all the way over George.

He was conscious of gigantic violence; of roaring and jolting and concussion; of choking clouds of dust, shot with lightning, about his head; he heard snapping sounds as loud as shots from a small pistol, and was stabbed by excruciating pains in his legs. Then he became aware that the machine was being lifted off of him. People were gathering in a circle round him, gabbling.

His forehead was bedewed with the sweat of anguish, and he tried to wipe off this dampness, but failed. He could not get his arm that far.

"Nev' mind," a policeman said; and George could see above his eyes the skirts of the blue coat, covered with dust and sunshine. "Amb'lance be here in a minute. Nev' mind tryin' to move any. You want 'em to send for some special doctor?"

"No." George's lips formed the word.

"Or to take you to some private hospital?"

"Tell them to take me," he said faintly, "to the City Hospital."

"A' right."

A smallish young man in a duster fidgeted among the crowd, explaining and protesting, and a strident voiced girl, his companion, supported his argument, declaring to everyone her willingness to offer testimony in any court of law that every blessed word he said was the God's truth.

"It's the fella that hit you," the policeman said, looking down on George. "I guess he's right; you must of b'en thinkin' about somep'm' or other. It's wunnerful the damage them little machines can do— you'd never think it—but I guess they ain't much case ag'in this fella that was drivin' it."

"You bet your life they ain't no case on me!" the young man in the duster agreed, with great bitterness. He came and stood at George's feet, addressing him heatedly: "I'm sorry fer *you* all right, and I don't say I ain't. I hold nothin' against you, but it wasn't any more my fault than the statehouse! You run into me, much as I run into you, and if you get well you ain't goin' to get not one single cent out o' me! This lady here was settin' with me and we both yelled at you. Wasn't goin' a *step* over eight mile an hour! I'm perfectly willing to say I'm sorry for you though, and so's the lady with me. We're both willing to say that much, but that's all, understand!"

George's drawn eyelids twitched; his misted glance rested fleetingly upon the two protesting motorists, and the old imperious spirit within him flickered up in a single word. Lying on his back in the middle of the street, where he was regarded by an increasing public as an unpleasant curiosity, he spoke this word clearly from a mouth filled with dust, and from lips smeared with blood.

... It was a word which interested the policeman. When the ambulance clanged away, he turned to a fellow patrolman who had joined him. "Funny what he says to the little cuss that done the damage. That's all he *did* call him—nothin' else at all—and the cuss had broke both his legs fer him and God-knows-what-all!"

"I wasn't here then. What was it?"

" 'Riffraff'!"

experiments in such gropings as those for the discovery of substitutes for gasoline and rubber; and, though his mood had withheld the information from Kinney, he had recently bought from the elder Akers a substantial quantity of stock on the condition that the chemical company should establish an experimental laboratory. He intended to buy more; Akers was anxious to please him; and a word from Eugene would have placed George almost anywhere in the chemical works. George need never have known it, for Eugene's purchases of stock were always quiet ones: the transaction remained, so far, between him and Akers, and could be kept between them.

The possibility just edged itself into Eugene's mind; that is, he let it become part of his perceptions long enough for it to prove to him that it was actually a possibility. Then he half started with disgust that he should be even idly considering such a thing over his last cigar for the night, in his library. "No!" And he threw the cigar into the empty fireplace and went to bed.

His bitterness for himself might have worn away, but never his bitterness for Isabel. He took that thought to bed with him—and it was true that nothing George could do would ever change this bitterness of Eugene. Only George's mother could have changed it.

And as Eugene fell asleep that night, thinking thus bitterly of Georgie, Georgie in the hospital was thinking of Eugene. He had come "out of ether" with no great nausea, and had fallen into a reverie, though now and then a white sailboat staggered foolishly into the small ward where he lay. After a time he discovered that this happened only when he tried to open his eyes and look about him; so he kept his eyes shut, and his thoughts were clearer. He thought of Eugene Morgan and of the Major; they seemed to be the same person for awhile, but he managed to disentangle them and even to understand why he had confused them. Long ago his grandfather had been the most striking figure of success in the town: "As rich as Major Amberson!" they used to say. Now it was Eugene. "If I had Eugene Morgan's money," he would hear the workmen day-dreaming at the chemical works; or, "If Eugene Morgan had hold of this place you'd see things hum!" And the boarders at the table d'hôte spoke of "the Morgan Place" as an eighteenth-century Frenchman spoke of Versailles. Like his uncle, George had perceived that the "Morgan Place" was the new Amberson Mansion. His reverie went back to the palatial days of the Mansion, in his boyhood, when he would gallop his pony up the driveway and order the darkey stablemen about, while they whooped and obeyed, and his grandfather, observing from a window, would laugh and call out to him, "That's right, Georgie. Make those lazy rascals jump!" He remembered his gay young uncles, and how the town was eager concerning everything about them, and about himself. What a clean, pretty town it had been! And in his reverie he saw like a pageant before him the magnificence of the Ambersons—its passing, and the passing of the Ambersons themselves. They had been slowly engulfed without knowing how to prevent it, and almost without knowing what was happening to them. The family lot, in the shabby older quarter, out at the cemetery, held most of them now; and the name was swept altogether from the new city. But the new great people who had taken their places—the Morgans and Akerses and Sheridans—they would go, too. George saw that. They would pass, as the Ambersons had passed, and though some of them might do better than the Major and leave the letters that spelled a name on a hospital or a street, it would be only a word and it would not stay forever. Nothing stays or holds or keeps where there is growth, he somehow perceived vaguely but truly. Great Cæsar dead and turned to clay stopped no hole to keep the wind away; dead Cæsar was nothing but a tiresome bit of print in a book that schoolboys study for a while and then forget. The Ambersons had passed, and the new people would pass, and the new people that came after them, and then the next new ones, and the next—and the next—

He had begun to murmur, and the man on duty as night nurse for the ward came and bent over him.

"Did you want something?"

"There's nothing in this family business," George told him confidentially. "Even George Washington is only something in a book."

———

. . . Eugene read a report of the accident in the next morning's paper. He was on the train, having just left for New York, on business, and with less leisure would probably have overlooked the obscure item:

LEGS BROKEN

G. A. Minafer, an employe of the Akers Chemical Co., was run down by an automobile yesterday at the corner of Tennessee and Main and had both legs broken. Minafer was to blame for the accident according to patrolman F. A. Kax, who witnessed the affair. The automobile was a small one driven by Herbert Cottleman of 2173 Noble Avenue who stated that he was making less than 4 miles an hour. Minafer is said to belong to a family formerly of considerable prominence in the city. He was taken to the City Hospital where physicians stated later that he was suffering from internal injuries besides the fracture of his legs but might recover.

Eugene read the item twice, then tossed the paper upon the opposite seat of his compartment, and sat looking out of the window. His feeling toward Georgie was changed not a jot by his human pity for Georgie's human pain and injury. He thought of Georgie's tall and graceful figure, and he shivered, but his bitterness was untouched. He had never blamed Isabel for the weakness which had cost them the few years of happiness they might have had together; he had put the blame all on the son, and it stayed there.

He began to think poignantly of Isabel: he had seldom been able to "see" her more clearly than as he sat looking out of his compartment window, after reading the account of this accident. She might have been just on the other side of the glass, looking in at him—and then he thought of her as the pale figure of a woman, seen yet unseen, flying through the air, beside the train, over the fields of springtime green and through the woods that were just sprouting out their little leaves. He closed his eyes and saw her as she had been long ago. He saw the brown-eyed, brown-haired, proud, gentle, laughing girl he had known when first he came to town, a boy just out of the State College. He remembered—as he had remembered ten thousand times before—the look she gave him when her brother George introduced him to her at a picnic; it was "like hazel starlight" he had written her, in a poem, afterward. He remembered his first call at the Amberson Mansion, and what a great personage she seemed, at home in that magnificence; and yet so gay and friendly. He remembered the first time he had danced with her—and the old waltz song began to beat in his ears and in his heart. They laughed and sang it together as they danced to it:

> "Oh, love for a year, a week, a day,
> But alas for the love that lasts alway—"

Most plainly of all he could see her dancing; and he became articulate in the mourning whisper: "So graceful—oh, so graceful—"

All the way to New York it seemed to him that Isabel was near him, and he wrote of her to Lucy from his hotel the next night:

I saw an account of the accident to George Minafer. I'm sorry, though the paper states that it was plainly his own fault. I suppose it may have been as a result of my attention falling upon the item that I thought of his mother a great deal on the way here. It seemed to me that I had never seen her more distinctly or so constantly, but, as you know, thinking of his mother is not very apt to make me admire *him*! Of course, however, he has my best wishes for his recovery.

He posted the letter, and by the morning's mail received one from Lucy written a few hours after his departure from home. She enclosed the item he had read on the train.

> I thought you might not see it,
> I have seen Miss Fanny and she has got him put into a room by himself. Oh, *poor* Rides-Down-Everything! I have been thinking so constantly of his mother and it seemed to me that I have never seen her more distinctly. How lovely she was—and how she loved him!

If Lucy had not written this letter Eugene might not have done the odd thing he did that day. Nothing could have been more natural than that both he and Lucy should have thought intently of Isabel after reading the account of George's accident, but the fact that Lucy's letter had crossed his own made Eugene begin to wonder if a phenomenon of telepathy might not be in question, rather than a chance coincidence. The reference to Isabel in the two letters was almost identical: he and Lucy, it appeared, had been thinking of Isabel at the same time—both said "constantly" thinking of her—and neither had ever "seen her more distinctly." He remembered these phrases in his own letter accurately.

Reflection upon the circumstance stirred a queer spot in Eugene's brain—he had one. He was an adventurer; if he had lived in the sixteenth century he would have sailed the unknown new seas, but having been born in the latter part of the nineteenth, when geography was a fairly well-settled matter, he had become an explorer in mechanics. But the fact that he was a "hard-headed business man" as well as an adventurer did not keep him from having a queer spot in his brain, because hard-headed business men are as susceptible to such spots as adventurers are. Some of them are secretly troubled when they do not see the new moon over the lucky shoulder; some of them have strange, secret incredulities—they do not believe in geology, for instance; and some of them think they have had supernatural experiences. "Of course there was nothing in it—still it *was* queer!" they say.

Two weeks after Isabel's death, Eugene had come to New York on urgent business and found that the delayed arrival of a steamer gave him a day with nothing to do. His room at the hotel had become intolerable; outdoors was intolerable; everything was intolerable. It seemed to him that he must see Isabel once more, hear her voice once more; that he *must* find some way to her, or lose his mind. Under this pressure he had gone, with complete scepticism, to a "trance-medium" of whom he had heard wild accounts from the wife of a business acquaintance. He thought despairingly that at least such an excursion would be "trying to do *some*thing!" He remembered the woman's name; found it in the telephone book, and made an appointment.

The experience had been grotesque, and he came away with an encouraging message from his father, who had failed to identify himself satisfactorily, but declared that everything was "on a higher plane" in his present state of being, and that all life was "continuous and progressive." Mrs. Horner spoke of herself as a "psychic"; but otherwise she seemed oddly unpretentious and matter-of-fact; and Eugene had no doubt at all of her sincerity. He was sure that she was not an intentional fraud, and though he departed in a state of annoyance with himself, he came to the conclusion that if any credulity were played upon by Mrs. Horner's exhibitions, it was her own.

Nevertheless, his queer spot having been stimulated to action by the coincidence of the letters, he went to Mrs. Horner's after his directors' meeting today. He used the telephone booth in the directors' room to make the appointment; and he laughed feebly at himself, and wondered what the group of men in that mahogany apartment would think if they knew what he was doing. Mrs. Horner had changed her address, but he found the new one, and somebody purporting to be a niece of hers talked to him and made an appointment for a "sitting" at five o'clock.

He was prompt, and the niece, a dull-faced fat girl with a magazine under her arm, admitted him to Mrs. Horner's apartment, which smelt of camphor; and showed him into a room with gray painted walls, no rug on the floor and no furniture except a table (with nothing on it) and two chairs: one a leather easy-chair and the other a stiff little brute with a wooden seat. There was one window with the shade pulled down to the sill, but the sun was bright outside, and the room had light enough.

Mrs. Horner appeared in the doorway, a wan and unenterprising looking woman in brown, with thin hair artificially waved—but not recently—and parted in the middle over a bluish forehead. Her eyes were small and seemed weak, but she recognized the visitor.

"Oh, you been here before," she said, in a thin voice, not unmusical. "I recollect you. Quite a time ago, wa'n't it?"

"Yes, quite a long time."

"I recollect because I recollect you was disappointed. Anyway, you was kind of cross." She laughed faintly.

"I'm sorry if I seemed so," Eugene said. "Do you happen to have found out my name?"

She looked surprised and a little reproachful. "Why, no. I never try to find out people's names. Why should I? I don't claim anything for the power; I only know I have it—and some ways it ain't always such a blessing, neither, I can tell you!"

Eugene did not press an investigation of her meaning, but said vaguely, "I suppose not. Shall we—"

"All right," she assented, dropping into the leather chair, with her back to the shaded window. "You better set down, too, I reckon. I hope you'll get something this time so you won't feel cross, but I dunno. *I* can't never tell what they'll do. Well—"

She sighed, closed her eyes, and was silent, while Eugene, seated in the stiff chair across the table from her, watched her profile, thought himself an idiot, and called himself that and other names. And as the silence continued, and the impassive woman in the easy-chair remained impassive, he began to wonder what had led him to be such a fool. It became clear to him that the similarity of his letter and Lucy's needed no explanation involving telepathy, and was not even an extraordinary coincidence. What, then, had brought him back to this absurd place and caused him to be watching this absurd woman taking a nap in a chair? In brief: What the devil did he mean by it? He had not the slightest interest in Mrs. Horner's naps—or in her teeth, which were being slightly revealed by the unconscious parting of her lips, as her breathing became heavier. If the vagaries of his own mind had brought him into such a grotesquerie as this, into what did the vagaries of other men's minds take them? Confident that he was ordinarily saner than most people, he perceived that since he was capable of doing a thing like this, other men did even more idiotic things, in secret. And he had a fleeting vision of sober-looking bankers and manufacturers and lawyers, well-dressed church-going men, sound citizens—and all as queer as the deuce inside!

How long was he going to sit here presiding over this unknown woman's slumbers? It struck him that to make the picture complete he ought to be shooing flies away from her with a palm-leaf fan.

Mrs. Horner's parted lips closed again abruptly, and became compressed; her shoulders moved a little, then jerked repeatedly; her small chest heaved; she gasped, and the compressed lips relaxed to a slight contortion, then began to move, whispering and bringing forth indistinguishable mutterings.

Suddenly she spoke in a loud, husky voice:

"Lopa is here!"

"Yes," Eugene said dryly. "That's what you said last time. I remember 'Lopa.' She's your 'control' I think you said."

"*I'm* Lopa," said the husky voice. "*I'm* Lopa herself."

"You mean I'm to suppose you're not Mrs. Horner now?"

"Never was Mrs. Horner!" the voice declared, speaking undeniably from Mrs. Horner's lips—but with such conviction that Eugene, in spite of everything, began to feel himself in the presence of a third party, who was none the less an individual, even though she might be another edition of the apparently somnambulistic Mrs. Horner. "Never was Mrs. Horner or anybody but just Lopa. Guide."

"You mean you're Mrs. Horner's guide?" he asked.

"*Your* guide now," said the voice with emphasis, to which was incongruously added a low laugh. "You came here once before. Lopa remembers."

"Yes—so did Mrs. Horner."

Lopa overlooked his implication, and continued quickly: "You build. Build things that go. You came here once and old gentleman on this side, he spoke to you. Same old gentleman here now. He tell Lopa he's your grandfather—no, he says 'father.' He's your father."

"What's his appearance?"

"How?"

"What does he look like?"

"Very fine! White beard, but not long beard. He says someone else wants to speak to you. See here. Lady. Not his wife, though. No. Very fine lady! Fine lady, fine lady!"

"Is it my sister?" Eugene asked.

"Sister? No. She is shaking her head. She has pretty brown hair. She is fond of you. She is someone who knows you very well but she is not your sister. She is very anxious to say something to you—very anxious.

Very fond of you; very anxious to talk to you. Very glad you came here—oh, *very* glad!"

"What is her name?"

"Name," the voice repeated, and seemed to ruminate. "Name hard to get—always very hard for Lopa. Name. She wants to tell me her name to tell you. She wants you to understand names are hard to make. She says you must think of something that makes a sound." Here the voice seemed to put a question to an invisible presence and to receive an answer. "A little sound or a big sound? She says it might be a little sound or a big sound. She says a ring—oh, Lopa knows! She means a bell! That's it, a bell."

Eugene looked grave. "Does she mean her name is Belle?"

"Not quite. Her name is longer."

"Perhaps," he suggested, "she means that she was a belle."

"No. She says she thinks you know what she means. She says you must think of a colour. What colour?" Again Lopa addressed the unknown, but this time seemed to wait for an answer.

"Perhaps she means the colour of her eyes," said Eugene.

"No. She says her colour is light—it's a light colour and you can see through it."

"Amber?" he said, and was startled, for Mrs. Horner, with her eyes still closed, clapped her hands, and the voice cried out in delight:

"Yes! She says you know who she is from amber. Amber! Amber! That's it! She says you understand what her name is from a bell and from amber. She is laughing and waving a lace handkerchief at me because she is pleased. She says I have made you know who it is."

This was the strangest moment of Eugene's life, because, while it lasted, he believed that Isabel Amberson, who was dead, had found means to speak to him. Though within ten minutes he doubted it, he believed it then.

His elbows pressed hard upon the table, and, his head between his hands, he leaned forward, staring at the commonplace figure in the easy-chair. "What does she wish to say to me?"

"She is happy because you know her. No—she is troubled. Oh—a great trouble! Something she wants to tell you. She wants so *much* to tell you. She wants Lopa to tell you. This is a great trouble. She says—oh, yes, she wants you to be—to be kind! That's what she says. That's it. To be kind."

"Does she—"

"She wants you to be kind," said the voice. "She nods when I tell you this. Yes; it must be right. She is a very fine lady. Very pretty. She is so anxious for you to understand. She hopes and hopes you will. Some-one else wants to speak to you. This is a man. He says—"

"I don't want to speak to any one else," said Eugene quickly. "I want—"

"This man who has come says that he is a friend of yours. He says—"

Eugene struck the table with his fist. "I don't want to speak to any one else, I tell you!" he cried passionately. "If she is there I—" He caught his breath sharply, checked himself, and sat in amazement. Could his mind so easily accept so stupendous a thing as true? Evidently it could!

Mrs. Horner spoke languidly in her own voice: "Did you get anything satisfactory?" she asked. "I certainly hope it wasn't like that other time when you was cross because they couldn't get anything for you."

"No, no," he said hastily. "This was different. It was very interesting."

He paid her, went to his hotel, and thence to his train for home. Never did he so seem to move through a world of dream-stuff: for he knew that he was not more credulous than other men, and if he could believe what he had believed, though he had believed it for no longer than a moment or two, what hold had he or any other human being on reality?

His credulity vanished (or so he thought) with his recollection that it was he, and not the alleged "Lopa," who had suggested the word "amber." Going over the mortifying, plain facts of his experience, he found that Mrs. Horner, or the subdivision of Mrs. Horner known as "Lopa," had told him to think of a bell and of a colour, and that being furnished with these scientific data, he had leaped to the conclusion that he spoke with Isabel Amberson!

For a moment he had believed that Isabel was *there,* believed that she was close to him, entreating him—entreating him "to be kind." But with this recollection a strange agitation came upon him. After all, *had* she not spoken to him? If his own unknown consciousness had told the "psychic's" unknown consciousness how to make the picture of the pretty brown-haired, brown-eyed lady, hadn't the picture been a true one? And hadn't the true Isabel—oh, indeed her very soul!—called to him out of his own true memory of her?

And as the train roared through the darkened evening he looked out beyond his window, and saw her as he had seen her on his journey, a few days ago—an ethereal figure flying beside the train, but now it seemed to him that she kept her face toward his window with an infinite wistfulness.

... "To be kind!" If it had been Isabel, was that what she would have said? If she were anywhere, and could come to him through the invisible wall, what would be the first thing she would say to him?

Ah, well enough, and perhaps bitterly enough, he knew the answer to that question! "To be kind"—to Georgie!

————

... A red-cap at the station, when he arrived, leaped for his bag, abandoning another which the Pullman porter had handed him. "Yessuh, Mist' Morgan. Yessuh. You' car waitin' front the station fer you, Mist' Morgan, suh!"

And people in the crowd about the gates turned to stare, as he passed through, whispering, "*That's Morgan.*"

Outside, the neat chauffeur stood at the door of the touring-car like a soldier in whip-cord.

"I'll not go home now, Harry," said Eugene, when he had got in. "Drive to the City Hospital."

"Yes, sir," the man returned. "Miss Lucy's there. She said she expected you'd come there before you went home."

"She did?"

"Yes, sir."

Eugene stared. "I suppose Mr. Minafer must be pretty bad," he said.

"Yes, sir. I understand he's liable to get well, though, sir." He moved his lever into high speed, and the car went through the heavy traffic like some fast, faithful beast that knew its way about, and knew its master's need of haste. Eugene did not speak again until they reached the hospital.

Fanny met him in the upper corridor, and took him to an open door.

He stopped on the threshold, startled; for, from the waxen face on the pillow, almost it seemed the eyes of Isabel herself were looking at him: never before had the resemblance between mother and son been so strong—and Eugene knew that now he had once seen it thus startlingly, he need divest himself of no bitterness "to be kind" to Georgie.

George was startled, too. He lifted a white hand in a queer gesture, half forbidding, half imploring, and then let his arm fall back upon the coverlet. "You must have thought my mother wanted you to come," he said, "so that I could ask you to—to forgive me."

But Lucy, who sat beside him, lifted ineffable eyes from him to her father, and shook her head. "No, just to take his hand—gently!"

She was radiant.

But for Eugene another radiance filled the room. He knew that he had been true at last to his true love, and that through him she had brought her boy under shelter again. Her eyes would look wistful no more.

A Note on the Type

The principal text of this Modern Library edition
was set in a digitized version of Janson,
a typeface that dates from about 1690 and was cut by Nicholas Kis,
a Hungarian working in Amsterdam. The original matrices have
survived and are held by the Stempel foundry in Germany.
Hermann Zapf redesigned some of the weights and sizes for Stempel,
basing his revisions on the original design.

Printed in the United States
by Baker & Taylor Publisher Services